THE SOUND OF GLASS

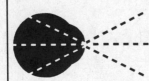

This Large Print Book carries the
Seal of Approval of N.A.V.H.

THE SOUND OF GLASS

KAREN WHITE

THORNDIKE PRESS

A part of Gale, Cengage Learning

GALE
CENGAGE Learning·

Farmington Hills, Mich • San Francisco • New York • Waterville, Maine
Meriden, Conn • Mason, Ohio • Chicago

GALE
CENGAGE Learning·

Copyright © 2015 by Harley House Books, LLC.
Thorndike Press, a part of Gale, Cengage Learning.

Thorndike Press® Large Print List Core.
The text of this Large Print edition is unabridged.
Other aspects of the book may vary from the original edition.
Set in 16 pt. Plantin.

LIBRARY OF CONGRESS CATALOGING-IN-PUBLICATION DATA

White, Karen (Karen S.)
   The sound of glass / Karen White. — Large print edition.
    pages cm. — (Thorndike Press large print Core)
    ISBN 978-1-4104-7953-2 (hardback) — ISBN 1-4104-7953-6 (hardcover)
   1. Widows—Fiction. 2. Family secrets—Fiction. 3. Large type books. 4. Domestic fiction. I. Title.
  PS3623.H5776S68 2015b
  813'.6—dc23   2015013913

Published in 2015 by arrangement with New American Library, an imprint of Penguin Publishing Group, a division of Penguin Random House LLC

Printed in the United States of America
1 2 3 4 5 6 7 19 18 17 16 15

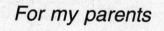

For my parents

ACKNOWLEDGMENTS

Thank you to the lovely people of Beaufort, South Carolina, for your kindness and warm hospitality, especially the staff at the Rhett House Inn and native Beaufortonian Nancy Rhett. A huge thanks and hugs to friend and fellow author Dee Phelps for the private tours and insider information on your beautiful hometown. This book couldn't have happened without you!

A special thanks to airline pilot Steve Weber for all the technical information about planes, flight paths, and basically anything I needed to know, and to Tracy Ferro, MSN, RN, PCCN, for your incredible help regarding all things health related in this story.

Thank you to Meghan White and Alicia Kelly, my "research buddies," who accompanied me on my trips to Beaufort and waited patiently as I asked endless questions of tour guides and read every inscription on every gravestone.

Last but not least, thanks to BFFs and authors Susan Crandall and Wendy Wax, whose insights help shape and perfect each book I write. Thanks for being there since the beginning and through the ups and downs of this crazy writing thing we do.

One need not be a chamber
to be haunted,
One need not be a house;
The brain has corridors surpassing
Material place.
— EMILY DICKINSON

PROLOGUE

Beaufort, South Carolina
July 1955

An unholy tremor rippling through the sticky night air alerted Edith Heyward that something wasn't right. Like a shadow creeping past a doorway in an empty house, or the turn of the latch on a locked door, the movement outside Edith's opened attic window raised the gooseflesh along her spine. Her breath sat in her mouth, suspended with anticipation as icy pinpricks marched down her limbs.

Her gaze moved from her paintbrush and the tiny drop of red paint she'd drizzled onto the chest of the doll's starched white cotton nightgown, to the sea-glass wind chime she'd made and hung just outside the window. The stagnant air of a South Carolina summer had stifled any movement for months, yet now the chimes seemed to shiver on an invisible breeze, the frosty blue

11

and green glass twitching like a hanged man from a noose.

She jerked her gaze to the locked door, wondering whether her husband had returned. He didn't like locked doors. The bruises on her arms, carefully placed and easily hidden under long sleeves, seemed to press against her skin in memory. Edith dropped her paintbrush, barely aware of the splatter of red paint on the dollhouse-size room she'd been re-creating, eager to unlatch the door and make it down to the kitchen and her mending basket before Calhoun had cause to wonder where she was.

She'd barely slid from her stool when the sky exploded with fire, illuminating the river and the marshes beneath it, obliterating the stars, and shooting blurry light through the milky glass of the wind chime. The stones swayed with the shocked air, singing sweetly despite the destruction in the sky behind them. Then a rain of fire descended like fireworks, myriad balls of light extinguished into hiccups of steam as soon as they collided with water.

Smaller explosions reverberated across the river, where the migrant workers' cottages clustered near the shore like birds, their roofs and dry postage-stamp lawns easy fodder for the hungry flames that fell from the heavens. A fire siren whirred as Edith leaned out the window as far as she could, listening to people shouting and screaming, and smelling something indiscernible. Something that smelled like the tang of wood smoke mixed with the acrid odor of burning fuel. She recalled the hum of an airplane from when she'd been working on the doll, right before she'd thought the earth had shifted, and imagined she knew what was now falling from the sky.

A thud came from above her head, followed swiftly by the sound of something heavy sliding down the roof before hitting the gutter. Then the sound stopped and she pictured whatever it was falling into the back garden.

Edith ran from the room, ignoring the shoe-size bruises on her hips that made it hard to walk, sliding down half the flight of stairs to the second story, where her three-year-old son, C.J., lay in his bed, blissfully unaware of the sky falling down around them. She scooped him into her arms, along with the baby blanket he'd worn thin but wouldn't give up, feeling his warm, sweaty skin against her own. Ignoring his whimpers, she moved as quickly as she could with the boy in her arms down to the foyer.

Edith threw open the front door to stand on her wide columned porch and stared past her garden and across the street to where the river seemed to bleed in reverse with rising steam. Her neighbors streamed toward the water, as if all the trauma were occurring somewhere else and not in their own backyards. She made her way to the street, but instead of following her neighbors she turned around to inspect her roof, expecting to see it lit with flames.

Instead she was met with the same sight she'd been seeing since she'd moved into her husband's home on the Bluff nearly eight years before, the dark roof outlined neatly against a sky that seemed dwarfed in comparison.

With her little boy tucked against her shoulder, Edith stepped gingerly through the garden gate at the side of the house by the driveway, looking for anything that might have fallen from the sky, wondering what she'd do if she found something on fire. Wondering whether she'd try to put it out with her son's blanket. Or throw it into the house and watch it burn.

She studied her flower garden, her only hobby that Calhoun approved of, smelling the tea olives and lemon trees that almost eradicated the odd smell of fumes that wafted toward her in waves. The full moon guided her along the white-stoned path, past her roses and butterfly bushes that nestled closer to the house and where she imagined whatever had fallen from the roof had landed.

Her foot kicked something hard and solid, reminding her that she was wearing only her house slippers. She started at the sight of a disembodied hand, its fist enclosing a rose. She pressed her hand against her chest to slow the heavy thud of her heart as she realized it was the arm from the marble statue of Saint Michael. He'd watched over her since she'd placed him there when she first realized she needed protection.

She spotted the rest of the statue lying faceup on the path among broken branches from the oak tree, his sightless eyes hollow in the moonlight. When she stepped forward to assess the damage, her foot collided with something hard and unyielding, hidden in the shadows beneath the fragrant boxwoods.

More sirens joined in the cacophony of sound that had invaded her quiet town, but as Edith knelt on the rocky path, she hardly seemed to notice, her attention completely focused on the brown leather suitcase that sat upright in her garden as if an uninvited visitor had suddenly come to call.

C.J. began to stir as Edith deliberated what she should do. Unwilling to separate herself from either her son or the suitcase, she pressed C.J. against her body with her left arm, ignoring the throbbing from the bruises that ran along her rib cage, then grabbed the handle of the suitcase. Gingerly she lifted it to test the weight, finding it lighter than it appeared. Walking slowly, she carried the suitcase up the back steps and into the empty kitchen.

After placing C.J. in the playpen, Edith returned to the brown suitcase, noticing for the first time the large dent in the bottom corner, the hinge badly damaged but not broken. Judging from the relatively good condition of the suitcase, she realized the canopy of oak limbs had broken its fall before it landed on the roof. A name tag dangled from the handle, practically begging her to touch it.

She should call the police. Let them know that she had a piece of whatever disaster had happened in the sky that night. Perhaps some survivor would be looking for this exact suitcase that now rested on her kitchen floor. Still, she hesitated. She wasn't sure why she felt the need for secrecy, but the thrill of the forbidden teased her senses, brought forth her rebellious spirit, which she'd learned years before was best left hidden.

She pressed her lips together with determination. She'd push the button on the latch to see whether it opened. It was probably locked anyway. Or the lock could be too damaged from the fall to open. Then she'd call the police.

She heard a sound from the playpen and saw C.J. watching her with his wide blue eyes. "Mama?"

She smiled. "It's all right, sweetheart. You go on back to sleep, all right?"

"Suitcase," he said around the ever-present thumb Calhoun had been demanding she make him stop sucking.

"Yes, darling. Now go on back to sleep."

He remained standing, watching her intently. She knew his rebellious streak came from her and she was reluctant to stifle it. "You can watch for a little bit if you'd like. I'll be right back."

Edith kissed his damp forehead as she walked out of the kitchen and to the front door, which she carefully opened to peer out. She was more afraid of her husband's return than of the band of angry people she imagined marching toward her door to find the errant suitcase. The smells and sounds were stronger now, the sky glowing orange across the river over the fields of okra and watermelon as sirens screamed into the night.

Edith retreated into her house and closed the door, turning the key in the lock, then returned to the kitchen and the suitcase. After a quick glance at C.J., who remained sucking his thumb and watching everything with his father's eyes, she reached for the luggage tag and tried to read the name and address. Moisture must have seeped beneath the plastic cover and the cardboard name tag, making the ink run like tears. The address was nearly illegible, but she could read the name clearly: Henry P. Holden. When she flipped up the handle, she saw that a monogram had been boldly stamped in gold: HPH. She imagined a middle-aged man in a dark suit and hat, with a wife and kids at home, traveling on business. She thought of where they were now, and how they might be notified of the accident. Wondered whether it was possible to survive such a thing as falling from the sky.

She pushed the button and the latch popped open. It was a sign, Edith thought as her hands moved to the two latches on the sides of the suitcase. One opened easily, but the one on the side with the dent took a few twists and tugs.

Without pausing, she opened the suitcase wide on her kitchen table. She unlatched the separators on each side and folded them up, revealing neat stacks of starched and pressed dress shirts and suit pants, bleached white undershirts, boxers, and linen handkerchiefs. Everything had been packed so tightly that there'd been little room for movement as the suitcase had tumbled to earth.

Edith recognized the scent of the detergent that wafted up to her as the same one she used, as if the clothes had come from her own washing machine. It had so obviously been packed by a woman that Edith almost laughed at the predictability of it, then sobered quickly as she pictured the faceless woman walking down a dark hallway to answer the ringing telephone.

She stared down again at the clothing, taking note of the quality of the thread count in the shirts, the soft linen handkerchiefs, the fine gabardine of Henry Holden's trousers, the thickness and brightness of the undershirts. Each handkerchief had a perfectly stitched monogram on the corner in bright, bold red: HPH. It all made sense for a man traveling on business. But as she stared at the suitcase's contents, something bothered her, something she couldn't quite

19

put her finger on.

Calhoun had once told her it was her analytical mind that had first attracted him to her. As the only child of a widower police detective, she'd never known any other way to be. So when the handsome lawyer Calhoun Heyward had come to her small town of Walterboro to try a case, she hadn't known that she would have been better off pretending to be a simpering female without opinions. Because, in the end, that was what he'd really wanted.

C.J. was sleeping standing up, his head cradled on the top rail of the playpen, his thumb in his mouth. Edith glanced nervously at the round metal clock over the sink. Calhoun could be home at any minute to find a locked front door and a man's suitcase on the kitchen table. She didn't stop to think where he'd been or with whom, or if he'd seen the airplane explode and had thought to worry about her and their son.

She quickly refastened the separators, the fasteners slipping through her fingers because she was going too fast and her hands shook. It was then that she realized what had been bothering her. The dopp kit. The ubiquitous men's toiletry kit was missing. No man traveled without one. She pulled

20

the cloth separators back again, looking at the neatly packed clothes, studying the side where the clothes had shifted slightly more than on the other. She reached in to shove a stack back to the side, revealing a small pocket where a dopp kit would have fit during the packing. She pursed her lips, thinking. Could Mr. Holden have removed it before boarding his plane, believing he might have need of something inside it during the flight?

Edith smiled to herself. These were the questions her father had taught her to ask until her inquisitiveness had become a part of her. During the years of her miscarriages and Calhoun's growing disappointment in her, it had become her saving grace. It had been what had made her ignore the censure of her friends and husband and reach out to the local police department and offer her services as an artist with an unusual talent. It had kept her whole.

Forgetting the time and the sound of an approaching siren, she reached into the suitcase and carefully began to shift the clothing, searching for the missing dopp kit. She searched the top half of the case first, and then the bottom, almost giving up before her fingers brushed against something that didn't feel like cloth. Careful not

21

to disturb anything further, she gently pushed away three pairs of neatly rolled-up dark socks to find a crisply folded letter.

She hesitated for only a moment before taking it out. It was expensive stationery, thick, heavy linen, the Crane watermark visible when Edith held it to the light. It wasn't sealed but had been tightly folded, as if the writer had pressed his or her fingers along the creases many times. When she flipped it over, a single word was written in thin black ink with elegant penmanship.

Beloved.

She paused, wondering how many boundaries she could cross, quickly deciding that she had already crossed too many to worry about one more. With steady hands she unfolded the letter and began to read the short lines written in the same elegant script as the word on the back.

She stared at the words for so long that they began to blur and dance off the page, until the letter fell to the floor as if the weight of the words were too much for Edith's fingers. She let it go, watching as it slipped beneath the new white refrigerator that had been delivered the previous week as an apology from Calhoun. She didn't try to retrieve it, wishing that the words could disappear from her memory just as easily.

She wasn't sure how long she stood there, staring at the small crack between the black and white vinyl floor tiles and the bottom of the new appliance, but she jumped when the hall phone began to ring. With a quick glance at the sleeping boy, she ran to answer it.

"Edith? It's Betsy. I'm so glad to hear your voice. We all ran to the river, but Sidney and I got worried when I saw that you and Calhoun weren't with us. Is everything all right?"

Edith was surprised at the calmness to her voice. "I'm fine. Calhoun is working late, so I was here alone." It never surprised her anymore how easily the lies spilled from her mouth. "I didn't want to leave the house because of C.J. He's been sick and was sound asleep. Didn't even wake up at the sound of the explosion."

"It was an airplane," Betsy said, her voice higher pitched, a tone usually reserved for neighborhood gossip. "They're saying it exploded — just like that. Sidney said it was probably an engine catching on fire. You know how dangerous airplanes are. I took a train to visit my parents in Jackson last Christmas even though Sidney told me I should fly instead, so he can't tell me I was wrong now, can he? It's just tragic, though.

All those people . . ." Her voice trailed off.

"How awful," Edith said, her hands still remembering the feel of the stranger's clothes, the image of a ringing phone in a dark hallway. The elegant handwriting in the letter. Her throat felt tight, as if the fingers of the letter writer were pressing against her windpipe. "Are there any survivors?"

"Sidney said he didn't think so. He was outside walking the dog when it happened, and he says it was pretty high up in the sky. But the authorities are handing out flashlights to all the men to go search the fields, the river, and the marsh for survivors. A solid beam for any sign of life, and a flashing light to indicate a . . ." Her voice caught. Betsy Williams was Edith's bridge partner, and they were neighbors. And Sidney Williams was their family lawyer. That was where their common interests ended. Betsy was content to live on the surface of life, to avoid any sharp edges that might force her to open her eyes a little wider. Betsy would tell people that she and Edith were best friends, but she couldn't tell them anything about her except for Edith's favorite flower and that she disliked chocolate.

"A body," Betsy continued. "That was a while ago. Sidney sent me home, but I'm too restless to do anything. I thought maybe you could use some company."

"No," Edith said, a little too quickly, thinking of the suitcase in her kitchen. "I'm exhausted from taking care of C.J., and I think I'm just going to go to bed. I'm sure Calhoun is out there searching, too, and can fill me in on the details when he returns."

There was a brief pause, and Edith pictured Betsy's small mouth tightening with disappointment. "All right. But call me if you get nervous and need me to come around."

Edith said good-bye and carefully replaced the phone back in the cradle, suddenly aware of the sound of voices from her front lawn. She'd already started back toward the kitchen when the doorbell rang. She stopped, unsure what to do. It wasn't Calhoun. He would have banged on the door when he'd discovered it locked. With an eye toward the closed kitchen door, Edith smoothed down her skirt and carefully tucked her hair behind her ears before opening the door.

Two police officers stood on her front porch, their hats in their hands. She wondered if she would be sick all over their polished black shoes that reflected her porch

25

lights or if she could make it to the side railing. How had they known about the suitcase?

"Mrs. Heyward?" The young officer on
the left spoke first. She thought she recognized him, but she was having a problem
focusing.

She smiled, forcing the bile back down
her throat. "Yes?" She struggled to suck a
breath into her lungs, the air now thick with
the scent of rain. While she'd been in the
kitchen, the moon and stars had disappeared as if ashamed to illuminate the
scene beneath them. The splat of raindrops
hitting her front walk and the leaves of the
oak tree that shaded most of the front yard
almost obliterated the sound of her heart
thrumming in her ears. "Can I help you?"
She knew she should invite them inside, just
as she knew she could not.

A figure moved from the shadows of the
porch, and she recognized the police chaplain as he stepped inside the arc of light.
She blinked in surprise, wondering why he
was there with the officers.

A flash of lightning lifted her gaze from
the three men to the scene across the river,
and she found herself holding her breath.
Dozens of blinking flashlights came from
the shore and from boats on the water like

26

hovering fireflies, spots of light marking the souls of the departed.

"Edith?" The chaplain stepped closer, so she could now see his kind eyes and the deep creases around his mouth placed there like scars during the war. "I'm afraid we have bad news."

"Mama?" C.J. called from the kitchen.

Edith turned to the chaplain in a panic. "I'm sorry; I have to see to my son. . . ."

He reached out to take her hands, his fingers as icy as hers. "There's been an accident. Calhoun's car was found off of Ribaut Road up against a tree. An eyewitness said it looked like he was distracted by the explosion." He paused. "He . . . he didn't survive."

She felt as if she were free-falling from the sky, the lack of oxygen making her lightheaded and strangely calm. She felt nothing. Absolutely nothing. "Was he alone?"

The men shuffled their feet in embarrassment, but it was the second officer who finally spoke. "Yes, ma'am."

Edith nodded, feeling inordinately relieved that they hadn't come because of the suitcase. Her son called out from the kitchen again, distracting her from the sight of the blinking lights. She knew she needed to say something, to pretend that she cared that

27

Calhoun was dead, to pretend that she felt anything except relief. She thought instead of the feel of her mother's cold hand in hers, and her father's voice saying something about her being free from pain. Edith let out a sob, then pressed her knuckles against her mouth.

The chaplain spoke again. "Can I get you anything? Or can I call someone to come stay with you?"

She shook her head, blinked back the tears. "No. I'll be all right. I just need to be alone right now with my son. I'll be in touch in the morning to see what needs to be done. Thank you, gentlemen." She closed the door on their surprised faces, her last glimpse that of the chaplain's knowing eyes.

The storm outside intensified as she pressed her forehead against the closed door, feeling guilty that instead of thinking of Calhoun dying alone on a darkened road, her thoughts were occupied with the letter under her refrigerator and the woman who'd written it. Edith felt an odd kinship with the unknown woman, the bond of a secret the other woman would never know she'd shared. A secret Edith knew she'd take to her grave.

Before she turned from the door, a gust of wind pushed at the house, unfastening a shutter on an upper story and slamming the limbs of the old tree against the roof of the porch. As she began walking slowly back toward the kitchen, she heard the wind chime cry out into the troubled night like a prayer to accompany lost souls to heaven. She shivered despite the humid night, then closed her eyes for a moment, hearing only the sound of glass.

CHAPTER 1

Merritt
Beaufort, South Carolina
May 2014
Fires can be stopped in three different ways: exhausting the fuel source, taking away the source, or starving the fire of oxygen. Whenever Cal was worked up or upset he would repeat small facts he'd learned at the academy like reciting a prayer. It sometimes worked, which is probably why I'd taken up the habit after he was gone.

My logical and organized curator's mind wouldn't allow me to completely push away the thought that my own recitation was some kind of unanswered plea for forgiveness. Because no matter what they told me, Cal's death wasn't an accident. I was reminded often that he was a firefighter and walking into burning buildings was what he did, and sometimes a roof collapsed and firemen got trapped. And they were right, of course, because that was how Cal had died. But it didn't explain why.

I looked up at the address on the thick white door casing of the old brick building, then back to the letterhead of the law firm Williams, Willig, and White, 702 Bay Street. I stared at the brass numbers, my mind still unwilling to grasp how I'd ended up more than a thousand miles from home.

I climbed the three steps, holding down my skirt so it wouldn't expose the ridged scar on the side of my leg. I pulled on a heavy brass doorknob, needing both hands to open the large door, then stepped into a well-appointed reception room that looked like it had once been a foyer to a grand home. Old pine floors, polished to a sheen that didn't quite obscure the centuries of heel marks and scratches that gave the wood character, creaked beneath my feet as I walked toward a large mahogany reception desk.

A brass nameplate with the name Donna Difloe introduced the middle-aged woman behind the desk. She looked up at me and smiled as I approached, her rhinestone cat's-eye glasses beneath a cap of frosted blond hair catching the light from her desk lamp. She smiled at me with brightly painted pink lips, and I wondered whether

I'd need to start wearing at least lipstick now that I'd moved down south.

"May I help you?" she asked.

"Yes. I'm here to see Mr. Williams. I have an appointment at eleven."

Her eyes quickly took in my navy skirt and white blouse and makeup-free face, but her smile didn't fade. "Merritt Heyward?" She said my name as if she recognized it.

I nodded. "I'm a little early. I don't mind waiting."

She rose. "He's expecting you. This way, please."

She led me down a hallway where a dark green runner had been thrown over the wood floors to cocoon all sound. Pausing outside a thick, paneled door, she said, "I'm sorry for your loss. I remember Cal when he was growing up. Such a sweet boy."

It had been almost two years since Cal's death, and her condolences surprised me. But no more so than her calling Cal a sweet boy. The person he'd grown into had been hard to know, an impenetrable character hiding inside the imposing body of a man strong enough to scale ladders and carry people out of burning buildings. A man whose own anger smoldered inside of him like a fuse, waiting for a spark.

"Thank you," I said, wishing I could tell

her that Cal remembered her, too, and had said nice things about Ms. Difloe. But he'd never spoken of her, nor of his family or Beaufort. And I had never asked, feeling it a fair trade to avoid questions about my own family. Ashamed, I looked away as she opened the door and stepped back.

The office was large, with a wall full of floor-to-ceiling bookshelves filled with the requisite heavy leather-bound legal texts, and framed diplomas decorating a side wall. A large desk, even larger than Ms. Difloe's, looking to be about the same vintage as the house, sat in front of the bay window facing the street but slightly above street level.

The man who stood to greet me was completely white haired, but appeared to be in his sixties. He looked like a lawyer should, complete with wire-framed glasses, a sweater vest, and the aroma of pipe smoke heavy in the room. He came from around his desk and took both my hands inside his large ones.

"Mrs. Heyward. So nice to meet you in person. And may I say again how sorry I am for your loss."

Like Donna Difloe, when he said my name it was with familiarity. I assumed he must have known Cal, too, as a boy. He led me to a chair on the other side of his desk and waited for me to sit before returning to his own chair. He didn't say anything at first, as if waiting for me to speak.

Unnerved, I smiled, then blurted out, "I didn't know Cal was from Beaufort. In the seven years we were married he never spoke about his family, or growing up here. I always assumed that he had no family."

Years of being a lawyer had schooled Mr. Williams's face into a smooth mask of concerned evaluation, hiding any emotions my words might have evoked. He patted his hands on a neat stack of papers, his only concession to his surprise. Clearing his throat, he said, "The Heywards are an old Beaufort family, since before the Revolution."

"Yes, you explained that on the phone. You said their house was built in the seventeen hundreds."

"Seventeen ninety-one, to be exact — although generations have made changes and additions so it looks more Greek Revival than Federal. It's why Cal's grandmother left it to him, wanting to keep it in the family, you see. She wasn't aware that he'd predeceased her."

I swallowed, as if the reproach I heard in his voice were directed at me. "Of course. Which must seem so odd to you now, to be

35

speaking with me about it."

His smile was gentle. "You were his wife, and I'm sure Cal would be pleased to know that his family's home is in good hands. Especially someone like you, who is an expert in old houses."

I blushed. "I was a curator for a small art museum in Maine. Although I have an advanced degree in art history, I don't think that makes me an expert in much of anything."

Again, the lawyer patted the stack of papers. "Yes, well, we are all glad you're here to see about things and settle the estate. As we discussed over the phone, I know the Beaufort Heritage Society would be interested in acquiring the property for a house museum. Of course, the distribution of the house and its contents is completely up to you, but I'm sure someone of your background is aware of its value in more than simply monetary terms."

"I was actually hoping to live in it." The words sounded even more ridiculous said out loud rather than just as jumbled thoughts in my head. They'd been the reason I'd left my job and sold my house and driven from Farmington, Maine. I was still surprised at how far a person could go fueled only by quiet desperation.

Mr. Williams cleared his throat. "Perhaps I didn't make it clear when we spoke. I was in the house last week to assess the situation." He closed his mouth, as if afraid something he didn't want to say might leak out. After a moment he continued. "Miss Edith was a recluse. And to my knowledge nobody's been inside the house in two decades — about the time Cal left. The last time I saw her was about a month before she died, when she came to see me about her will. She knew she was ill, and wanted to get her things in order."

I adjusted myself in my seat as he waited for me to say something. But I was a New Englander, more comfortable with silence than small talk.

He cleared his throat again. "There's one other thing I preferred to speak to you about in person. Although Miss Edith left Gibbes a generous sum, she left the house and all its contents to Cal, since he was the eldest. Since Gibbes was raised in that house, I thought that perhaps I could prevail upon you to allow him to choose an item or two of furniture. We'd have it appraised, of course, and he would reimburse you for the value, but I know he'd appreciate having a part of his childhood."

"Gibbes?"

"Cal's brother. Ten years younger than Cal."

I imagined that my look of surprise mirrored his own. "Cal has a brother?"

Mr. Williams's face remained impassive, but I detected a slight raising of his brows. "Yes. He's a pediatrician here in Beaufort. Didn't Cal . . . ?" He stopped, his words suspended between us, mocking me. Mocking my marriage to an apparent stranger.

"No," I said, struggling to hide my embarrassment.

Mr. Williams smiled, making him appear as the warm grandfather he probably was. "I'm sorry, Mrs. Heyward. My family's firm has been legal counsel to the Heywards for more than four generations, but even I wasn't privy to their private matters. I know Cal left suddenly and it broke Miss Edith's heart. There was some sort of estrangement but she never spoke of it. I don't mean to pry into your life or Cal's life. I'm just glad you're here to settle things for the Heyward family, and do what you think is fitting. To lay old bones to rest, so to speak."

He continued to smile, but the chill that swept down my back at the mention of old bones made me shiver.

"Mrs. Heyward . . . may I call you Merritt?"

I nodded, glad to hear my name spoken aloud, needing something solid to anchor me to this place of strangers who were telling me things that couldn't possibly be right.

"Merritt. Miss Edith and my mother, Betsy, were best friends, and I was sort of a father figure for Cal and Gibbes after their parents died. You could say I loved them both like my own." His eyes misted. "I've been very eager to meet the woman who finally managed to tame our Cal."

I looked down at my hands, feeling very close to tears. "I didn't tame him, Mr. Williams," I said, knowing that such a thing would have been like pushing back a hurricane wind with my hands. I paused, taking deep breaths as he waited for me to speak. "I killed him."

Loralee
McDonough, Georgia
May 2014

In her thirty-six years on earth, Loralee Purvis Connors had learned the three main truths about life: Time was a slippery thing, pain was temporary, and death wasn't something to be afraid of. This last one she hadn't learned from all the tent revivals her mama had dragged her to when she was a little girl. Life itself had taught her that

39

when somebody you loved died, it was almost a relief not having to worry anymore when it would happen. Because we all die eventually. Finally knowing the answer of when took away the unbearable part of wondering.

She had also learned that being born dirt poor didn't mean you had to stay that way, and that it wasn't a sin to use the face and figure God gave you to get ahead in life, as long as it was legal. Although those things were important, they weren't the things that she wrote down in her *Journal of Truths* each day. The journal was meant to go to Owen one day, and she didn't figure he needed to know about using his physical assets to get ahead. He wouldn't need to. With his mama's looks and his daddy's brains, he would do just fine.

She shoved the last piece of luggage into the back of her Lincoln Navigator, breaking a long red nail in the process. After making sure her ten-year-old son wasn't within hearing range, she let out an expletive while she examined the damage and tried not to cry. It wasn't the biggest tragedy of the past year, just the latest in a long line.

When she'd been a flight attendant for Delta she'd taken such pride in her hands. She'd considered it a job requirement and had always received compliments. Robert had said it was the first thing he'd noticed about her. He'd been so handsome in his pilot's uniform that she'd thrown his compliment back in his face, sure he told that to all the girls. He'd been genuinely hurt that she'd doubted his sincerity. They were married six months later in her hometown of Gulf Shores, Alabama, by a justice of the peace. Robert's daughter from his first marriage hadn't been there for the wedding, nor for any event in the intervening eleven years. Not even for his funeral.

Loralee studied the house they'd bought together, the driveway looking bare without Robert's car or Owen's bicycle and insect terrariums, the lawn naked without the family of cement bunnies she'd purchased at a garage sale because she'd known they'd be perfect in front of their house. She'd dressed them up for the various holidays until the homeowner association had made her stop.

The front door stood open, allowing the hot sun to spill into the empty entranceway, illuminating the bare rectangles on the stairwell where a happy family had once smiled at visitors.

"Owen? Come on. It's time to go." She'd always told Owen it was bad manners to yell, but she didn't want to go back into the house. She'd already said good-bye and was afraid that if she had to go inside again, she might never be able to leave. With her high heels clicking on the pavement, she tapped her way up the walk and climbed the three steps to the front door but went no farther. "Owen? We really need to get going. We've got a long drive ahead of us, and you know I don't like driving at night."

The emptiness of the house echoed like a continuous sigh. But somewhere in the depths of the small house, Loralee thought she heard a sob. Dropping her pocketbook on the threshold, she ran as quickly as she could in heels up the stairs and into the only bedroom Owen had ever known.

He was kneeling inside his empty closet in front of the access panel to an attic crawl space. He held a LEGO airplane in his hands as carefully as he could while his shoulders shook with sobs. Without a word, Loralee knelt beside him on the carpet. Out of habit she took off his glasses and cleaned them on the edge of her skirt before settling them back on his face.

"Did you forget to pack something, sweetie?"

Owen nodded. "Daddy and me made this together. I put it back here so it wouldn't get broken."

"I remember. It's a seven forty-seven, right?"

Owen rolled his eyes. "It's an MD-eighty."

Loralee smiled. "Glad you got your daddy's brains."

Owen didn't look up. "What if it gets broken in the car? I might not know how to put it back together."

"I bet the two of us could figure it out."

Owen looked at her as if she'd just said she was only going to wear flats from now on.

"We could try," she offered in her defense, although it was more of an attempt to make him stop missing his daddy so much.

"I don't want to move to South Carolina."

Loralee shifted from her knees so that she was sitting on the carpet, anticipating another long conversation. "We've already gone over this, sweetie. It's time for you to meet your sister."

He looked at her again as if she were speaking a foreign language, as if he knew how desperation could make a person do crazy things. Like driving to another state to meet a sister who never wanted to know you existed.

"Besides, it could be worse. We could be driving all the way up to Maine. Lucky for us Merritt has just moved to South Carolina and will probably be happy to know somebody in town. I'm sure she'll be happy to have us there to help get her settled." Loralee tried to make her smile appear natural, as if she actually believed everything she'd just said instead of worrying whether Merritt had even had a chance to move into her new house yet. Not that it mattered. Loralee and Owen were leaving that day no matter what. Loralee had simply run out of time.

"Does Merritt want to meet me?" His bright blue eyes stared at her from behind his thick glasses.

"Who wouldn't want to meet you, Owen? You're smart and funny and always have something interesting to say. She'll love you the moment she sees you."

"The kids in my class didn't."

She reached over to smooth down the cowlick that refused to be tamed. "That's because they're just a bunch of rednecks who don't appreciate intellect."

He gave her that look again and she wondered how long it would be until he just quit listening to her. "Will I have to be homeschooled in South Carolina, too?"

Loralee concentrated on combing her fingers through his thick, dark hair so that she wouldn't have to meet his eyes. "Probably not. But it's not so bad, is it? Just you and me at the kitchen table?"

She kissed the top of his head, pretending that he wasn't rolling his eyes again. "We need to go, sweetie."

He twisted away, his eyes hopeful. "Maybe I can change my name, since we'll be in a new place."

When he was born, all she'd wanted to do was give him a name as far away as possible from the trailer park where she'd been born. His daddy was a pilot, and the boy shouldn't be stuck with a name like Bubba for the rest of his life. She'd read the name Owen in a *People* magazine a passenger had left behind on a flight, and had torn out the page and stuck it into her *Journal of Truths* for future reference. She'd wanted a name that sounded sophisticated and couldn't be shortened or ruined by adding an *-ie* at the end. She'd just had no idea that choosing a name that began with the letter *O* would be considered abuse in some circles. Like fourth grade. Or that Owen's myopia would require him to wear glasses that boys in his class said made him look like an owl. It didn't help that he was so much smarter than most of the other kids and that he'd compensated by deliberately failing tests and not turning in homework. When he'd come home with the name *Owen the owl* painted on his backpack, she and Robert had decided she would homeschool.

"Maybe," she said, a part of her reluctant to let go of her original dream. "Or maybe kids in South Carolina appreciate intelligence and won't care that your name starts with the same letter that the word *owl* does."

His sigh shook his narrow shoulders, his gaze focused on the LEGO plane. "I'm going to leave this here." He leaned into the crawl space and carefully placed the toy on the floor, tucked against the wall to the left of the opening.

"You don't have to, Owen. I promise to drive carefully so that it doesn't get broken."

He looked at her again with magnified eyes. "It belongs to the old Owen. I'm not going to be him anymore when we get to South Carolina."

Tears pricked the back of her eyes. He *was* wise, but she knew he was sensitive about that word and its connection to owls. Instead, she nodded and reached past him to close the little access door for the last time.

She hugged him, feeling his small bones beneath her hands, noticing how his jeans were too short because he was growing too fast for her. She hadn't bought new ones because she didn't want to acknowledge the fact that he was getting older. Loralee kissed the top of his head, promising herself that they would stop at a mall before they reached South Carolina. It was important to Loralee that Owen's sister didn't think his mother wasn't taking good care of him.

"It's all going to be fine," she said. She made a mental note to add one more thing to her *Journal of Truths. Sometimes it's necessary to tell a lie when the truth will break a heart.*

They walked out of the house together, neither one of them turning around, as if they both knew that some good-byes were forever. After making sure that Owen was buckled securely into the backseat, Loralee put the SUV in drive and made one more note to add yet another newfound truth to her journal.

Sometimes bravery can be just another face of desperation.

CHAPTER 2

Merritt

The auto-ignition temperature of any material — including paper — is a function of its composition, volume, density, and shape, as well as of how long it's exposed to high temperature. I remembered Cal telling me that once as the reason he hated the title of Ray Bradbury's *Fahrenheit 451:* because it was misleading. I repeated the words to myself one more time before opening my eyes.

I wasn't sure how I'd ended up sitting on the leather sofa in Mr. Williams's office, or when Ms. Difloe had entered with a tall glass of water, its sides weeping with sweat. And then I remembered my impromptu confession and how I'd started gasping for breath.

I closed my eyes for a moment, remembering gentle hands leading me to the sofa, and I felt my shoulders hunch with embarrassment. My eyes felt raw and swollen, as if I'd been crying for the last one thousand miles, but I knew I hadn't. I was an expert at keeping all my emotions inside. Had been for years. But there was something in the way Mr. Williams had looked at me, something that reminded me of my father and the little girl I'd once been before everything changed.

Ms. Difloe placed the cold tumbler in my hands and I brought the glass to my lips, dripping water down my chin because I couldn't steady my fingers. Mr. Williams brought out a pressed linen handkerchief from his trouser pocket, and as he gave it to me I noticed his embroidered monogram in navy in the corner. It told me everything I needed to know about Mrs. Williams, and I felt oddly comforted.

"Thank you," I said, dabbing at my chin but ignoring my eyes, as if I could hide my tears by blinking them away.

Ms. Difloe quietly exited the room while Mr. Williams sat patiently in a pulled-up chair that matched the nail-head couch I was propped up on. He looked at me expectantly, and I thought about how Southerners were supposed to be so slow about everything, and I suspected he'd sit there waiting indefinitely until I finally spoke.

After taking another sip from the glass, I

put it on the side table on a delicate lace coaster that I also imagined Mrs. Williams had strategically placed to protect the antique furniture in her husband's office.

I clutched the handkerchief, watching my knuckles whiten as I tightened my fist around it, then looked up in surprise when Mr. Williams spoke first.

"When we talked on the phone, you said Cal had died in a fire. That he was a fire-fighter and his unit was responding to an emergency when he died."

I nodded. "Yes," I said, my voice barely louder than a whisper.

"Were you there?" he asked gently.

"No."

He patted my arm. "Then it was an accident, see? It's normal to want to blame ourselves when a death is unexpected."

I pulled my arm away from him and stood. "Thank you," I said, forcing a smile. "I'd like to see the house now, if I could. Before it gets dark. All of my things are in my car, and I'd like to unpack while I can still see."

Mr. Williams glanced out the wide window. "Did you haul a trailer or leave most of your furniture in storage?"

"I only brought what I needed. I sold or gave away everything else."

His eyes were compassionate, as if he understood the meaning behind my words. "Really, Merritt, please stay with Kathy and me at least for tonight, and as long as you need to while you decide what you're going to do. I promise you that the house isn't in move-in condition."

I looked at him as the reason for his reluctance became clear to me. "Did Edith die in the house?"

He seemed taken aback at my direct question, but quickly composed himself. "Yes. In the front parlor. I had a professional team come and do a thorough cleaning and dispose of the sofa. The house was completely aired out, and the ventilation system sanitized."

I realized what he was trying to say without actually saying it out loud. I didn't glance away, although I had the impression that he wanted me to. "How long was she dead before they discovered her body?"

He reached into his pocket for the handkerchief he'd already given me, his hand stilling as I held it up to him. He took it and hastily folded it before returning it to his pocket. "The coroner estimates she'd been dead between a week to ten days. Heart attack. Her neighbor noticed her newspapers stacking up on her porch steps and called the police."

"That's horrible," I said, finally glancing away. I wiped my palms against my skirt as if what I'd just heard had made them dirty. "You don't have to come with me. Just give me the address so I can plug it into my GPS."

His face softened, and I imagined him recalling our phone conversation when I explained to him that I had no family except for Cal. "It's no bother at all, and it would be an honor to show you the house. It truly is a fine example of some of the beautiful architecture here in Beaufort. Let me grab my car keys and the house keys, and we'll be on our way. I'll call my son to bring your car in a little bit so you can enjoy the scenery on the way to your new home."

I was relieved that he didn't expect me to drive yet, as my hands were still a little shaky. He smiled, but he couldn't hide the look of worry behind his eyes. And I was too exhausted to explain to him that I was no stranger to sadness, and that it had become second nature to wake up each morning expecting the worst. I didn't want to be surprised anymore. Hearing the story of an elderly lady I didn't know dying alone merely pinged at the glass wall I'd erected without even leaving a chip.

We exited through a rear door that opened up to a small parking lot that faced a large green park area and behind that a wide expanse of water. I shivered despite the temperature, watching cars traverse a long bridge to another spit of land, while boats wandered aimlessly beneath it like a scene in a postcard from somebody else's life. Heat rose from the asphalt, baking the soles of my shoes, and I shifted my feet.

"That's the Beaufort River," he said to my unasked question. "You can see it from your house."

I nodded to show I'd heard, then followed him for a short distance until he stopped in front of a black Lincoln Town Car.

He opened the door and stood back. "It's a hot one, that's for sure. Don't touch any metal, and I'll get the air-conditioning going right away." He pressed a button on his key fob and the car windows lowered. I breathed deeply, trying to catch a cross breeze as it moved through the car. "This Lowcountry heat takes a bit of getting used to," he said apologetically as he started the engine.

He drove slowly, so slowly that I found myself pressing an imaginary accelerator on the floorboard in front of me. Not that he could have driven faster. Everybody else seemed content to plod along at or below the speed limit. We left the downtown area as we drove parallel to the river, where the houses became larger and older, with lush gardens full of unfamiliar blooms that most likely couldn't survive a New England winter. The reds and pinks seemed brighter, the greens deeper, as if I'd stumbled into an exotic, foreign place. Compared to my small, three-bedroom, midcentury ranch, I realized I probably had.

I spotted an enormous tree whose trunk seemed as wide as the Lincoln, and whose branches were dressed in frothy green moss. It was something out of a movie set, and I half expected to see a woman in a corset and hoop skirt step out from behind it. I was so busy staring at it that I was barely aware of Mr. Williams pulling into a gravel driveway leading to a detached garage with a drooping roof. The bays had tall, arched entrances, making me think it had once been a carriage house. Only the bravest or best insured would actually park a vehicle inside it.

But the garage was quickly forgotten as my attention was drawn to the enormous house that dwarfed it. Six large Doric columns supported double porches the width of the house and a hipped roof with three visible chimneys. The porch railings and spindles had once been white, but now were mostly peeling. Several spindles were missing, making the porches resemble Halloween jack-o'-lanterns. Divided steps made out of what appeared to be cement led up to the front porch from a raised basement and to a massive front door that hadn't seen a coat of paint for decades. A clear fanlight with a cracked pane and rectangular glass sidelights surrounded the door, the glass murky, as if passing time had left its fingerprints in a layer of dirt.

I stood beneath a limb of the enormous oak tree, relishing the respite from the beating sun, and stepped back to see two dormer windows in the roof, possibly in an attic, and I wondered how hot it would be now in the middle of summer. A lone air-conditioning unit in an upstairs window flipped on, disturbing the quiet.

I looked up at the house and it seemed to be considering me, too. A broken path led around to the side, where a wooden door with peeling white paint sat within a high wall with crumbling plaster, blocking my view of what lay behind it. A flowering vine had flung itself over the top of the wall like an escaping prisoner. There was an air of expectation, a held breath, as if the house and I were both waiting for something to happen.

"The house is in good structural shape, although, as you can see, there are quite a few aesthetic issues. Edith's husband died in 1955 — in a car accident — and I don't believe she made a single improvement to the house since. I'm afraid there's no central air, but there is indoor plumbing, of course, and a functional kitchen." He rubbed his hands together like a father trying to convince a child that a piece of fruit was just as desirable as a candy bar. Mr. Williams continued. "If you'll turn around, you'll see the real beauty of the property."

I felt reluctant to turn my back on the house, but I did and quickly understood what Mr. Williams had meant. The house had been built on a rise that afforded a wide vista of the river, the view framed by the thick-trunked oaks and their shawls of moss.

The lawyer wore a pleased expression, as if he'd finally found a reason for me to smile. "This part of Beaufort is called the Bluff for obvious reasons. Most of the houses are about the same age as this one, between one hundred and fifty to two hundred years old, and a few even older than that."

I listened with only half an ear, too mesmerized by the flicker of sunlight off the water, and the graceful shape of the land as it gently knelt toward the river, and the grand house that sat in proud desolation and watched over it all. It had been Cal's home, where he'd been born and spent his childhood. He'd lived inside the old house's walls, had seen what lay behind the crumbling garden wall, and probably saw the view of the river every day of his life. Yet he had left it all behind two decades before and never looked back. Had never thought to tell me about it, or to bring me there to share the beauty of it. I shivered again, as the thought I didn't want to voice pricked at my conscience. *What happened to Cal here to make him want to forget?*

The heat seemed to roll at me in waves, bringing with it a scent I didn't recognize. "What's that smell?" I asked, tilting my face to capture the scent that wasn't pleasant or unpleasant, but had an earthiness to it that made it oddly alluring.

"That's pluff mud. Basically rotting vegetation that gets left behind at low tide in the marsh. People from here call it the scent of home."

I nodded as we turned back toward the house, wondering whether Cal had ever missed the scent of the pluff mud or the exotic vegetation that seemed to explode all over the yard. Our house in Farmington had been small, with a tiny yard. It had been one of the things he'd specified to the Realtor when we'd been house hunting, claiming he had no time or patience for a yard or garden.

As we climbed the steps Mr. Williams offered his arm, and I took it after a brief pause. Looking down to avoid a large crack bisecting the bottom step, I realized that the steps weren't made of cement as I had originally thought. There were small rocks and shells embedded in the material, coarser than cement, with a sandier hue.

"That's tabby," explained the lawyer. "Old sea-island building substance made of lime, water, sand, oyster shells, and ash. In the old days it was the most economical building material because of its ready availability and durability. You'll notice that your chimneys are also made of tabby."

I smiled at his use of the word *your,* as if I were the rightful owner and not just the unknown wife of a favorite son who'd disappeared from this place twenty-one years before. Maybe it was the way of the South to welcome home wayward family members who had no claim to such a piece of history except for a willingness to adopt it as their own and a shared last name.

A strong breeze blew up from the river, cooling the sweat that had begun to drip down my neck, and I could see the shimmying of the leaves and moss of the oak tree reflected in the dull sidelight windows. A melodic tinkling sang above me, and I looked up in surprise. Lining the peeling blue porch ceiling were about a dozen wind chimes made of what looked like blue and green stones.

"Edith made those. They're on the upstairs balcony, too. She liked to collect sea glass and figured this was a good way to display her favorite pieces."

I looked closer, frowning. "They look like stones."

"They do. That's because they've been tumbled about the ocean for many years, which gives them that cloudy look. That's what she liked about them. Edith said that any glass that could withstand such a beating without crumbling was something to be celebrated." He smiled to himself as if recalling an old conversation. "She always said that only fools thought all glass was fragile."

Another breeze chased us up the steps, bringing a respite from the heat and making the glass dance and sing. I frowned, contemplating the wind chimes, and tried not to think of the old woman who'd made them. "They're charming, but I wonder if the noise will keep me up at night."

Mr. Williams slid a large brass key from his pocket. "Oh, maybe the first few nights, but I expect you'll get used to it after a while, to the point that you'll find it hard to sleep without them."

I took one last look at the long row of wind chimes, wondering whether I'd need to go buy a stepladder so I could remove them, then stepped past Mr. Williams holding open the large door and into the foyer of my new home.

My first impression was of vastness, of high ceilings and thick baseboards, of a wide and deep foyer with four tall, thick doors opening on two sides, a narrow hallway leading toward the back of the house. A delicate banister of dark wood held aloft by slender spindles curved its way to the second floor, cradling an enormous crystal chandelier that had more cobwebs than working lights. It smelled of dust and age and neglect, and I finally understood Mr. Williams's reluctance to allow me to move right in.

But I saw beauty, too, hidden under the dust and dark shadows. I saw it in the intricately carved ceiling medallions and door cornices, in the broken inlaid wood floors of the dining room and marble pilasters that separated the two parlors. It was there in the graceful sweep of the solid-wood banister and in the tall rice poster beds of the bedrooms upstairs.

Everything reeked of dust, but I couldn't help remembering the feeling I'd had staring up at the house, as if it were considering me as much as I was considering it. The sense of expectation, of us both waiting for something to happen. The feeling dogged my steps until I realized I was holding my breath and imagined the house doing the same thing.

Mr. Williams opened a door to the main bathroom upstairs, and I stayed back, having already been warned — and knowing from seeing just inside the door the chipped marble floor tiles and antiquated claw-foot bathtub — that although the house had modern plumbing and electricity, nothing much had changed in a very long time.

"Which was Cal's room?" I asked, my voice sounding loud in the quiet house.

"This one," the lawyer said as he moved to the end of the hallway and pushed open a door. The heat poured out of the room, keeping me at the threshold just long enough to see the twin bed and a large chest at its foot. LEGO models covered bookshelves and a small desk under the window, sharing room with school textbooks. A dog-eared copy of *Huckleberry Finn* sat on the nightstand. I stared at it, not recalling ever seeing Cal read a book.

"It's like he never left," I said, unaware I'd spoken out loud.

"When he left so suddenly, it broke Edith's heart. She'd never been a happy person, but her grandsons brought a lot of light into her life."

"What about Gibbes — Cal's brother? Did he have a good relationship with Edith?"

We stepped out of the room and Mr. Williams closed the door, pausing with his hands on the doorknob for a moment while he thought. "They did. Up until Cal left. Gibbes was only about ten at the time, but I think he blamed Edith for making Cal leave. As soon as Gibbes went off to college and med school, he barely came home. Sometimes he would stay with us instead of staying here on his school breaks — he and my sons were good friends. And I don't think it was all his choice, either. After Cal left, Edith just sort of . . . closed up shop, I guess. She told me . . ." He stopped as if remembering to whom he was speaking.

"She told you what?" I asked. "I'm sorry to be so blunt, but Cal was my husband. I'm just . . . I'm trying to make sense of all this."

He nodded slowly. "She said that Gibbes was better off with us than with her. That she'd failed twice to raise good men and she wanted Gibbes to have a chance. This was still his home, but Edith made sure that he spent a lot of time with us. She thought that we were his only chance to have a happy, normal life. I'm not sure I agreed, but there was nothing I could do to persuade her otherwise. And Gibbes seemed to enjoy having brothers around, especially after Cal left." He paused, his thoughts turned inward. "I do know that she loved Gibbes very much. Enough to send him away."

I could see that Mr. Williams didn't understand what she'd meant any more than I did, so I didn't press. "But why would Gibbes blame Edith? What could she have done to make Cal leave?"

Mr. Williams shrugged. "She never confided in me." Patting my arm, he said, "And I guess now we'll never know."

We were headed back toward the staircase when I paused in front of a closed door that we hadn't gone through yet. "What's in here?"

Mr. Williams tried the knob. "I'm not really sure, to be honest. I imagine it's the stairs to the attic, since we haven't run across those yet. Don't know why the key's missing, though. All the other doors have their keys in the locks, and I know I wasn't given any extras. I know a good locksmith and I'll send him over. I'm sure it's only old furniture and clothes up there, but you never know." He winked, as if a surprise in the attic might make up for the rest of the house.

I put my hand on his arm. "It's fine, you know. The house. I think . . ." I stopped myself from telling him that I felt the house had been waiting for me, that maybe we had been waiting for each other, each needing our dust and cobwebs cleaned out. "I think I'll enjoy setting it all to rights."

He smiled, looking relieved. With one last look at the locked door, we made our way down the stairs, Mr. Williams holding my elbow whether I needed it or not.

It was at least twenty degrees cooler downstairs with the air-conditioning units in the dining room and front parlor blowing out air that, while not exactly cold, was better than the heat from upstairs.

"Do you garden, Merritt?"

I shook my head. "No. Not that I wouldn't want to learn, but I've never had the opportunity. Cal and I only had a small yard, and he hated to spend any time working in it, so it was pretty sparse."

The old lawyer looked at me oddly. "Follow me through the kitchen. Edith really loved her garden, although as you can see, it became too much for her in the end."

We walked through a kitchen with appliances that were decidedly midcentury but, as Mr. Williams explained, were all in fine working order — including the refrigerator and stove, which looked like they'd been ripped out of a scene from the fifties TV show *Leave It to Beaver.*

He opened the back door and waited. I smelled the garden before I saw it, a sweet, heady fragrance of flowers I was not familiar with, mixed with a rich green aroma not unlike the pluff mud. There was a narrow porch and then a wide flight of tabby steps, and I stood on the top one, staring at the magical place in front of me. Four wind chimes dangled from the porch, and I found their presence somehow unnerving, their soft sound like a constant whispering where you couldn't understand the words.

"What's that?" I asked, pointing to a narrow door at the end of the porch.

"The entrance to the basement. Nothing you need to see. Mostly cobwebs, I expect. Still has the dirt floors and timber rafters. Slave quarters back in the day, I suspect. Not much use for it now except for a wine cellar, most likely." He winked.

I turned my attention back to the garden. A winding brick walkway meandered its way through patches of brightly colored shrubs and flowers, skirting the high wall I'd seen from the front yard. It was covered with a climbing vine that drew me to it with its scent. I stood before it and couldn't help but smile.

"That's Confederate jasmine," Mr. Williams offered. "Has a short growing season, but every garden has at least some of it."

"It's gorgeous," I said, taking in a deep breath.

"Cal put in this bench for Miss Edith, so she could sit and enjoy her garden. He made it just for her."

Behind me, against the side garden wall, surrounded by potted flowers that seemed to have run amok, was a pretty curved wooden bench with a high back and wide arms big enough to rest a glass of lemonade or a cup of tea on.

I touched it, wondering who this Cal had

been. My Cal claimed to have no knowledge of how to wield a hammer or nail. Or how to plant living things and make them grow.

I looked around at the wild beauty of the garden, imagining Cal there. "You said Cal used to help Edith with the garden?"

Mr. Williams nodded. "Yes. He'd do all the heavy lifting for her, but he also liked to help with the planting." He paused, as if measuring his words. "He said it was the only place he could find that would calm his soul."

Our eyes met, and I couldn't help but wonder to what extent Mr. Williams knew of Cal's troubled soul. And to what lengths Cal would go to find the peace he so desperately sought.

I looked away, not wanting to know the answer, and my eye touched on the statue of a saint standing lopsided between two billowing rosebushes, one of its hands missing.

"Saint Michael," Mr. Williams provided.

"The protector," I added quietly. "Cal put a small Saint Michael by our front door." I stared at the stone face, at the eyes turned heavenward, knowing why Cal had thought we needed one. And wondering why his grandmother had thought the same thing.

I bent to smell a rose, its scent pungent in

the afternoon heat. "Were Cal and his brother close?"

I felt Mr. Williams shrug before turning to look at him. "They were ten years apart, so Cal was raised almost like an only child. It must have been a shock for him when Gibbes arrived. But even if they'd been closer in age, I don't know how close they might have been. Cal was like his father. Very . . . physical. Both were high school football stars — did Cal tell you that?"

I shook my head, pretending to examine the roses more closely.

He continued. "And Gibbes was more like their mother. More introspective and inquisitive. Before his job took over his life he was big into sailing — did a great deal of it in high school — loves the complexities of cheating the wind, I suppose. No time for it anymore, but he and my sons still spend time on the water when they can." He chuckled softly. "I taught Cal and Gibbes how to play chess, thinking it was something they could do together. It was a terrible idea, of course. Cal would start off using his queen to barrel through his opponent's pawns and then lose her early on. Gibbes would strategize his next five moves and win the game in six. Most of their games ended with Cal throwing the board across the room."

My finger stung, and when I looked down at it I saw I'd pricked it on a thorn. I sucked on the pad, tasting copper and remembering Cal. Squeezing my finger and thumb together to stop the bleeding, I said, "I hope you don't mind my asking these questions. I'm sure it seems odd to you that Cal never told me anything. I don't blame him. Really, I don't. I was relieved, I think, because then that gave me the excuse to never talk about my own past."

"You have no family," he said, his face so sympathetic that I felt the sting of tears and had to look away.

"No," I said, turning my head so that I faced the stone saint. "How did their parents die?"

He took a deep breath. "Their mama, Cecelia, fell down the stairs and broke her neck. It was New Year's Eve and she was wearing a long gown. C.J., their daddy, said he thought her heel had caught in the back of the skirt. She was dead by the time he reached the bottom of the steps. Gibbes was only five and Cal fifteen — terrible ages to lose a mother. C.J. died three years later. He was a heavy drinker and smoker, so it was no surprise that he died of a heart attack at forty-six. But my wife believes he died of a broken heart."

I nodded silently, wondering whether such a thing was possible and wishing that something Mr. Williams had told me explained why my husband had left this place and never wanted to share his past with me.

We both looked up at the sound of car doors slamming. Mr. Williams began walking toward a rusty iron gate disguised by the climbing jasmine on the garden wall. "It might be members from the Heritage Society bringing casseroles in the hopes of getting a peek inside the house."

He lifted a heavy latch and turned a small doorknob before pulling on the gate, the vines and time blocking his efforts. "I'll find some pruning shears and cut these away this Saturday, if you like. Let's go back through the house to the front door."

As we stood inside the foyer, I heard a woman's voice outside and the sound of footsteps crossing the wooden floorboards of the porch. I threw open the door before anyone could ring the doorbell.

I found myself staring into large blue eyes that were surrounded by what could only be false eyelashes. She had on fresh pink lipstick, and her blond hair was worn long and wavy with a pouf at the crown. Her silk blouse looked expensive but was unbuttoned one button too far, and her slim skirt revealed a long expanse of legs — legs ending in impossibly high heels.

I was so busy staring that I didn't see the young boy standing beside her until I heard him speak. "Merritt?"

A small breeze teased the wind chimes, making them all sing in unison, the sound more like an alarm bell to me as I stared at the boy. He had a slight build, and seemed far enough from puberty that his cheeks still had a little baby fat despite his lean frame. He had thick, dark hair with a cowlick that parted his hair at an odd angle. His eyes, hidden behind thick-rimmed dark glasses, were bright blue, enlarged and blinking at me like an owl. I couldn't stop staring at him. I'd seen eyes like that before. And the same dark hair. They were just like my father's. They were just like mine.

The woman put her arm around the boy's shoulder and smiled, and I saw how beautiful she was, and was reminded again that she was only five years older than me. "We wanted to surprise you, Merritt. We were going to go to Maine, but when I called the museum where you used to work, they told me you had moved to South Carolina. When I explained to the woman who I was, she gave me your lawyer's name. And when I stopped by the lawyer's just now, the woman there gave me your address." She smiled even more broadly, as if she were delivering a much-anticipated gift, and moved the boy to stand in front of her. "This is your brother, Owen."

I was too stunned to speak, my tongue heavy in my mouth. The boy stepped forward and offered me his hand to shake. "Actually, I'm going by Rocky now. Rocky Connors."

I stared down at his hand, soft and pale with bony knuckles just like our father's, then took it. His grip was surprisingly strong, his skin warm. He blinked up at me through the thick lenses of his glasses with uncertainty, but his handshake wasn't tentative. I imagined my father teaching him how to shake hands like a man. It was the kind of thing he'd once taught me.

Mr. Williams cleared his throat, waiting to be introduced, and I turned to him, trying to find a way to explain that I had no family regardless of the two people standing on the front porch.

The boy slid his hand from my grasp and turned to the lawyer. "I'm Rocky Connors, sir. It's nice to meet you."

"I'm Mr. Williams. It's nice to meet you,

too, Rocky." He turned to Loralee with a hopeful expression, as if she might want to explain who they were and why they were there.

But she'd stepped past us and was looking up at the row of sea-glass wind chimes, her expression like a child's on Christmas Day. "Mermaid's tears," she said, clasping her hands together over her Barbie-like chest. "I don't think I've ever seen anything so beautiful in my whole life."

Mr. Williams smiled at her as if he'd never seen anything as beautiful as she was, and I wanted to shout at him, to warn him that charming older gentlemen was something she was really good at.

"My mother used to call them that, too," he said, smiling a smile that wasn't grandfatherly at all. "You must have been raised by the ocean."

"Yes, sir, I was. In Gulf Shores, Alabama, not too far from the gulf." She stuck out an elegant, well-manicured hand with a broken index fingernail. "I'm Loralee Connors. Merritt's stepmother."

Mr. Williams took her hand, but looked at me with raised eyebrows, his expression letting me know that I had some explaining to do.

A stiff breeze blew at us and the house

73

and the wind chimes, making the glass stones sing. The long day and the stress of the last few months were finally too much for me, and my knees just buckled.

Loralee was closest and caught my elbow, and she and Mr. Williams led me to a wicker chair with an indented seat. I nodded my thanks, but, in my embarrassment, couldn't look at either of them. Instead, I kept my gaze focused on the scarred floorboards of the porch, listening to the wind as it picked up speed and shook the chimes, showering us all with the sound of glass.

CHAPTER 3

Loralee

Blood isn't always thicker than water. As Loralee watched Merritt hesitate before finally shaking Owen's hand, that was the first thing she thought, and she moved a bracelet to her other arm to remind herself to add it to her *Journal of Truths* later. But then Loralee saw that Merritt's eyes were the same color as Robert's and their son's, except just a shade darker. It was like all the hurts in Merritt's life had settled there. Loralee thought they probably created shadows in front of everything Merritt saw in life, and felt herself soften toward her stepdaughter. But Loralee knew she could never let on that she'd seen Merritt's weakness, that she knew Merritt felt the hurts more than most people and thought she'd figured out how to hide them from those who knew where to look.

Loralee knelt down by the wicker chair so

she could see Merritt's face. "If you tell me where the kitchen is, I'll go fetch you some water."

Merritt looked at her with an expression Loralee had seen on a fox her mama's bluetick hound, Roscoe, had cornered outside their chicken coop. It was hunger, and hopelessness, but tucked way back was the tiny glimmer that there was still a chance to escape.

"Why are you here?" Merritt asked, her Northern accent at once jarring and familiar to Loralee.

"I figured it was time you met your brother. Your daddy would want that." Loralee hoped that she was better at hiding her real feelings than Merritt was.

Merritt struggled to get out of her chair and Loralee knew better than to offer help. It would be like trying to help a rattler by moving a rock off its tail. It would bite you just because it was hurt and didn't know the cause of it.

She fell back into the seat and glared at Loralee. "What makes you think that I give a" — she glanced at Owen before continuing — "hoot what my father wanted? He didn't care what I wanted, so I guess that makes us even."

Loralee wanted to tell her something she'd

already written in her *Journal of Truths* — that life wasn't about keeping score — but she didn't think Merritt would appreciate it just then. Loralee knew she should take Owen by the hand and go find a hotel, to give Merritt time to get used to the idea of their being there. But she was running out of time, and a category five hurricane wind couldn't have blown her from her spot on the porch.

She felt Owen's worried eyes on her, and Loralee knew she had to make this work. "Your daddy said that you and Owen are like two peas in a pod. Always has his nose in a book and loves to swim. He's on the summer rec swim team. He hasn't won a ribbon yet, but he signs up every summer so he can try. Your daddy said you did the same thing."

Merritt looked at Owen, and they regarded each other with matching eyes. Loralee felt a glimmer of hope, as if she'd somehow found a rip in Merritt's duct-taped heart that allowed a little light to shine in. "He loves to draw and paint, too, and he's so creative. You should see what he can do with a bunch of LEGO bricks."

Brother and sister continued to stare at each other without Merritt saying anything, and Loralee began to fish through her brain for something else she could try to convince her stepdaughter to allow them to stay. She was about to mention how they both ate their Oreos cream-first (according to Robert) when Owen reached into his pants pocket and pulled out a folded piece of paper.

Handing it to Merritt, he said, "I drew this for you. It's not very good, because I was only six. But that's when I found out I had a sister."

Loralee watched as Merritt's mouth softened, which made her believe that Merritt would take the piece of paper. Because if she didn't, Loralee didn't know if she could be held accountable for what she might do.

Owen took a step forward and slid the paper from his fingers to hers. She opened it slowly, then spent several moments staring at it without saying anything. Mr. Williams shifted his feet as Loralee and Owen held their breath, waiting for Merritt to say something.

"It's very good," she said, her words sounding like they'd been tumbled with cotton. "Even for a six-year-old," she added, and her lips tilted upward in what probably passed for a smile in some parts of the country.

The three of them let go of their breath as

Merritt's gaze settled back on Owen's face and her features softened as if she'd put on a mask. Loralee wondered whether Merritt did it on purpose, or if she was so used to hiding her feelings from other people that the mask appeared without her knowing. "It's nice to finally meet you, Owen. And I'm glad you've come for a visit. I'm sure there are hotels in town. . . ."

"We have the same eyes," he said, studying her the way he watched the ants in his ant farm. Like he had to study her to figure out how she worked. Loralee decided that he probably had that right.

Merritt's eyes darkened, and Loralee thought of the cornered fox again. Merritt blinked rapidly as she stared back at Owen as if she were going to cry. But Loralee knew she wouldn't. Merritt had probably practiced how not to cry in front of other people for years. Loralee had figured that one out when Robert told her how Merritt had gone to her mama's funeral with dry eyes, and then spent the wake bringing people punch and straightening the pillows on the couch. Loralee thought of something else to add to her journal: *Some people hide their grief by pretending it's not there.*

Loralee shifted her feet, wishing it were just her shoes that were making it hard to stand, and needing another breeze. Mr. Williams touched her elbow. "You all right there, Mrs. Connors?"

She gave him her flight-attendant smile, the one she'd used to greet passengers. "I'm fine, thank you. It's just a hot one today, isn't it?" She punctuated her words with a heavy fanning of her hand. She was about to ask again whether Merritt wanted her to get some water when Owen spoke.

He was looking up at the line of sea glass strung across the entire porch like an ocean had just thrown up all over the front of the house. "I like the wind chimes. Daddy made one for our backyard in our old house, but I think we forgot to bring it. Can I have a room where I can hear them from my bed? I'd like to hear the sound in the morning when I wake up. Sort of like I'm still in my bedroom and Daddy's downstairs."

Merritt must have heard his voice break a little, too, because she leaned forward, almost as if she wanted to reach out and touch him. But she didn't. Her lips tilted upward again, and Loralee wondered whether her smiling muscles would hurt the next day from being used too much.

"He made one for me, too, when I was a little girl. It would keep me awake, so he put it in the front yard, where I could hear it when I went to the school bus in the morning. He traveled a lot and I used to say it was his way of saying good morning even when he wasn't there."

Loralee put her hand on Owen's shoulder and squeezed, trying to show Merritt that they were a package deal. "I promise we won't be any trouble. And I'll be happy to put clean sheets on beds, or I could sleep on a couch — whatever is easiest for you." Her mama would be rolling over in her grave at her lack of manners for inviting themselves to move in with this stranger, even if she was Owen's blood relative.

Mr. Williams cleared his throat. "I really don't think the house is ready to be moved into right now, and there is plenty of room at my home —"

"You can stay here," Merritt interrupted, dropping Owen's picture in the seat of the chair next to her before standing. Directing her words to Loralee, she added, "I suppose you can stay for a couple of days. I just need to find some clean sheets for the beds and a few cleaning supplies."

Loralee felt Mr. Williams looking at her with expectation, but she knew her offer of help wouldn't be welcomed. Taking care of the details was probably how Merritt took back control, and Loralee wondered whether every girl who lost her mother did the same thing when life got muddier than a puddle. At least it had been that way for her.

She was about to mention that they might be staying longer than a few days, perhaps leaving out the details that she'd sold their house in Georgia along with all the furniture and had no place else to stay, when Mr. Williams pulled out his phone. "Let me call my wife and see if she can round up some supplies, or maybe even call her cleaning lady to see if she can come by. . . ." He stopped, his flip phone held in midair, and watched as a recent-model black Explorer pulled up at the curb.

The lawyer replaced his phone in his pocket and began quickly walking down the path toward the visitor with a worried look creasing his forehead.

Just as he reached the truck, the driver stepped out and stood facing the house, watching Mr. Williams approach. "Hello, Sidney," the man said, and Loralee understood for the first time what her mama had meant when she'd described a man as a tall drink of cool water.

He was young, early thirties, with light brown hair and tanned skin, as if he spent a lot of time outdoors. He was lean, but not thin, with broad shoulders and legs that filled out his khaki pants just right.

"I'm not sure now is a good time," Mr. Williams said to the visitor. "Why don't I set up a meeting at my office, and I'll let you know . . ."

But the younger man had shifted his focus from Mr. Williams back to the house, where Loralee stood with Owen and Merritt, and had begun walking up the path toward them. When he got closer, Loralee could see that his eyes were golden brown, like the color of Robert's favorite brandy. She could also see that he wore a smiley-face pin on his breast pocket, a wardrobe choice that seemed out of place with the expression on his face.

He made a beeline toward Loralee, but was distracted by a small, strangled sound from Merritt. Her face had gone even paler than it had been, and she was holding both of her hands to her face. She looked like a person who was seeing a ghost.

"Cal?" The one word seemed to suck the rest of her color from her face and the man stopped, his expression turning to one of worry as Merritt dropped back into the porch chair like a bag of rocks.

Loralee pushed on Owen's back. "Go find a clean glass and bring Merritt some cool water, sweetie. And hurry."

Mr. Williams rushed to Merritt's side and laid a fatherly hand on her shoulder. "No, Merritt, this is Gibbes. Cal's brother."

Her breath was coming in shallow gasps, and it looked like she might faint. Loralee wondered whether Merritt would ever forgive her for witnessing weakness. She figured that to Merritt, nearly fainting in front of three strangers would be right up there with being caught locked outside naked as the day she was born.

Without saying anything, Gibbes took Merritt's wrist in one hand, then glanced at his watch on his other arm like he was checking her pulse. That was when Loralee noticed his Mickey Mouse watch and the wrapped tops of three lollipops sticking out of his shirt pocket. Out of habit, left over from her days as an airline attendant, her eyes drifted to the empty ring finger on his left hand. She found herself wishing that she'd known he was coming over, because she would have tried to talk Merritt into a little bit of mascara and maybe a swipe of lipstick. First impressions were the most important. She'd put that one in her journal right after she'd met Robert.

Merritt snatched her hand out of his grasp, and Loralee was relieved to see two spots of red appear on her cheeks. "I'm fine," Merritt said, but she didn't try to get out of the chair, probably because she wasn't sure she could be steady on her feet and didn't want Gibbes to see. Thankfully, that meant Merritt had at least a bit of vanity, or at least enough for Loralee to work with.

Owen came through the doorway holding a tall aqua aluminum tumbler, an identical match to the ones Loralee's grandma had once owned, purchased with Green Stamps and used only for company and special occasions. The sides had already begun to sweat when he handed it to his sister.

Merritt took her time drinking, her eyes darting around, and she was looking like a giraffe at a watering hole filled with alligators Loralee had once seen on TV. She and Owen watched a lot of *National Geographic* so she'd know things she hadn't learned growing up in Gulf Shores, Alabama.

Mr. Williams's phone rang and he stepped off the porch to answer it, leaving Loralee to fill the silence. That was another thing she was good at, besides serving peanuts in small packets and pouring drinks. "I'm Loralee Connors, and this is my son, Owen."

Owen stepped forward and put out his hand just like his father had taught him and shot his mother an annoyed glance. "I'm going by Rocky now. It's nice to meet you, sir. Mama and I have just moved to Beaufort to live with my sister, Merritt."

Merritt choked on a sip of water, coughing as she held a delicate hand to her mouth.

Gibbes sent her a worried look, then took Owen's hand. "It's nice to meet you, Rocky. I'm Dr. Heyward." They shook hands. "You've got a nice grip for a ten-year-old. You play baseball?" His voice was slow and Southern, and Loralee felt reassured somehow, as if she were still in familiar territory.

"No, sir. I was in Little League for a while, but I got tired of handing out water bottles, so I thought I'd try to find a sport I was good at."

"And did you?"

"No, sir. But I'm still looking." Owen tilted his head like he did when he was hurt or confused. "How did you know I was ten?"

The man smiled, his teeth white and even. "I'm a pediatrician. It goes with the territory."

With a hard glance at Loralee and a swipe at a small wet spot on her blouse, Merritt placed the tumbler on a wicker table that held a pot with a dead stem and dried-up dirt inside it, then took a deep breath before standing quickly.

Holding out her hand to Gibbes, she said, "I'm Merritt. Cal's wife. He never told me he had a brother."

He stared at her hand for a long moment before taking it, his large hand dwarfing hers. The spots of color reappeared on her cheeks and she quickly slid her hand away.

His words were clipped. "I guess that makes us even, then, because Cal never told me he had a wife."

Merritt tilted her head, just like Owen had. "Did he ever call or write to you?"

Gibbes gave her an odd look. "He wrote a short note to me about once a year, letting me know he was still alive, but not much more than that. He stopped about nine years ago — I'm guessing around the time the two of you got married. Because he never mentioned you." He indicated the lawyer still speaking on his phone. "And Mr. Williams has informed me that you now own our grandmother's house."

Merritt stared at him openly. "Yes, it appears I do."

He looked up at the wind chimes that were busy shimmying in the wind. "How nice for you." Their eyes met, leaving Loralee to wonder who would look away first.

They both did as Mr. Williams came up the porch steps. "That was Kathy. She's sending her cleaning lady over now, and I'm to bring you all over to our house for supper. You're invited, too, Gibbes."

Gibbes slowly looked over at Merritt before shaking his head. "Please give my thanks to Mrs. Williams, but I have other plans."

The look on his face made Loralee think his plans were something pressing, like organizing his sock drawer or cleaning out his tackle box.

Addressing Mr. Williams, he said, "I'll call tomorrow to set up an appointment to go through the house. Assuming the new owner agrees."

Merritt crossed her arms over her chest. "The new owner can give you an answer if you'd care to ask her directly."

His jaw pulsed and Loralee wasn't sure whether he was trying not to smile or was clenching his teeth.

Instead of answering, Gibbes nodded, and without directing his words toward anybody in particular, he said, "It was a pleasure to meet you all."

Everybody watched as he walked back toward his truck while Loralee slowly backed into one of the chairs and sank down into it, sighing quietly so no one would hear her. The sun had begun to dip, casting long shadows onto the porch, and she rocked back into one of them, happy to be able to take cover for a moment, thankful for the distraction of the departing truck to hide how very, very tired she was.

She felt something beneath her leg and pulled out the picture that Merritt had dropped in the chair. It was a crayon drawing of a table with two people, a boy and a girl, sharing a glass of milk and a bag of cookies that looked like Oreos. They both appeared to be twisting the Oreos apart to eat the cream first. Loralee smiled, glad Owen had thought to bring it, and feeling hopeful for the first time. She focused on holding on to her smile, knowing that if she lost it, she might never find it again.

CHAPTER 4

Merritt

The sea-glass chimes crashed against one another outside on the porch as I attempted one more time to press a pillow over my head without suffocating. Although as I lay wide-eyed and sleepless, suffocation seemed like a good alternative. But then I thought of Cal, and how they said he'd died, and I felt guilty just for the thought.

I added another item to my mental shopping list right under earplugs: a ladder. Those damned wind chimes were coming down or I would be known as the second crazy lady who lived in the Heyward house.

After dinner with the Williamses, Loralee and I had driven to a grocery store with the improbable name of Piggly Wiggly to pick up supplies, and I remembered her putting a gallon of milk for Owen — or Rocky, as he seemed to want to be called — in the cart. I'd never tried it before, but I'd heard that warmed milk helped a person sleep. I'd have to find a pot to heat it on the ancient stove, because I didn't recall seeing a microwave.

The grocery-shopping trip had been an oddly silent one. Owen had slept in the car to and from the store, then walked like a zombie along the fluorescent-lit aisles. Loralee had been unusually silent, and I wondered if it was because she was tired, too, or because she'd realized that her heavy Alabama accent and nonstop chattering were giving me a headache. There could have been another reason, but I'd been too tired and my mind too full with the day's events to care enough to ask.

I threw off the covers — all freshly laundered and put on the beds by Kathy Williams's cleaning lady — and slid from the tall four-poster bed. This had been Edith's room, and her bed, and the only reason I'd been persuaded to use this bedroom was because Mr. Williams had told me that she had died in the downstairs parlor.

But her presence was everywhere. Her clothes remained in the tall antique armoire against the wall and in the closet; her silver-backed hairbrush, with long gray hair still wound around the bristles, rested on the dresser. I hadn't unpacked yet, because I was unsure I would remain in this room, with its view of the river from the front windows, and that of the garden from the side. I wasn't sure I wanted to wake up each morning and see the water. Even at this distance it made me uneasy. But I imagined that during cooler weather in the spring, when everything was blooming, the scents from the garden would rise up to this corner bedroom. For now, this was Edith's room and her house, and before I could start claiming space in it, I needed to convince myself that it was actually mine — something I hadn't really considered until I'd met Dr. Gibbes Heyward.

I heard a sound from inside the house and I stilled, straining my ears. I heard it again, like metal against glass, and I froze, thinking only of Edith and how she'd lived alone in this house for so long, and died within its old plastered walls. I relaxed only a little when I remembered that there were two other living, breathing people in the house with me who were capable of making noise.

It was a tall bed, and I had to slide off the side a bit until my feet touched the floor, my oversize New York Giants jersey reaching to my knees. I'd bought it for Cal our first Christmas together, but he'd told me to keep it, saying he preferred the Atlanta

Falcons. His rejection had hurt my feelings, but I'd felt better after realizing that it made the perfect nightgown for me. All these years later, I couldn't bear to part with it, clinging to it like a child might cling to a security blanket. If only it had made me feel secure.

Barefoot, I crossed the wood floor and pulled open my door, sticking my head out into the corridor. A plastic Darth Vader night-light had been stuck in a baseboard outlet, looking ridiculously out of place in the elegant yet shabby decor of the hallway. But Loralee had insisted, saying that all three of us might need it if we woke up disoriented. She'd said "we," but she'd shifted her eyes to Owen. Apparently my half brother and I shared more than a love for eating Oreos cream-first.

I'd learned to compensate for my fear of the dark since my marriage to Cal. He didn't like any show of weakness and had banned night-lights not just from our bedroom and bathroom, but from our house. He'd been right, of course. No adult should harbor childish fears, no matter how justified their source.

The noise came again, and I was pretty sure it was from the kitchen. I peered down the hallway, seeing that Owen's bedroom door, to what had been Cal's room, was closed, but that the door to the room next to his was open.

I made my way down to the first level, then toward the back of the house to the kitchen. The swinging door had been left propped open, and I stopped right before the light of the kitchen hit me to observe.

Loralee, wearing a ridiculous long silk leopard-print peignoir set with matching kitten-heel slippers, stood at the peeling Formica counter stirring a light brown liquid in a large Tupperware pitcher with a wooden spoon. A bag of sugar — from our trip to the store — sat open in front of her, and as I watched she picked it up and poured the remainder of the bag into the pitcher, and then the entire thing into a large pot on the stove. I hoped that meant the stove was working.

"What are you doing?" I asked, forgetting my plan to back away and head back upstairs before she spotted me.

She jerked a little in surprise, then widened her perfect mouth into a genuine smile. "I couldn't sleep, so I decided to make sweet tea so that we have some tomorrow. I hope I didn't wake you. I was trying to be real quiet."

I didn't return her smile, as I was too focused on what she was doing. "Do you need a measuring cup? Because I can't believe you just poured that much sugar in the pot." ° °

She waved a hand at me like I'd just made a joke and began dragging the wooden spoon through the pot. Grinning even more broadly, she said, "There's no such thing as too much sugar in your sweet tea. My mama said that when I was a girl she'd take my little finger and dip it in her glass to make it just a little bit sweeter." Her smile softened. "I told that to your daddy, and he did the same thing with Owen. I have it on a DVD if you ever want to see it."

I looked away, and not just because I was uncomfortable with her mention of the man who connected us, but because of the absurdity of this woman standing in my kitchen. Loralee looked like she was dressed to appear in a television commercial, complete with shiny, thick hair tumbling down the leopard-print silk, and what looked like full makeup. Even the way she was posed by the counter, with a slender knee peeking out from the opening of her robe, seemed staged.

I thought of my mother in her flannel pajamas and fluffy robe, with brown hair that frizzed in the summer and flattened against her head while she slept. She had died when I was twelve, but when I thought of her now I knew the word *sexy* had never been used to describe her. She was the kind of mother who baked cookies and volunteered for the PTA, packed your lunch and made sure you had a sweater if she thought it was too cool outside. She would never make a drink that had more than the month's allotment of sugar, or wear something low-cut that would make her stand out from your friends' mothers. She didn't wear makeup, and her hair was always worn short, because it was easier to take care of. She was the kind of mother I was proud of — the kind of mother who saved her child even when it meant there was no time to save herself.

I began opening cabinets, looking for a pan to heat my milk, eager to keep myself occupied so Loralee wouldn't see my anger. "Do you sleep in makeup?" I asked, unable to resist.

She laughed. "No — but it looks like I do, doesn't it? I had my eyebrows and eyeliner tattooed so that when I woke up in the morning, Robert would still think I was beautiful."

I gritted my teeth at the mention of my father's name, but she didn't seem to notice, because she continued. "He always said I didn't need any makeup, but that's because he never saw me without it. My mama always said that everybody could use a little help."

I didn't look up, but I felt her looking at me, and my irritation grew. Finding a warped pan with scald marks on the bottom, I slammed the cabinet door a little too loudly. I faced her, ready to tell her bluntly that I didn't need any help from her about makeup or anything else, but stopped with the words still in my throat.

She was gripping the edge of the counter, and her face was screwed up as if she had eaten something that didn't agree with her. Her porcelain skin seemed even a shade lighter.

"Are you all right?" I asked, keeping my distance, unsure what I should do.

She remained where she was for a few more moments before opening her eyes and meeting mine. Her smile was shaky. "I think I just had a sugar rush — been tasting this tea too much." With her back to me, she turned off the stove and placed a lid over it so the contents could cool. With a washcloth, she began wiping up the counter, her movements slow and deliberate, while the bell-shaped sleeves of her robe billowed out like the arms of a conductor conducting a symphony.

Trying to avoid her as much as I could in the small kitchen, I placed the pan on the stove before reaching into the refrigerator for the milk. Somehow my hand slipped from the handle of the gallon jug, sending the entire thing crashing to the floor and spewing milk on the black and white checked linoleum, the cabinets, the stove, me, and the leopard-print silk peignoir.

We both stared wide-eyed at the milk pooling on the floor and dripping off the cabinets and refrigerator drawer. I had the oddest sensation that I needed to laugh, but I held back, unable to find the energy to utter any sound at all. Loralee quickly started opening various drawers until she found one full of faded and frayed dish towels. She tossed a handful to me and took more for herself. Without a word, she slipped off her robe, leaving only the skimpy nightie that was too short to get milk on the hem, and began mopping up the white liquid.

I knelt on the floor opposite her and began to do the same thing. Without looking at me, she said, "Were you making warm milk to help you sleep? My mama always said that an herbal tea and a warm bath —"

I didn't let her finish. "You know, Loralee, I don't really care what your mama used to tell you. None of it pertains to me or how I want to live my life. And right now, I've chosen to move to South Carolina to live by myself while I figure out what I'm supposed to do next. Forgive me if I'm not overjoyed with your sudden visit. And regardless of what you might have told Owen, this is a visit. A short one. I have no idea what you were thinking, just showing up on my doorstep expecting to stay with me."

She blinked her eyes at me several times, her long black lashes fanning her cheeks. I couldn't help but wonder whether those had been artificially implanted, too. Sitting back on her legs, she said, "When I called your office to find you, they told me that you'd inherited your husband's family home in Beaufort and that's why you were moving here. I kind of put two and two together and figured out your husband must have died. With us being widows, I thought maybe we had something in common besides your father. It's a hard thing to deal with, and I thought we could help each other. I thought we could be friends."

"How can we be friends, Loralee? You were married to my father for eleven years, and I saw you maybe three times before you got engaged and not once after the wedding. There's a reason for that. So, no, I don't think we can be friends. We're practically strangers, and I'm happy to leave it at that."

Her smile dimmed. "My mama used to say that strangers are only friends we haven't yet met." She put her hand over her mouth. "Sorry. That just popped out."

I sighed. "I'm not good at relationships — family or otherwise. I'm glad you brought Owen — I am. He seems like a great kid. I'll make sure that I send him a birthday and Christmas present every year. But I can't pretend that I want either one of you in my life — there's no room."

"What are you talking about? This house is huge. You've got plenty of room — and you'll need help taking care of all this space." She held up her long, slender hands, my father's huge engagement ring sparkling on her finger, nestled against a simple gold wedding band. "And you've got an extra pair of hands to help right here."

She smiled again, but there was a brightness missing, as if she was aware that we both knew that my having no room had nothing to do with the size of the house.

The strong breezes of the afternoon and evening had given way to a full-blown storm, and a gust of wind and rain struck the house, making the wind chimes shriek.

"Did you hear that?" Loralee asked, her voice full of expectation.

"I've been hearing it all night — I think you'd have to be dead or a ten-year-old boy not to. As soon as I can find a ladder, they're coming down."

Loralee looked stricken. "Oh, no. Don't do that — they're so beautiful. When I was a little girl, I really believed they were mermaid's tears. I think I still do. Maybe that's why I like them so much — because they remind me of what it was like to be a child and believe in magic."

I had another memory, of my mother planting the lima bean I'd brought home from school. I told her that it was a magic bean that would grow to be huge and I could climb all the way up to the clouds on it. She hadn't said anything as we'd planted it together, and I had watered it religiously, staking it with a Popsicle stick. But it had never gotten any bigger than a lima bean plant no matter how much care I gave it. In a fit of anger and frustration, I'd ripped it out by the roots and run to my mother, who'd comforted me with her arms around me and a gentle pat on the back. As the years passed, I began to understand that as a mother she'd just been trying to ease me into the reality of what life was, to help me understand that magic wasn't real no matter how we wished differently.

"It's just broken glass, Loralee."

She tilted her head. "I know that, Merritt. But I think sometimes even adults — especially adults — need to believe in magic. Do you know the legend of the mermaid's tears?"

"No, and I really —"

As if I hadn't spoken, she continued. "The story goes way, way back, and is about a beautiful mermaid who fell in love with a sailor. To save his life she calmed a storm, which was forbidden. As her punishment, she was banned to the bottom of the ocean, where she is to this day, crying her heart out for her lost love, and we're reminded of her every time we find a bit of sea glass on the shore."

I wanted to tell her she was being ridiculous, that mermaids weren't real. But the softness in her face, and what she'd said about us needing to believe in a little bit of magic, stopped me.

I took a deep breath. "You can stay a week. That should be plenty of time for me to get to know Owen before you head back to Georgia."

"We're not going back to Georgia. We were thinking that since you're here, this might be a good place to settle down." She smiled, but it was different somehow. Like she was holding two conversations and I could hear only one of them.

"Why don't you go back to Gulf Shores? I'm sure your mother would be happy to see you."

"Mama died when I was twenty. I've been on my own ever since. Robert and Owen are the only real family I've ever had. And now you."

She didn't say it with self-pity, and I respected her for that. But it didn't make me want to like her any better. She was still an over-made-up, underdressed, big-haired woman who'd snared herself a man nearly twice her age despite the fact that he had a daughter just five years younger than she was who didn't approve. I couldn't bring myself to care too much where she went next.

Throwing my towels in the sink, I said, "I'll mop this up in the morning — I'm too tired to deal with it right now. I'm going to bed — see you tomorrow." I turned to go.

"Good night, Merritt. Sleep tight, and don't let the bedbugs bite."

I stopped and turned around, then took another deep breath, wearier than I'd been when I'd come downstairs. "Let me guess

— that's something your mother used to say."

She gave me a wide grin. "Uh-huh. But I say it to Owen every night now, too. I guess you could say it's sort of a family tradition."

I nodded, then headed toward the stairs, remembering how my mother had always said, "Sweet dreams," before she closed my bedroom door, and how it had been a long, long time since I remembered how to dream.

CHAPTER 5

Loralee

The smell of frying bacon filled the small kitchen, reminding Loralee of the tiny trailer she'd shared with her mother all those years ago. Loralee had never been allowed to go anywhere before she'd had a home-cooked breakfast, and it was something she'd continued to do for Owen. Her mama had always smelled like bacon grease from the diner where she worked two shifts every day. She was always there for Loralee when she came home from school, and each morning ready and dressed in her uniform and apron. She'd be standing at the two-burner oven in the corner of the trailer they called the kitchen, frying up bacon or flipping flapjacks from batter that the diner's cook had slipped Desiree in a small Tupperware bowl.

Loralee gripped the edge of the counter and leaned on her arms as she closed her eyes. The smell wasn't agreeing with her this morning, stealing what little appetite she still had. She heard Owen's steady steps down the hallway and quickly straightened and put a smile on her face. She placed two fried eggs on a plate and then selected a couple of strips of bacon, arranging them so it looked like a smiley face.

Owen entered the kitchen and blinked sleepily at her before settling in at the old Formica kitchen table. Out of habit, Loralee took his glasses from his face and cleaned them with the hem of her skirt. He was wearing the new pair of jeans she'd bought the previous day, the crease in the middle still sharp. His knit golf shirt with the little man playing polo stuck on the left corner was buttoned up to his neck.

As Loralee replaced his glasses, she resisted the pull to unbutton the top button and to rumple his hair, which had been parted and combed down with water. He liked it that way, he'd told her, because his daddy had worn his hair like that.

"Good morning, Owen," she said, kissing the top of his head, relieved that he hadn't pulled away when she kissed him. She knew that was part of growing up, and she accepted that. She just wasn't ready for it yet.

"Good morning, Mama," he said, staring

down at his plate. He put both elbows on the table and let out a heavy sigh.

"What's the matter?" she asked, stopping at the side of the table.

He shrugged a bony shoulder. "I like the smiley face — I really do. But if I go to a real school here, don't do that with anything you pack in my lunch box, okay?"

"Sure," she said, smiling although it hurt her to do it. "I understand." And she did. It was just too soon.

"So you're already talking about schools here?"

They both turned to see Merritt standing in the kitchen doorway. She wore another shapeless skirt that was too long for her, and a beige blouse that did nothing for her coloring. Her beautiful dark hair was scraped off her face into a low ponytail, and her face was bare of any makeup. Her skin was pale but perfect, and Loralee itched to sit her down and put some color on her lips and cheeks. She didn't even have earrings in her earlobes, leaving Loralee to wonder whether she didn't have her ears pierced, or maybe there wasn't a mirror in her bedroom and she hadn't noticed that she'd forgotten to accessorize.

Loralee pulled out a chair across from Owen. "I'm making breakfast — eggs, bacon, toast, and I've got blueberries just in case you have a hankering for blueberry pancakes."

Her stepdaughter looked as if she would refuse the chair until she saw Owen's hopeful expression. She sat down on the edge of the chair as if she didn't plan to be there for very long, and said, "Just coffee, please. I usually don't eat breakfast."

Loralee walked over to the old percolator and poured steaming coffee into a chipped china cup before bringing it over to the table. "But breakfast is the most important meal of the day. My mama . . ." She stopped when she saw the look on Merritt's face. "Cream or sugar?" she asked instead.

"Just black," Merritt said, then added, "Thank you," as if remembering her manners. She blew across the top of her cup and took a sip, looking up at Loralee as she did so. "So, what's this about looking for schools? You've been here less than a day. I'm sure there are other places you should consider before making a decision."

Loralee turned her back to the table and cracked two eggs in the skillet. "Yes, well, schools will be a big part of our decision. We figured that while we're here we should go ahead and check out the public and private schools. Owen's been homeschooled for the last year but wants to get back into what he calls 'real' school again."

"Mama, I'm going by Rocky now, remember?"

She adjusted the heat under the pan. "If that's what you want everybody to call you once you're in school, that's fine. But to me you'll always be Owen, all right? It would be like me suddenly asking you to call me Daisy instead of Mama."

Owen laughed, making Loralee smile.

Merritt said, "I set my alarm so I could get up and come down here and mop up the rest of the milk I spilled last night, but for some reason it didn't go off."

Loralee flipped the eggs, the melted butter crackling in protest. "I turned it off because you wouldn't wake up, so I let you sleep, seeing as how you probably needed it after your long drive. And that nice-looking doctor called and said he'd be here at ten with Mr. Williams."

"You what?"

Loralee turned around at the sound of a kitchen chair being scraped on the floor as Merritt shot to her feet. "What time is it now?"

"It's nine forty-five. And I already mopped the floor, and I made some cookies for the doctor when he gets here —"

Merritt cut her off. "There will be no entertaining him, all right? The man doesn't like me very much, and I don't think my opinion of him is much better. He's coming over to decide what he wants to take from his childhood home, and then he's leaving. And hopefully that will be the last time we need to see each other."

Loralee slid the eggs, bacon, and toast onto a plate and turned to set it on the table. "Well, you'll need your energy if you're going to tussle with him, so you might as well sit down and eat. I'll be happy to answer the door when they get here."

Merritt stared at her for a long moment before slowly sitting down again. She looked at her plate suspiciously. "It's smiling at me," she said, her voice not amused.

"Just go with it," Owen said, putting a forkful of eggs in his mouth.

Loralee dropped the pan in the sink and began to run the hot water.

"Aren't you going to eat, Mama?" Owen asked.

"I already did," she said, adding one more lie to the list. "And don't talk with your mouth full." She turned the faucet as far as it would go, but only a lukewarm drip of water rewarded her efforts. "I think you're going to need a plumber, Merritt. Unless

110

you like cold showers and greasy plates. I could ask one of the neighbors for a recommendation when we go over to introduce ourselves. . . ."

Merritt coughed and Loralee looked over her shoulder in time to see coffee sloshing over Merritt's cup as she roughly set it down on the table. "Excuse me? Even if I thought that knocking on a stranger's door unannounced were something expected here, I can't imagine why you'd be accompanying me."

"So they could meet Owen," Loralee said, squeezing dishwashing soap onto the new sponge they'd bought the night before. "Since he's family and all."

"She baked cookies 'cause she figured you probably didn't know how and she wanted to make a good impression." Owen's words were garbled, and Loralee wanted to tell him again about not speaking with his mouth full, but she was too busy being embarrassed.

Keeping her back to the table, she continued scrubbing the now-clean pan. "Robert said you never liked to spend any time in the kitchen; that's why I thought you wouldn't want to do any baking. But they're chocolate-and-peanut-butter-chip — Owen's second-favorite cookies — so I thought you'd like them, too. And don't tell me you're counting calories, either. You're so skinny, when you turn to the side and stick out your tongue you look like a zipper."

Loralee cringed at the sound of a kitchen chair being scraped back, and she was pretty sure it wasn't Owen's.

Merritt's words were tight, as if she was measuring them carefully. "I appreciate your cleaning up the milk and making me breakfast — I do. But I don't want you to do anything else for me, all right? And if you're going to be staying here for a week, we're setting some ground rules, the first being that my room and alarm clock are off-limits. As are my neighbors and any plumbers or electricians or whoever else I might need to come work on the house. You and Owen are guests here, and all I'll need you to do is stack your sheets and towels on the floor of the laundry room when you leave."

Loralee had finally gotten control of her face to turn around. "Actually, Merritt, the washing machine isn't working — I tried to wash those towels we used to mop up the milk last night and it just made this sound like an old pickup truck trying to start on a cold morning. That load of sheets Mrs. Williams's cleaning lady did for us must have been the washing machine's swan song.

There's a stack of Yellow Pages in the garage, so I looked up a number and a serviceman will be here between one and five. I would have looked it up on my phone, but I only had one bar and there's no Wi-Fi connection. I can call somebody for that, too, if you'd like."

Loralee smiled her flight-attendant smile, the one even the crankiest passenger couldn't help but respond to. But Merritt was different, and instead of smiling back she seemed to be getting angrier as bright red spots of color appeared on her cheeks. Loralee wanted to take a picture with her iPhone so that she could show Merritt what she'd look like with a little bit of blush on her cheeks, but she figured this probably wouldn't be the right time.

Merritt barely moved her lips while she spoke. "I can't talk with you right now. I'm going upstairs —"

The doorbell interrupted whatever she'd been about to say.

Loralee forced herself to smile even brighter. "That must be Mr. Williams and the doctor. I'll go get the door if you want to run upstairs and change — you can take the back stairs. You've got such a cute figure, and it's a shame to be hiding it under that skirt."

Merritt held up her hand and Loralee could see it shaking a little bit. "Not one more word. Please. I'll go get the door."

As soon as Merritt left the room, Loralee pulled out a china platter from the pretty wood hutch and began transferring cookies from the baking sheet. "Owen, could you please get some plates and napkins? I'm going to bring these to the front parlor in case anybody's hungry."

Loralee hurried, her heels tapping against the wide-planked floors until she reached the foyer, where Merritt was alone with the doctor, the two of them looking like two dogs circling a bone.

"Well, good morning, Dr. Heyward," Loralee said in greeting.

The handsome doctor responded with a wide grin that got even wider when he spotted Owen coming up behind her with the plates and napkins. "Hey, there, Rocky. Nice shirt."

Everybody seemed to notice at once that Owen and the doctor were wearing matching shirts, although if Loralee was being honest with herself, she'd have to admit that Dr. Heyward filled his out a lot more nicely than her son did.

Owen smiled shyly. "Thank you, sir."

"Where's Mr. Williams?" Loralee asked as

she placed the plate on the hall table instead of waiting for Merritt to play hostess and invite everyone into the parlor.

"He had an emergency at the office and couldn't come. He was going to call and reschedule, but I said I was sure Mrs. Heyward and I could do this without any blood drawn."

Merritt stood with her hands clasped together like a schoolteacher, but the spots of color on her cheeks had returned. "That's very brave of you, considering you don't know me at all."

Dr. Heyward turned to Owen. "Does she bite?"

Owen was trying very hard not to laugh, but when he glanced at his mother she gave him the look that meant it would be very bad manners if he did.

Loralee placed a cookie on a plate and handed it to the doctor with a napkin. "Would you like a cookie, Doctor? They're chocolate-and-peanut-butter-chip."

"My favorite," he said. "After Oreos, of course. Thank you." He took a bite and closed his eyes. "Delicious, Mrs. Connors. You have a gift."

"You're very kind. And please call me Loralee."

"Only if you call me Gibbes."

Loralee beamed, feeling like she'd made a new friend. "I just brewed a fresh pot of coffee if you'd like a cup."

Before Gibbes could respond, Merritt said, "I'm sorry to interrupt your social hour, Doctor, but I've got a lot to do, so maybe you can schedule your coffee klatch for after we're done."

"Absolutely, Mrs. Heyward. And you can call me Gibbes. We're family, after all, and it feels strange calling you by my grandmother's name." He paused as if expecting Merritt to ask him to use her first name. When she didn't, he took another cookie from the plate and smiled at Loralee. "I guess I'll take a rain check on that coffee, but thanks for the cookies." He ruffled Owen's hair. "Save at least one for me, okay?"

"Mama always hides some in the freezer just in case, but I'm not supposed to know that."

Loralee looked up at the ceiling and smiled. "I guess we're going to have to find you a sport soon, so you can burn off all those calories. Or I could just stop baking."

Owen turned to her, unsure whether she was joking or not. "Mama!"

"Do you like to fish?" Gibbes asked.

Owen shook his head. "I've never tried it,

sir. But I think it sounds fun."

The doctor nodded his head slowly. "I think so. Maybe next time I take out my boat, if you and your mother" — he paused and lifted his gaze to Merritt — "and your sister would like to go, I could bring you with me. I usually spend most of my time off work on the water when the weather's good, but we're temporarily shorthanded right now, so I haven't had too much boat time."

"Oh, Mama, could we?" Owen was nearly jumping up and down with excitement.

Loralee had to smile really hard so the tears that threatened wouldn't spill over. It had been so long since she'd seen him so excited about anything that she'd almost begun to believe his grieving had become as much a part of him as the color of his eyes or the way he pulled at his lower lip when he was deep in thought. "That would be lovely. Thank you."

She felt Merritt's gaze and turned to find her stepdaughter staring at her with thinned lips. "I have a lot to do in the house, and I'm sure Loralee will be busy checking out the area to see if this is a place she wants to consider living. Maybe even going to the library to check out atlases of other states."

Owen's shoulders slumped and Loralee

wanted to reach over and shake Merritt until her hard shell cracked wide-open so everybody could see the hurt child inside. But she didn't. Robert had told her how Merritt's mother had died, and she knew Merritt carried the wound inside her heart, picking at it so it wouldn't heal. Instead Loralee reached her arm around Owen's shoulders. "I think we can do both, don't you?"

Gibbes nodded. "Absolutely. I'll work around your schedule. I'll give you my phone numbers before I leave." Turning toward Merritt, he said, "So disappointed you won't be able to join us."

As if realizing she'd thrown cold water over Owen's excitement, she ignored the doctor's comment and instead gave Owen a small smile. "As long as Owen gets to go and has a good time, that's all that matters." Turning toward Gibbes, she gave him a hard stare. "Let's get this over with, shall we? The sooner we start, the sooner we'll be done."

"I was assuming you'd need an appraiser to come in first before you'd allow me to take anything. I don't want you to think I'm cheating you out of your inheritance."

Merritt lifted her chin. "Despite what you might think, I married Cal because I loved him. I didn't know about this house or his grandmother or that he would die at age thirty-nine. So whatever you want is yours, because none of it was ever meant to be mine. I'm here because I wanted to leave my old life and all of its bad memories behind me, and this was the opportunity I needed. I just want to get all this business taken care of and to be left alone."

Loralee glanced at Owen to see whether he'd heard what Merritt had said about being left alone, but he was busy stuffing cookies into his pockets. She felt her own heart burn a little, and before she did something stupid like cry, she placed a cookie on a plate and practically shoved it into Merritt's hand.

"I'm sure you don't mean that, Merritt. We're just so happy to finally get to know you. Owen's talked of nothing else since I mentioned moving away from Georgia. Isn't that right, Owen?"

He heard his name and glanced over at her with a worried look, nodding his head while crumbs dropped from his full mouth. Merritt just stared at her cookie as if Loralee had handed her a dead fish.

Gibbes shoved his hands deep inside his pockets, his eyes narrowed. "You're not the kind of woman I imagined Cal marrying."

Merritt sucked in a breath, as if his words had physically assaulted her. "When Mr. Williams told me that Cal had a brother, I wondered what you'd be like, too. Because Cal didn't just leave this town, or this house, or his grandmother. He left you, too, didn't he? And I figured there had to be a reason why."

A tic began in Gibbes's jaw, but he didn't say anything, and Loralee thought it might be because he was aware of Owen, who'd stopped chewing and was straining his head forward to listen.

Clutching the paper plate, Merritt headed for the stairs. "Let's start upstairs and work our way down."

Loralee picked up the plate of cookies to take back to the kitchen. "I'm going to go clean out the kitchen cabinets and put that new liner paper inside that we got at the Piggly Wiggly last night. I should probably wash all the dishes, too."

Merritt placed her hand on the thick wood banister where it swirled at the bottom of the steps and where Loralee had placed her pocketbook the previous evening. "You don't have to do that."

"I know. But it's my small way of thanking you for letting us stay. For a little while," she added quickly.

"Thank you." Merritt put her first foot on the bottom step and began walking up. Her hand must have caught the pocketbook's strap, because before Loralee could tell her to be careful, her purse had plopped to the ground on its side, with all of its insides spilling out onto the floor.

Multiple tubes of lipstick, her compact, brush, small toothbrush, and tweezers slid to a stop at the edge of a faded blue rug, but four prescription pill bottles and a tube of antacids rolled in the other direction, stopping at Dr. Heyward's feet.

"I'll get it," she said, taking a step forward, but she was too late. Gibbes had already picked up all four bottles, casually looking down at them before meeting her eyes.

"I've got ulcers, and a few other pesky issues I'm dealing with right now," she offered in explanation, waving her free hand in the air. Brushing aside Merritt's apology, Loralee stooped down to pick up her pocketbook with her free hand and held it up for the doctor to dump in the bottles.

"If you're going to be staying here for a while and need doctor references, I'd be happy to help. Just let me know."

She smiled with relief. "That would be real helpful — thank you. I'll let you know."

Merritt continued up the stairs and Gibbes followed, staring at Merritt's straight back as if he were trying to read something written on her shirt.

Loralee handed the plate to Owen. "Can you please take these back to the kitchen while I hunt around for the rest of my stuff?"

His eyes gleamed and she knew there would be fewer cookies on the plate by the time it reached the kitchen, but she didn't say anything. When he was grown, she wanted him to look back on his childhood and remember these small things that made him happy.

She knelt on the rug and began picking up the tubes of lipstick, thinking about Merritt's straight back and the reason Cal had left his brother and his life behind him and never looked back. She clutched the tube of Passion Pink in her fist, poised to drop it into her pocketbook, and thought of one more thing to add to her journal: *Everybody carries their hurts in different ways, but everybody's got them. Everybody. Some people are just better at hiding them.*

Using the spindles to help pull herself up, Loralee walked slowly toward the kitchen, her heels tapping across the floorboards as her smile found its way back to her face before Owen saw her.

CHAPTER 6

Merritt

I felt Gibbes's eyes on my back just as surely as if he were pressing two fingers into my flesh. I paused at the top of the elegant stairs. "Where would you like to start?"

"My old room, I suppose. I'm assuming my grandmother didn't throw anything away, and there are a few things in the closet I'm hoping are still there."

I led the way to the room Mr. Williams had indicated had belonged to Gibbes and that Loralee was now staying in. I wondered what Gibbes was hoping to find — perhaps an old chess set or baseball glove. Nothing that meant more than recalling his youth. "Judging from what I've seen so far, I don't think much has been thrown out or changed since you lived here."

I made the mistake of looking at him and saw a glimpse of vulnerability and tenderness there, neither one an emotion I wanted to associate with my brother-in-law. I quickly looked away and pushed open the bedroom door. ♠ ♠

The bed had been neatly made, a homemade quilt in the blues and greens of the ocean neatly tucked under the wooden slats on the side of the pencil-post bed. A small corner of Loralee's leopard-print nightgown stuck out from where it had been folded behind a pillow. On the bedside table next to a roll of antacids was what appeared to be a journal, covered in hot-pink vinyl. I imagined that the pages would be mostly blank, Loralee using them only to record what she wore each day so she wouldn't repeat an outfit.

A neatly arranged array of cosmetics sat in gilded attention on the dressing table. I was in the middle of squinting at the tubes and jars to see whether there was something I might recognize when I was distracted by Gibbes opening the closet door.

The closet was oddly shaped, and jutted out from a corner of the room like a gaudy piece of oversize furniture, having apparently been carved from the bedroom in an attempt at modernization. I'd noticed this with all the bedrooms, and wondered whether the construction of closets in the last century or so had been the last time the house had undergone any updates.

Loralee's suitcases had been neatly stacked in the back of the closet, their contents apparently emptied and hung with military precision on the single rod. Multiple shoes, all with high heels, were lined up in rows in front of the suitcases.

But above the rod was a deep shelf the width of the closet with piles of boxes that went up to the twelve-foot ceiling, stacked in three rows of varying widths.

"Looks like she kept everything," he said out loud, although I wasn't sure he was speaking to me. Turning around to look at the bed, he said, "I don't think she changed anything at all."

"That's not such a bad thing," I said, tucking the leopard nightgown out of sight.

He paused to look at me. "Because . . . ?"

I blushed, having no excuse for why I would have blurted that out. I wasn't one to share my family's dirty laundry, especially with this man. We might share the same last name, but he was a stranger to me.

I shrugged, pretending to straighten the pillows on the bed. "When I left for college, my father sold the house I'd grown up in and moved into a small condo. He got rid of everything — furniture, Christmas decorations, clothing. Even sheets and blankets."

"And your mother let him?"

I felt light-headed for a moment, the bruise of my mother's loss still as fresh as the day she'd died. "She died when I was twelve."

He considered me for a moment. "My mother died when I was five. Cal would have been fifteen. It was hard. I don't think it matters how old you are when you lose a parent; you still feel like you've lost a limb."

I stared back at him, recalling how I'd told my father the same thing after my mother's funeral. And how ever since I'd limped through my life as if I'd been walking on a phantom leg. I quickly turned back to the closet. "You're welcome to any of the boxes up on the shelf. Leave what you don't want and I'll sort through them to give away or toss. I can't imagine there's anything I'll need."

"What's that?" he asked.

I stepped toward him just as he raised his hand to point at an unmarked corrugated box. I caught myself before I uttered a sound, but my body, honed by instinct, flinched as I covered my face with my arm.

He dropped his hand quickly, his eyes searching mine.

"Sorry," I said, stepping back and lowering my gaze, suddenly aware of how much

126

his eyes resembled Cal's.

He didn't say anything, but I felt him watching me. I walked toward the door and flipped on the electric switches, the overhead light and fan turning on. "It's so hot in here," I said, waving my hand in front of my face.

"You'd probably be a lot cooler if you weren't wearing long sleeves."

I looked down at my blouse, wondering how long I'd been dressing in beige. And why I still did.

The surge of anger was unexpected, and I knew I had to get out of the room. Ignoring him, I said, "Put the boxes you want in the hallway so we can keep it all together. I'm going ahead to Owen's room to make sure it's presentable."

"Oh, it is," he said, turning back to the closet.

I found his matter-of-fact attitude annoying. "How would you know?"

"In my experience, most children who've lost a parent tend to go overboard with their best behavior so their other parent doesn't leave, too."

I thought for a moment, remembering how I'd been after my mother's death, trying to be the best student, the best daughter, the best housekeeper so that my father wouldn't notice my mother's absence so much. And it had worked for a long time, too. Until he'd met Loralee.

"But you probably already know that." He reached up into the closet to pull down whatever it was he'd seen, allowing me to stare. He was so different from Cal, and I wondered why I'd thought I'd seen my dead husband when Gibbes had appeared at my doorstep the day before. They had the same sandy-colored hair and deep-set eyes of golden brown, and they both walked with the same confidence. But whereas Cal had been built like a football player, broad and strong, Gibbes was taller and leaner. So much alike, yet so different. I recalled Mr. Williams saying how Gibbes favored their mother and Cal their father. It made me wonder whether other things besides physical traits could be inherited, too.

I hovered in the doorway, eager to get away yet not wanting him to get the last word. "You don't know anything about me."

He didn't even glance at me. "I know enough," he said dismissively.

I bit my lip and breathed deeply, mentally reciting what Cal told me was the first thing they learned at the academy: *The triangle represents the three components that fires need to exist: heat, oxygen, and fuel. If one of these components is missing, a fire can't ignite.*

"Are you all right?"

I was embarrassed to realize I'd closed my eyes, as if I could hide inside myself and not be noticed. Another habit I'd picked up during my marriage. "I'm fine."

"Why don't you sit down?"

"I said I'm fine. I really just want to get this over with."

"Is it the New Englander in you that makes you so stubborn, or is that just you?"

Too angry to respond, I headed toward Owen's room and had reached the threshold when a crash came from the room behind me. I raced back to see the unmarked box from the closet shelf lying on the wood floor on its side, its top flaps opened like lips, regurgitating a stack of yellowed newspapers.

Gibbes squatted in front of the box and righted it. "It was heavier than I thought. Doesn't look like anything broke."

Curious, I stepped forward. "It's just newspapers?"

He nodded. "Yeah — and they're not mine. It's the only box I didn't recognize, which is why I tried to pull it down from the shelf."

He began picking up the scattered news-

129

papers and restacking. I leaned down and scooped up one that had slid nearly to the door. Glancing down, I read the date on the front page. *July 26, 1955.*

"This one's pretty old," I said, handing it to him and watching as he added it to the stack.

"They're all pretty old," he said as he stood, flipping through the pile. "They all seem to be from the same year." He pulled out one from the bottom. "From July and August." He shrugged. "Must be somebody's graduation or wedding or something my grandmother wanted to put in a scrapbook and never got around to." Leaning over the box, he dumped the newspapers inside, then bent over to fold the lid flaps before hoisting it into his arms.

"If it's all right with you and Loralee, I think I'll just stick this in the corner of the room along with anything else we find that can be thrown out. That way they won't be confused with the boxes of stuff I want to keep that I'll be stacking in the hallway."

"Fine with me. And Loralee won't mind — she's only here for the week."

He shot me a look that made me want to close my eyes again. "You seem pretty sure of that."

"Of course. She told me they're just here

130

for a visit, and I'm sure she's eager to find a new home for her and Owen."

He studied me for a moment before walking to the corner of the room and dumping the box on the floor.

"You don't look anything like him, you know. Except for the eyes. And the color of your hair." I bit my lip, but it was too late to call the words back. As a child I'd always spoken before I thought, something my mother had tried to curb but my father had found amusing. Cal was the one who'd finally made me stop. Until now.

"So I've been told. I hadn't seen him since I was ten, but everybody always said that he looked like our daddy, although we both had our mother's eyes. Which always made me happy, since I didn't remember her eyes at all."

He couldn't completely hide the hurt in his voice and looked away.

"What happened to your leg?"

My hand immediately went to my skirt, where I tugged on the hem as if I could make it longer, which was pointless, since he'd already seen the scar.

"I was in an accident when I was a little girl."

If I'd hoped that would stop his questions, I was wrong.

"An accident?"

"A car accident."

I turned and led the way across the hallway to Cal's former room, effectively ending a conversation I had no intention of having.

I hadn't yet walked inside this room, somehow sensing that Cal wouldn't have wanted me there, as if to see his childhood possessions would make him seem less the man he wanted to portray himself as to the world. But Cal was dead. I'd seen him buried and could still feel the grains of dirt that clung to my palm after I'd opened my fist, unable to dislodge them, just as I was unable to free myself of my memories of him. I just couldn't stop imagining him around each corner, waiting for me to say or do the wrong thing.

After pausing briefly on the threshold, I walked into the middle of the room, forcing myself to breathe normally.

Gibbes had been right: Owen had left the room spotless. The bed would have made even Cal approve, the bedclothes pulled so tight a quarter would have bounced off them. I imagined the corners of the sheets under the bedspread were folded with military precision.

Gibbes walked past me, then squatted in

132

front of a clear plastic boxlike structure tucked back against the wall.

"It's a terrarium," a voice said from the doorway.

We turned to see Owen, with his starched pants and buttoned-up shirt, watching us openly. I knew he was only ten, but he was like a little man, with his grown-up clothes and big words. I had no experience with children, but something in me wanted to rumple his hair and buy him a pair of faded jeans with patches on the knees.

"What's a terrarium?" I asked, although I already knew. I thought it had probably been a while since anybody except his mother had cared enough to show any interest in his hobbies. He looked so fragile all of a sudden, as if he were a small leaf hanging precariously from a tree branch.

He looked from me to Gibbes and then back again, as if waiting for one of us to tell him I was joking. Taking a step into the room, he said, "Technically, a terrarium is a miniature ecosystem for plants. You're not supposed to put bugs or animals inside them, but I like to collect interesting insects and spiders and watch them through a magnifying glass. But I always make sure I let them out after a few hours."

"Do you like catching and observing

133

Lampyridae?"

He looked at me with surprise.

I cleared my throat and thought back to the many summer mornings in our brightly lit kitchen, where my father and I would peer into my own insect cage and he would teach me the proper names of the winged and six-legged critters I'd collected from my mother's garden.

"Lampyridae is a family of winged insects in the beetle order Coleoptera. They're called lightning bugs because their bodies use bioluminescence to attract mates or prey." I gave him a crooked smile.

He smiled back, and I noticed how his front teeth slightly protruded over the others and he'd probably need braces at some point. Just like I had.

"Did our daddy teach you that?" Owen asked.

Something sharp and deep tugged at my chest. "Yeah. I guess he gave that to both of us."

"Did the kids at school laugh at you because you knew all the scientific names for insects?"

I frowned for a moment, remembering. "They did at first. And then, when I picked up a big spider from Terri Zerbe's backpack and took it outside, the kids thought I was pretty cool."

"Really?" His face was so bright and hopeful that I had to laugh.

"Really. Believe it or not, most people are afraid of large bugs, especially spiders — although technically they're arachnids and not bugs. My husband was a big and strong firefighter, but he was afraid of even the tiniest of spiders." My smile faded as I recalled how angry Cal had been when I'd calmly scooped up a little house spider and set him out on the windowsill. Cal had crushed it with a flowerpot, and I'd learned quickly to never allow myself to acknowledge his fear.

I looked up and caught Gibbes watching me carefully, and for a moment they were Cal's eyes, and a small fissure of fear threaded its way down my spine.

Unaware of the undercurrent of tension in the room, Owen said, "Spiders are pretty cool, but I like the fireflies the best. Sometimes I catch enough that when I turn out the lights in my room, it's like having a night-light."

The sound of chattering glass came from outside the open window. A rusty screen with more holes than wire separated us from a wind chime suspended outside the bedroom window by a board nailed to the windowsill.

I sighed. "I thought all I needed was a ladder, but I think I'm going to hire somebody to remove all of these wind chimes. I can't imagine why a person would want so many."

Owen rushed to the window, putting himself between me and the chime as if he expected me to reach out and knock it from its perch. "I like them. Could we keep this one at least?"

I thought of the racket the previous night and how I'd hardly been able to sleep.

As if reading my thoughts, Gibbes said, "In a few days you won't even hear them."

"We'll see," I said noncommittally, aware of Owen's eyes on me.

Gibbes moved toward the closet and opened the door while my eyes scanned the room, settling again on the LEGOs I'd noticed the day before. I stepped closer, studying the various primary-colored vehicles and structures made out of the ubiquitous blocks, trying to imagine a young Cal having the patience to make them one brick at a time. I couldn't.

"Do you think it would be all right if I played with them?" Owen asked. "I promise to be careful, and if anything breaks I can fix it."

I opened my mouth to say yes, but paused. They didn't belong to me. Not really.

136

They'd been Cal's, and I was his widow, but I'd never known the boy who'd made these. That boy was a stranger to me.

"Wow."

Owen and I turned toward Gibbes, who stood in the doorway of the closet, his hand still on the door handle. The deep closet, a twin to the one in the previous bedroom, appeared empty except for Owen's suitcase, which sat tidily in the back corner, and a dark blue backpack with a monogram in red resting on top. The shelves that stretched across the closet rose up to the tall ceiling, all of them glaringly empty except for one.

In my mind's eye I could see Cal taking everything out of the closet and throwing it away, angrily tossing into big black plastic bags the memories of his childhood. Plucking clothes from the rack and hurling them in the bags without bothering to remove the hangers. He never did things by halves, or with muted emotions. It's what made him a great firefighter, a saver of lives — because he never thought twice about what he needed to do. Yes, I could see him discarding his childhood into garbage bags. But I had yet to understand why.

"Wow," Owen echoed as he spotted what must have caught Gibbes's attention.

On a high shelf was another LEGO structure, its blue and white bricks glaring against the faded paint of the closet walls. It was huge, much bigger than anything else on the bedroom shelves, and not as cleanly formed. It seemed as if this one had been made freestyle, without an instruction sheet that explained which brick to place where. It was hollow on the inside, large enough for small LEGO people to sit inside, their sightless stares looking out through holes in the bricks that acted as airplane windows.

"It looks like a DC-six," Owen said matter-of-factly. Gibbes glanced at Owen with raised eyebrows.

"Our father was an airline pilot," I explained. *Our father.* The words had stuck on my tongue for a moment, as if to release them meant I couldn't consider myself an only child anymore. I'd known it for ten years, but this was the first time I'd had to acknowledge it.

"I want to be an aeronautical engineer when I grow up," Owen said. "So it's important I know this stuff."

I wondered whether he announced those kinds of things when he was out on the playground with other boys, and I felt another urge to mess up his hair and undo his top collar button.

We watched as Gibbes gently took the

LEGO plane from the shelf and placed it on the desk. "You're more than welcome to play with any of the LEGOs, Rocky. I know you'll take good care of them." He looked at the boy as if he, too, wanted to rumple the dark brown hair.

Gibbes eyed the tall chest of drawers. "I wonder if there's anything in there."

Owen shook his head. "No, sir, there's not. When I folded my clothes and placed them in the drawers, I saw that they were all completely empty."

Gibbes's eyes met mine again, and I couldn't help but wonder whether he was picturing his brother in this room, erasing himself drawer by drawer, hanger by hanger. But he'd left his LEGO creations, and a part of me wanted to know why.

"Have you not been in here since Cal left?" I asked.

He hesitated. "No. He didn't like me messing with his stuff when I was little, and I guess after he left I figured he wouldn't want me in here." He paused, and it was as if a ghost passed between us. "I'm guessing this is exactly how Cal left it." His voice held something indefinable, something that bridged wistfulness with loss, and I thought again of the husband I'd known and how I'd felt neither at his passing.

Gibbes headed back into the hallway, scanning the art on the walls, pausing to touch a frayed section of wallpaper, the edges curling in on themselves like the legs of a dying spider. He continued to the locked attic door and turned the knob, looking at me with a frown.

"Mr. Williams doesn't know where the key is and said he would send over a locksmith."

He stared at the closed door for a long moment. "My grandmother had a workshop up there when I was little."

"A workshop?" I asked. "What kind?"

He shrugged. "I'm not sure — I wasn't allowed in the attic, and then, after Cal left, my grandmother locked the door and didn't go up there anymore. I think that's where she made her sea-glass wind chimes."

I wanted to ask him why — why Edith had made so many wind chimes, and why she'd stopped going into her attic workshop. And why Cal had tried to erase himself from this house and his previous life. But I'd come to realize that Gibbes had probably been asking himself the same questions for two decades.

His phone vibrated and he removed it from his pocket. After looking at the screen, he said, "We'll have to finish this another time — I've got to head back to the office.

Apparently there's some kind of stomach bug going around the under-twelve set and they're inundated. I'll call you later to set up a convenient time to come back."

I held back a sigh. "I'll be happy to look through closets and drawers between now and then. Obviously anything of personal interest or value will be up to you, but maybe if you could give me an idea of what you're looking for, that would make this process go a little faster."

The look he gave me was part amused, part annoyed, and I had to stop myself from flinching.

"Old photo albums. My mother was an amateur photographer and I remember her putting pictures in the albums up until the time she died. There are photos of Cal and me when we were kids. I'd like to see them again."

His words surprised me. I hadn't expected him to be sentimental, to want to peer into a past he seemed to have moved beyond, or see photos of a brother who'd left him behind.

We'd reached the top of the stairs and he paused to let me go ahead of him. I walked to the front door and pulled it open. "Let me know when you can come back to finish, and I'll see if I can find any of those albums."

"And the key. Let me know if you get into the attic. I've always wondered what my grandmother did up there." He stepped out onto the porch. "Please tell Loralee I had to go and I'll take a rain check on the coffee."

I nodded and was about to close the door when I thought of something. "Was Cal allowed up in the attic?"

Gibbes looked at me oddly. "Yes, as a matter of fact. He was."

We regarded each other in silence, and again I thought of Cal's spirit walking between us, casting shadows like smoke blocking the sun.

"Good-bye," I said suddenly, closing the door before Cal's name was said again, conjuring a ghost neither one of us wanted to see. D-H.

CHAPTER 7

Loralee

Loralee leaned back on the pretty garden bench and closed her eyes. Owen — she couldn't think of him as Rocky no matter how much she tried — was upstairs in his room playing with LEGOs. He wouldn't take apart the pieces that had belonged to Merritt's husband, but instead used his own to make an airport, a runway, and other planes to play with alongside the original ones. When she'd asked Owen whether he was keeping Cal's planes intact so Merritt wouldn't be sad, he'd shaken his head and told her that he wasn't taking them apart because he felt that Merritt would do it herself when she was ready.

Merritt was upstairs in her room taking everything out of the dresser drawers, armoire, and closet, cataloging everything in a notebook before placing it all in boxes marked TOSS, GIVE AWAY, and GIBBES. Loralee slid her feet out of her shoes, feeling it was safe with nobody looking. Her mama had taught her that lipstick, manicured nails, and high heels would always make you feel better than you actually did. And she'd been right, to a point. Lately nothing made Loralee feel good or less tired, but that didn't mean she wouldn't keep trying.

Opening her eyes again, she found herself staring into the face of the crooked stone statue, sticking catawampus out of the dirt like it had been carelessly tossed from heaven. She placed her journal, which she'd been sketching in, next to her on the bench and leaned toward the statue, wondering whether he had a name. He looked like one of those saints that Molly O'Brien — her best friend from Gulf Shores — had all over her trailer. Her mama was Catholic and was always asking for Saint So-and-so to find her keys or Saint What's-his-name to send her a good man who was easy on the eyes and long in the pocket. She'd also asked for a saint's help to make Loralee's mama better when she got sick, but Desiree would have none of it, saying if it was her time to go, it was her time to go, which was probably why she continued to smoke three packs a day until the day she died. Mama had had a strong faith, but had never cared too much for religion, although she'd had more than one come-to-Jesus meeting with her daughter during Loralee's wild years in high school.

"Loralee?" The back screen door slammed shut as Merritt made her way down the steps into the garden.

Loralee quickly slid her feet into her heels and stood. The sudden movement made her light-headed, and she gripped the back of the bench while remembering to smile. "I'm over here," she said, not wanting to risk her balance by waving. Waving would probably annoy Merritt anyway.

Merritt approached the bench, then stopped, her hands on her hips. "There's a stone rabbit statue on my front porch. Do you have any idea where it came from or why it's there?"

"I found it at Walmart over on Robert Smalls Parkway when I took Owen to the grocery store this morning, and all of their garden statuary was on sale. Isn't he adorable? I left him there so you could decide where you'd like him, although if you ask me, I'd say this old guy here could use some company."

Merritt blinked rapidly, like she was hoping each time she opened her eyes she'd see something different.

Loralee continued. "You can dress him up for each holiday. I actually have a Santa outfit and an Uncle Sam hat and jacket. I think it makes a house look more festive for the holidays."

Merritt didn't smile. "I find that hanging out a flag or putting up a Christmas tree usually does the trick."

Loralee had a brief flash of her old homeowner association meeting, where she could insert Merritt at the head of the table. Loralee sat carefully, her eyesight still spotty. "Yes, well, you don't have to put the bunny in the front yard. Like I said, I think it would look great back here."

Merritt was about to speak, but her attention was distracted by something next to Loralee. Loralee followed her gaze to her pink book, held open by the elastic band.

"Do you like it? It's just a rough sketch, but I wanted to show you what your garden is supposed to look like." She picked up her journal and held it out for Merritt. "You can still see the original beds, and I recognize a lot of the plants, since they also grow in Gulf Shores. Same climate, I guess.

"Anyway, when we knew we'd be in the same place for a while, Mama always grew pretty flowers, and she had a nice vegetable garden so I wouldn't miss out on eating my

146

greens. When we moved into the trailer, we had flower boxes so we wouldn't notice the rust so much. I think I could make this place look real nice again. A lot of the work will be removing all these weeds, although I hate to do that, because I feel like I'm judging which plant is right and which is wrong, and I was raised not to judge, because then I might be judged." She forced a smile, trying desperately to get Merritt's face to soften, to stop looking as if she were always bracing for a crash. "I thought maybe I could help you bring the garden back to its original beauty, give you a nice place to sit and read or drink sweet tea. There's even enough green space for a little pitchback for Owen. He's not great at baseball, but maybe he just needs more practice."

When Merritt still didn't smile, Loralee felt her own smile faltering. Desperate, she blurted out, "My mama always said that to plant a garden meant you believed in tomorrow."

"A pitchback for Owen?" Merritt asked through lips that looked like they were made of glass.

Loralee was relieved Merritt chose to mention the pitchback instead of bringing up her mama again. She relaxed. "Yes. I think once we get all the overgrowth cleaned up, there will be plenty of room. . . ." The last word trailed off as she watched Merritt's expression.

She cleared her throat and tried again. "We'll make sure that it's not near any windows, if that's what you're worried about."

Merritt sat down heavily on the bench and took a deep breath. She flattened her hands, with their short unpolished nails, against her shapeless black skirt. "You're planning on staying longer than a week, aren't you?"

Loralee bit her lip, tasting lipstick, and realized her mistake. It seemed all her hopes and plans had lunged ahead of where she actually was. Which was nowhere, really. She'd made it past the front porch and inside Merritt's house, but not really much farther than that. Definitely not far enough to where she could tell Merritt that she and Owen planned to stay awhile.

Loralee considered denying it, but knew there was no point. The truth would come out eventually. It always did — something else her mama had taught her. So instead she nodded, not taking her eyes from Merritt's, almost afraid that if she did, Merritt would bolt like a scared deer.

"Yes. But like I said before, I promise you we won't be any trouble. I'll cook and clean

148

for you and you won't even know I'm here. Mostly I just want you to get to know Owen. Your daddy would have wanted that. I'm sure he would have put it in writing if he'd known some tractor-trailer was going to plow into his car that day on his way to work. But he talked about it a lot, and that's why I knew I had to bring Owen." She swallowed nervously but didn't lower her gaze. "Since we gave up waiting for you to knock on our door."

Merritt didn't move or say anything for a long while, which made Loralee nervous. It had been her experience that people who thought for a long time before they spoke usually had something to say that Loralee didn't want to hear. And that meant she always wanted to postpone the response with chatter.

"I was thinking that it looks like this saint statue was placed on a tree root or a rock, which is why he's all crooked. I bet standing that way all day long gives him a headache! Anyway, I was thinking we could dig him out and reposition him so that it looks like he and Mr. Bunny are having a conversation back here under this big oak tree. . . ."

"Is it money? You said my father left you enough money that you didn't need to worry, but I'm wondering if you just said that so I wouldn't guess the real reason you're here. But it has to be money; otherwise why would you have packed up your lives and ended up here with me?"

"Money . . . ?" Loralee stared back at Merritt, wondering whether she'd missed part of the conversation, thinking she might have been distracted by imagining what a little mascara and lip gloss and a blouse in any color other than beige might do to enhance Merritt's appearance and probably her attitude.

Merritt continued. "Was the life insurance not enough? Or did you already go through it? My settlement was generous, but I assumed my father had left the bulk of his estate to you and Owen. He was the kind of guy who'd make sure you were taken care of. Did you spend it all?"

Loralee blinked, trying to erase the sting of tears. She gripped her pink notebook to her chest, squeezing hard and wishing she could open it right then and there and write down what she really wanted to say to Merritt. *Jumping to conclusions is often the only exercise some people get, and is always easier than finding the patience to discover the truth.*

She opened her mouth to defend herself, to tell Merritt she was wrong. But a river breeze had found its way to them in the forlorn garden, playing with the wind chimes and twisting the oak leaves so their silver undersides seemed to wink at her as if they were in on a joke.

Loralee lifted her chin. "You're right. We're broke. I have no means to support my son, and I'm desperate to find a place to stay until we can get back on our feet again."

Merritt looked at the dancing leaves, too, but instead of seeing winking leaves she appeared to see something else she couldn't take charge of or make go away.

"Does Owen know?"

Loralee thought quickly, then shook her head. "No. I kept money aside for Owen's expenses, and that's what I've been using to buy him clothes and food, and the gas that got us here."

"Did you sell your house?"

Loralee nodded.

"And the money from that, where did it go?"

Loralee kept her chin and voice steady. "We had a lot of debt. Mostly credit cards. They're all paid off now."

"And your medications? How are you paying for those?"

Loralee felt like she'd swallowed a cotton boll, wondering how Merritt knew. She relaxed slightly when she remembered her purse falling and the pill bottles rolling across the floor. "I'm covered for another couple of months and then I'll have to figure something out."

Merritt nodded, her gaze focused on the statue. "Why didn't you tell me the truth right at the beginning?"

Loralee didn't pause. "Because I thought you'd turn us away if it looked like we needed more from you than you were ready to give." She watched as the shadows in Merritt's eyes darkened as she realized that Loralee was right. It reminded Loralee of Owen as a toddler, with crumbs on his face and chin, denying that he'd eaten a cookie. *Just because you say something over and over and believe it with all your heart will never make it true.* It was one of the first truths she'd written in her journal.

Softly Loralee added, "You have your own burdens, and it was never my intention to add to them. I'd hoped that we could help each other until I got on my feet again, and that it would bring you and Owen closer. He's your flesh and blood, Merritt, even if I'm not. Unfortunately, we're a package deal, but I'm hoping you can overlook that."

Merritt stood, smoothing her hands on her dull skirt as if wiping away a stain. An ugly plastic headband held back her beautiful hair but couldn't control it from blowing in the breeze, shifting in the muggy air like an impatient child hopping from foot to foot. The thought made Loralee want to smile, recalling a photograph of Merritt as a little girl wearing sparkly red shoes and a pink tutu she'd made herself. Loralee was sure that girl was still inside Merritt somewhere. What she didn't know was whether the little girl who loved bright shoes and designing her own outfits was buried under too many years of sorrow to find her way out. She hoped not. For Owen's sake, she really hoped not.

Merritt's voice was strong, almost as if she'd been practicing saying the words in her head. "Despite what you might think, I loved my father. We were all the other needed for a long time after my mother died. Until you came along and he didn't need me anymore, although I still needed him. I never forgave him, but I never stopped loving him."

She paused, and Loralee imagined all the words in Merritt's head falling into neat, orderly columns like numbers, rounded and even and organized before she allowed them out.

"I'll do it for Owen. Because he's my

brother and because our father would want me to. And, as you reminded me, the two of you are a 'package deal.' Fine. You can stay here, too, until you can get on your feet again. Just don't expect me to forge a relationship with you. I never forgave my father, so don't expect me to forgive you."

She'd said all this with her back to Loralee, and Loralee was glad, since that meant Merritt couldn't see the small smile on her face. Somehow, and quite by accident, she'd gotten what she'd wanted. What Owen needed. For the first time in months the terror and uncertainty began to shrink back like the ocean at low tide, calling the waves home.

Merritt began walking toward the kitchen door, but Loralee's words stopped her. "I loved him, you know. And he loved me. Yes, he was old enough to be my father, but as my mama used to say, love can't tell what color a person is or how old they are. Love just happens. I know you don't want to hear that, but you need to. We were very happy together. The only thing missing was you. You would have made our family and happiness complete, and we never stopped hoping that would happen."

Without a word, Merritt made her way to

the back steps and into the kitchen, the screen door shutting behind her like a slap.

CHAPTER 8

Merritt

Looking down from my spot on the bluff, I saw the ribbon of river shift from light to shadow, dodging the sun as a sailboat made its way toward the bridge. I sat in a rocking chair on the front porch and drank my first cup of coffee, as had become my habit in the last week, trying to identify what was so different there, what made the light seem drenched in yellows instead of the gray-white light of home.

I hadn't grown up on the water in Maine, but close enough that I could sense its nearness, the frothy power of it, the dark depths of it that could swallow a boat while the waves continued to rise and fall as if nothing had happened. My mother had grown up on the coast in Stonington, in a family of fishermen. Maybe it was my mother's story of an uncle whose boat had been lost at sea during a storm that made me eye the ocean with suspicion. Or maybe it was the fact that my mother happily moved inland when she married my father and never ventured near it again.

In college I'd gone to Higgins Beach on spring break with a friend. Low tide made an old shipwreck visible not far from shore, and that had been enough to keep me close to land. I'd gotten only as far as my ankles into the water before proclaiming it too cold, and then spent the rest of the break under an umbrella worrying I'd get sunburned, and avoiding looking at the spot where the water claimed the ship again at high tide. That was the first and last time I'd ever gone to the beach. Every once in a while I wondered whether it was because I really hadn't enjoyed the experience, or if my reluctance to join my friends under the waves had more to do with my mother — with her avoidance that could have been as much about the water as it was about her childhood memories of growing up with my difficult grandmother.

Bringing the cup to my face again, I breathed in the aroma of fresh-brewed coffee. I'd grown up with instant coffee — two scoops and hot water in the microwave. Not because it tasted better or even the same as real coffee, but because it was faster and

easier. True to her word, Loralee had breakfast on the table and a steaming cup of
percolated coffee for me each morning,
somehow managing not to chatter and to
disappear from the room when I entered. It
made me feel uncomfortable, guilty even,
but I had no idea how to change things
without her thinking I had forgiven anything, or forgotten that she was living in my
house when all I wanted to be was alone.

The wind chimes swayed overhead as I
took another sip from my steaming coffee,
knowing Loralee would be there with the
pot to refill my cup before it even had a
chance to grow cool. I knew I should get up
and get it myself before she came out again,
but I was reluctant to leave. There was
something about the light there, the soft
brightness that made it seem as if I were
looking at everything through a snow globe
where nothing was quite real. I'd even
begun leaving my curtains open at night so
that I'd awaken to the morning light streaming into my room, something Cal never
would have allowed. I wondered whether
that was the real reason I did it now.

I thought of Cal, of him sitting in this very
spot, thinking of leaving and not coming
back, and I wondered again why. There was
something otherworldly about the air, about

the river, about the way the waiflike Spanish moss dripped from the oak trees at the water's edge, their placement almost intentionally geared toward a perfect reflection in the water, two sets of arms reaching toward each other to form an oval. In places it seemed these were the openings to secret caves beneath the water, an invitation to dive inside. I wondered, if I weren't afraid of the water, what it would be like to dive between the wavering arms to find the other end of the cave. It would be reckless and silly, two things my young self had been full of — two things my married self hadn't allowed me to be.

The front door opened and I braced myself, expecting to see Loralee again, creeping around silently so that I wouldn't notice her. I turned around to tell her it was okay, that she didn't need to tiptoe, when I spotted the familiar dark head of my brother peering around the open door.

"Is it okay if I come out here? I promise I won't bother you."

I felt as if I'd had that promise made to me more times in the last week than I'd had in a lifetime.

"Of course. And you're not bothering me." I wanted to tell him that my distance had nothing to do with him, and how it had been so much easier to dislike the idea of him before I'd even met him, and that now all I could feel were the cold fingers of regret. But I couldn't. Not because I thought he was too young to understand, but because I was afraid he might.

My brother was ten years old and I'd never seen him before, and I wanted to explain to him that now was just the wrong time. Not that there'd ever been a right time, not while Cal was alive, but not now, when I'd begun to reclaim my life — a life I had no intention of sharing with anyone, especially not a stepmother and little brother I only occasionally thought about, like half-forgotten characters from a book I'd read long ago.

Owen sat down in the rocker next to me, holding a mug identical to mine. "Is that coffee?" I asked.

"No, ma'am. Hot chocolate." He screwed up his face. "Mama says coffee will stunt my growth, so she's making me wait until I'm eighteen. I figure if I'm old enough to vote, I should be old enough to drink coffee."

"That's for sure," I agreed, wondering whether Owen was what I'd heard some people call an "old soul." I glanced at his pressed jeans and clean boat shoes, and another polo shirt — this one striped — with a pressed collar. He was sipping his hot chocolate from a coffee mug — steaming despite the temperature outside — and looking like a miniature man. "Do you own a pair of shorts, Owen?"

He shook his head. "No, ma'am. I had some but they got too short, so Mama gave them away. She says she keeps meaning to buy me more, but forgets."

I smiled at him, remembering what Loralee had said about her lack of funds. "I'm sure there are malls near here, and everybody always runs sales around Memorial Day. I've been wanting to go to get a few new things myself. Maybe you'd like to come with me?"

He stopped mid-sip and his eyes widened. "Yes, ma'am. That would be nice. I'd like a pair of skater shorts."

I didn't know what those were, but I had a feeling they weren't the kind of shorts worn with a pleated crease and pulled tight with a belt. "And you don't have to call me ma'am. My name's Merritt."

Owen stared into his mug for a moment. "Okay. And you can call me Rocky."

I hid my grin. "I'll try to remember. It's just that I think you look more like an Owen than a Rocky."

He frowned. "I know."

"It's a good thing. Owen is a fine, strong name. It's a smart name for a smart boy. Why try to hide that behind a name like Rocky? There's about one hundred IQ points between those two names."

He was still frowning, making me realize that I was no good talking with children. I was way out of my league. I leaned back in my chair with a sigh, remembering watching the movie *Rocky* on TV with my father. I didn't remember much about it except for Sylvester Stallone's almost unintelligible dialogue. "Yo, Adrian," I muttered under my breath.

Owen snorted, then choked and coughed on his hot chocolate before turning to me with a wide grin. "That was funny."

I looked at him with surprise, then found myself grinning, too. "It wasn't meant to be, but thanks. I think."

We both looked up at the sound of car doors shutting. A light blue pickup truck with WEBER & SON LOCKSMITHS written on the side was parked behind a white Cadillac sedan, circa 1980. A tall man wearing a khaki uniform with a name tag on the front pocket was walking across the lawn, headed toward the front walk, where two older ladies, both with short, permed gray hair and wearing sensible shoes and floral blouses, bore down on the porch carrying casserole dishes. Behind the women, hidden almost out of sight except for a pair of riding pants and sparkly blue Mary Janes, was a little girl who looked to be about Owen's age.

Owen stood and I quickly followed, impressed with Owen's good manners. The man took off his cap, revealing an almost marinelike haircut with spiky salt-and-pepper hair. Using his hat, he indicated for the women to precede him up the steps.

Apparently people dropping in unannounced was just something I needed to get used to. Or I needed to spend more time in my back garden, where I couldn't hear the doorbell. Although that would mean staring at that rabbit monstrosity that had somehow managed to find its home beneath the oak tree.

"Good morning," the two women chimed in together. "Welcome to Beaufort," they said in unison, holding out their casserole dishes. The little girl squeezed in between them and held out her own Tupperware container.

"Good morning. And thank you." I glanced down at my house slippers, appalled to be seen in them. They had holes in the

163

toes, and the navy color had faded to a hospital-room blue. They were hideous, but it was against my New England upbringing to replace them while the soles were still attached to the tops.

"I'm sorry, I would have finished dressing, but I wasn't expecting visitors." I reached out and took one of the proffered casseroles, and Owen took the Tupperware from the little girl. Her brown hair was worn in braids on either side of her head, and her bronzed skin was covered with freckles that accented her bright blue eyes. Though slight, she had long, lean limbs like a colt, and looked like she spent a lot of time outdoors. She smiled at Owen, revealing a dimple on each cheek.

"I'm Merritt Heyward, and this is my . . ." I paused, unused to introducing him to strangers.

"I'm Rocky," he said. "Merritt's brother."

The women raised their eyebrows and smiled. The one with the slightly whiter hair and beaked nose looked at me and said, "You're not from around here, are you?"

I wasn't sure whether she could determine that from my slippers or from the fact that I was a newcomer and wasn't expecting visitors. "I'm from Maine. My brother and his mother are from Georgia."

They both nodded in unison, calling to mind dashboard bobble heads.

The one with glasses and tightly permed hair spoke. "I'm Cynthia Barnwell, and this is my sister-in-law, Deborah Fuller. And this" — she placed her hand on the little girl's shoulder — "is my granddaughter Maris Ferro. We're with the Beaufort Heritage Society, and on behalf of everyone at the BHS, welcome to Lettuce City."

"Excuse me?" I said.

Deborah, who seemed to be the more serious of the two, and whose skin was brown as leather and heavily lined, as if she spent a great deal of time in the sun, said, "It's an obscure reference that only us true historians really use anymore, but it dates back to the early twentieth century and the beginning of truck farming in the area. Lettuce was a big crop back then."

"Oh," I said, confused. "I was told that Beaufort is called 'Little Charleston.' "

The two women frowned at me, and I wondered whether they'd both been schoolteachers at some point. I had the sudden urge to find the principal's office.

Cynthia spoke up. "Actually, for those of us who live here, Charleston is known as 'Big Beaufort.' Which is better than 'Home of the Catfish Stomp,' which is what they call Elgin."

She looked serious, so I just nodded.

The man stepped closer. "And I'm Steve Weber. Mr. Williams called me to come look at that door upstairs and see if I can't get it open and make you a new key."

"Oh, thank you," I said. I looked around, wondering how to proceed, when Cynthia took the casserole from my hand.

"Why don't we have Owen lead us to the kitchen so we can put this all in the refrigerator while you show the gentleman where the lock is?"

"Sure," I said, moving toward the door and opening it. "Just in case you've already left by the time I return, thank you for coming. And for the food."

They stared at me for a moment, and I wondered what I'd said wrong.

Owen took the door from me and held it open. "My mama makes the best cookies in the world. Why don't you come on back and have some with a cup of coffee? Merritt can join us when she's done." He smiled brightly at me, and I wasn't sure whether I wanted to hug him or shake him.

The women filed past us, followed by Maris and Steve Weber. Owen closed the door and led the group toward the back of the house. I stared after them, doubting my

166

decision to move there sight unseen, with the belief I could somehow live my new life in peace and solitude.

"This way," I said to the locksmith, leading him upstairs to the attic door. "All the other doors have antique locks, too, but their keys are still in the locks. This is the only one that's missing, and the only door that's locked."

The locksmith got down on one knee and eyed it warily. "Well, that dog won't hunt."

"Is that good or bad?" I asked.

"Depends," he said, straightening. "This is a real old doorknob and lock — probably original to the house, I suspect. Thick door, too." He wiped his forearm across his forehead as if I needed to be reminded how hot it was upstairs. "It's going to be a custom job. It could take a while, and it'll be pricey." He looked up and down the hallway, probably trying to find a thermostat.

"Or?"

"Or if you want this to be a quick fix, I could take this whole thing off and replace it with a new modern doorknob with a simple lock. I could get one in brass to sort of match the other doors."

We turned toward the top of the stairs at the sound of a deep intake of breath. Deborah Fuller stood there with her hands over her heart and her eyes wide, and I thought she'd seen a ghost.

"Are you all right?" I asked.

"I'm fine, really." She took a moment to catch her breath before walking toward us. "I was just looking for the powder room. The lovely Loralee told me the one downstairs is leaking and to use one up here. They'll be up in a moment to start the house tour."

"The . . . ?"

As if she hadn't heard me, she turned purposefully toward Steve Weber. "I'm quite sure Mrs. Heyward will want to retain the historical integrity of this house and do what is necessary to get a replacement key for the existing lock. Isn't that correct, Mrs. Heyward?"

She faced me and I was once again reminded of being sent to the principal's office for speaking out of turn — something I'd once done with the frequency of somebody who thought she had something worthwhile to say. "I'm . . ." I paused. "I'll need to have more information — more specific prices and time frame first."

The locksmith scratched the back of his head, and I noticed the sweat stains under his arm. "Yes, ma'am. When I head back to the office I'll look up a few things and get you a quote. Can I e-mail you?"

I thought of the ancient laptop computer that I hadn't even unpacked yet and the old e-mail account that I'd shared with Cal. "I'm between Internet service providers, so why don't you give me your card and I'll e-mail you tomorrow? Does that work?"

"Yes, ma'am. That works just fine." He reached into his pocket and handed me a business card, then hurriedly closed his toolbox as if he couldn't wait to get into the cooler air outside.

"But surely you could open the door now."

We both turned to Deborah, who stared back unapologetically. I had no idea why I hadn't thought to ask. Maybe because the heat upstairs was nearly unbearable, and I was as eager as Mr. Weber seemed to go somewhere else. Or maybe it was because Edith Heyward had locked this door and possibly hidden the key. There was something up there she didn't want others to see, and like a child reluctant to wind the Jack-in-the-box, I was unsure I was ready to climb the stairs to the attic to see what was there.

Almost reluctantly, Steve put down his toolbox. "Of course. I was going to suggest it, but then I figured it's probably hotter than Hades, so you'd be in no rush to get up there."

I wanted to agree with him and tell him to come back later, once we'd decided on a course of action, but there was something in Deborah's expression that made me stop.

"Yes," I said. "Why don't you go ahead and get it open? We'll be in the kitchen if you need anything — take a right at the bottom of the stairs and go straight back."

I moved toward the steps and Deborah followed me, apparently having forgotten about using the powder room, although she looked back twice at the closed attic door as we headed downstairs. I paused at the bottom, and Deborah stopped next to me. When I looked into her face, her expression surprised me. Her eyes were wide with anticipation, but there was a glint of apprehension, too.

Steve came down the stairs behind us. "I've got to run to my van to get a special tool — it's an old lock and I don't want to break anything. I'll be right back."

I waited until the front door closed behind him. "Do you know what's up there?" I asked.

She shook her head. "No." She looked at me closely, as if determining whether she could tell me something. She seemed to find

170

what she was looking for and continued. "When I was a girl, whenever I passed by the house at night I'd glance up and see a light on in the attic, and sometimes I'd see Miss Edith looking out the window. A few times I waved, but she never seemed to see me."

Laughter came from the kitchen, reminding me that we needed to join the others. But I was reluctant to move forward. There was something in Deborah's voice that made me hesitate.

"Do you know what she was doing?"

She paused. "She made her sea-glass chimes up there, among other projects. As I grew older she and I became friends, but she never showed me what she did up there, and only mentioned a big project she was working on. She was very secretive about it and always kept the door locked. Just about everybody in town seemed to have a few thoughts on what she was doing in that hot attic. But one thing we did know for sure." She pressed her lips together in a tight line. "She wasn't mourning her husband."

The door to the kitchen opened, and Owen ran past us up the stairs with a quick hello and a surreptitious glance over his shoulder. I heard his door shut hard right before the kitchen door opened again and

Maris stuck her head out, looked around, and then, apparently not finding what she was looking for, slowly withdrew her head again.

I barely noticed, Deborah's last words still hanging in the air. "What do you mean?" I asked.

The locksmith reentered the house and headed toward the stairs. Deborah's eyes followed him before she turned to face me again. "I'm not one to gossip, but my mama played bridge with Miss Edith when I was a little girl, and she'd bring me along sometimes. She was a nice lady, really lovely, and with beautiful manners. I watched her little boy, C.J., sometimes when I got a bit older. I guess he would have been your father-in-law. Anyway, I remember she always wore long sleeves, even in the summertime." She paused. "We had a secret that not even my mother knew about. Actually, until now I don't believe I've ever told anybody." With a soft smile she said, "When she found out we had a beach house on Sullivan's Island, she asked me to be on the lookout for sea glass and she'd pay me a penny for every piece I could find. I'd pile them in the corner of the porch when I was out riding my bike, and then she'd slip pennies in my pocket when Mother brought me again. I

172

didn't know why she wanted them — there weren't any wind chimes back then, only the one hanging from the attic window. I suppose she was working on them up in the attic. All I know is that she didn't want Mr. Heyward to know what she was doing."

"Why?" I asked, my voice suddenly tight.

Her eyes settled on me, but whatever else she was going to say was interrupted by the kitchen door swinging open again as Loralee, Cynthia, and the little girl, Maris, came toward us. I noticed that Loralee had gone heavy on the blush so it looked like she was trying to hide her skin — something I had yet to see without makeup. My mother had had beautiful skin, creamy in the winter and freckled in the summer, and she'd never worn makeup except for parties and special occasions. That was what mothers were supposed to look like, not Barbie-doll wannabes who wore animal prints and high heels.

Deborah placed a hand on my arm, the fingers worn with calluses, her touch like rough burlap. I looked again at her floral blouse and saw the sunspots on her cheeks and nose and thought she was probably in a gardening club, too. Maybe she could help Loralee with the garden.

I stopped my thoughts, seeing them lead in a dangerous direction. *My mama always said that to plant a garden meant that you believed in tomorrow.* I wasn't sure I believed enough in the future to even resurrect the garden, and I especially didn't imagine Loralee there for the long term to see it through.

Leaning toward me, Deborah spoke softly. "Stop by the Heritage Society offices next Wednesday — they're on Carteret Street. I work from eleven to four. I have something to show you that you might be interested in."

She squeezed my hand and smiled, her warmth bringing a smile to my own face. There was something familiar about the way she spoke that reminded me of home.

"Are you ready for the grand tour?" Cynthia asked, her blue eyes sparkling. "Deborah here is ashamed to admit that we ladies over at the Heritage Society have been dying to get into this house for years, but it's the truth. It was built by the same architect who built the John Mark Verdier house, you know. Quite famous back in the day." She clasped her hands together. "Just look at that cypress paneling and the cast-plaster mantel," she said, indicating the fireplace in the front parlor. "And the melodeon," she added with excitement, brushing her hand against a small pianolike instrument between two windows in the front parlor. "Not many of them exist anymore, you know. I have the name of a lovely man who specializes in melodeons if you need any repairs to it." She pursed her lips and in a hushed whisper added, "He's been institutionalized, but I'm sure as soon as he's released he can come look at your melodeon."

She walked around the front rooms, touching various pieces of furniture. "I just knew this house would be full of treasures! I'm hoping you'll allow us to include it on the fall home and garden tour. You wouldn't have to lift a finger, I promise. We do everything. . . ."

I caught movement from the corner of my eye and turned in time to see Loralee sway before catching herself on the edge of the hall table. Her skin appeared bleached under her makeup, and I was pretty sure that if the table hadn't been there, she'd have slid to the floor. I remembered the pill bottles, and her explanation of ulcers and other "pesky problems," and had the uncharitable thought that if she spent less time spending my father's money and more taking better care of herself, she wouldn't currently be looking as if she were trying to blend into the white wall.

I'm fine, she mouthed.

I didn't completely believe her, but I stepped between her and the two women, wanting to keep their prying eyes from Loralee. Despite our differences, I knew too well as a motherless child what it was like to be stared at. "I'm so sorry, but now isn't a good time for a house tour. I completely forgot, but Loralee and I have an appointment. Can you come back another time? And then we'll have the attic open, too."

Both women looked disappointed as I herded them to the door. "Just call ahead so I can make sure I'm home."

They looked back toward Loralee, who managed a smile and a wave before I escorted them out onto the front porch, where Steve Weber joined us. Before closing the door I glanced back to see Loralee reclining on the upholstered settee in the foyer, her color still pale but better than it had been. She gave me a thumbs-up, and I found it oddly reassuring.

The locksmith's face was a mottled red, and his hair and khaki uniform looked as if he'd been tossed into a pool. "The attic door's open, Mrs. Heyward, but I don't recommend heading up there just yet. It's hotter than a pepper patch in July, and you should probably get an HVAC guy out here to install an attic fan and probably another window unit or two upstairs before you go anywhere near that attic. I like to have burned my eyebrows off halfway up the steps before I gave up."

I nodded, relieved that I could postpone my trip to the attic, even if just for a few days.

"I'll add today's service and parts to the bill after we make the key, if that's all right with you." His voice sounded hopeful.

I got the impression that he couldn't wait to get into his truck and blast the air-conditioning, and I didn't want to keep him from it. "That's fine. I'll send you an e-mail later."

He tipped his hat and headed for his truck.

"Can I come back to see Owen?"

I looked down to see Maris, noticing again her sparkly blue shoes. When I'd been her age, and even past that — at least until my mother had died — I'd had an affinity for bright shoes, and sparkly headbands, and beautiful fabrics that could be made to do magical things with the right stitches from a sewing machine. The memory made me smile, and Maris smiled back, her freckles dark against her skin.

"I'm sure he'd love it. He doesn't know anybody here yet, so maybe you can introduce him to more children your age."

She looked relieved, and I recalled Owen running up the stairs and shutting his door, and felt a twinge of remorse.

I thanked them for the casseroles again before we said our good-byes, and I watched as they piled back into the Cadillac. I stood on the porch for a long moment, acutely aware of the unlocked door of the attic, like an open mouth breathing hot air on my neck.

I looked up at the wind chimes, remembering what Deborah had told me about hiding the sea glass from Edith's husband. The chimes were still now, the air stagnant and heavy. I squinted into the sun to see them better, remembering Mr. Williams explaining that the glass was cloudy because the pieces had been tumbled about the ocean for years. *Edith said that any glass that could withstand such a beating without crumbling was something to be celebrated.*

I rubbed my arms, feeling goose bumps beneath my fingertips, as if it were November instead of May, then went inside to check on Loralee to make sure she was all right, finding the idea preferable to going upstairs to stare up into the attic and wonder what waited for me there.

CHAPTER 9

Loralee

Loralee stood at the bottom of the stairs contemplating — just for a moment — taking off her heels before heading up. Gripping the two Coke bottles, she slowly climbed the steps, pausing at the top to catch her breath. Her gaze scanned the upstairs hallway, resting on the attic door, closed until the HVAC man came. Merritt hadn't been up there, although at night, when it was cooler, Loralee had seen her standing outside the door with her hand on the knob. The first time she'd seen Merritt there, Loralee had quietly gone back into her room and had written in her *Journal of Truths. The weight of fear goes away as soon as we face our monsters and realize they weren't as scary as we thought.* Thinking of Owen, she underlined that one, hoping he'd read it first.

Merritt's door was half-open, with no

sound coming from inside. Thinking she might have gone somewhere, Loralee stuck her head around the corner and saw the closet door wide-open, stacks of clothes and shoes and labeled boxes lined up against the walls. Merritt sat on the high bed thumbing through what looked like an old photo album, the kind where the pictures were stuck onto the pages and then covered with clear plastic. Four more albums were stacked on the bench at the end of the bed, all different sizes and colors, as if they'd never been intended to be part of a set.

Loralee lifted her hand to tap on the door, but paused when she heard Merritt sniff, then raise a tissue to her eyes. Loralee took a step back and was rewarded with the answering groan of an old floorboard protesting her weight. Merritt's surprised eyes met hers, and Loralee could think only to smile.

Pretending she hadn't heard or seen anything, she said, "I brought you a snack. You've been up here most of the day and I figured you could use a perk-me-up." Without waiting to be asked inside, she walked toward Merritt and handed her one of the Coke bottles.

Merritt blinked, trying to hide her reddened and wet eyes, and Loralee knew enough not to say anything. Her first instinct was to plop down on the bed beside Merritt and throw her arms around her in a big hug before forcing her stepdaughter to tell her what was wrong. Most people would probably start talking during the hug, but Merritt was different. And it wasn't just because she was from Maine; it had more to do with a childhood that had ended too early and a life full of more hurts than most people could survive. But Merritt had. With scars, and bruises, and prickly parts as reminders of where she'd been, but she'd survived. Not that Merritt would ever want to hear it, but Loralee admired her for her strength, and prayed every night that Owen was made of the same stuff.

Merritt took the bottle and stared at it suspiciously. "I usually don't drink soda." She tilted the bottle slightly and looked at the label. "And when I do, I drink Moxie."

Loralee repressed an involuntary grimace. In her travels as a flight attendant, she'd tried the state drink of Maine, a bitter concoction that tasted like root beer poured over cotton and laced with battery acid. Loralee leaned forward as if she were whispering to her best friend at the desk next to hers in fourth grade. "If I were you, I wouldn't say that too loud around here.

First of all — it's all Coke. Whether you want a Coke, a Fanta, or a Mountain Dew, you ask for a Coke — and then you tell them what kind. But don't ever ask for a Pepsi. That's just wrong."

"That's just odd," Merritt said, her eyes narrowed as she tried to determine whether Loralee was teasing.

"It's just Southern, which is sometimes the same thing as odd, but that's how we like it. Keeps our Northern brothers and sisters guessing."

Closing one eye, Merritt peered into the neck of the pale green bottle, her forehead creased. "What's floating in there?"

Loralee brightened. "Peanuts! Haven't you ever put peanuts in your Coke?"

"Never." She looked at Loralee as if her stepmother were trying to poison her.

"Look," Loralee said, lifting Owen's bottle to her lips. "You want to drink it when the Coke is ice-cold and the peanuts are still crunchy and salty. The first couple of sips are always the best."

She closed her eyes as the cool, bubbly liquid hit her tongue, quickly followed by the hard, salty taste of peanuts. She was immediately taken back to summer afternoons sitting next to her mother on the cinder-block steps in front of their un-air-conditioned trailer, their faces sticky with sweat, the smell of dry mud and hot grass clinging to the metal sides of the trailer like bread crumbs on chicken.

It wasn't a bad memory, but it made her sad for her mama, who never got to meet Owen or see Loralee living in an up-and-down house with a real yard and two nice cars in the attached garage.

She opened her eyes in time to see Merritt swigging her first sip, awkwardly holding the bottle as if she'd never drunk from anything besides a glass before. Her throat moved as she swallowed before lowering the bottle from her mouth.

"That wasn't too bad," Merritt said, leaving the impression that she would have smacked her lips if Loralee hadn't been there.

"It's a great afternoon snack, too — the Coke gives you the caffeine you need and the peanuts give you the fiber and protein. I had all the Delta pilots I worked with drinking it."

At the mention of pilots, Merritt leaned over and placed her bottle on the nightstand before shoving the album off of her lap. "Thank you," she said, sliding off the bed. "But I need to get back to work. Edith was a bit of a pack rat, so there's a lot to get through. Gibbes is supposed to come back tomorrow to go through the rest of the house, but I haven't even made it out of this bedroom."

"I could help," Loralee offered, trying to keep her voice neutral. Merritt didn't like asking for help, and technically she wasn't asking. But Merritt would look at it that way just the same.

After a short pause, Merritt said, "If you're looking for something to do, there are a lot of boxes in the closet in your room that Gibbes said belong to him. If they're too heavy, wait until he gets here to remove them. If they're not, could you stack them in the hallway with the other boxes that are marked with his name? If there are any more with newspapers inside, just stack them on top of the one in the corner of your bedroom. We'll take them to be recycled, but I'll wait to make sure that's all of it." Merritt looked down at Loralee's feet. "I found a stepladder in the pantry downstairs you can use. Just make sure you take off those shoes first."

Loralee glanced at Merritt's shoes, the worn house slippers she wore whenever she wasn't wearing her sensible loafers, which didn't even have tassels for decoration. "All right. I'll just deliver Owen's Coke and get started. And since you're going to throw out those newspapers, is it okay if Owen keeps a few? He's been reading them and has found a few articles he wants to hang on to."

"Sure. He can keep them all if he wants."

Loralee's gaze fell on the open photo album Merritt had pushed off her lap, curious as to what had made her cry. They were photos of two boys in a small metal boat, both of them sandy haired and golden eyed, sitting with their arms slung around each other despite a great difference in height. She looked closer at the photo, recognizing the smaller boy. She'd always found it interesting how some people still looked like their baby pictures into adulthood, while others changed so much you could no longer see the child inside. She wondered whether that was intentional, whether you could bury that person you once were just as easily as you could pack your bags and move away.

"Is that your husband?" she asked, pointing to the taller boy.

For a moment Loralee thought Merritt wouldn't answer. Finally she nodded. "Yes. These are mostly pictures of Cal and Gibbes. I found these albums in a box at the back of the closet. I thought I'd go through them before I gave them to Gibbes." She reached over and shut the album, blocking the photos from view.

"I'm sure Gibbes wouldn't mind if you took some of the photographs to be copied. Then you could frame them. . . ."

"No. I have enough photos." She let her hand linger for a moment on the closed album. "I never knew this boy." She met Loralee's eyes. "It would be like having photos of Gibbes around the house. Or you." She looked away, as if the words hadn't belonged to her at all. "I'm sorry. I didn't mean it the way it sounded."

"I understand. I do. I'm a widow, too. It's hard to lose the person you thought would always be with you." Her chest burned for a moment as she thought of Robert. She forced her smile to be even brighter. "It's like your life has become some sort of game where they changed all the rules in the middle. But it's not the end. My mama used to say that when you lose something from your life it just means that you're making room in your heart for something new."

Merritt closed her eyes and began breathing deeply, her hands clenched into tight balls. Owen used to do that when he was a toddler and was on the verge of a meltdown. She wished Merritt would throw a big caterwauling, screaming-and-jumping-and-throwing-things kind of tantrum. It wasn't good to hold everything inside, even if you were from Maine and thought you were supposed to.

Through very thin lips, Merritt said, "Please leave. And don't say another word. You can't help me. Nobody can, and not for lack of trying. Why can't I just be left alone so I can work through things on my own?" She turned back to the closet, and Loralee thought for a moment that she'd walk inside and shut the door and maybe not come out.

She wasn't sure whether Merritt wanted an answer, but Loralee had one anyway. "Because you seem lost. And most people can't let it alone when they see someone bumping into walls."

"Merritt?"

They both turned to see Owen in the doorway. "There's a man at the front door saying he's here to fix the air conditioner. Can I let him in?"

Merritt looked like she'd just gotten a stay of execution from the governor's office. "Yes, thank you. I guess we didn't hear the doorbell."

She walked past them into the hallway. Loralee watched the back of her prim white blouse as Merritt descended the stairs, knowing it was high time for Merritt to have a hissy fit, to clench her fists and then grab something and hurl it across the room, watching each piece explode against the wall like a raindrop in dry dirt. Loralee had done it several times during her thirty-six years and knew for a fact that watching the pieces scatter was like seeing all of your hurts lessened somehow, each part finally made manageable and bearable. Yes, Merritt was due a hissy fit, and hopefully soon. At least before Loralee had one more hurt to lay at her feet.

Loralee leaned heavily on the buggy at the Piggly Wiggly as she studied the organic produce in front of her, weighing her decision of what to buy between how healthy it was and how likely it was that she'd get Owen to eat it. Merritt would eat anything that was put in front of her, although in rabbit-size portions. Robert had said that Merritt ate like a linebacker when she was a child to fuel her appetite for climbing trees and running races with the neighborhood boys. All while wearing sequined tops with matching headbands. Loralee had seen the photographs or else she wouldn't have believed it.

According to Robert, the climbing and racing had ended with Merritt's mother's death, but not the designing part. Not even Loralee's marriage to Robert had grounded Merritt's creativity. Loralee wasn't sure when that had stopped, and when this new Merritt with the tight lips and ill-fitting clothes had begun, but she was starting to think it had to have been around the time of Merritt's marriage to Cal.

Loralee picked up a package of organic kale and tossed it into the cart without looking at it. She needed to be quick, before the last spurt of energy left her completely. She thought of her mother and how long she'd been sick before she died, and how she'd wished for a pill to just get it over with. Loralee understood that now, how dying was such a *process.* How the end would come sooner or later but it would come. Some mornings she felt so bad that she wished it could just be over. But it was too soon. There was Owen to think about, her precious boy, who would be an orphan. Who would need somebody to take care of him. That thought alone gave her the energy she needed each day to put one foot in front of the other, to smile, to cook breakfast, to do all the things that made it look like everything was fine in her world. Except, of course, that it wasn't.

She leaned all her weight on the handlebar, pretending to study a package of baby carrots like they were the instrument panel in a 747 while giving her body a little rest. Just for a moment. If she didn't think she'd be noticed, she could have easily slid to the floor, pressed her cheek against the cool laminate, and gone to sleep immediately.

"Loralee?"

She jerked her head up, automatically smiling as she recognized the voice. "Dr. Heyward. So nice to see you." He held a six-pack of beer in one hand and a bunch of bananas in the other. Even if she hadn't already known he was a bachelor, that alone would have tipped her off.

"It's Gibbes, remember?"

"Gibbes," she repeated, admiring how nicely he filled out his light green polo and how his gold eyes and white teeth looked in his tanned face. *He's bigger than life and twice as handsome.* Loralee almost giggled out loud as she recalled what her mama used to say when they spotted a good-looking man.

"I'm glad I ran into you. Outside of the house, that is," he said.

He glanced around and waited for a woman with a tight gray perm to push her cart out of produce and into the dairy section. Loralee kept smiling, but her insides froze.

"My offer is still good for sharing any doctor recommendations you might need."

"Yes," she said. "How nice of you to remember."

He looked at her closely for a moment before continuing. "If Rocky will be starting school here in the fall, he'll need a physical and a doctor's sign-off that he's had all his shots. My practice does free school checkups the last week in July, which should give you plenty of time to get his current pediatrician to send over his medical records. There are lots of other pediatricians in the area, so feel free to check them out, too. Just wanted to give you the heads-up."

"Thank you, Gibbes. I appreciate it." She continued to smile, waiting for her insides to thaw.

"I know lots of other doctors in the area, too," he went on. "You'll probably want an internist or a GYN. A dentist. Whatever you need, I'm sure I know one I could recommend. Please don't hesitate to let me know." His voice was light, but his eyes held a serious glint. "You want to make sure that you're under a doctor's care, with your ulcers."

"Yes, of course. Just give me a few more days to get settled and I'll give you a call."

He continued to look at her without speaking, and it was almost like they were daring each other to be the one to look away first.

Still studying her, he said, "I'm not on call this weekend and was planning on taking my boat out — maybe just to ride around in so you can check out your new home. We can fish next time. The invitation still stands if you and Rocky are interested."

"He'll love that — we'll love it. Thank you. What should I bring? I'll pack a picnic basket — there's one in the pantry that looks like it's still in good condition."

"You don't need to, but I have a feeling that you're going to bring one anyway."

She returned his smile, although it did nothing to melt the frozen spot inside her. "Can you ask Merritt to come with us again?"

He tilted his head, the way some people did when they couldn't understand her accent. "I was under the impression that she'd rather sew her head to the carpet than spend any time in my company."

She thought just for a moment, remembering what her mama had said about how it was always easier to ask for forgiveness than for permission. "I think the reason she said no was not so much because of you, although I won't lie and say that's not part of it. It's more about the boat. And the water in particular."

He looked at her with dawning understanding and she hoped, just for a second, that he would understand enough so she wouldn't have to say it out loud. Merritt was such a private person that she would probably turn to stone if she knew what Loralee was about to tell Gibbes. But Merritt needed somebody besides Loralee to know, and Loralee just didn't have the time to wait the fifty or so years she imagined it would take Merritt to warm up enough to anybody to tell them herself.

"Merritt's mother drowned. She and her mother were driving over a bridge in a storm at night, and the car went over. Sarah managed to get Merritt free, but Sarah died."

Gibbes looked stunned for a moment, then nodded his head. "Ah. Well, that would explain why she wouldn't want to go out on the water. And I can't say I blame her."

"I know. But I think if she gives it a chance, she'll find the water is different here. It's still the Atlantic, but down here — except during hurricanes, of course — the ocean seems so much more forgiving. It's warmer, calmer; the colors are green and blue and not black and gray. Growing up in Gulf Shores, I always found the water to be a place of refuge and renewal." She looked past him, through the sliding glass doors that showed blue sky outside, remembering. "When my own mama died, I spent a lot of time on the beach staring at the water until I learned what I was supposed to. And I did. I finally figured out that when the waves come ashore and wipe away all the footprints, it's like God telling you that starting again is part of life. It saved me."

"And you want to save Merritt?"

Loralee dipped her head, examining her gold metallic strappy sandals. They had been Robert's favorites, and they made her happy when she wore them. With a strength of conviction that came from deep inside of her, she said, "We all need saving."

"Good luck with that. Something tells me that Merritt isn't the type who enjoys a good ol' coffee klatch with her girlfriends."

Loralee almost laughed at the mental image of her and Merritt wearing fluffy slippers and bathrobes with towels in their hair, curled up on a couch drinking coffee while sharing confidences. She had the disloyal thought that she'd see Owen playing professional football before that ever happened.

She and Gibbes ended up at the checkout even though Loralee still had grocery items on her list. But her energy reserves were below empty, and she was glad she'd had this conversation with him. He was an unlikely ally, but one she felt good about.

He placed his two items on the lip of the conveyor and began loading her purchases onto the belt. She wanted to tell him to go ahead, that she could do it herself, but knew she'd be lying. "Thank you," she said instead, handing her credit card to the cashier.

Gibbes bagged her purchases and put them in her buggy before buying his own items, then escorted her out to her car, pushing the buggy and even loading her car. He didn't ask permission. She liked that about him. He saw what needed to be done and did it. It reminded her of Merritt, although Loralee would rather dip her head in honey and lie down on a red-ant hill than say that aloud to either one of them.

"Thank you," she said as he opened her door and she climbed in behind the wheel. She hit the start button and rolled down the windows, taking deep breaths of cool air.

"Are you sure you'll be okay?"

"I'll be fine — please don't worry about me." She looked up at him, recognizing the same shadows she saw behind his eyes that she saw in Merritt's. "And I'm sorry for your own loss. First your grandmother and then you find out that your brother is gone, too. I know you hadn't seen him for a while, but I'm sure you're grieving. It might help if you talk about him with somebody. Just let me know — you know I love to talk, but I'm a good listener, too."

"You're a nice person, Loralee. I hope living with Merritt doesn't change that."

She laughed softly. "Oh, don't you worry about that. I understand Merritt. More than she thinks I do. She's just one of those people who thinks they have to live with their toes pressed against the edge of disaster. She's been pushed over it so many times she just comes to expect it. I think this place will be good for her. Every time I hear the mermaid's tears I think they're clapping to welcome Merritt."

He raised his eyebrows. "Mermaid's tears?"

"That's what my mama called the sea glass." Her smile fell at her next thought. "I hope you're not upset that your grandmother left the house to your brother and now his widow is living in it. Especially since you grew up there."

Gibbes shuffled his feet, uncomfortable. "Family tradition and all. Cal was the oldest son and so the house should rightly have gone to him — or his heirs. And she's welcome to it." He looked at Loralee, but she was pretty sure he was seeing something else. "If my grandmother had left it to me, I would have torn it down."

He stepped back and closed her door, his hands braced on the frame. "Remember to let me know about any doctor recommendations you might need. Call me anytime."

"I will. Thank you, Gibbes." On impulse, Loralee touched his arm. "And remember to call me anytime you want to talk. I really am a good listener."

"I'm sure you are. I'm just not sure anybody's ready to hear what I have to say." He pushed off from the car, his smile back in place. "I'll let you know about the boating."

After a final wave, he picked up his grocery bag and headed toward his truck. She rolled her window up as she watched him walk away, wondering what demons he still saw lurking in the dark corners of the old house, and if they knew the ones Merritt was running away from.

Slipping her pink journal out of her purse,

she opened it at the spot she'd marked with her pen and began to write. *The scariest things in our lives aren't always the bogeymen under the bed. It's the fear that the small bird with bound wings that lives in the darkest place in our hearts will one day find a way to break free.*

She put on her seat belt, then drove back to the house on the bluff, thinking of the dark places in her own heart, and how much time she had before she had to face her biggest fear.

CHAPTER 10

Merritt

I walked slowly through the dining room, my fingers lightly skimming the top of an elegant eighteenth-century sideboard with Queen Anne legs and detailed marquetry bordering the small drawers. A heavily tarnished silver tea service sat on top, and I'd already discovered that the drawers were filled with sterling flatware with handles embellished with vines of roses and the letter "H."

As I'd taken inventory of all the rooms, I realized that the old house contained a fortune in antiques and art, presumably acquired by a family that had called this place home for generations. But Gibbes didn't seem to have warm feelings about it, as if there were too many dark spaces clouding his memories. I felt them, too, the shadows that seemed to move and twitch right beyond my field of vision. But I also felt a warmth, a sense of family and belonging that must have been included in each floorboard and each nail when it was built all those years ago. It was almost as if the house were waiting for someone to shine light into all of its corners.

I had been an art history major and then a curator of a small art museum in Farmington, Maine, but that made me no expert. The museum also contained pieces of furniture donated or collected from the area, the legs thicker and bolder, the wood darker and grainier than the almost dainty furniture in this house. It had made me think of the long, hard winters in Maine, and I couldn't imagine this delicate furniture surviving in such a brutal environment.

These were family heirlooms, treasures that I owned but had no real claim to. Gibbes had expressed no interest in anything except personal mementos, but I would have to insist. I didn't want any burning resentment to link us together. I wanted to give him what was his and cut ties completely. I wanted to be alone, *needed* to be alone. I'd already spent a lifetime loving people and losing them.

I sat down for a moment on a Chippendale sofa with faded blue and white Chinese silk upholstery, resting my clipboard on my lap. I was waiting to show Gibbes the inventory list I had made, and had even included a column for him to check off the items he wanted. I tilted my head back, not minding the whir of the new air-conditioning unit as long as the cold air blew on my face and dried the sweat on my cheeks and forehead. The HVAC man had looked at me oddly when I mentioned that it surely couldn't get any hotter outside than it already was. He'd reminded me that it was only May.

I was the happy owner of six unsightly window units, which would make the house bearable while I determined when the best time to install the new central heating and air system would be. The estimate I'd received was more than I'd been expecting, but at that point he could have charged me three times the amount and I would have gladly paid it. For somebody with a genetic predisposition to keep the wallet strings tightened at all times, that was saying something.

The doorbell rang and I spent a moment mentally preparing myself before standing up and answering it. Gibbes smiled when he saw me, but it was the kind of smile one gives to his dentist right before a tooth is pulled.

He paused in the foyer under the beautiful fluted arch that separated the doorway from the rest of the entrance. "Is that a cool breeze I feel?"

"It is. I had new AC units installed in the study and front parlor to create a cross breeze, and I added a new one in the dining room, two more upstairs in Owen's and Loralee's bedrooms, and one in the attic. It makes the house almost bearable."

"It's not that hot, you know. It's still spring. You might want to leave the windows open so you can get acclimated before summer gets here."

I wasn't sure whether he was trying to prepare me or scare me, so I didn't say anything. Instead I handed him the inventory list. "Here's everything in the house — excluding the kitchen and garden. You're welcome to go through those yourself if you think there's anything there you might want. Or I'm sure Loralee would be happy to do it."

He looked at me sharply, and I wondered whether my tone of voice had given me away. Loralee had been so excruciatingly helpful with the inventorying. She was like a diligent little worker bee who did what was needed and didn't require any direction. She was efficient, organized, and —

for lack of a better word — cheerful. She took frequent naps, but her sleeping habits didn't interfere with her productivity any more than her propensity to wear high heels and makeup every waking hour did.

To my shame, I knew I was looking for reasons to dislike her — as if I didn't have enough — but kept coming up empty. Even more shameful was that that just made me even more put-out. I responded by avoiding her as best I could, which turned out to be easier than I'd anticipated. It had only just occurred to me that she might also be avoiding me.

"Where is Loralee? I wanted to let her and Owen know that we're definitely on for boating this weekend." He opened his mouth to say something else, but hesitated, his expression like that of a person who'd just bitten into something rotten. After a moment, he said, "And I'd like to extend the invitation to you, too."

"No," I said quickly. Then added, "Thank you. I have work to do here. Besides, I don't like the water very much."

He continued his cajoling, even though his expression looked like he was sucking on a lemon. "That's because you've never been on the water down here in South Carolina. And we won't go near the ocean

203

— just stick to the creeks and marshes and possibly the river. We'll fix you up with a life jacket and a hat and a bunch of sunscreen and all you'll have to do is sit down and enjoy the ride."

"I don't like the water," I repeated, surprised at the power the merest suggestion that I go near a body of water still had over me. I felt cold all over, as if I'd been plunged into the frigid north Atlantic, and it had nothing to do with the air-conditioning.

"Okay, I get it. Just thought I'd ask." He sounded too relieved, enough so that I began wondering about his motives.

"And to answer your question, Loralee took Owen to the nursery to get supplies for the garden. She's planning on re-creating it the way it was. Maybe you can give her some insight, since you probably remember it. She wants to finish with the garden before she finds a job."

Gibbes regarded me with serious eyes before glancing down at the inventory list. He flipped through the pages, giving each one a cursory glance before handing the clipboard back to me. "Nope. Nothing here I want. It's all yours, and you're welcome to it."

"Didn't you see my value estimations next

to the items? There's a fortune in furniture and paintings in this house. Not to mention heirloom silver. We can talk to Mr. Williams and see if we can work something out. . . ."

"I told you. I'm not interested in anything in this house except for a few personal items. That's it. I don't need the money, and I don't need the furniture. I don't *want* any of it. It's yours. You won it fair and square."

I felt the blood rush to my head. "I didn't *win* anything. My husband died."

"You're right, of course. I was out of line and I'm sorry." He didn't look the least bit sorry, but I let it go.

I placed the inventory list on the circular table in the entranceway. Eager to move on, I said, "I think I found the photo albums you were looking for. They're upstairs in the hallway with the rest of the boxes marked with your name." I hesitated just for a moment before adding, "I haven't been up to the attic yet. There's a window unit up there now cooling everything off. You're welcome to go up with me now if you have time."

I felt foolish all of a sudden, like a child afraid of the dark. But every time I approached the door I heard Deborah Fuller telling me about secretly gathering sea glass for Edith Heyward, keeping it from her husband, and seeing Edith's face in the attic window. When I placed my hand on the doorknob I felt a little bit like Pandora, but with the benefit of hindsight. Maybe I *was* afraid of what I might find. Or maybe I was simply discovering the small pleasure of deliberately ignoring the little voice in my head that I knew was Cal's goading me to do something I didn't want to.

"You haven't been up there yet?"

"No," I said as I turned away toward the stairs, not wanting him to see my cheeks flush. "So we might as well get it over with now."

We climbed the stairs, the rising warm air upstairs seeming to press into us, adding to my feeling of gloom. Gibbes glanced down the hallway at the piles of boxes with his name on them, then stopped next to me by the attic door. Stalling, I said, "I had the new AC in the attic set at sixty-eight. It's a horrible waste of money, but I couldn't stand the thought of going up there otherwise."

He widened his eyes, as if to remind me that the new AC had been installed almost three days before.

I took a deep breath, concentrating on my loafers and how the tips were badly scuffed.

More people die from smoke inhalation than flames. Fire can suck all of the oxygen from a room and fill it with poisonous smoke and gases before flames even reach a room. I didn't have to wonder why that particular nugget of fire-academy wisdom had come to me at that moment.

With a confidence that was completely artificial, I turned the knob and the door swung open into the hallway. A tall, narrow flight of stairs, made of wood stained only by time, led the way up. They were steep steps, making them difficult to climb and impossible to see what lay beyond the top step.

"I should go first," Gibbes said, putting a foot on the first step.

I bristled. I knew about Southern boys, and I needed to shove his chauvinism back where it came from. "Just because I'm a woman?"

He looked at me and it seemed as if he were trying very hard not to smile. "Well, it would be good manners. But mostly it's because you're wearing a skirt." He indicated the steep steps in front of us. "I figured we're already as well acquainted as we need to be."

The air left my lungs in a sudden rush, meeting the blood heading toward my cheeks, and for a moment I saw stars. "Just go," I finally managed, pointing toward the stairs.

A lopsided and decidedly boyish grin lit his face before he jogged up the steps. I grabbed hold of the banister and slowly began my ascent, taking each steep step one at a time.

The first thing I noticed were the dust motes in the shafts of light from the two dormer windows, dancing in the disturbed air like summoned spirits. Gibbes stood within the light, surveying the room around him, his hands on hips making him look like a pillaging pirate. The ceiling was high in the center, giving even a tall person like Gibbes plenty of room to walk about without banging his head on a rafter.

The ceiling and walls were unfinished — and uninsulated — which made me wince as I considered all the air-conditioned air I was paying for that was apparently seeping through the cracks and single-paned windows. The HVAC man had expressed reservations about the wisdom of running the window unit, and had suggested I come up to look, but I'd refused, explaining it was just a temporary fix anyway. It was still warm in the attic, but bearable for a short period of time.

I thought of Edith up there sweltering, wondering how she'd managed it. Even with open windows and a fan or two, it would have been broiling in the summer. Deborah had said she'd seen a light on in the attic, so there must be electricity up there, which made me think Edith must have had a dozen fans. But still, even with the wall unit blasting, it was sticky and hot, suffocating. What had been so important to her that she would spend periods of time up there? Or had it been less about what she was doing and more about escaping something?

Gibbes looked up at an ancient ceiling fixture with a chain dangling from it. He pulled the chain but nothing happened. At least the light from the windows would be enough for me to see during the daytime, but I'd need to replace the bulbs if I wanted to be able to see at night. Not that I wanted to be up there after dark. There was something in the air up there, something beyond the dust and staleness, something more oppressive than even the heat. If the house had been a living, breathing thing, I might have said I'd found the dark place at its heart. But it wasn't, of course. It was just an old house.

There was a long wooden ledge that extended across the wall below the dormers with an ancient fifties-style kitchen chair sitting in front of it, yellow foam erupting from the turquoise vinyl seat. Woven baskets in varying sizes littered the top of the table like offerings for some unknown entity. They were set up in a deliberate line, a measure of tidiness not expected on a worktable. I stepped forward involuntarily, wanting to see inside the baskets but knowing already what they contained.

Milky glass of varying hues lay dully in their woven homes, listless without the wind and sun to bring them to life. They were separated by colors — varying shades of white, blue, green, brown — each as lifeless as the next. I wondered how long it had taken to collect them, imagining that it must have been years. I thought of the dedication, the purpose required to collect something as rare and precious as sea glass. My mother had had a small dish on her dressing table filled with a small handful of glass she'd collected on childhood visits to Old Orchard Beach with her cousins. They were the only reminder I had that she had once loved the ocean, and the great waves that sometimes left gifts of glass behind.

"What on earth could this be?" Gibbes walked toward the wall opposite the attic door and perpendicular to the dormer wall.

Faded white sheets billowed softly from the blast of the air conditioner, undulating like ocean waves. Whatever they were concealing protruded in random bumps and lines, little fists of prisoners begging to be let out.

"Hold your breath for a moment — I'm going to yank these down."

I realized I'd already been holding my breath, and just nodded. He reached up to the topmost corner and gave a sharp tug, the sheet releasing its hold on whatever it had been hung up on. Slowly Gibbes walked down the line, tugging the fabric from the top, until three large flat sheets had slipped down to the floor in a puddle of cotton and dust.

We both stepped back as the dust motes thickened, holding our hands over our noses and mouths. I choked on the air when I finally took a breath, nearly gasping. We waited for a moment for the dust to clear before stepping forward.

Crudely made shelves, consisting of two-by-fours and thin planks about three feet deep, covered the entire wall from floor to ceiling. They were constructed of raw wood, unstained and unadorned, crooked in places, with bent nails peeping out from various sections. I didn't want to stand too near, afraid they might come crashing

211

down, because despite the fact that the unit had obviously been there for a long time, it was apparent that an amateur who knew nothing about construction had made it.

As odd as the shelves were, they weren't what drew our attention. It was the row upon row of what appeared to be large shoe boxes without lids — perhaps intended for short boots — tipped on their sides so that the openings faced out, that transfixed us.

"Dollhouses?" I was the first to speak, then regretted it. These were definitely not dollhouses — at least not like any dollhouse that I'd ever seen. Each box was a sort of tableau of a single room, but different from the other boxes, so that they didn't all appear to come from the same house.

We peered closer, amazed at the intricate details of each little room, from the miniature furniture with tiny tubes of lipstick and a perfume bottle, to shoes with untied laces, and dressers with half-closed drawers. Tiny people with real hair and eyelashes lay in odd positions in the various boxes or, in one box, sat slumped over in an upholstered chair whose plaid fabric was faded in the way one would imagine a real chair that sat near a window might be. Right above the chair was a wall calendar with the bottom right corners curled up, the month and year emblazed in bold, black letters: May 1953.

"What in the . . . ?"

I found Gibbes staring into one of the boxes, an odd expression on his face. I moved next to him and peered inside. It was a replica of a 1950s-era bathroom, with separate hot and cold faucets — each tiny porcelain handle marked with a blue "C" or "H" — and an old-fashioned toilet. But it was the tub that was the center of attraction, and not because of the clawed feet or the chipped porcelain, but because of the figure of a woman whose top half was submerged in lifelike water, her pale blue eyes staring up at the ceiling in silent horror.

I stepped back, my gaze darting to the dozens of boxes that crowded the shelves, focusing on the miniature dolls and registering why they were strewn about in such odd poses. A man in a business suit with a pocket square in his jacket lay faceup on an oval braided rug, a puddle of red surrounding his head right behind a deep gash on his forehead. Red splotches on the wood floor in the shape of footprints led out the door.

Another was of a woman apparently asleep in her bed, the floral quilt neatly tucked under her chin, an empty vial of pills with a tiny label on the side on the nightstand.

213

Rose-printed wallpaper above a woman bent halfway into a kitchen sink was peppered with red spray opposite a window with a clean round hole surrounded by a cracked web of glass.

"What is this?" Gibbes asked, his voice quiet, as if he didn't want to disturb the dead.

I shook my head. None of the scenarios I'd gone over in my head of what I might find in the attic had come close to this. Nothing in my worst nightmares had come close to this. "I've never seen anything like this in my life. It's . . . macabre." I wanted to say *sick and twisted,* but I had to remind myself that Edith was Gibbes's grandmother.

"I think I've seen enough," I said, slowly backing up toward the door, unable to look away from the scenes of carnage in front of me.

"Wait. There's something else."

I took one more step toward the door, not completely sure I could handle seeing anything else.

On the floor to the far left, in the corner between the wall and the side of the shelves, was an oblong object about the size of a table lamp. I couldn't tell what it was from where I stood, but I could at least be certain it wasn't another dollhouse box.

Gibbes stooped down and picked it up, then carried it over to the table, brushing back the line of baskets with his forearm to make room.

"It's a model airplane, but it's missing its wings," I said, hearing the surprise in my own voice.

"Yes, it is," he said slowly. Very carefully, he tilted the wingless plane on its side, displaying navy-colored stripes with no insignia on the tail and a gaping hole on the right side of the fuselage. "And look," he said, pointing to the mosaiclike side where pieces alternated between transparent plastic and something that was a hard, pasty white. "There are people inside, and luggage still below."

He considered something for a moment. Pulling out his phone, he flipped on the flashlight and returned to the corner where he'd found the plane. Squatting down to see into the dark space, he then pulled out an old brown paper bag.

Returning to the worktable, he placed it on top.

"Let me," I said, reaching for the bag and hoping it wasn't crawling with those large flying cockroaches they called palmetto bugs in South Carolina. As a child I'd loved

215

surprises and discovering new things. Maybe that part of me hadn't completely disappeared.

The old paper felt soft in my hands as I unfurled the top. Gibbes flipped on his flashlight again as I pulled apart the edges and gently leaned forward. Staring up at us were about forty or so doll miniatures of people dressed in 1950s-era clothing. Some were strapped in plane seats; others were missing limbs or had grotesque wounds on their heads or bodies; most had grass or dirt clinging to their hair, skin, and clothes. What looked like two wings, also made in a mosaic fashion with two separate materials, were intermingled with the figures, the detritus of a catastrophe I couldn't comprehend.

Our eyes met, and I wondered whether the same lost and scared expression I saw in his eyes was reflected in my own. "What is all this?" I asked. I knew he didn't have the answer, but saying it out loud made it somehow more real and less dreamlike. Because I could handle reality no matter how brutal. I had a harder time with dreams.

"I have no idea," Gibbes said softly, not taking his eyes from mine. I was reminded again of how during a fire it was what you couldn't see that killed you and not the fire.

It seemed to me that all of this was the fire in the attic we'd only sensed, the poison leaking out undetected for years.

I looked out one of the dormer windows and saw the wind chime dangling from a long metal bar. The outside was hot and heavy, the sea glass still. But I could imagine it clinking together, its music like words trying to tell me something in a language I didn't understand.

CHAPTER 11

Edith
April 1961

Edith sat in the stifling attic and took a long drag from her cigarette before stabbing it out in the small porcelain dish with the crimson climbing vines and the large "H" painted in the middle. Calhoun wouldn't have allowed her to smoke, much less use his precious heirloom china as an ashtray, but he wasn't there to stop her. He'd allowed her to pack his cigarette case, and to light his cigarettes, taking one puff to get it going, but she was never allowed to have her own.

She'd started smoking the day after he'd died, the day the tremors started each time she heard a plane rumble in the sky. Each time she thought of the suitcase and the note still under her refrigerator.

While all of her friends were buying the latest in home appliances — Betsy had a new pink Frigidaire with a matching stove — Edith kept her refrigerator, its white door damaged where C.J. had banged his toys against it or run his tricycle into it with an intensity Edith hadn't expected from a small child. She'd attributed it to the fact that he was a boy, and she, having been raised an only child with a gentle, brooding father, had no experience with little boys or children in general. Still, when she'd heard him thumping his head against his crib rails, sometimes for as long as an hour, she'd wondered. Betsy and even her doctor told her that many children did this as a soothing mechanism, finding comfort in the steady rhythm the way other children sucked their thumbs or wore a hole in a favorite blanket with constant scratching.

And it usually worked, and he'd settle down into a long sleep. But sometimes, usually after he'd heard the sound of a plane or thunder in the sky or a siren in the distance, he'd become agitated, and the head thumping would erupt into a complete and all-out tantrum.

His doctor told her that when he threw his tantrums she should leave him in a safe place and let him do it and not, under any circumstances, pick him up and coddle him, in order to avoid rewarding bad behavior.

But she loved her son, and remembered that terrible night they had shared. Sometimes, when his screaming and thumping became too much for her to stand, she'd go into his room and pick him up, worried that he was remembering that night, too, and she'd cup the back of his head, his hair sticky and damp with sweat and tears, and allow him to bang his head against her. She would be left with a small bruise, a fist-size smear of blue and green right under her collarbone, but Edith hardly noticed. It wasn't because she was overly familiar with bruises; it was more that she'd had a say in it, and therefore it was all right.

"Mama! Where are you?" Nine-year-old C.J. shouted from somewhere in the house. His restless energy hadn't dissipated at all, and Edith found it exhausting yet not worrying. He was a growing boy, and needed to run about and be loud and physical and make dents in walls. *Even after they grow into men.*

She brushed her hand through the air to erase the thought and the smoke and stood. "I'll be right down," she called, but not too loudly. Even though Calhoun had been dead for so long, there were still things she couldn't bring herself to do. Like shouting. Or wearing anything too loud or too short.

Cutting her hair even though it was past her waist and so very hot in the summertime. Or driving. She'd like to drive, but she'd have to buy a car, and she hadn't the first idea how to do that by herself. Her friends' husbands would surely help her out, but she was uncomfortable being alone with them, and couldn't imagine sitting inside a closed car with one.

"Mama!"

Edith's gaze strayed to her pack of cigarettes, wishing she had time for another, and then past it to her current project. It was, of all things, a back balcony in an apartment building involving a clothing line, a block of firewood, and a woman. She examined the doll's face for a moment, wondering whether she'd made it just the right shade of blue, and whether the print on the blouse was accurate enough. She wanted to hurry and finish it so she could go back to her biggest project, the one that consumed most of her waking thoughts. She was so close now to an answer that it was hard for her to focus on anything else.

It would have to wait until the following day when C.J. was at school. He didn't like her spending time in her workshop any more than Calhoun had. He wasn't allowed up there, and she was careful to lock the door when she left, putting the key in its hiding place in her closet. To make a prohibited place less appealing, she'd told him it was hot and stuffy, that there were lots of spiders, and all she did was work on her sea-glass wind chimes. She hoped she'd made it sound boring enough to him that he wouldn't be interested in finding the key.

She took her cardigan off the back of her chair and slid it over her shoulders before heading down the attic stairs, being careful not to trip in her high heels. After carefully locking the door and pocketing the key, she found C.J. in the upstairs hallway, bouncing a small rubber ball against the wall, which she'd told him not to do at least a dozen times.

"I'm here," she said, reaching over and grabbing the ball in mid-bounce.

He looked annoyed. His shirt had a tear at the hem and the neck had some unidentified food stain. His dungarees had holes in the patches on his knees, and his high-top sneakers looked exhausted, with their tongues and laces dangling over the sides. But she didn't say anything. Betsy had told her that the modern method of child rearing in that book by Dr. Spock was about choosing battles. C.J. played hard; that was all. Edith could accept that.

"Jimmy wants me to come over for dinner."

"I'm sorry, sweetheart. But you know Tuesday is bridge night. Debbie Fuller is coming over to babysit, and I've got a Swanson TV dinner in the oven already."

"No," he groaned. "I don't like Debbie Fuller, and I hate TV dinners."

This was how he generally responded when things didn't go his way. "I'm sorry that's how you feel, C.J. But Debbie is responsible and reliable and I like her." *She's also the only babysitter who will still come stay with you.* "And I think you'll like this TV dinner. It has a dessert — an apple cobbler."

"I *hate* apple cobbler," he shouted, rushing past her to the stairway and sliding down the banister. She'd told him too many times to count not to do that, that it was dangerous, but it didn't seem to matter. He was like his father that way, a rushing, boisterous *presence* in a room. She'd loved that about Calhoun — once, a long time ago. She didn't want to erase it completely from his son.

The doorbell rang and Edith answered it. Debbie Fuller was only four years older than C.J., but about a foot taller and years older in terms of maturity and poise. She wasn't frivolous like those other girls who were suddenly no longer available to babysit when Edith called. Debbie was a serious girl, her hair always crimped back in a tight ponytail and heavy bangs over thick, dark glasses. She was the oldest of six and the only girl, which was probably the reason she wasn't daunted by watching C.J. the few times Edith left him.

"Hello, Mrs. Heyward," Debbie said, her expression serious. She looked like one of those girls who was born old, as if their life's plan were already laid out in front of them and they followed those plans with the seriousness of a nun. Edith might even have envied that about her, the knowing what the future held. Maybe then she might have done things differently.

"Thanks so much for coming, Debbie. I've got two TV dinners in the oven for you and C.J. I hope you like meat loaf." She closed the door behind her.

"Yes, ma'am," Debbie said without smiling. "That will be fine." She held a stack of heavy schoolbooks, and Edith admired her optimism. The only time she ever got anything done with C.J. around was when he was at school, watching *Gunsmoke* and *Dennis the Menace* on television, or sleeping.

She led Debbie toward the kitchen. "Why

don't you come put your books down on the kitchen table while I go find C.J. Mrs. Williams will be here any minute to pick me up. We'll be at the Butlers' house tonight, and I've written her phone number on the pad by the phone."

She put her books down while Edith opened up the back door and called for C.J. When she turned back to Debbie, she was watching Edith closely. Edith ran her tongue over her teeth, making sure they weren't smeared with lipstick. She was patting the back of her chignon to check for loose bobby pins when Debbie finally spoke.

"This might be the last time I can come babysit."

"Oh, no, Debbie. Why? Am I not paying you enough?"

The teenager shook her head, her lank ponytail shaking, too. "No, ma'am. That's not it. It's just . . ." She fidgeted, turning her Keds-clad feet outward onto the sides of the soles.

"It's okay, Debbie. You can tell me."

She looked at Edith with pale blue eyes and she suddenly knew what Debbie was going to say. "Last time I was here, he hit me. On the arm. Hard enough to make a big bruise. Mama saw it and said I couldn't come back here unless you promised that

C.J. wouldn't hit me anymore."

It was as if Edith had turned to ice, as if one small tap anywhere on her would make her crack into a thousand little pieces. *Sins of the father.* She managed to hold on to her composure. "I'm so sorry, Debbie. So truly sorry. I'm sure he didn't mean it. I'll talk to him. Tonight — before I leave — and I'll make him promise to never hit you again."

With a tentative smile, she nodded. "Thank you. I know he didn't mean it. We were playing cards and I was winning. . . ." She stopped, either because she knew what she was saying wasn't making it any better, or because she suspected that Edith didn't want to hear it.

Edith opened up the back door and called for C.J. again, her voice more strident. She pictured him hunkered down beneath the oak tree, digging in the dirt with the penknife he'd found in his father's desk. Since he was a small boy, C.J. had always hidden in the garden when he was upset, finding refuge beneath the heavy arms of the oak tree and within the fragrance of the gardenias and roses Edith tended with a mother's care. She thought it was because as a baby she'd set up his playpen in the oak's shadow while she tended her garden, and that must have brought warm memories to him. But sometimes, when he looked at her with his father's eyes, she saw the dark sky exploding in fire all over again, as if he were remembering things he shouldn't.

Edith eventually found C.J. on the ground by the garden wall, whittling on a stick. They had their talk, and he seemed penitent enough that Edith chose to believe him. He didn't protest when she asked for the knife, or when she told him he shouldn't use his fists when he got angry. He even allowed her to hug him and he hugged her back, his soft, "I'm sorry," choked with tears. He was truly sorry; she knew this. Just as much as she knew that he was his father's son.

When Edith finally pulled away from the house in Betsy's Buick, she'd glanced up at the dormer windows, an orange glow coming from the light she'd left on. She probably wouldn't be able to sleep again tonight and would spend most of it working on her special project in the attic. She needed it to be done with, for the answer to her question to be found. It was what kept her going, besides her son. She had to believe that there was an answer, a reason. An explanation more complicated than anything she'd come across before in her work. More than that, it was a labor of love, a show of solidarity with a woman she'd never met. It would be her crowning glory, a nod to her own past. A promise to a secret kept.

She slid a cigarette and her lighter out of her pocketbook, catching sight in the side-view mirror of the lit attic window one last time before Betsy turned the corner and the old house disappeared from view.

CHAPTER 12

Loralee

Loralee was standing in the kitchen wrapping the quartered watermelon slices in plastic wrap when the doors swung open. Owen's feet were bare, and he wore a long-sleeved swim shirt with an SPF of fifty along with a bathing suit with characters from *The LEGO Movie.* He looked about as comfortable as a long-tailed cat in a room full of rockers. "Dr. Heyward called and said he's on his way."

With a sidelong glance, Loralee took out a twenty-dollar bill from her apron pocket and slid it across the counter. She hated resorting to bribery, but she'd already tried going the honest route, and Gibbes had had no better luck in convincing Merritt what was best for her than Loralee had. "We went over this enough last night that you know what to do. Just don't take no for an answer."

Owen gazed down solemnly at the bill. "Yes, ma'am. I'll save this toward my college education."

Loralee sighed. His father's side of the family hailed from New England, after all. "Or you could just blow it on LEGOs and candy. It's up to you."

Owen stared at her as if she'd stopped speaking English.

Without looking at Owen, she asked, "And Maris is coming, too?"

She imagined Owen's shoulders slumping.

"Yes. Dr. Heyward said he'd be happy to bring her. I don't know why you made me invite her."

Loralee held back a sigh. "To begin with, she's your first friend in Beaufort, and she'll be able to introduce you to more children your age so you'll know people at school. She's a darling little girl. I don't know why you're making such a fuss."

His fingertips tugged at the bottom of his swimsuit. It *was* too short, even though she'd bought it at the beginning of summer. She wasn't ready for him to get taller, but she would swear on a stack of Bibles that she wasn't making him wear too-small clothes on purpose. And it wasn't because she'd loved his baby years, when it had been just her and Robert and Owen. They'd been so happy, the days full of wonderful memories. Would it be such a bad thing if she was holding on to them in any way she could?

"That's the problem," Owen said in a small voice she hadn't heard in a long time.

"What do you mean?" she asked, opening the picnic basket and carefully placing the watermelon inside on top of ice packs. She'd read in *Parenting* magazine that sometimes the best way to have a conversation with your children was to be busy doing something else so you didn't have to make eye contact. Her own mama had held her by the ponytail and spoken to her almost nose-to-nose to get her points across, and that had seemed to work pretty well. But this was a new era, and she figured *Parenting* knew best.

Still tugging at his bathing suit, he said, "It's a problem because she's pretty, and fun, and smart." He paused, studying the plastic-wrapped plate of Loralee's homemade chocolate-and-peanut-butter-chip cookies. "When she finds out how not cool I am, she won't want to be my friend. I figure if I stay away from her all summer, by the time school starts she'll think I'm an enigma, which is a lot better than her knowing I'm a loser."

Loralee studied her son for a long moment, wondering how he knew the word *enigma* and if it was even a word a ten-year-old should be using. Or *loser* for that matter. Especially a ten-year-old boy who was painfully shy and desperate for friends. She threw the dish towel down on the counter. Screw *Parenting*. Getting down on her knees, she took Owen by the shoulders. "You are not a loser. Just because some other boys decided to call you that does not make it true. You are smart and funny and interesting. And I bet that once Maris gets to know you, all the other boys won't seem half as cool. Besides, smart girls like smart boys." He didn't look completely convinced, but she thought she'd at least given him something to think about.

She stood slowly, keeping her hands on his shoulders as support.

"Why doesn't Merritt want to come with us?"

Loralee took the glasses from his nose and cleaned them on the hem of her blouse before replacing them. "Because she's afraid of the water."

His eyes scrunched behind his glasses. "But I thought you said we should respect other people's fears."

She turned back to the counter and began

slathering bread with mayonnaise, wrinkling her nose at the smell of it, at the turning of her empty stomach. "I did. And we should. It's just that some people need a little push in the right direction. Some people use their fears as a wall, an excuse for not moving forward. It's not on purpose — just human nature, I guess. Usually I let people figure this out on their own, but Merritt's a little slower than most."

Owen snorted and she sent him a stern glance. "I don't mean that in a bad way. She's been through a lot and thinks that moving to a new place means all the bad stuff gets left behind. But it doesn't. We travel with the same packed bags we've always had, until we take the time to unpack them."

She glanced to the small laminate table where her pink journal sat, recalling what she'd written in it just that morning. *There are times when fear needs to be in the driver's seat. The best learning and growing happens when wisdom is won from pain.* And then she'd written, *Brush your teeth every morning and every night before you go to bed. Clean teeth and fresh breath will give you a reason to smile.* She figured practical advice should go in her *Journal of Truths,* too.

"Is that why we're here? To help her?"

Loralee stared into those beautiful eyes and saw his father. "Mostly," she said softly, turning her focus to slicing the tomatoes for the sandwiches.

The doorbell rang and Owen ran toward the kitchen door but stopped. "I forgot. Maris is with him."

"Either way, you need to answer the door."

He looked so panic-stricken that she wiped her hands on a paper towel. "Wash your hands and then put a handful of chips into five plastic bags. I'll go get the door."

Merritt had already opened the door, where Gibbes and Maris waited. She greeted the little girl with a warm smile, but looked oddly at the doctor. Ever since they'd gone up into the attic, there had been a strange undercurrent between them, like two fiddler crabs who'd decided that walking sideways didn't suit them anymore, yet were unsure how to walk any other way.

Loralee stepped forward, trying to ease the awkwardness. "So glad you could join us today, Maris. And thank you, Dr. Heyward, for allowing Owen to bring a friend. Maris, I spoke to your mother and she assured me that you're a great swimmer and a regular on a boat."

"Yes, ma'am. We have a motorboat that we like to swim and waterski from — not at the same time, of course — and we usually go sailing with my uncle when the weather's good. I also like to go shrimping and crabbing, and I always catch more than my brother even though he's two years older. Mama says she thinks I was born with webbed feet, because I love the water so much, even though I love horses just as much."

She apparently had used a single breath to get all the words out, her cheeks pink from the exertion.

"That's good to know. Owen's in the kitchen helping make lunches. Why don't you go back and join him?"

The little girl's eyes lit up, and Loralee noticed they were the same color as her sparkly blue bathing suit and cover-up and the sequined bows on her flip-flops. Her hair was braided again and held back with blue ribbons. She held a beach bag that was almost as big as Maris, with a horse emblazoned on its side.

"Yes, ma'am!" Without further prompting she ran toward the back of the house, where an unsuspecting Owen waited.

Before the kitchen door swung shut behind Maris, Loralee added, "And please tell him that Merritt is downstairs."

Loralee closed the front door, wondering

whether Merritt had taken the time to admire Gibbes in his Bermuda swim shorts that exposed his tanned and muscular legs. He wore a white T-shirt that fit him just fine, and if Merritt *hadn't* noticed, then Loralee had more work ahead of her than she'd thought.

Turning to Gibbes, she said, "Our picnic is almost ready. Just give us about five minutes to get it all packed up."

On cue, Owen came from the kitchen, closely trailed by Maris. After a quick glance at his mother, he turned to Merritt. "Where's your bathing suit?"

Merritt looked down at her skirt and blouse as if expecting to see something different. "I'm not going. I have too much to do here." His face fell, and for a moment Loralee thought he might cry.

He was really working for his twenty dollars, and he might even get a tip with this performance. "But I really, *really* want you to come with us. It won't be any fun without you. And Mama said she wasn't feeling good, and if she has to leave we all have to go home early, because it's not safe for just Dr. Heyward and two kids to be on the boat."

He used the puppy-dog eyes that he usually reserved for getting extra dessert, and

Loralee admired his ad-libbing. She would definitely have to give him a tip.

Merritt looked at him as a person would look at a yipping little dog, unsure whether it was just for show or a real threat. "That's very nice of you to say, but I'm just not comfortable in a boat. . . ."

Gibbes cleared his throat. "I thought we'd take my jonboat. Stick to the small waterways. Maybe explore the creeks and see if we can spot any turtles."

"I love the turtles," Maris said, jumping up and down. And then, as if she were in on Loralee's plans, she said, "I'd really be sad if we couldn't stay long because Mrs. Connors got sick." Her dimples were even more pronounced when she frowned, which didn't make any sense at all.

"But I'm . . . not comfortable on the water," Merritt said. "And I don't even know what a jonboat is."

Owen piped up. "It's a flat-bottomed boat that was originally used by the old fur traders, but is still used today for traveling in shallow creeks and marshes."

"We call them stump-knockers, too, because that's what you do with them in the shallow water. They used to be called *bateaux,* which means *boats* in French," Maris added. Owen looked at her with surprise and she gave him a smug smile.

"And I have a life jacket for everyone —
including two children's jackets — and I'm
a really good swimmer. There is absolutely
nothing to worry about." Gibbes sounded
like a man offering to feed a rattlesnake,
and Loralee sent him her mama look to get
him to quit.

She had once seen a movie about the
French Revolution with a scene of a woman
being led to get her head chopped off.
Merritt looked a little bit like that woman.

Her face lit up briefly. "I don't have a
bathing suit."

"Just shorts and a T-shirt is all you need,"
Gibbes said.

"I don't have that either."

Loralee almost expected Merritt to swipe
her hands together like she'd finished a
complicated task and was ready for something else.

"I do," Loralee almost shouted. "And you
can borrow anything you want. I'm pretty
sure we're the same size."

Merritt and Gibbes looked at Loralee as if
she'd just told a bald-faced lie. They would
have to wait and see, because she was
confident that Merritt had a body hidden
under those drab clothes and it was time to
let the world know.

"*Please*, Merritt," Owen whined, using a tone that usually got him sent to his room. "Daddy had a boat, too, and he used to always take me out on the lake to go fishing or just ride around. It was our favorite thing to do. It would be real neat going out on a boat with you. Kind of like Daddy being right there with us." Owen had never been fishing in his life, but Loralee was prepared to let the lie slide unremarked.

Loralee winced, hoping Merritt didn't remember Owen telling Gibbes that he'd never been fishing before. Still, if they'd been alone, Loralee would have hugged her little boy for such a performance. But something in his face told her he wasn't completely playacting. She wished they'd had more time to mourn Robert, for her to give Owen his chance to grieve instead of taking him away from the only home he'd known. One day he'd understand. She didn't allow herself to second-guess her belief that one day he would. Because he would just have to.

Merritt must have seen that in his face, too, because her own face softened just like Owen's did right before he fell asleep.

"Unless you don't mind a ten-year-old girl in pigtails showing you up. Of course, you might prefer staying here to inventory the attic." Gibbes's voice was filled with a challenge, baiting her.

Merritt gave him a hard look before turning to Owen. "If we're not going anywhere near the ocean, and we stick to the little creeks, we should be okay. I'm sure I have a pair of old pants. . . ."

Loralee didn't let her continue. Instead, she grabbed her by the elbow and began leading her to the stairs. "Owen, please take Maris back to the kitchen and finish packing up the basket. Merritt and I will be down in ten minutes." She glanced at Merritt's pale, pinched face. "Maybe closer to fifteen," she added.

They were halfway up the stairs when Owen called up. "Maybe we'll see some dolphins."

Merritt's arm stiffened under her fingers, but Loralee just gripped harder, pulling her along. She dragged her into her room and sat her down on the step stool she'd found in the pantry and had placed in front of her dressing table.

Loralee began rummaging through one of her drawers, tossing possibilities on the bed.

"Absolutely not," Merritt said, pointing to the hot-pink strapless two-piece bathing suit. "Don't you have Bermuda shorts, or capri pants? And something with sleeves in case it gets cool?"

Loralee looked up at Merritt for a moment to see whether she was serious, then went back to rummaging, finally deciding on something they could both agree on. Handing the shorts and shirt to Merritt, Loralee said, "Take these and put them on. I'm going to dig in my cosmetics case to see if I've got something that would work."

"I am not wearing makeup to go out on a boat. That's ridiculous."

Loralee sighed, finally letting her exasperation out. "It's got an SPF of fifty, and I'll make it look natural so nobody even knows you're wearing any."

"So what would be the point? It's a waste of time. Don't you have any zinc oxide?"

Loralee sighed inwardly, wondering whether David had ever complained that much to Michelangelo while he was being sculpted. "I have a wonderful foundation that's moisturizer and sunscreen. You'll need sunscreen to go out on the boat." She glanced down at Merritt's pale legs and arms. "Actually, we'll need to stop by a drugstore to get you some pretty strong SPF for your body. And probably a hat. Have you ever been in the sun before?"

Merritt crossed her arms and looked so much like her little brother that Loralee almost laughed. "I'm from Maine. My sun exposure was . . . limited."

"That's why your skin looks like porcelain, and I'm trying to keep it that way by using the right products."

Merritt stood and crossed the room toward the door.

"Where are you going?"

"To my room so I can change."

"Don't be silly," Loralee said. "It'll be quicker if you do it here. I promise I won't look."

Merritt seemed to consider it for a moment before heading toward the closet and pulling open the door so she could stand behind it. First a skirt was thrown out from behind the door, and then the hateful beige blouse. "I don't know what game you and Gibbes are playing by dragging me out on a boat. You both know I'm afraid of water, and I suspect you know why."

Loralee straightened, dumping several tubes and bottles on the dressing table. "I would never make anybody do something I thought wasn't the right thing to do. Besides, you could have said no."

It was silent behind the closet door, and Loralee could picture Robert's stubborn jaw in his daughter's face jutting out to show how riled up she was. They were so much alike that it shouldn't have been a surprise to anybody who knew them how they could have remained estranged for so many years. If Loralee had known it then, she would have dared Robert to never see Merritt again and they would most likely have been on the next flight to Maine.

Merritt came out from behind the door, pulling and tugging at her clothes like they were covered in fleas. "I don't think this fits."

The sleeveless top was in a soft sky blue that looked lovely against Merritt's dark hair. The smooth knit skimmed over her slim body, hugging where it was supposed to. The shorts were the most conservative ones Loralee owned, purchased for Boy Scout events, where the other mothers didn't seem to appreciate any other clothing choices Loralee had previously worn. They were navy blue and cuffed at the hem, hitting midthigh and showing off Merritt's long, slender — and appallingly white — legs.

"It fits you just fine. Now come over here so I can put something on your face so you don't get sunburned."

Merritt crossed her arms. "No. I'll stop by a drugstore and get a hat and a high-SPF lotion I can put on my face and body. That's all I need."

Loralee didn't smile with relief at the discovery that the girl with opinions Robert had told her about was still inside Merritt somewhere. Instead she just nodded, then led the way to the door.

"Won't I need a sweater out on the water? This shirt doesn't have any sleeves."

Loralee didn't even pause. "I promise you that you won't need a sweater. Not until October, most likely."

Loralee kept walking, knowing that Merritt would follow her, just as she knew Owen would figure out how a LEGO model was put together no matter how many times he threw it against the floor because it was wrong.

The children were in the front yard when they came down, and Gibbes was in the foyer with his head bent over his cell phone, typing a message. He glanced up and his eyes got that look Loralee remembered from her flying days, when she brought a scotch and soda to a first-class passenger without being asked. "Oh," he said.

Merritt plucked at her blouse. "Loralee says I won't need a sweater."

"No."

Merritt didn't seem to notice that Gibbes was acting like he'd fallen out of the stupid

244

tree, hitting every branch on the way down, and Loralee figured it was probably a good thing. Merritt had enough on her mind right then.

"I'll get the picnic basket," Merritt said, her voice hopeful, like she was looking forward to carrying the basket in front of her as some kind of barrier.

Gibbes cleared his throat. "It's already in my truck." He moved to the door and held it open while Merritt grabbed her pocketbook from the hall table.

Loralee paused as she stared out into the new day, the river golden in the morning light, glassy and bright like a promise. She hoped Merritt felt that, too: that each morning should always feel like a promise regardless of where you'd been the day before. She remembered the safety training she'd received as a flight attendant, how if they found themselves in water to roll on their backs and lead with their feet so they could see where they were going instead of where they'd been. She'd always thought that was a good way to approach life, too.

"We need to talk about the attic," Gibbes said to Merritt.

She frowned up at him. "Not today. I can only handle one scary thing per day."

She said it seriously, but the corner of his

mouth turned up. "Me, too."

Loralee grabbed her own purse from the hall table and followed Merritt out the door, wishing she could tell her what she'd written in her journal that morning as she was thinking about her coming out on the river that day. *You are stronger than you think.* She couldn't, of course. Most people just needed to figure that out on their own.

She joined everybody out on the porch, pausing a moment to catch her breath, and waiting for the sound of the door closing behind her.

CHAPTER 13

Merritt

I could have said no. I had once been a young girl who'd grown into a young woman with opinions and a strong will, both of which the years had leached from my bones, an embalming of the spirit. But I still could have said no.

Maybe it was Owen's obvious pleas that had made me agree to go along. I knew he'd been prompted by Loralee, or Gibbes, or maybe both, making me curious as to their motive. Or it could have been the memory of my father gently suggesting a family beach vacation, and my mother's stubborn refusal to revisit a part of her unhappy childhood she wanted left in the shoe box of photos she kept under her bed. A perverse part of me wanted to find out whether our fear was genetic, something I'd inherited along with her dark hair and slender feet. Mostly, I thought, I wanted to prove Cal wrong in his belief that all fears are permanent, that, like bone fractures, they will heal but leave a hairline shadow.

But I could have said no.

Gibbes drove his Explorer with Loralee in the front seat and Owen, me, and Maris in the back. I'd insisted on the seating arrangement as soon as I realized that we would have to drive over the river to get to Lady's Island, where Gibbes lived. I knew only that his house was on the marsh, and he had a dock, and that Lady's Island had once been the home of large agricultural plantations before the Civil War — although Loralee had called the war something else. She might have said more, but I'd stopped listening, too intent on watching her toddle on incredibly high heels as we walked toward Gibbes's SUV.

Where I'd lived inland in Maine, bridges hadn't really been an issue. I didn't travel far, and when I did, I would go to great lengths to avoid them. But there in the Low-country, the land seemed borrowed from the ocean. With strips of islands separated by creeks and salt marshes, avoiding bridges would be like avoiding snow in Maine in January.

Before my decision to move to Beaufort, I'd gone to the box of books I'd inherited from my maternal grandmother, who'd moved inland when my mother died to take care of me when my father was flying, and had died when I was in college. She was quiet, not unlike my mother, but always wore an aura of wariness, always overly cautious around strangers, events, and emotions. Which was why I'd been surprised to find that she owned a AAA South Carolina travel guide and road map. In all the years I'd known her, she'd never expressed any interest in knowing what might exist outside the small corner of her New England world. I'd felt ashamed, as if I'd never really bothered to know her. But then, she'd never offered, deflecting my questions with a dismissive flick of her wrist. It wasn't until after I'd married Cal that I began to realize that we rarely really know everything about those whose lives we share.

I'd spread open the map of South Carolina across my kitchen table as if seeing the land itself would make my undertaking somehow real. As if by following red and blue highways with my fingers, crossing bridges, and driving alongside vast bodies of water, I was as good as gone. I was my mother's daughter, after all. By her own admission she wasn't a great cook, but an adequate one who surprised herself every once in a while with a flash of genius. Her recipe box was filled with minute, step-by-step instructions on how to make even the most basic item. It was her road map in the unfamiliar territory of the kitchen, just as my map would guide me through an even more foreign place.

I sat in the middle between Maris and Owen, listening to Loralee and Gibbes talking about fishing, something they were apparently both familiar with, having grown up by the coast, and Maris's constant question bombardment aimed at a desultory Owen. He responded by narrating a litany of random facts that he'd either found interesting and wanted to share, or that were his way of dealing with being so close to Maris. I focused on the bright bows on Maris's flip-flops, aware of Gibbes's SUV heading toward the bridge and not wanting to know exactly when we'd get there.

If I were to live there, I knew I couldn't avoid driving over bridges forever, but I was glad it was Gibbes behind the wheel instead of me. A therapist had shown me how to use breathing techniques and helpful thoughts to manage the few times I'd had to navigate a small bridge back home. I'd have to remember them, go look for my notes and practice in the quiet of my bedroom. I didn't imagine I'd ever get used to it no matter how many times I had to cross the rivers and byways of my new home, but I'd manage. I'd simply recall Cal's voice telling me I couldn't do it and I would prove him wrong. One thing I knew for sure, however, was that I could never do it during a storm. And never, ever at night.

"This is the Woods bridge," Gibbes said, turning slightly toward the back seat. "Also known locally as the Beaufort River Bridge, and the Sea Island Parkway. It's a swing bridge."

"What's that?" Owen asked, sitting forward so that his seat belt strained across his chest.

"They have a man in the operations station in the middle of the span to swing the bridge open to allow boats through that are too tall to go beneath it."

"Cool," said Owen, looking intently out the window as we approached. A shiver ran through me as I imagined the bridge swinging open just as we reached it.

"Please keep your eyes on the road." I realized I'd said it out loud when Gibbes's eyes met mine in the rearview mirror. I closed my eyes and tried to disappear into the back of my seat.

"Did you know that this year August will

have five Fridays, five Saturdays, and five Sundays? This happens only once every eight hundred and twenty-three years. The Chinese call it 'silver pockets full.' It's supposed to be good luck or something." Owen's voice sounded loud in my ear, but not loud enough to block out the change in sound under our tires as we began a small ascent onto the bridge.

The bridge rumbled under the tires of the SUV and my hands took hold of the edges of the seats in front of me, as if they would hold me aloft while the brakes squealed and the side rails of the bridge gave way with the force of a vehicle crashing through them. As if they could save me from falling into freezing water that lapped below like the tongue of a hungry animal. *Breathe. Breathe. Fill your lungs with air. Everything's fine.*

"Did you know that when you're playing rock, paper, and scissors that you have a higher probability of winning if you always go with paper? That's because most people don't like making a scissors with their fingers, so they use rock because it's easier, and paper always covers rock." Owen was staring out the front window as if talking to no one but himself.

Maris bounced up and down in her seat,

her beach bag rubbing against my arm. I didn't pull away, happy to have a reminder that I was in South Carolina, crossing the Beaufort River, that the sun was shining and the water beneath was warm.

Fingers pressed against mine and I looked up to find Loralee watching me, her hand on mine. I was embarrassed and let my hand slip from hers as I sat back in my seat, prepared for free fall.

I stifled a sigh of relief as we reached the end of the bridge and headed away from the river, although I sensed its nearness. I was quickly learning that there was no escaping the water there, its presence as perennial as the sky. Gibbes's gaze met mine again in the mirror and he gave me a quick nod and a smile, as if saying, *Good job.* I looked away, wondering how much Loralee had told him about my mother, and realized he probably knew everything. I wasn't mad at her, merely relieved that I wouldn't have to explain to one more person why there were things I could not do.

Gibbes's house was down a dusty road with few neighbors, towering oaks on both sides, with swinging moss that hung lazily from knobby branches blocking the sun as we drove through. We passed a house with large, colored Christmas lights dangling from the porch right before he turned onto an unmarked driveway that led us far from the main road.

Gibbes's house itself surprised me, although maybe it shouldn't have. It was a midcentury modern with sparse landscaping and Christmas lights — these smaller and clear — still hanging from the gutter above the one-car garage. He gave us a brief tour inside, including a state-of-the-art kitchen and a family room with a television screen almost as wide as the wall. It was as different from the home he'd grown up in as it could have possibly been. Which, I supposed, was the point.

We stored the basket in the kitchen after deciding we'd have our picnic on the dock later, and followed Gibbes down toward the water, where a very decrepit-looking flat-bottomed boat waited.

"Is it safe?" I asked, eyeing it dubiously.

Gibbes looked offended. "I certainly hope so, since I'm planning on putting all of us in it. It's an heirloom — used to belong to my grandfather, and then my father, and then Cal and I used it when we were boys."

The mention of Cal's name stole the fight from me, and I didn't mention any other reservations I had about getting into such an old boat, instead surreptitiously checking for holes in the bottom and sides.

As Gibbes maneuvered the ancient boat closer to the dock, I slathered on even more sunscreen. I eyed Loralee's perfect sun-kissed skin and how she didn't seem to be sweating. Even her hair was unfazed by the humidity, falling around her shoulders in soft waves. My only consolation was the thought that if she were up in Maine, her teeth would be chattering once the sun set and the temperature dropped below sixty.

As promised, Gibbes had life jackets for all of us. He took over putting the ones on the children while Loralee assisted me with mine. She tightened the straps so that it wouldn't slip off over my head if I managed to find my way into the water — which, Gibbes assured me, wasn't going to happen while he was captain of the boat — then turned around so I could adjust hers.

I tugged on one of the side straps and she began to giggle.

"What's wrong?"

"The front buckle doesn't seem to want to stay buckled."

I moved in front of her and figured out the problem immediately. Her bust was simply too large. We both looked down at the two straps that circled her waist and she giggled again. "I don't think I need to worry about that top one — the other two won't be able to slide past my chest anyway."

I blushed, unable to think of a response that wouldn't make me blush harder. Gibbes gently moved me aside and began adjusting Loralee's straps so that all the buckles would work. His fingers were sure and steady and never paused even when they passed over her chest. He was a doctor, and though he just treated children now, I knew that during med school and his residency he'd probably seen lots of patients of both sexes and all ages in various stages of undress. Still, I couldn't look, wondering at my irrational anger, and blaming it on Loralee, whose biggest success in life was apparently attracting men. I thought blaming her would make me feel better, but it didn't.

I was relieved to see she'd at least changed into flat-soled sandals, so I didn't have to worry about her top-heavy self tumbling into the water. Owen stepped into the boat first as Gibbes held it steady from the dock. Owen began scooting toward the rear seat when Maris, still standing on the dock, cleared her voice loudly while crossing her arms and looking at him expectantly through blue plastic sunglasses.

"Owen," Loralee said, lowering her chin

and sending him a meaningful glance.

With a heavy sigh, he braced himself before reaching his hand out to the little girl. Maris was strong and agile despite being so petite, and it was obvious to anyone other than the blind that she could get into the boat without any help. I turned my head so he wouldn't see me smile, only to find that Loralee and Gibbes were doing the same thing.

Loralee got in next, with help from both Owen and Gibbes. She seemed unsteady, which surprised me, since I knew she was used to boats. Gibbes held on to her forearm with a tight grip, not letting go until she'd sat down.

"Thank you," she said to Gibbes, flashing him a brilliant smile.

He turned to me and paused, as if unsure how to handle me.

"I'm sure I can do it myself," I said, not agreeing at all but wanting to somehow separate myself from Loralee. As if he couldn't tell we were completely different just by looking at us.

I moved forward but, as if he hadn't heard me, he held out his hand. "Humor me, okay? We've already gone to all this trouble to get this far, and it would be a sad thing to end our outing before we've even left the dock."

"Why would we end our . . . ?" I stopped, understanding dawning on me. Holding back a choice word or two in deference to the two children, I put my hand in his and was surprised to find Owen taking my other in a firm grip.

The boat rocked gently, my equilibrium thrown completely off balance, my feet seeming suspended in air for a long, nauseating moment. Gibbes held on tightly until I sat down.

"You okay?" he asked.

I nodded, trying to look confident, and not speaking so he wouldn't hear how out of my league I really was.

He sat at the rear of the boat, near the tiller, and paused a moment until we were all settled. After my heart had stopped its irregular thudding, I could hear the sounds of the marsh, the odd snapping and clicking noises from dozens of unseen creatures. I thought of Owen's terrarium, and how fun it would be to capture a few specimens for us to look at, but knew it would be a while before I would gladly release my hands from the side of the boat to trawl the waters for unusual plants and insects.

"Maybe we'll see a dolphin!" Owen

shouted.

I prayed that we wouldn't, but I kept my thoughts to myself, grasping the sides of the boat just in case one decided to jump up out of the water and tip over the boat.

"Or an alligator!" Maris shouted, just as loud.

I jerked my hands into the boat. "An alligator?"

"Don't worry, Merritt," Gibbes said. "If we don't bother them, then they won't bother us." His voice was low and calm, like the one I imagined he used before giving a shot to a small patient.

"But if you see babies, stay away," said Maris, her face serious. "Because where there are babies, there are mommics."

I looked at the dock, wondering whether I could jump out of the boat safely. But I thought of Cal, and when I met Gibbes's eyes I straightened my shoulders.

"Everybody ready?" Gibbes asked, waiting for all of us to nod before starting the motor, the sound abrupt and jarring. After the initial jolt, the motor settled into a steady, low thrum that I grew accustomed to, and didn't completely override the marsh music.

The first thing I noticed was the smell, the same one I remembered from standing in the front yard with Mr. Williams. *Pluff mud.* That was what he'd called it. It was a peculiar odor that was green and earthy, part salt and part sea. It was alien and exotic, almost unpleasant, but completely intoxicating and unlike anything that I'd experienced at home.

We'd meandered into a widening creek, the tall grasses that had at first brushed the boat now farther away as we skirted through the marsh on a watery path. Gibbes was true to his word and kept out of open water, always within easy reach of the sandy hammocks that protruded from the marsh like underwater serpents, their salty-soil backs exposed to the relentless sun as the tides ebbed and flowed around them every six hours and six minutes.

I'd never seen a place of such contradictions, barren yet lush, monochromatic yet teeming with unexpected shades of color. It was a constantly changing landscape where nothing was the same, yet nothing was truly altered except for the rise and fall of the tides.

"This is my favorite place in the world," said Maris. "I don't think I'll ever want to leave it." She kept her voice quiet, an unspoken agreement between all of us that this was a place as sacred as a church, where hushed voices were required.

"Do you have beaches or is it all this grassy stuff?" Owen asked.

Gibbes glanced at me and then over to Owen. "We have beaches, but we'll save that for another day. Remind me to take you to Hunting Island someday. I spent a lot of summer days and nights there with my friends as a teenager. They have a lighthouse, and you're allowed to climb to the top."

A secret smile lit Gibbes's face, and I wondered at his memories. I imagined they involved beer and music and girls. I could see him doing all those things I imagined teenage boys did: saw him tossing a football with a friend or diving into the ocean headfirst. It was easy to picture Gibbes as the carefree kid raised by the water who took for granted suntanned skin and bleached hair and shirtless nights. But I couldn't see Cal doing any of those things, no matter how hard I tried.

"I like this," Owen said slowly. "It's just . . . different from Lake Lanier at home. Like all the plants out here haven't had a chance to grow very tall."

Gibbes slowed the boat, the engine just a low murmur. "In a way that's true. To survive out here as a plant you have to be tough. They've adapted to take all they need from nature while at the same time fight it back. It's not easy to be covered with water for half the day, and then baked in the broiling sun for the other half. They couldn't survive if they behaved like ordinary plants."

Owen frowned for a moment, his mouth twisted as he thought. "Actually, they're really just ordinary plants. But they've learned to survive unordinary events, which makes them like the strongest plants in the world. That's pretty cool."

"Pretty cool," Gibbes agreed, speeding up the boat again. "You see examples of that all over the plant and animal kingdoms."

He kept his focus in front of him, but I felt that his words had been meant for me. I thought of Cal again, and how two brothers raised in the same place could be so different. How one could survive and thrive and the other not.

I soon forgot the sounds of the marsh creatures and the thrum of the motor as we entered the river. I was transfixed by how easily the land gave way to the water, the marsh a wide transition separating closely related cousins. It was hard to reconcile this place with the Maine shoreline of my memory, the large granite boulders that defied each frothy wave that crashed against

262

them. The Atlantic coast of Maine had been chiseled by the relentless forces of wind, ice, and water, its craggy face the result of sheets of ice for thousands of years gouging the reluctant granite. But this place of marsh grasses and long-legged birds seemed to have been placed on the Earth by gentle hands, a remedy for the rest of the world.

A shift in the light drew my eyes upward and an involuntary sigh seeped from my mouth. The blue sky sparkled, the sun hanging perfectly above us, its yellow heat making me more languid than hot. I tried to put my thoughts into words, to order them into sentences that would make sense. Several times I opened my mouth, only to have my tongue trip me.

"The sky is different here," I said, but that was all wrong. It wasn't what I'd meant to say at all. I tried again. "I wanted to say that the sky is so big, but that isn't quite it." I contemplated the view from the boat as our wake trickled back toward the marsh and the grass, moving it gently, as if an unseen hand were brushing the tops. The horizon grew in front of us as we slowly made our way forward, the sky and water melting together.

"It's that the water is wide," Gibbes said softly.

"Yes," I said before I could think. Before I realized it was Gibbes who spoke the words that were still dancing in my brain and I hadn't wanted him to know.

Owen slapped his arm, lifting his hand to reveal a squashed mosquito. He dangled his hand in the water to rinse it off. I'd seen Loralee douse him and Maris with bug repellent, but apparently, like me, he was too much of a mosquito magnet for it to make any difference. I slapped one on my ankle, where a telltale pink bump had already made its mark.

"Do you have mosquitoes in Maine?" Owen asked.

"Oh, yes. The mosquito is the unofficial state bird of Maine, I think."

He grinned. "Daddy used to say that about Georgia."

"Well, South Carolina's is the palmetto bug, just in case you were wondering." Gibbes moved the tiller on the boat, turning us sharply to the left. A bubbly spray shot up over the side while my hands searched for something to grasp as my heart wedged itself somewhere between my chest and my throat.

"Sorry," Gibbes said, actually sounding contrite. "I thought it was time to head back to the dock and eat."

I nodded, embarrassed to find my hand pressed against my heart. I turned my head, my gaze captured by the alabaster poise of a white bird with black legs standing in the water. Her head didn't move, and she didn't appear to be looking at us, but I sensed she was aware of us the way a person sees in the dark. Long, dainty white feathers extended from her tail, and I held my breath, not wanting her to fly away.

She was such a thing of beauty and grace and strength, and I was glad that I'd been forced to come out on the boat Gibbes called a "stump-knocker" to see her, to see even a fragment of the natural wonders of this place. Each golden-tipped strand of marsh grass, every slim-throated bird and wide-watered vista, were like gossamer threads tugging at my wounded heart. I watched as the bird's orange beak drilled with perfect precision into the water, extracting a small fish. The boat glided past her as she ate her meal, and I wanted to applaud her cleverness.

"That's a great egret," Gibbes explained. "Their eggs usually hatch in June, so there's most likely a nest nearby. We'll come back in a month so you can hear the babies ask for food. It sounds like they're saying, 'Me first.'"

"No way!" said Owen, tilting his head back as the giant bird stretched her wings and flew over us, her feathers rippling like ribbons of smoke, more elegant and regal than any man-made flying machine could ever hope to be.

"It's true," Maris said. "I've heard it. I'll come back with you and we can listen for it together."

"Sure," Owen mumbled. His ears pinkened but I didn't think it was from the sun. My eyes met Loralee's and we shared an insider's smile before I remembered who she was and looked away.

Gibbes docked the boat and we all managed to disembark without incident. Gibbes took my hand, and I held on tightly as I tried not to look down at the small space between the dock and the edge of the boat. I stretched my legs wide, holding back a shout of victory when my foot found purchase on the wood of the dock.

"Mrs. Heyward? Look — I have one, too."

I turned to Maris, who was pulling up the edge of her cover-up and displaying an impressive scar on her knee. I looked down at my own leg, where my shorts had ridden up on my thigh, displaying a six-inch line of puckered skin. Every year it faded just a little, the skin becoming smoother, the pink tint of it lightening. But it would never go away completely, and I was glad. There were some offenses where a brief punishment wasn't enough.

"I was jumping with my horse and I fell off. How did you get yours?"

Her question was so innocent, the inflicted hurt so unintentional, that I knew I shouldn't be angry. But I was — suddenly angry at the reminder of why I hated the water and hadn't wanted to come out in the first place. Angry that the memory outshone anything I'd just seen.

She continued to stare up at me, her eyes hidden behind her blue sunglasses, and I struggled to find a calm voice. "It was an accident. When I was twelve. But that was a long time ago."

I felt Gibbes's eyes on me but I didn't look up, instead pretending to focus on unbuckling my life jacket, and then helping the children with theirs as Gibbes and Loralee left to retrieve the picnic basket from the kitchen.

When Loralee first spread the red and white checked tablecloth on top of the deck so near the water, I almost asked for my life jacket back, but when nobody else seemed concerned I remained silent. I wondered to myself whether alligators could jump, but kept that thought to myself, too.

We all helped Loralee remove the plastic-wrapped and Tupperware-covered items from the basket, setting them on the cloth. I was busy taking off lids and wrappings when Loralee bumped into me. We were on our knees, so I wasn't taken off balance, but I instinctively reached out to steady her. Her face was pale under her makeup and her skin clammy.

"Are you all right?" I asked, realizing that I was the only thing preventing Loralee from toppling into the water.

Gibbes moved quickly to her side, his fingers finding her pulse. We were silent for a moment as he counted. "I think she needs to get out of the sun. I'm going to bring her inside where it's cooler and get her some water before I make her lie down on the sofa for a bit." He turned to Owen. "She'll be fine," he said, and I felt absurdly grateful that he'd thought to reassure Loralee's son.

She could barely walk, and by the time they'd reached the end of the dock, Gibbes was carrying her, lifting her as if she weighed no more than a pillow. Her long, manicured fingers rested on his shoulder, and I quickly looked back at the picnic spread, although it took a while for the image to go away.

We were busy loading our plates with food

when Gibbes returned.

"How is she?" I asked, glad to hear my voice sounded neutral.

"She'll be fine. Her meds cause her to be dehydrated, which makes her overheat easily. She drank a tall glass of water and she's already feeling much better. I set the clock on the stove to wake her up in an hour."

"Good," I said, watching him closely, wondering why he was avoiding eye contact.

He sat down next to me on the blanket and rubbed his hands together. "So, who wants some watermelon?"

"I do, I do!" the kids shouted in unison, their hands and faces smeared with mayonnaise from their sandwiches, half-moons of yellow on their upper lips from the lemonade.

I reached into the basket, surprised to find it empty.

"What are you looking for?" Gibbes asked.

"Knives and forks. How else are we supposed to eat the watermelon?"

The children began laughing and I saw that Gibbes was trying very hard not to. "Have you never eaten watermelon before, or had a contest for who could spit a seed the farthest?"

I thought for a moment, then shook my head. "I know we had watermelons in the grocery store, but I can't say I've ever actually eaten it. And the watermelon I remember wasn't anywhere near as red as that. But I can say with certainty that I've never spit any seed out of my mouth, intentionally or not."

I was being silly, almost flirtatious, yet I didn't stop to think about why. I felt the sun on my skin; I was in the middle of a salt marsh where nobody seemed to care that I was wearing an old lady's floppy hat and three coats of sunscreen, or that I was wearing a pair of shorts for the first time in a very long while.

Gibbes seemed to pick up on my mood. As if he were a surgeon exhibiting a precise technique to medical students, he carefully unwrapped a wedge of watermelon. Holding it up like a prize, he then leaned forward and bit right into the middle of it. Watermelon juice seeped from the fruit, past the rind, and onto his hand and wrist.

"Pardon me, Merritt, but this is a necessity when eating watermelon." He bunched his lips together and without further warning ejected a seed from his mouth. I watched with guarded fascination as it carried out over the water, landing at a good distance.

"Nice one, Dr. Heyward," Owen said, high-fiving the doctor. Holding his hand up,

Gibbes then lightly patted Maris's palm with splayed fingers.

"What a talent," I said, hoping I wouldn't also be asked to perform.

"Why, thank you, ma'am. I was the watermelon-seed-spitting champion at the Water Festival three years in a row when I was a boy."

"That being on your résumé is probably what got you into med school. What happened the fourth year? Got too old and lost some teeth?"

The laughter in his eyes died. He looked down at the watermelon in his hands, but didn't seem to notice the juice still dripping down onto his crossed legs. "No. Cal left, and I didn't feel like going to the Water Festival anymore."

"I love the Water Festival!" Maris said, oblivious to the sudden tension in the air. "It's every July and it's *so* much fun. There's games and music and lots of really great food." She turned to Owen. "You can come with me and my family — we go every year, because my dad has to enter the sailing regatta even though he's never won. He says somebody has to come in last, so it might as well be him."

Owen just nodded numbly, as if unsure whether any response was really required, or whether his attending the festival with Maris and her family was already a foregone conclusion.

Gibbes handed a slab of watermelon to Maris and then one to Owen and then, finally, one to me. He held it up like a challenge and I took it. Even though I was dying to wad up a pile of the napkins Loralee had packed but that had so far gone untouched, I took a bite out of the watermelon, closing my eyes at the unexpected sweetness that accompanied the crunch.

I chewed in silence, savoring every bite until all that was left were a few of the flat seeds in my mouth. Since it seemed expected, I moved them all to my lips and ejected them one by one. None were as impressive as Gibbes's effort, but not bad for a first-timer. I eagerly picked up a second piece.

My victorious grin faded as I spotted a man on foot downstream from us standing on solid ground right on the edge of the marsh. He wore an Atlanta Braves baseball cap, jeans shorts, and a white T-shirt, and he was slowly coming down toward the water, waving with sweeping strokes in front of him what appeared to be a metal detector.

Gibbes leaned back on his arms, watching. "You'd be amazed at the treasures you find in the marsh. With the influx of new water and material every high tide, it's not that surprising. Especially after a bad storm, when all sorts of things get dredged from the bottom. My brother got a metal detector for Christmas one year, and he and I used to treasure-hunt all the time."

"Neat!" Owen scrunched his eyes at the sun, and I noticed that the tip of his nose was getting pink. "Did you ever find anything?"

Gibbes kept his gaze on the stranger. "We found lots of things — mostly junk. Beer cans, bottle openers, hubcaps — stuff like that. But sometimes we'd find cool things, too." He stopped, his brows furrowed as if he were trying to remember something. "We found a Civil War bullet once. We were so excited when we brought it into an antique store on Bay Street and the man verified it was definitely from the Civil War era."

"Do you still have it?" Owen asked, his eyes wide.

Gibbes shook his head. "No. Cal kept it, but I don't know what happened to it."

I turned my focus from the man with the metal detector to Gibbes, something he'd just said jarring my memory.

"What other cool things did you find?"

Owen asked, leaning forward with his arms around his knees. Both were also turning pink, and I was about to tell him he needed to put on more sunscreen when Gibbes spoke again.

"Part of an airplane. It was a bolt with a little strip of charred metal on it. We had no idea what it was when we found it, but we brought it in to the same antiques dealer and he said he thought it might have come from a plane. He said back in the nineteen fifties a plane crashed into the marsh and we must have found a part of it."

"Can we see it?" Owen asked, presumably including Maris, who was as wide-eyed as he was.

"I'm afraid I don't have it either. Cal kept it with the bullet in a shoe box under his bed. He must have gotten rid of it when he moved away."

"He didn't," I said, my throat suddenly dry. "He kept it."

I remembered finding the shoe box in our closet after Cal had died. He'd never spoken about the box or its contents to me, and I'd almost included it in the bags I took to Goodwill before I moved. At the last moment I'd pulled out the shoe box and kept it, one of the few remnants I had of my late husband.

274

"I brought it with me. I'll show it to you when we get back to the house."

They were all looking at me, making me self-conscious. I discarded my half-eaten piece of watermelon and reached for a napkin and a clean plate. "I'm going to bring some food to Loralee. I'm sure she'll want to eat when she wakes up."

Gibbes cut another slice of watermelon from one of the quarters and placed it on the plate. Our gazes met and held, as if we were both remembering the same Cal, the boy who searched the marsh for hidden treasures with his younger brother.

But as I walked down the dock carrying Loralee's food, all I could think of was the magic of this place into which Cal had been born and raised, and why all he'd cared enough to take with him when he left was an old bullet and burned wreckage from a crash.

CHAPTER 14

Loralee

Loralee's skin felt tight, a surefire way to tell she'd been in the sun too long. Her mama had never believed in sunscreen, telling Loralee over and over that the only way to keep your skin wrinkle-free was to stay out of the sun altogether. She'd ignored her mama and had happily coated herself in baby oil throughout her teens and twenties, trying to get as dark as she could. It was only since she'd become a mother that she'd started using sunscreen and had become a convert — at least on her face. She let her limbs get as brown as they wanted, but she'd never allow a ray of sun to touch the skin on her face. That was what makeup was for.

But today she'd *needed* to feel the sun on her face and body. It had almost been as strong as the cravings she'd had for fried pickles and Krispy Kreme doughnuts when she was pregnant with Owen. It was as if the sun's rays held healing properties that her body needed and that she couldn't supply. She made a mental note to add to her journal later, *Wear sunscreen every day. Except when you really need to feel the sun on your skin.*

Loralee leaned against the edge of her bed and pointed past Gibbes to the closet. "Merritt said all of those boxes are yours, so take them if you want them. Anything to be recycled goes with the boxes over there." She pointed toward the corner of her room.

After they'd dropped off Maris and returned home, Loralee had invited Gibbes to come inside and have a cool glass of sweet tea before heading back to his house. She'd felt Merritt's hard stare on the back of her head but had just smiled at Gibbes when he'd said yes. Loralee knew everybody was hot and tired and in dire need of a shower, but she'd been reluctant to let the day end. It had been too long since Owen had had such a carefree day, one where he laughed out loud often and didn't seem to be missing his daddy so much. Loralee wanted to make it last as long as she could, just so he'd always remember it.

Gibbes removed a box from one of the shelves, and she enjoyed the play of muscles

under his shirt. If Merritt didn't start noticing Gibbes's fine assets soon, Loralee was
going to drive her stepdaughter to the eye
doctor herself.

He opened up the top of the box and
leaned down, then lifted a boxed game.
"Wow — I haven't seen this in a while."

Too tired to stand, Loralee craned her
neck to see while Gibbes tilted the box
toward her. "Battleship," she read out loud.
"I've heard of it but never played. Is it fun?"

"It can be — if your opponent doesn't
hate losing and get mad and throw pieces."
He studied the cover of the box, his index
finger playing with a frayed piece of masking tape holding one of the corners together.
"Cal and I played it a lot when I was a kid."

He took out the box and put it aside
before pulling out two more and showing
them to her. "Stratego and Clue — both
classics." Looking up at Loralee, he said, "I
was going to give these away, but I'm thinking maybe Owen might like them. Nice to
have on rainy days."

"Thank you, Gibbes — Owen will be
thrilled. Maybe even Merritt might want to
play with him." She chewed on her lower
lip, deciding whether to ask Gibbes, and
then the words just forced their way out.
"Do you think Merritt is getting along okay

with Owen? Do you think she's feeling a connection with him?"

A side of his mouth quirked up. "It would be hard not to — he's a great kid. But, yeah, I think they're getting along fine."

He didn't say anything else as he placed the games in a pile. "I'll bring these and anything else I find that Owen might like to his room when I'm done." He paused. "Are you sure you don't want me to come back later? You should probably rest."

She shook her head. "Only if you want to. I was going to ask you to stay for dinner." She tried to smile but managed only a slight lift of her lips.

"I'll stay if you let me order pizza. You shouldn't be making dinner."

"Pizza!" Owen shouted from the hallway, his footsteps coming toward them at a run. "Did somebody say pizza?"

Gibbes gave her an apologetic shrug. "I guess it's decided. Pizza for dinner."

"Pizza?"

They all turned to find Merritt standing behind Owen. Her hair was still damp from her shower, and she'd changed back into her uniform of blouse and skirt. Despite the hat and sunscreen, she'd still managed to get a kiss of sun on her nose and cheekbones. She looked less severe, less like the pale and lost Merritt that Loralee and Owen had first met. Younger, too, much more like the girl in the pictures Robert had kept in frames around the house, the girl in bright colors with a mischievous smile who hadn't yet lost her mother. Loralee itched to swipe pink lipstick on Merritt's mouth but kept her hands to herself. She didn't want to scare Merritt right when they were beginning to make progress.

"My treat," Gibbes said. "I know a great place, and I'll order just as soon as you all tell me what you like on your pizza."

Owen began listing all of his favorite toppings, but Loralee could tell Gibbes wasn't listening. He stepped toward Merritt. "Where did you find those?"

She held up two pickle jars with faded yellow lids, rusty holes poked in the top. "I was looking for Cal's shoe box. I'm pretty sure I brought it in from the car, but with all the sorting I've been doing I can't remember exactly where I put it. But I found these in the back of Edith's closet and thought Owen might want them to catch fireflies with a friend."

Gibbes took one from her and peered inside. "These were mine and Cal's. My grandmother must have saved them all these years."

Owen looked inside the glass at the nearly translucent carcass of a long-dead insect lying at the bottom of the jar. "There's a dead firefly inside that one. Isn't that supposed to be bad luck?"

Gibbes rumpled Owen's hair. "Nah. We all make our own luck." He turned the jar upside down before reaching for the other one and doing the same. "This one was mine," he said, handing the second one to Owen. "I'll let you use it."

Owen frowned, staring at the jar and turning it over. "How can you tell?"

"Because I had to get a replacement and this one's newer. See how the shape's different? The pickle company changed their jars in 1990 and this is the new shape."

"What happened to your old one?" Owen asked. Loralee was proud of Owen and his questions. She and Robert had taught him that there was no shame in asking questions, only in remaining ignorant. She'd made sure that was in her journal, but thought that there might be room for another one, too: *Never be afraid to ask a question, even if you're not sure you want to hear the answer.*

Merritt's gaze caught Gibbes's and it looked like she already knew what Gibbes was going to say.

"Because my brother broke mine." He

paused for a moment, as if deciding whether he should say more. "He didn't like that I'd caught more fireflies than he did, so he smashed mine on a rock."

"That's mean."

"Yeah, well, afterward he felt sorry enough to go buy a jar of pickles from his own money and eat them all in one sitting to punish himself before giving me the empty jar."

Owen studied the jar for a long moment before turning to Merritt. "Sometime when you're not busy we can go catch fireflies. We don't have to have a contest if you don't want, but let's catch a bunch and use the jars as lights."

Merritt dipped her head as if searching for a message in the holes in the lid, and for a brief moment Loralee thought she might say no. Instead, Merritt smiled and her cheeks seemed to pinken even more. "Sure. That sounds fun. It's been a while since I've done it, so you might have to give me a refresher course."

With a serious nod, Owen said, "I don't mind. I can show you."

Stifling a grin, Gibbes picked up the pile of games and handed them to Owen. "Go put these in your room for now — I'll teach you how to play later. Maybe you and Maris

282

can play a little Stratego on the next rainy day."

Owen blushed as he took the games, balancing the jar on top of the stack, and headed back to his room. Gibbes pulled out his cell phone and was in the middle of dialing the pizza restaurant when a loud crash came from Owen's room. Loralee reached Owen's bedroom right behind Merritt and Gibbes.

The large LEGO airplane lay on the ground without one of its wings and with small pieces scattered around it like lost luggage. Owen's eyes were wide with panic as he faced Gibbes. "I'm sorry, Dr. Heyward. I think I must have bumped it with one of the boxes when I walked by."

Gibbes put his hand on Owen's shoulder, then bent down to look at the plane. "Don't worry about it, Rocky. It was an accident." He picked up the two pieces of the wing and tried to fit them together. "It's an easy fix — especially for a pro like you." His smile stopped halfway, his gaze wandering over the blue and white plane.

"What kind of a plane did you say this was, Rocky?"

"A DC-six. Actually, a six-B if you want to be technical. That just means it was only used for passenger service, because it doesn't have cargo doors. They were made from the mid-forties to the mid-fifties. I know that for sure because my daddy used to have a model of one on his desk at home. It's in storage now, but Mama said we could have it shipped to us here after we figured it was okay with Merritt."

Loralee felt Merritt's eyes on her.

"How can you tell?" Gibbes asked, standing slowly.

"Well, because of a couple of things. It was made after WWII, when passenger planes took over from military planes, and all the manufacturers decided to make longer fuselages so they could fit more passengers."

Loralee smiled to herself as he used his first two fingers to indicate the fuselage, just as she'd done as a flight attendant when indicating the locations of the exits.

Owen continued. "The nose is a lot rounder than today's planes, which kind of dates it, and though it's possible it could be a couple of other models, maybe even the DC-seven, which came later, the DC-six outsold Lockheed's Constellation and pretty much everything else out there at the time. It wasn't the prettiest but it was the fastest."

He looked around to make sure he wasn't

talking too much — a habit Robert and Loralee had taught him to be aware of — and when he noticed that everybody was still listening, he continued. "On my dad's model, which has a lot more detail, you can tell what it is because it's got piston engines. That technology was pretty much as good as it was going to get by the mid-fifties, when the piston engines got replaced by the turbo props, which were a lot faster and smoother."

"Do you think it's the same kind?" Merritt asked quietly, looking at Gibbes.

Gibbes shrugged. "I'm not sure." Handing the wing parts to Owen, he said, "I'm going to bring something down from the attic for you to take a look at, if that's okay." He glanced at Loralee and she nodded, not sure she wanted to see what had been in the attic, judging by Merritt's and Gibbes's reactions the previous day, but if Gibbes thought it was okay, then it was.

He continued. "Maybe you can tell me what kind of a plane it is."

Owen nodded eagerly. "I can try. I've got a book that has pictures of all the different kinds of planes, so we can check to be sure. But I'm not usually wrong."

Loralee put her arm around Owen, proud of how smart he was, but wishing that in addition to his smarts he'd also been given a filter that would tell him when it was okay to say things like that and when it wasn't. Like right then, surrounded by adults who needed his help, it was okay. At the lunch table with boys his age he wanted to be friends with, maybe not so much. Her heart squeezed in her chest for a moment as she thought of all the things she still needed to teach Owen, and she hoped her journal had enough pages.

Gibbes returned with a large and hand-made model of a wingless plane and placed it on Owen's neatly made bed, next to two battered wings that might have once been attached to the plane if there had been a place without holes to put them. If she hadn't been told beforehand what it was, Loralee would have thought it was some kind of a time capsule, like the one city councilmen liked to bury in the foundations of new government buildings. When she still lived in Gulf Shores, she'd submitted her favorite tube of lipstick as well as a pair of newly invented SPANX for the capsule that was being cemented in the foundation of the new city hall, but had been disappointed when they'd been rejected in favor of an iPod and an American flag. She'd thought her submissions had been a lot more about who they were as individuals, but it was clear the councilmen lacked imagination.

She stepped forward, noticing the hairline cracks that looked like black threads covering the fuselage, like Humpty Dumpty after all his pieces had been put together. Small oval windows dotted the two sides of the plane, some with clear cellophane-looking windows still intact, a few with jagged tears, but most missing completely. Loralee walked to the other side of the bed and saw the uneven hole in the plane's side. The edges were curled outward, as if something from the inside had blown out the hole. It looked like a toy that had been played with really roughly. Or that had been in an actual crash.

"Cool," Owen said slowly as he walked around his bed, peering into the little windows and the hole, then picking up one of the wings and turning it over before replacing it on the bed.

Loralee took a peek into one of the windows, then jerked back when she realized there were miniature people seated inside. "This was in the attic?"

Merritt nodded. "Not exactly what I thought I'd find. There are also baskets of sea glass and other materials to make wind chimes, along with a few other items." Her lips pressed together the way people do on planes when they were about to be sick.

Loralee covered her mouth, hoping to direct her words out of Owen's hearing. "It's a little creepy, isn't it?"

"You have no idea."

Their eyes met and Merritt even smiled a little before looking away, as if she'd become aware that they'd just shared a confidence.

"Is this the same kind of plane as the LEGO one?" Gibbes asked.

Owen nodded. "It's kind of hard to tell, because it's so messed up, but I think so. See, the engines on this wing are fatter and rounder, and short from front to back. Hang on a sec."

He ran to a stack of books on the bedside table and pulled out a thick volume. He flopped it onto the bed and began flipping pages before coming to a stop and turning the book around so they could all see the picture. "This is a DC-six — it looks just like it. See how the engines are kind of stubby-looking?"

Gibbes scratched the back of his head. "And these were used until about when?"

"The mid-fifties. That was the beginning of the jet age, when everybody started making the new turbo props. Like these." He flipped through the book and stopped on a page. "This is a Vickers Viscount British turbo prop — it was a passenger plane they used here in the U.S. in the late fifties. The engines are skinnier than the DC-sixes. They're round but more streamlined — see?" He showed them the page and then flipped through the book again until he found what he was looking for. "And this was the first really successful commercial jetliner — the Boeing seven-oh-seven. It's way different-looking from the DC-six, isn't it? I think those started in 1959."

Gibbes stared at Owen for a long moment that made Loralee's heart swell with pride. "You're a really smart kid, Rocky. Thanks for all your help."

Owen beamed, and Loralee had to look away so nobody would see the tears in her eyes.

Gibbes rubbed his finger along the top of the plane. "What is this made of?"

"Papier-mâché," Loralee announced. "I know for sure because Mama and I went through a craft-making period when I was in middle school and made lots of stuff from papier-mâché. We made a Nativity set, but the baby Jesus ended up looking like the Pillsbury Doughboy, so we moved on to making pot holders using spandex head-bands."

Merritt began coughing, her face turning red as she faced away from them until the fit stopped. Gibbes just looked at Loralee with bright eyes and a big smile.

After clearing his throat, he said, "Well, somebody must have used an X-ACTO knife or something like that, because this plane has been cut apart and pieced back together."

"But why put it together with clear parts?" Merritt asked, her brows knitted. Loralee wanted to press her thumb in the spot above her nose like her mama used to do, to smooth out any wrinkles.

Gibbes studied the plane. "Good question. But if I were to guess, I'd say if somebody were putting together a crash recreation, they'd want to be as accurate as possible, showing which pieces had been found, and which ones were still missing." He met Merritt's gaze. "But why a crash recreation would be up in the attic, I don't even have a guess."

"What's with the hole in the side?" Owen asked, his eyes huge behind his glasses.

"I'm not sure," Gibbes said slowly, his fingers gently probing the furled edges. "Does anybody have tweezers?"

"I do!" Loralee said without hesitation. To Owen, she said, "Sweetie, can you go get my pocketbook? I left it on the hall table downstairs." As Owen ran out of the room she said, "My mama always told me to never go anywhere without tweezers, lipstick, and a roll of duct tape."

Merritt was looking at her oddly again, but she didn't look angry like she usually did when Loralee mentioned something her mama had told her. Instead, it looked like she was just confused.

Owen raced back into the room and handed her the pocketbook. It took her a couple of minutes to find the tweezers at the bottom, but she proudly held them up before giving them to Gibbes.

Leaning over, he reached inside the hole on the side of the plane and stuck the tweezers inside. Slowly, Gibbes plucked out a passenger seat with a man in a striped tie still strapped into it, the little white dot pattern of the cloth seat clearly visible. He held it up to eye level and examined it closely.

"This is remarkable. Each seat has those little white head covers on them, and the ashtrays in the armrests actually open," he said, using the tweezers to demonstrate.

"And he's got a little dopp kit on his lap," Loralee pointed out.

"A what?" asked Merritt.

"It's like a cosmetics bag for men," Loralee explained. "Although I guess the guys would prefer to call them 'toiletries.' When I was a flight attendant I saw them all the time. I'm sure men still use them, but I'm not sure if they're called dopp kits anymore."

Gibbes carefully placed the man and his seat on the bedspread next to the plane. Owen got down on his knees to be at eye level, his elbows on the bed and his chin resting on his hands. His dark brows were angled over his forehead as he studied the man very carefully. "Why would the dopp kit be on his lap?" he asked.

"I was just asking myself the same thing, Rocky," Gibbes said. He gently pinched the dopp kit between his thumb and index finger and tugged. "It's glued down. Must have been a pretty heavy-duty glue for it to still be stuck." His eyes narrowed slightly as he studied the man in the business suit, the vivid stripes on his navy blue tie, and the white handkerchief in the breast pocket. "When I travel, my toiletry bag goes inside my suitcase. I certainly wouldn't carry it on my lap."

They all stared at the plane model for a long moment, the silence finally interrupted by Owen.

"Mama?"

Loralee looked down at her son and resisted the impulse to lick her fingers and smooth back his hair. "Yes, sweetheart?"

"This doesn't have to stay in my room, does it?"

"No, sir. And I don't blame you, Rocky," Gibbes said as he replaced the man and seat and then lifted the plane and wings from the bedspread. "I'm going to go stick it back where we found it."

Owen let out a breath of relief as Loralee gave in and put her fingers to her mouth before plastering down that stubborn cowlick that would never lie flat no matter how hard she tried to coax it.

"I'll call in the pizza order just as soon as I put this back, okay?"

"Pizza!" shouted Owen, and Loralee and Merritt laughed.

Merritt carried the two firefly jars to the door. "I'll go put these in the kitchen by the back door so they're handy when you're ready to use them. Although it looks like they're old enough for a museum."

"Speaking of which," Gibbes said, "when is your appointment to go see Deborah Fuller at the Heritage Society?"

"Tomorrow morning." She eyed him suspiciously. "Why?"

"She was a good friend of my grandmother's and I haven't seen her for a while. I wouldn't mind tagging along, if that's all right with you."

Merritt took a moment to respond, but Loralee noticed that her face didn't get that closed-off look that she'd grown used to seeing, the face that made it clear that Merritt was making sure you were kept a stranger. "Sure. I'm meeting her at ten o'clock."

"Great. I'll pick you up at nine forty-five." He smiled, and it didn't even look like he was getting ready to shoot his favorite dog.

Loralee put her arms around Owen's shoulders, noticing again that his head was now as high as her shoulders and not remembering when that had happened. She sighed, feeling more tired than she'd ever been, but happy, too. She considered the day and all that had happened, her thoughts resting on Cal's shoe box that held the old bullet and an airplane bolt, and remembered something else she needed to write in her journal. *To really know a person, find out what they choose to take with them, and what they leave behind.*

She listened to Merritt's footsteps fading down the stairs and thought of Cal and wondered what kind of person he must have been to have saved only those two things.

And whether Merritt had ever known him
well enough to understand.

CHAPTER 15

Merritt

I reluctantly turned around to see myself in the mirror over the dresser in Loralee's bedroom. Before I could protest, she yanked the rubber band out of my ponytail hard enough that it broke. She picked up a brush and pulled it through my hair, arranging it around my shoulders.

"See? Doesn't that look better?"

"It looks heavier and hotter, and like it's going to get in my face and annoy me. Where did you put my headband?" I searched the top of her dresser where I thought she'd tossed it.

"It must have slipped behind the dresser. Sorry."

She didn't look sorry at all, and I was about to suggest we pull the dresser out from the wall when the doorbell rang.

"That must be Gibbes," she said, eyeing me critically. "Let me just put a little dab of lipstick . . ."

"What for? I'm just going to the Heritage Society, and Gibbes is coming with me."

"You're widowed, Merritt. Not dead. Why not put your best foot forward? My mama used to say . . ."

She caught my gaze in the mirror and closed her mouth. Although I don't think I would have stopped her if she had continued. I'd begun to almost anticipate the little pearls of wisdom she felt obliged to drop at random intervals throughout the day. I'd somehow moved beyond being annoyed to being amused, to now actually listening to the grains of truth she and her mother had managed to learn from their lives in a trailer park in Alabama. It made the world seem smaller, made me feel connected by these universal truths. Maybe even made me feel a little less lonely.

I pushed the hair behind my ears. "You don't need to be my friend, okay?"

"Why? Because I'm your stepmother?"

I looked down at my worn loafers, realizing how ridiculous they must look with Loralee's dress. And seeing again how very different we were — how different she was from my own mother. "Because I never invited you into my life." I paused, regretting my harshness and tasting shame on my tongue. In the last weeks my old anger had shifted like an arrow in a bow without a string, useless despite its potential to wound. If I were one for introspection, I might even say that my anger over life's injustices had managed to become self-directed.

Her smile dimmed but didn't fall completely.

"It's not that you're not a likable person, or that there aren't people out there who I'm sure would love to have you in their lives. I'm just not one of them. We're way too different."

Loralee placed the hairbrush carefully on the dressing table. "And I married your daddy even though you thought the two of you already had a team and didn't need new members. I get that. But I also believe that we have more in common than you think."

I met her gaze in the mirror and almost laughed. With her blond hair, tanned skin, and bright lipstick, we looked like we had as much in common as a loaf of bread and a shoe. The doorbell rang again and I moved toward the bedroom door, eager to end our conversation before anybody's feelings got hurt.

"You've got a big and generous heart, Merritt, and you need people in your life, no matter how much you tell yourself different."

I shook my head, trying to find the words to let her know that my heart had been closed up for years. It made life easier that way. I reached the doorway, grateful to have escaped.

"You could have told us to leave."

I paused in the doorway without turning around, Loralee's soft voice doing nothing to deaden the impact of her words. Anger, shame, and loss flooded my lungs, making it impossible to breathe.

I clenched my eyes, remembering something Cal had once told me, and how I'd often thought of it when he became angry. *Fire is an event, not a thing. Heating wood or other fuel releases vapors that quickly combust with oxygen in the air, resulting in a fiery bloom of gas that heats the fuel even more, releasing more vapors and continuing the cycle.*

"I still can," I finally managed.

"But you won't."

I didn't respond as I made my way down the stairs to the door. Gibbes was leaning against the railing, his hands shoved into his front pockets, his long legs crossed casually at the ankles. I noticed the way he stood because Cal had never leaned like that.

He'd always stood with his feet apart, balanced on his toes, almost in a wrestler's starting pose. I'd always thought he looked like an animal getting ready to pounce.

Gibbes straightened as his gaze flickered over me. "Nice dress."

"It's Loralee's." I tugged on the hem of the skirt that was a good four inches above my knees, and tried not to think about how much of my scar was showing. "For some reason, she chose to wash all of my clothes today and nothing is dry. She lent me this. Apparently she doesn't have anything longer than streetwalker size. I'm just thankful my feet are a half size smaller than hers."

He slowly scanned my body from the low V-neck of the white knit wrap dress to the short hem that made me think maybe it wasn't actually a dress but a long shirt and I should go get a pair of pants to wear under it. Except I didn't have any that weren't wet.

"I don't see anything wrong with it."

He said it with a straight face, but I was sure I heard a hint of laughter in his voice. I marched past him and down the steps, still tugging at my hem and hoping he'd put on sunglasses so the sun reflecting off my legs didn't blind him.

He held open the passenger door and helped me in, averting his gaze as I climbed in and the wrap of the dress widened alarmingly. He turned on the car and the air-conditioning blasted. Leaning toward me, he reached out to adjust the fan's direction, and I flinched without even being aware of it until I'd done it. He looked at me oddly and I thought he was going to say something, but quickly changed his mind.

"The Heritage Society is just down on Carteret, so it should take us only about five minutes, depending on how many tourists are jaywalking across the street. We have time, so if you'd like, I could take you the long way around and give you a little tour of the backstreets."

Besides a few necessary trips to the grocery store and drugstore, and once to Hilton Head to buy shorts for Owen at the mall, I hadn't seen much of the immediate neighborhood. I'd looked at a street map, so I knew that Beaufort was relatively small, with neatly laid-out streets in straight lines, the water forcing a slight rounding at the edges of the grid to accommodate the river and marshes that surrounded the city.

The water was everywhere, a constant presence that reminded me of a bear in the woods that needed to be kept at bay. From my front porch I could see the ebb and flow of the tides, the river leaching the water from the marsh twice a day, and then refilling it with stealth. It fascinated me as much as it terrified me, and I'd gotten in the habit of looking up the time for high and low tides during the day to reassure myself that the water wouldn't come any closer to my house. Maybe that was why I hadn't strayed too far, fearing that the water would creep too close if I weren't there to keep watch.

"That would be nice. Thank you."

Gibbes pulled out of the driveway and took a right on Bay Street, away from the downtown area, driving slowly so I could get a good view of the antebellum mansions that perched on the bluff like proud matrons surveying their domains.

He slowed in front of several of them, pointing out historical facts about the owners and about events that happened in the houses during the Revolutionary and Civil wars. The white clapboard Federal-style homes reminded me of Maine, but only briefly. The palmetto trees and giant magnolias in their front yards were an easy reminder that I was far from home.

"They call this one the Secession House," Gibbes said, pointing to an antebellum mansion on Craven Street with a pink-painted first floor. "There's an inscription on the basement wall in this house saying that the first meeting of secession in South Carolina was held there."

I nodded, only half listening. Not because I wasn't interested — I was. I loved history, and had enjoyed visiting historical sites with my father when I was a girl. There was something about the past; the reassurance that others had lived and loved and survived before me gave me something to cling to in the present. And Southern history was new to me. I'd studied the Civil War in school, of course, but to see the small Confederate flags on graves as we passed St. Helena's churchyard made it somehow more relevant.

But mostly I was busy studying Gibbes and the relaxed way he held the steering wheel with only one hand, the other arm resting on his door. Cal had gripped the wheel with both hands, his jaw set as if he were ready for battle. And we'd rarely spoken on car trips. Saying the wrong thing in the small confines of a car would have had consequences I hadn't wanted to contemplate.

"Merritt?"

I jerked my eyes to meet his and for a second I thought it was Cal. But only for a second, until I realized that just the eyes were the same. Ever since our trip into the marsh, I'd stopped seeing Cal when I

303

looked at Gibbes. The marsh had exorcised that ghost, at least. Or maybe it was Gibbes himself who'd done that.

I realized he'd asked me a question. "I'm sorry. I must have been woolgathering. What were you saying?"

"I was asking how you and Cal met."

"Oh." I stared out the window at a small white clapboard church with colorful stained-glass windows. "There's nothing much to say, really. It's all in the past."

"Those who refuse to acknowledge the past are condemned to repeat it."

I glared at him. "You're starting to sound like Loralee."

"I'll take that as a compliment."

I didn't argue. Gibbes turned on his signal to take a left on a small street with weeds and grass escaping from large cracks in the asphalt. I felt an odd affinity for the spots of green, knowing what it felt like to think you'd escaped, only to be hit by the next oncoming car.

"My brother is dead, Merritt. But I started missing him a long time before that. I just want to know a little bit about him, about his life after he met you." He paused, his fingers thrumming on the steering wheel to a beat only he could hear. "I'm not trying to make you uncomfortable or sad."

I looked down at my hands, wanting to tell him about the Cal I'd first met. The man who sensed my loneliness and filled up all the empty spaces in my heart. At first. But I couldn't tell Gibbes any of that without telling him the rest. *I don't want to hurt you.* I turned back to the window. We were back on Bay Street, passing the marina with the sleeping sailboats rocking lazily on the water, their sails folded like window shades. The tide was high, only the tips of the sea grass visible, and for a moment I imagined they were holding their collective breath, waiting to be pulled from the water.

I cleared my throat. "He came to the museum where I worked. He said he was there from the fire department and was doing a safety inspection." I remembered myself stammering and flushing, completely taken off guard by the tall, strong fireman who couldn't seem to stop looking at me. "He asked me out to dinner that night. We were married five months later."

Gibbes didn't say anything, and when I looked at him he seemed deep in thought.

"It's funny, really," I continued. "Because I found out later that he wasn't officially a fireman yet — he'd applied, but he hadn't been offered the job. After we were married, I was going through some paperwork and saw that the dates didn't make sense. When I asked him, he said he'd seen me on the street and followed me to the museum and figured out an excuse to meet me."

Gibbes parked the car in front of the Heritage Society offices, a converted Victorian house with pink fish-scale tiles and a green roof. He pulled the key from the ignition, but didn't move right away. Finally he turned to me. "Didn't you find that odd?"

"My fingers plucked at the skirt of Loralee's dress. "Not at first. I thought it was romantic. It wasn't until . . . later. After we'd been married for a while. It was as if . . ." I stopped, remembering to whom I was speaking.

"It was as if what?"

It was getting warm in the car with the air conditioner off. I lifted my hand to my throat as if that would help me breathe. "It was as if he were a child who wanted a toy very badly, but then lost interest as soon as it was his." I met Gibbes's eyes. "Every time he looked at me, it was like he expected to see somebody else."

The words stung as they exited my mouth, and I realized I'd never spoken them out loud before. Maybe being a doctor made Gibbes a good listener, or maybe I was desperate to dissect my marriage, to understand where I'd gone wrong, and it didn't matter who was available to listen.

"The man you're talking about wasn't my brother."

I reached for the door handle, eager to get out of the truck and suck in the thick, heavy air. The metal slipped from my hands twice until Gibbes reached across and pulled it for me. I slid from the SUV and leaned against the door, breathing heavily, my skin clammy with sweat.

"I'm sorry, Merritt. I didn't mean to upset you. It's just . . ." He shook his head. "My brother was so shy around girls. He always had a girlfriend, but that's because they usually threw themselves at him so that he couldn't say no. And they . . ." He stopped.

"They what?" I prompted.

"They weren't like you at all. They weren't like any girls we went to school with, or even like my grandmother or her friends."

"What do you mean?" I asked, thoroughly confused.

Gibbes glanced at his watch. "Come on. We're going to be late."

I didn't press him for an answer as we headed toward the front door, but only because I wasn't sure I wanted to hear it.

The building smelled like an old house — of wood polish, cedar, and the faint aroma of ashes from the fireplaces. Heavy Victorian furniture filled the foyer and was set up much like I imagined it would have been when it was a home, complete with lace doilies thrown over the backs of upholstered chairs.

Cynthia Barnwell was in the front parlor at a large rosewood desk with heavily carved legs, an ancient computer monitor and keyboard on top. I heard the *click-clack* of the keys as we walked in, and she peered over bifocals at us and smiled.

"So good to see you both. I can't tell you how much my granddaughter enjoyed last Saturday with Owen. She just can't stop talking about it. I warn you, though: She's already planning your next outing."

"We all had a good time, and Maris is a lovely girl," I said. "I'm so glad Owen's met a friend before school starts."

Cynthia's face got serious. "I know it's early, but I would suggest putting in his application for Beaufort Academy as soon as possible. I'll be happy to send a recommendation."

"Thank you," I said. "But I'm not sure Loralee wants to send Owen to private school. Regardless, the decision really isn't mine."

Cynthia frowned. "Well, she definitely

expressed interest in Beaufort Academy when I spoke with her, and she asked me to send her some information. It's where Maris goes, and we couldn't be happier with her education."

I wasn't going to discuss Loralee's financial status, so I let the subject drop, making a mental note to ask Loralee about it later. "We have an appointment to see Deborah. Is she in?"

"Oh, yes, and she's expecting you. Her office is at the top of the stairs, first one on the right."

We thanked her and headed up the long, straight staircase, holding on to the thick, dark wood of the banister as the old steps creaked beneath our weight.

Deborah's office more closely resembled a library's archive room, with four walls covered with shelves, leaving space only for the window and stacks of papers teetering on and around the perimeter of a metal teacher's desk. I didn't spot her until a loud thud came from a spot in the room behind us, and we turned to find Deborah standing on a tall stepladder, her arms overstuffed with books, the one on top threatening to join its partner in crime on the floor, where it lay with spine splayed, like a dead bird.

Gibbes reached up and took the stack of

books from her, then stayed beside her while she carefully made her way down the steps. "Thank you," she said, peering over her glasses at him. "If you could put them on my desk, I'd appreciate it."

There were no exposed parts on her desk, so I began carefully stacking folders and books to make room. I noticed two small frames perched precariously on the edge, both containing photos of the same two cats. There were no photos of children or grandchildren, just the cats. I wondered whether, after Loralee and Owen were gone, and Gibbes had finished taking what he wanted from the house, and I was alone again, I'd need to get a cat or two to keep me company. The thought stung more than I cared to admit.

Deborah wore a quilted vest with appliqués of cats and balls of yarn. Her khaki pants were pulled up higher than current fashion dictated, and she wore the same sensible shoes she'd had on when she visited the house. But her eyes were bright with anticipation, and when she clasped her hands in front of her, I almost expected her to rub them together with glee.

"Thank you both for coming. And it's so good to see you, Gibbes. I haven't seen you since your grandmother's funeral."

"Yes, ma'am. I've been working hard. One of the doctors has been out on maternity leave, so we've all been a little busier than usual."

She'd said it so bluntly that I wondered whether she wasn't originally from Beaufort. I knew she'd babysat for Cal's father, but that would have been when she was a teenager. And she didn't sound anything like Loralee — or Gibbes for that matter — where syllables were added to even the shortest words, and consonants were sometimes dropped completely.

"Are you from Beaufort, Ms. Fuller? I can't place your accent."

Her eyes continued to sparkle, and I could describe them only as mischievous. "I'm a true Beaufortonian. My family has owned land here since the original land grants. As for my accent, my mother taught me how to speak correctly, without a lazy drawl, and to clip the ends of my words. Some people mistake it for a New England accent."

I smiled, thinking I knew now why I'd taken a liking to her when I'd first met her. "The last time I saw you, you said you had something here that I might be interested in seeing."

She nodded eagerly. "Oh, yes. And Gibbes, too, I would suspect. Follow me."

311

She took a lanyard off a hook screwed into the side of one of the bookshelves, about a dozen keys dangling from the end. It looked handmade, with needlepoint cats marching up and down the length of it.

Deborah stopped in front of a closed door and turned to us with a secret smile before sorting through the keys. "We only open up this room by appointment. It's full of miscellaneous historical artifacts that have been either purchased for or donated to the society by residents who wish to preserve a piece of their family history." She stuck a key in the old lock, then opened the door, letting it swing wide in front of us. "Take a look."

Gibbes and I stole a glance at each other before heading inside. It took me a moment before my eyes adjusted to the dim light. Heavy shades were drawn over the windows to block out the harsh South Carolina sun, and the double-bulb light fixture in the porcelain shade on the ceiling did little to illuminate the room and its contents.

Small vitrines were set against one wall, displaying pieces of jewelry, portrait miniatures, and pocket watches. Larger pieces of furniture were set randomly around the room, with handwritten descriptions on cardboard plaques set in ornate wood frames. An antique rocking horse, a baby's cradle, and a modern mannequin wearing a nineteenth-century dress complete with hoop skirt and feathered bonnet were crowded in one corner of the room, allowing for a labyrinthine path through the artifacts.

I met Gibbes's gaze and he shrugged, confirming that, like me, he had no idea what we were looking for. He lifted a corset from a pile of linens and waggled his eyebrows, and I smiled before I could stop myself.

I turned to Deborah. "Ms. Fuller, was there something in particular that you wanted us to see?"

"Absolutely," she said, not bothering to mask a simmering excitement. "Over here." She walked toward a heavy rocking chair that looked like it had been made for a giant, and began tugging on the arms to slide it backward.

"Let me," Gibbes said, taking over and moving it easily on the wood floorboards, revealing a small end table behind it. On top of the table sat a large open shoe box on its side that was suddenly and horribly familiar.

"Where did this come from?" Gibbes asked, his voice clipped.

"The Beaufort Police Department. Your grandmother made it."

Gibbes stared at the older woman. "I'm afraid I don't understand. What is this?"

"She never told you?"

He shook his head. "No."

It was her turn to stare at him. "It's a crime-scene re-creation based on a real case. Surely you've heard of Frances Glessner Lee."

"I really have no idea what you're talking about," Gibbes said.

Her lips clamped together, like a teacher disappointed with a star pupil's performance. She took a deep breath. "Edith's father was a detective in the Walterboro Police Department, and she was always interested in his work and probably would have become a detective herself if she'd been born later. In those days it was unheard-of for a woman to have such a profession. But she was quite artistic and studied art in college. It was there that Edith found out about Frances Glessner Lee. Frances founded the Department of Legal Medicine at Harvard in 1936 — a precursor to modern forensics in this country."

She looked at us, expecting us both to nod our heads in recognition. When neither of us did, she continued. "Frances created her crime-scene boxes in order to train detectives to assess visual evidence. She called them the Nutshell Studies of Unexplained Death, after a well-known police saying: 'Convict the guilty, clear the innocent, and find the truth in a nutshell.' Edith, with her background in art and her knowledge of detective work, began making her own for her father's cases and then, after her marriage, for the local police department."

Gibbes and I moved closer to study the contents of the shoe box. It was a 1950s-style office, with no electronics in sight, but with a black telephone on the corner of a wooden desk, its coiled cord neatly wrapped around the neck of a male doll lying on an Oriental rug next to the desk. A miniature pencil holder had been upended on the desk, tiny pencils scattered on the surface like toothpicks. A framed photo of a woman with two children was placed prominently in the center of the desk, right in the middle of the pencils. The man's eyes protruded slightly from his cloth face, the knot of his necktie still taut around his blue-stained doll neck.

"In this particular case, the man was stepping out on his wife with his secretary, and she caught them together. The wife came into the office when her husband was working late at night and made sure that he wouldn't be doing that anymore. She would have gotten away with it, too." She pointed to the framed photo. "That was the biggest clue — the placement of the frame, obviously done after she'd strangled him. Notice how his chair is facing away from the desk. She was able to overpower him because of the element of surprise."

Gibbes and I regarded Deborah Fuller with renewed interest.

"You're very familiar with my grandmother's work?" he asked.

The older woman nodded. "I dropped out of law school and returned to Beaufort to nurse my mother in the last years of her life. Edith and I became good friends, even though she was closer to my mother's age than my own. That's how I first learned about her work for the police. She was very private about it."

Gibbes shook his head. "I had no idea."

"Yes, well, not many people knew. She kept it mostly to herself. Her husband didn't approve, you see. There were more, but after Cal left she asked the police department to return them to her. She never told me why. This one was being used at a police academy in Georgia, which is why it was left behind. I was hoping that perhaps you'd find the rest in the house."

She looked at me with hopeful eyes.

I swallowed. "Yes. We found them. In the attic. I'd say about ten of them. It was quite a surprise."

"They're extraordinary, aren't they?" she said. "And the attention to detail is really remarkable. Pencils actually write, rocking chairs rock back and forth to the exact degree as the original, and every detail — a newspaper headline, blood splatter on the wall, an outdated wall calendar — becomes a potential clue to the crime."

Remarkable wasn't the word I would have used, but I let it go. "You're welcome to stop by and take a look at them," I said. "It's hard to sleep at night knowing they're up there."

"Just consider them works of art," Deborah said. "And I'd love to come see them. I suppose I could have just asked whether you'd found them, but it's rather hard to explain. Better to see it in person." She pressed her hand over her heart. "Finally, after all these years, we know what became of them. I had the horrible feeling that she'd destroyed them."

"Why did you think that?" Gibbes asked.

She frowned again. "Because after Cal left, she changed. Not only did she reclaim all the ones she'd donated to the police department, but she stopped going out and didn't answer her door or return phone calls. I never saw the light on in the attic anymore. She made a few more nutshell studies after her husband's death, and continued to make wind chimes. She always gave those to her friends — I have five of them myself. She was working on some big project that she said was a secret. But everything stopped after Cal left. I guess I'll never know what her special project was, or why it was such a big secret." She peered closely at Gibbes. "And you knew nothing about her work?"

"No. I wasn't allowed up in the attic. After Cal left, she didn't go up there anymore. I knew she was upset that Cal had gone, but she was so sad, too. Now that I know what it is, I'd say she was probably depressed." He stared down at the doll with the cord around its neck, deep in thought. "She told me she didn't want me spending too much time in the house with her, telling me that I was her last chance and she was going to save me. That's pretty much when I began spending so much time at the Williamses."

His voice sounded stiff and agitated, but it was more than masking pain from an unwelcome memory. There was something else, something that made him stand still in the middle of the room, his gaze turned inward. I waited for him to say something, aware that an uncomfortable silence had fallen.

I wanted to ask Deborah about the plane we'd found with the shoe boxes, whether she knew anything about it, but before I could, Gibbes leaned forward and kissed Deborah's cheek, making her color. "Thank you, Miss Fuller. This has been very interesting."

We said our good-byes, and I had to almost run to catch up with him as we made our way down the creaking stairs. I paused long enough to say good-bye to Cynthia with a promise to have her over soon to see the rest of the house, and then ran outside onto the hot sidewalk. Gibbes stood motionless as passersby walked around him. Heat seeped through the soles of my loafers, and sweat dripped down my back. I wondered how long it would be until I found the heat and humidity bearable. And whether I ever would.

"What is it?" I asked.

He looked at me as if he'd forgotten I was there. He blinked several times before taking my arm and leading me back to the Explorer. He turned the key in the ignition and put the AC on full blast. We sat in silence with just the sound of the air-conditioning for a full minute.

"Are you going to tell me what's wrong?" I asked. I wanted to tell myself that I didn't really care, that it didn't matter, but I couldn't. *Because after Cal left, she changed.* The mention of my husband's name had reminded me that his ghost connected Gibbes and me in ways I didn't yet understand. And that I would never be free of either of them until I did.

He rubbed both hands over his face, his palms rasping the stubble on his cheeks. "I was ten when Cal left. I always thought that either I was clueless and unaware of any tension between my brother and my grandmother around the time he left, or maybe I've just blocked it all out, because I've never been able to remember any of it.

"Cal and my grandmother were close, although I always got the feeling that she kept him close to keep an eye on him, to keep him reined in, I think is what Mrs. Williams said. You can still see the marks on the windowsill in Cal's bedroom where he threw a chessboard after I beat him." A sad smile lifted his lips, then faded just as quickly. "So that's probably why I don't remember much. But just now . . ."

His chest rose and fell, pushing the past from his lungs. *Those who refuse to acknowledge the past are condemned to repeat it.* I sat, waiting, afraid to hear what he would say just as much as I was afraid I'd miss it.

"Just now," he continued, "listening to Deborah, I remembered something. Something I never remembered before. I'd come home from school and the door to the attic was open, as if my grandmother had just come down. Cal had been working in the garden and I heard him dragging something inside — but I didn't see what it was because I'd already gone upstairs. She told me to go to my room and not come out. I was walking down the hallway toward my room and I heard Cal yelling at my grandmother."

His eyes met mine. "What did he say?" I asked softly.

A sickly breeze teased us as it blew by, bringing with it the scent of the pluff mud. "He called her a murderer."

We stared at each other for a long time, horror mirrored in the other's eyes. Finally I spoke. "Did you ever ask Cal?"

Gibbes shook his head. "He was gone the next day. My grandmother told me I'd misunderstood, and that I should never mention it again. And I didn't."

Facing forward he put the SUV in drive and drove us home with only the cold blast of the air conditioner to cushion the weight of his words.

CHAPTER 16

Edith
April 1972

Edith sat on the garden bench and pulled in a long drag on her cigarette. With her other hand she rubbed her lower back and watched Debbie Fuller — now Deborah, since she was a mature twenty-five — yank out another clump of weeds. It had been a rainy spring, the dampness bringing with it a bumper crop of mosquitoes and weeds.

Deborah caught Edith watching her and sat back on her heels and smiled. "Cigarettes are really bad for you, you know. They can even kill you."

Edith took a long last drag, then dropped the cigarette in the dirt before smashing it with the toe of her shoe. "Don't be so dramatic, Deborah. I figure if life hasn't killed me by now, I've still got a long road ahead of me. Besides, according to Lord Byron, 'Whom the gods love dies young.' "

Edith found the need every once in a while to remind Deborah that she wasn't the only one with a good education whose life's plans had been thwarted by circumstance. It was why she requested Deborah's help in the garden: They both needed the mental stimulation.

Deborah frowned, and Edith forced her face to remain serious. Deborah's mother, Martha, had once said that her daughter had been born a forty-year-old nun, with a sober outlook on life and a seriousness of purpose. Her being the eldest of all those children was most likely to blame, but Edith wondered, too, if it had been a self-fulfilling prophecy. Deborah had graduated with honors from the University of South Carolina and was in her first year of law school when her mother became ill. As the eldest child and only girl, she'd taken the responsibility of moving back home and tending her mother. Almost two years later, nothing had changed, and, knowing Martha, it didn't appear that things would.

Edith picked up the trimmers on the bench next to her and moved to her azalea bushes. The blooms had been weak and paltry, their edges already turning brown by the time they'd opened. Which was fine with her, really. It matched her own lack of anticipation over the coming summer, when C.J. would be back from his second year at Carolina.

She missed him — she did. He was her son. But she didn't miss his moods, or the way she had to creep around her own house, afraid she'd upset the precarious peace she'd worked so hard to maintain. Or the way it sometimes made her feel as if Calhoun were still alive, her skin prickling with the knowledge that he would open the door at any moment.

It would be good to have C.J. back, to have the house full of his friends again, to hear their footsteps clattering on the porch at night and their car tires rolling over gravel on their way out to one of the islands for a midnight bonfire. Her biggest hope would be that he'd meet a nice girl, a strong girl. Someone who could soothe away the hurts he'd been born with, the hurts that emerged every time thunder cracked the night sky, a fissure of light illuminating their memories of a night long ago.

Deborah sat back on her heels, then wiped the sleeve of her blouse across her forehead, dislodging her glasses. She picked them up from the dirt and cleaned the lenses on her dungarees. "When C.J. gets home, I think you should have him pull out a few of your crape myrtles and plant orange trees instead. I've heard they keep the mosquitoes away."

Edith thought of telling her that the days of C.J. helping her in the garden had long passed, packed up and folded away like outgrown pants, toy army men, and his need to apologize and be comforted. She missed that part of her son the most and prayed each day that it would return as he became a man.

She nodded, murmuring evasively, then returned to attacking the azaleas with the trimmer.

"How's your big secret project, Mrs. Heyward?"

Edith had told her many times to call her by her first name, but apparently the rule follower in Deborah couldn't be overruled. She could imagine Deborah as an old lady, still living at home with her mother, and calling Edith "Mrs. Heyward."

"I'm afraid I've hit the doldrums with it. There's too much missing information, and I don't want to mess up everything I've already done with just guessing."

"Is it another crime scene?"

Edith opened the trimmer as wide as it would go and stabbed at a drooping branch, its dying blooms bowed in the heat. "I don't know why you keep asking me that, Deborah, because my answer never changes. It's a personal matter, and there's really only one person I believe I'll ever show it to." Edith smiled to herself. *And I've never even met her.*

"I'm just curious is all. Daddy said that the police department wanted to give you an award to thank you for all your help with advancing crime-scene investigations, but that you refused. I told him before he even asked that you'd say no."

Edith straightened, regarding the younger woman with narrowed eyes, recalling that Deborah was the daughter of a policeman, too. "You sound very sure of yourself."

Deborah reached behind her to deposit a pile of weeds in C.J.'s old Radio Flyer wagon. Edith eyed it ruefully, remembering how C.J. had never wanted to be pulled in it, but instead had used it to create crashes of epic proportions involving all of his stuffed animals and the large oak that was unfortunately positioned at the end of the driveway. Both the wagon and the tree still bore the scars.

Deborah placed her gloved hands on her thighs and looked up at Edith. "Because ever since I've known you, you've liked to keep things to yourself."

Edith just nodded, refocusing her attention on the azaleas as more and more wilted blooms plummeted to the ground at her feet like little sacrifices at the altar of truth.

Realizing that particular conversation was over, Deborah said, "Did you hear about the eight-foot alligator they caught in a shrimp net at Harbor Island last weekend?"

"I read that in the paper. They're lucky none of those shrimpers lost a finger — or worse."

"That's not all they caught in the net, you know." Deborah moved to the right, closer to the lopsided statue, rolling the wagon with her. "They called my daddy to go see, which is how I know about it. I don't think they put it in the paper yet, because they thought it was just trash. They'll probably print it later in the week, once they file the police report."

"What was it?"

"Daddy thinks it might be part of a plane that exploded over Beaufort in 1955. Do you remember that? I was only eight at the time, but I don't think it's something a person ever forgets. My mother was screaming up and down the hallway for all of us kids to get out of the house. She thought the roof was on fire."

Edith stilled, the trimmer stalled over an

azalea branch like a stay of execution. "What makes him think it's from a plane?"

"There was still some paint on the metal — navy, he said. And it looked like the letter 'N.' He had to go look it up, but the plane that blew up was Northeast Airlines."

Edith put down the trimmer. "Would you like some iced tea or lemonade? I need to go get myself a glass. This heat makes me so parched."

"Yes, ma'am — whichever one you're getting for yourself. Thank you." She sat back on her heels, her eyes straying to the statue of Saint Michael. "He's crooked. You should have Cal or somebody smooth out the dirt beneath him, or else I think he might fall over in the next storm. He's already missing a hand; wouldn't do for a saint to lose both. How could he perform miracles then?"

She'd said it lightly, but Edith couldn't find the humor in a powerless saint. She forced a small smile, then went inside. She had just pulled out the pitcher of lemonade from the refrigerator when the door to the kitchen swung open and C.J. walked in, pulling on the hand of a petite sandy-haired girl who trailed behind him.

"Hello, Mother," he said, his father's grin spreading across his face. He stepped closer and kissed Edith on the cheek. "I've decided to come home for the weekend and brought somebody special."

The girl waited until C.J. pulled her forward, putting his arm around her shoulders in a proprietary way. "Mother, this is Cecelia Gibbes. She doesn't like to be called CeCe except by me, so everybody else calls her Cecelia. Isn't that right, sugar?" He squeezed her to him and kissed the top of her head, and for a brief moment Edith thought she recognized something in the girl's eyes, something that reminded her of the panicked look of an animal caught in a cage.

Cecelia held a hand out to Edith and she took it, feeling small bones as delicate as a bird's. Her eyes were a warm golden brown, the color of the marsh grass in winter. "It's a pleasure to meet you, Mrs. Heyward." She met Edith's eyes briefly before turning them back to C.J.

The girl seemed dwarfed by him, and not just in size but in personality. She looked at C.J. with adoration when he spoke, and seemed to wait for his approval before she said anything. Edith felt her heart sink, seeing her younger self standing in the same kitchen and meeting Calhoun's mother. The only thing that had changed in the intervening years was the wallpaper.

"It's good to meet you, too, Cecelia." Edith looked down at her crumpled and dirty skirt, then up at C.J. with reproach. "I wish I'd known you were coming so I could have cleaned up and had a room prepared for our guest."

"You look just fine, Mrs. Heyward," Cecelia reassured her. "And I'll be happy to put sheets on my bed. I don't want you to go to any trouble."

C.J.'s affable smile dimmed. "She doesn't mind, CeCe. What else does she have to do?" He faced his mother with a wide grin. "What's for dinner? It was a long drive from Columbia and I'm starved."

Edith's thoughts were jumbled for a moment, refusing to settle. "I've got some shrimp and rice, and some wonderful tomatoes I got yesterday in Frogmore. . . ."

"Great. Just make it fast. I'm going to show CeCe the rest of the house. She's from outside of Greenville and swears she's never seen such grand houses as we have here in Beaufort."

The back door opened and Deborah entered the kitchen, stopping suddenly when she saw C.J. and Cecelia. C.J.'s expression hardened as Deborah closed the door slowly behind her, then stopped with her back against the door facing Edith's son, the two of them like fighters claiming their corners.

Deborah had continued to babysit for C.J. until he was old enough to be left alone, despite his protests that he hated her. Edith soon realized that he wasn't using that as an excuse, but he truly had a dislike for his babysitter. It hadn't taken Edith long to understand it was because Deborah didn't put up with any of C.J.'s bullying. Deborah was tall for a woman, with large bones and big, capable hands, and she was used to taking care of her siblings. This meant she wasn't susceptible to C.J.'s charm or cajoling, and was intimidating enough physically to make sure C.J. complied with her rules. C.J. hated rules and had spent most of his childhood circumventing them despite Edith's best efforts. Even without his father there, Edith had always felt outnumbered.

"Hello, C.J.," Deborah said. "It's good to see you."

"Hello, Deborah." C.J. just nodded at her, and didn't introduce Cecelia.

Ignoring the snub, Deborah turned to the girl. "I'm Deborah Fuller. I used to babysit for C.J. I must admit to being surprised that he survived childhood."

Cecelia gave a small laugh that was cut off by an abrupt squeeze from C.J. Sobering quickly, she said, "It's nice to meet you. I'm Cecelia Gibbes. I'm at Carolina with C.J., studying nursing."

"Not for long, though, isn't that right, sugar?" C.J. kissed the top of her head as Edith's unease grew.

"Is there something I should know?" Edith tried for a lighthearted tone, but she'd never been able to fool C.J. He looked at her as a person might look at a bug on a wall.

"Not yet, Mother. But you'll be the first to know."

She looked back at Cecelia and felt her heart shrink. She wanted to shout at her to run, to finish her nursing degree and find another life that didn't involve her son. She hated herself for such disloyal thoughts, but she'd long since stopped praying for forgiveness.

C.J. reached into the fruit bowl on the counter and grabbed an apple. He rubbed it on his shirt, then took a big bite before offering it to Cecelia. She took a bite, although it didn't seem like she wanted any. "I'd like to show CeCe my favorite fishing spot over on Lady's Island, but they've got the road blocked off. Any idea what's going on?"

Deborah turned on the faucet and began washing her hands in the sink. "They think they found parts of a plane that crashed over the marsh a while back."

C.J. chewed thoughtfully. "Was I alive back then? I don't think I remember that."

"You were almost four," Edith said quietly, watching him closely. She'd never spoken of that night to him, not wanting him to recall any memories that might still linger, or bring his nightmares into the daylight. And she'd never mentioned that it had happened on the night his father's car crashed into a tree, because that would have invited the questions of where he'd been going, and what had distracted his attention from the road. There were some things best left unsaid.

C.J. took another bite of the apple, the sound loud in the small kitchen. "What happened?" he asked with a full mouth.

Deborah turned off the faucet and wiped her hands with a dish towel. "They're not sure. I remember people finding bits and pieces of the plane in the river and the marsh for weeks afterward." She paused for a moment, her brow furrowed, her lips tightening. "We had a baby doll fall into our front yard, and my mother cried and cried when she found out all those people were killed."

Cecelia's face had paled, and she had a

hand to her mouth while C.J. kept eating the apple.

"Please excuse me," Edith said, smoothing her palms on her skirt. "I'll just go freshen up the guest room for Cecelia and then see about supper."

Edith ran upstairs to her room and pulled out her cigarettes from the nightstand. It took her three tries to light her cigarette, because her hands were shaking so badly. She moved to the front window and stared out at the sky above the river, seeing instead a black night illuminated with fire. She took a long drag, feeling the nicotine calm her, felt it seep through her blood like poison.

For the first time in a long time, she thought of the faceless woman packing her husband's suitcase, folding each shirt, each pair of pants, rolling each pair of socks and tucking them carefully inside. Edith saw her writing the letter and placing it among the clothing, each letter, each word in perfect penmanship, the ink thick and black on the paper from pressing too hard. She saw the woman closing the suitcase and locking it, knowing her husband would never read the letter — the letter that remained under Edith's refrigerator and likely would stay there forever.

Edith took another long drag, closed her

eyes, and imagined she could see the night exploding and hear the river hissing as it welcomed the dead and dying as they fell from the sky. But when she opened her eyes she saw only the sea-glass wind chime outside her window, singing softly in the spring breeze.

CHAPTER 17

Loralee

Loralee stumbled into the house, closing the door behind her with her foot, her arms overloaded with shopping bags she needed to hide before Merritt saw them, wanting to avoid the question about where the money had come from. Her hair dripped onto the shoulders of her raincoat and the paper bags as she shuffled them behind the blue and white sofa in the front parlor. She'd wait until Merritt left the house and then ask Owen to help her bring them upstairs. They were all for him, anyway. Except for two skirts, a bathing suit, a pair of shorts, a dress, and a couple of knit tops for Merritt.

She leaned against the back of the sofa for a brief moment to catch her breath. She should have brought Owen with her so that she would have been guaranteed a correct size, but she'd had a doctor's appointment beforehand and she hadn't wanted to drag him in with her. All those ladies' doctors always had pictures on the walls showing parts of women's bodies that Owen was happily ignorant of, and he would — hopefully — remain so for at least a few more years.

After a deep, sustaining breath, she pushed herself away from the sofa and went back out onto the porch. The heavy sky lit up again with a fork of lightning as the rain fell in sheets. Loralee turned her face upward, breathing in the scent of the rain-soaked marsh and the salty air, wishing she could bottle the fragrance. She'd make a million dollars selling it to all the displaced residents of the coastal South who longed for home.

Smiling to herself, she moved to one of the wobbly wicker tables on the porch, where she'd set her prize find. She'd been on the way from the doctor's office near Beaufort Memorial when she'd passed a garage sale. Her mama's words had seemed so loud that for a moment Loralee thought she was in the Navigator with her. *One person's trash is another person's treasure. Some of the most priceless finds have no real value except for the amount of love and memories they hold.* Loralee had written that down in her journal as soon as she'd found a parking spot.

It was a Singer sewing machine. Not one of the old black metal ones with a foot pump like her mama had had, but one that was probably from the seventies, with an electric cord. It was cream-colored plastic and metal but was in perfect working order, according to the woman selling it, who had happily run a piece of fabric through just to prove it.

There was a photograph in one of Robert's albums that showed a young Merritt with her mother at a kitchen table covered with bolts of fabric and a sewing machine that looked a lot like this one. Loralee knew she was taking a chance, rushing things with Merritt. But life was like that, keeping time on a clock with fewer hours on it than what you'd come to expect.

She lifted the machine and brought it into the house, leaving it on the foyer table. She was winded and looked longingly at the sofa in the parlor, wondering how long she could lie down before somebody noticed her. Owen shouted from the kitchen, followed by another shout that was definitely from Merritt.

Moving as fast as she could, and ignoring the dripping water from her raincoat and the wet footsteps from her high-heeled boots, she made her way into the kitchen, pausing at the threshold for a moment before anybody saw her.

Merritt and Owen sat next to each other with their backs against the kitchen table, facing the large window over the sink. The window framed the streaks of lightning as they flitted across the sky, Merritt and Owen spectators with their own personal viewing. Owen was afraid of storms, which was why Loralee had rushed home when the sky had first started rumbling. She'd imagined him under his bed with a flashlight and a book instead of in the kitchen watching the storm's impressive light show.

Merritt and Owen each held a glass Coca-Cola bottle, and an opened bag of salted and shelled peanuts sat on the table behind them. Loralee watched as Owen took a sip of his Coke, then sucked in his cheeks for a moment before swallowing. "Wow!" he shouted. "It's like it just popped in my head. Are there bubbles coming out of my ears?"

Merritt looked at her brother, her face serious. "Not yet. Maybe you need to take another sip."

Owen shook his head. "It's your turn. You have to take a big sip, and make sure you get a bunch of peanuts on your tongue."

Merritt tilted her head back, the Coke bottle to her mouth, and clenched her eyes.

After taking the bottle from her face she began chewing and then swallowed, sucking in her cheeks just like Owen. "Wow!" she said, just as loud as Owen. "You're right. Do I have bubbles coming out of my ears?"

Owen giggled so that he didn't even notice the flash of light outside, or the roll of thunder that quickly followed, and Loralee was certain that was Merritt's intention. Just as she was sure that the peanuts and Coke had been Merritt's idea.

She must have made a noise, because Merritt turned her head and spotted her. Loralee smiled, hoping Merritt knew how thankful she was.

"It's a real gully-washer outside, that's for sure," Loralee said as she shrugged out of her raincoat. She folded it over the back of an empty chair, then slid gratefully onto the seat. "I hope you don't mind, but I've got to get these boots off my feet. They're soaked through."

As she unzipped the first boot, Owen sprang from his chair. "Merritt said she didn't like storms and wanted company, so we decided to come down to the kitchen together and wait for it to be over. She said when she was little her mama used to say that thunder was just the sound of angels bowling and that lightning happened when one of them made a strike, and that made her not be afraid anymore." He laughed and took another drink from his bottle.

"That would do it," she agreed, meeting Merritt's eyes. Merritt smiled softly before looking away.

Loralee slid off the second boot and wiggled her toes, wishing she didn't have to stand up ever again.

"You know, Loralee, your feet wouldn't hurt if you wore sensible shoes. I'll never understand why you wear those high heels." Merritt's serious expression was softened by the small trace of Coke bubbles on her upper lip.

"Maybe you should try them sometime, so you'll know why so many women wear them." She imagined Merritt in five-inch Louboutins, strutting about feeling tall, powerful, and sexy, and the thought didn't make her want to giggle.

Merritt looked at her doubtfully as she slid her chair from the table. "It's time to get dinner started. I bought three lobsters — I *do* know how to do that, at least. I thought we could celebrate."

"Celebrate what?"

"I got a job today. At a small museum in Port Royal. I hadn't expected to find one in my field so quickly, to be honest. I saw the ad in Sunday's paper and sent in my résumé. I interviewed today and they hired me on the spot. I guess my degree and work experience really paid off."

Or maybe they just liked you, Loralee wanted to add. But she knew that Merritt wasn't good at taking compliments, and Loralee had begun to suspect that it was because she wasn't used to them.

Merritt continued. "It's only part-time for now, with not too many hours, but that's fine until I get more settled here and decide what kind of renovations I want to do to the house." She bent over one of the lower cabinets where the pots and pans were located and opened it. Without looking at Loralee, shc asked, "How's your job search going?"

"Oh, I've sent a few résumés, and while I've been out running errands I've checked out help-wanted signs in stores. Nothing yet, but I know the right job will come along soon."

Merritt nodded, her silence meaning only that she was thinking of the next thing she wanted to discuss with Loralee. Eager not to repeat the conversation they'd had regarding Owen's education and whether Loralee could afford private school, she forced herself to stand, leaning heavily on the table.

"I bought something for you today that I think you'll enjoy. Don't worry — it wasn't expensive. I found it at a garage sale. And if you don't like it, I'll sell it on craigslist."

Merritt eyed her suspiciously. "I hope it's not clothes. I don't think you and I share the same taste."

Loralee bit her lip so she wouldn't say the first thing that came to mind: *Thank goodness for small mercies.* "No. But close." She held out her hand. "Close your eyes — it's a surprise."

For a moment Loralee thought Merritt would refuse to take her hand, and maybe she would have if Owen hadn't been there. After a small hesitation, Merritt put her hand in Loralee's and allowed herself to be led through the kitchen door.

"Can I look, Mama?"

"Come on, Owen — just don't say anything until Merritt opens her eyes."

Owen jumped up and down behind them. "Tell me when and I'll let Merritt know when she can open them."

Loralee led them to the foyer, where the sewing machine sat on the table, looking as out of place on the fancy antique as a potbellied pig sitting in first class. She stood behind Merritt and took her shoulders to move her in the right position. "Okay,

344

Owen. Go ahead."

"Open your eyes," he commanded.

Merritt's eyes opened and she stared at the sewing machine without saying a single word.

"It's a sewing machine," Loralee explained, thinking that maybe it had been a long time since Merritt had seen one.

"I know what it is," she said, her eyes focused on the machine. "I just . . ." She faced Loralee. "Why is it here?"

"There was a photo of you and your mama, and you were making something with the sewing machine. I thought . . ." She stopped, alarmed at the wetness in Merritt's eyes and wondering whether she'd made a very big mistake.

With clipped and very deliberate words, Merritt said, "It was her mother's sewing machine." A slow smile softened her face. "My mother did a little bit of sewing, but my grandmother was really good with it — she could do monograms that looked like they were hand-stitched. She could make anything, really — I guess that's where I got the interest. It always amazed me, because she couldn't move two fingers of her right hand — nerve damage, she said. But she managed pretty well." Merritt placed her palm on top of the sewing machine very lightly, as if she were petting a dog that might bite her.

"After my mother died, my grandmother moved near us and would take care of me when my father had to fly. And then one day . . ." She turned to Loralee, her eyes distant. "I can't believe I'm remembering this now — I haven't thought about it for years." She rubbed her eyes with the heels of her hands. "One day she got a package with a letter, and inside the package was a handkerchief with a monogram on it — and it looked just like one she'd made. She threw it all away, and then packed up her sewing machine and I never saw it again. And we never made anything together after that."

"What did the letter say?"

Merritt shook her head. "I have no idea. She tore it up into little pieces and then shoved it back into the package with the handkerchief. She was crying — something I'd never seen her do before. She'd always told me that crying was only for weak-willed people, and I knew never to bring it up — so I didn't. Then I forgot about it. Until now."

Loralee shifted on her bare feet, not sure what to do. "Like I said, if you don't want it I'm sure I can sell it."

Merritt's attention returned to the sewing machine, but she didn't touch it again, like a girl being offered a large diamond ring but not sure whether she wanted to get married. "Why did you get it for me?" she asked quietly.

Loralee shrugged, recalling what she'd written in her journal on the first day she'd met Merritt, looking like she'd been licking the same wound for years so that it never got better. *Turning the page is always better than rereading the same page over and over.* "Your daddy used to tell me how creative you were, how you could make anything, but that you'd stopped. I figured now might be a good time to rediscover something you used to love."

Merritt just stared at her, which made Loralee nervous. And when she got nervous, she talked. "Since you're starting your life over, sort of. You're in a new town and a new house, with new people in your life. And you even have a new job. Maybe now you can forget about why you stopped and find the joy again that it used to bring you."

"Joy?" Merritt repeated like she'd never heard the word before.

"Like at Christmas, right, Mama?" Owen asked as he bent down to examine the working mechanisms of the machine. "It means happiness," he said to Merritt. "Like when I make something new with my LEGOs."

"You must think I'm pretty pathetic," Merritt said softly.

"Oh, no. Not at all. I just saw this sewing machine. . . ."

Merritt picked up the machine, and Loralee held her breath, expecting her to drop it on the floor. She could already see the bobbin rolling across the wood floor, unspooling the thread like a long, thin red tear.

"I'm going to set this up on the table in front of the window in the dining room overlooking the garden. You get the morning sun there." Merritt was halfway to the dining room when she stopped. "Thank you," she said. She waited, as if she wanted to say more, then seemed to change her mind and continued carrying the sewing machine to the back of the house.

"You're welcome," Loralee said to her departing back, knowing she'd done a good thing, and hoped Robert was watching.

She put her arm around Owen. "Come on, sweetheart. Let's go set the table and make some sides to go with Merritt's lobster. Don't tell her I said this, but I have doubts about her ability to cook an edible meal, so let's make sure we don't leave the table starving."

Owen put his hand over his mouth and laughed, and for the first time in a long, long while Loralee truly believed that her journey had finally moved from a steep hill to a flattened path. She just hoped a cliff wasn't waiting at the end of the road.

Loralee wiped her lips on her napkin, trying not to be obvious about the food she was transferring from her mouth. The lobster had been delicious, especially dipped in melted butter. She just had no appetite and had felt as full as a tick after the first bite. But she hadn't wanted to tell that to Merritt, or to allow her to think that the food wasn't good.

At least Owen had scraped his plate clean, eating everything that was edible from his own lobster and earning himself a smile of appreciation from his sister.

Loralee balled her full napkin in her hand. "That was very good, Merritt. Your daddy never told me what a good cook you are."

Merritt stood and started collecting plates. "That's because he didn't know. I started cooking when I was in college and never really had a chance to show him." She avoided Loralee's eyes as she took her plate.

Loralee touched her arm, causing Merritt to pause. "You didn't need to stay away

349

because of me, you know. I always made sure that I'd be away flying during your school breaks so I wouldn't interfere. Your daddy would put fresh flowers in your room and make lists of things the two of you would do while you were home. I didn't know until much later that he never told you that — that he just expected you to know that he wanted you to come home. To meet your new baby brother and spend time together as a family."

Merritt placed the dishes in the sink, then looked out the window into the garden. "I guess I know where I got my stubborn streak." She gave a little shrug. "And no, I never knew. It didn't even occur to me, really. I just thought . . ." She turned on the faucet and let the water run over the plates in the sink. "He had you."

Loralee tried to remember something her mama had once said about wanting to redo the past, but drew a blank. Probably because her heart hurt too much. "There was more than enough room in his big heart for both of us. And for memories of your mama, too. He wanted you to know that. He wrote you letters, but they all came back unopened."

Merritt's hands gripped the edge of the sink, her knuckles white. It was to keep from crying. Loralee knew this because Owen always did the same thing. She just hoped Merritt knew she wasn't accusing her of anything — there was so much hurt between Merritt and her daddy that Loralee never took a side. She just wanted Merritt to know that Robert had tried.

Owen, bored with the conversation, said, "May I be excused?"

Loralee sighed. "Not until we clean up the kitchen first. Merritt, leave those dishes alone. You cooked, so Owen and I will clean. You go relax. Gibbes is coming over later to pick up some of his boxes, but you probably have time to brush out your hair."

Merritt finally turned around, a small smile on her lips. "You never give up, do you?"

Loralee beamed her brightest smile, the kind she'd always greeted passengers with — especially those traveling with small children. "Mama always said that the point of life was to spend it trying. Only quitters quit."

Merritt wiped her hands on a dish towel. "And my mother always told me that the smartest people always know when it's time to quit." As she walked toward the door, she said, "I'm going to get Cal's box to show Gibbes. I found it on the floor of the backseat of my car." She paused as they both watched a reluctant Owen pick up the iced-tea pitcher from the table and move as slowly as possible to the refrigerator.

Loralee stood, trying not to lean too heavily on the table. "I guess we were both raised by a couple of really smart women."

What could have been taken as a snort came from Merritt just as Owen yanked open the refrigerator door, then stood there, confused. "The light's off and it's not really cold in here."

Merritt's shoulders slumped. "Not that I'm surprised — that thing has got to be at least fifty years old. I just can't believe it waited until tonight."

Loralee stuck her head into the refrigerator, agreeing with Owen that it was definitely not as cold as it should be. "Mama always said troubles are sometimes a blessing in disguise. Just think how nice it will be to have one of those new stainless refrigerators."

Merritt gave her a look that would have wilted kudzu.

"Can we get one with an ice dispenser in the door?" Owen asked.

Merritt closed the refrigerator door and waited a moment, then opened it again. The light flickered on and the motor started whirring. "Well, that's reassuring. Although

I think it just fired a shot across the bow. I'll call somebody to come take a look in the morning, but I have a feeling we'll need to replace it. I was planning on gutting the kitchen, anyway — just not so soon. Although it would be nice to have a dishwasher."

The doorbell rang, and if Loralee had been a betting woman, she would have bet her favorite push-up bra that Merritt's face actually brightened.

"I'll get that," Loralee said. "You go on up and get that box for Gibbes, Merritt." She hoped that Merritt would take the hint and do something with her hair. The next time Merritt left the house, Loralee promised herself she'd go into Merritt's room and burn every single one of those hideous plastic headbands.

"Owen, you stay here and finish scraping food into the garbage and rinsing off the plates, all right? I'll come back and help in just a minute."

Loralee looked at her soaking boots, then over at Merritt's discarded house slippers. Before she could imagine what she might look like, she slid on the slippers, then went to answer the door.

Standing next to Gibbes on the front porch was Deborah Fuller from the Heritage Society, whom Loralee had met before. She greeted them warmly and held the door open. The sky behind them had brightened, yellow beams of sunlight struggling to get through the clouds even though a heavy drizzle continued to fall. "Looks like the devil's beating his wife," Loralee said as she stepped back.

"What does that mean?"

They all turned to find Merritt coming down the stairs, her expression wary. It was Deborah who answered her. "That's what you say when the sun is shining while it's raining."

A crease formed between Merritt's eyebrows. "That's an odd thing to say." A forced smile lifted her lips. "If I'm going to live here, I should probably get a translation dictionary." She crossed the foyer to the front door, carrying a white shoe box with a dark blue lid, two rubber bands crisscrossed over the top to hold it closed. When Loralee looked closer at Merritt, she had to try very hard not to smile. The white plastic headband was gone, and her dark hair had been brushed over her shoulders in a perfect natural wave. It was prettier hair than most wigs Loralee had seen, and she'd seen a lot. She almost did a double take when she saw Merritt's lips. They were the palest pink with just a little bit of sheen to them. Lora-lee smiled to herself, remembering the lip gloss she'd given Merritt, telling her it was SPF protection, figuring Merritt would need a practical reason to wear it.

But there was something in the way she approached Gibbes, a wariness that reminded Loralee of a person driving down unfamiliar streets without a map. Or a teenager on her first date. Which was strange, because Merritt had been married for seven years. If there was one thing Lora-lee had taken away from all those years of being a flight attendant, it was her ability to see past what people wanted you to see. She scrutinized Merritt, remembering the photos of Cal she hadn't wanted framed, and began to consider what Merritt might not want the world to see.

"Hello, Deborah. It's good to see you again," Merritt said after giving just a quick glance and nod to Gibbes.

"Hello, Merritt. I ran into Dr. Heyward at the Piggly Wiggly, and he said he was on his way over. I invited myself to come see the nutshell studies."

"Yes, of course. The sky's brightened a bit, so it shouldn't be too dark in the attic."

"Wonderful," Deborah said, her eyes darting toward the stairs. "I can't tell you how excited I am to see them. I'm even hoping that if we can reach an agreement, you might loan them to the police department for educational purposes."

"I'm sure we can work something out," Merritt said, heading for the stairs and then remembering the box in her hand. She held it out to Gibbes. "This is for you — it's Cal's box. I figure it means more to you than it does to me, so I want you to have it."

He took it from her, then slowly rolled off the rubber bands. One of them broke and snapped back, slapping his hand. He placed the box on the hall table and lifted the lid. They all peered into it like they'd just dug up a buried treasure.

Inside was a dome-shaped bullet with three scored rings at its base, the lead oxidized to almost white, and a large steel bolt still connected to a jagged piece of blackened metal. He was silent for a moment, as if he were watching a movie in his head where he and his brother were the main players. "Yep. This is exactly what I remembered. I just can't believe these were the only two things he thought were important enough to take with him when he left home." Gibbes reached inside the box and took out the bullet, dislodging an object that had been stuck beneath it. A simple gold ring rolled to a corner of the box, then fell flat against the cardboard.

"I forgot that was in there." Merritt picked up the gold band and held it in the palm of her hand. "It's Cal's wedding ring. He didn't like to wear it because it interfered with his doing his job. So he put it in the box."

Her fingers closed over the ring, and she seemed to be considering what to do next. "I should probably keep this." Her tone reminded Loralee of when Owen said something just because he thought it was what his mother wanted to hear.

Merritt slid it into the pocket of her skirt, then led the way to the stairs, Deborah and Gibbes following her. Gibbes watched her closely, as if Merritt were a puzzle and he couldn't figure out how all the pieces fit together.

Owen's voice came from the kitchen as he sang the theme from *Gilligan's Island* at the top of his lungs. They'd both become addicted to the old TV show when they'd seen an episode on one of the children's cable channels, and Loralee had purchased the entire series on DVD. They'd memorized the lyrics of the theme song just by watching it so many times, and when Loralee told

Owen that singing sometimes helped unpleasant chores go faster, he hadn't needed
to be prompted. He would never be a singer
— not that talent had anything to do with
making records anymore — but the sound
always made her smile.

She moved into the open doorway and
paused. The rain had stopped, the sun glint-
ing off the wet pavement and the river, the
tips of the grass sparkling like tiny diamonds
in the front yard. A rainbow arced across
the sky in a brightly hued bridge, its end
fading somewhere behind Lady's Island.
Loralee took a deep breath, her exhaustion
gone for a moment. Rainbows always gave
her hope — hope that something beautiful
waited for those strong enough to survive
the storm.

Loralee quickly closed the door so she
could go write that down in her pink journal
before she forgot. Or before she stopped
believing it was true.

CHAPTER 18

Merritt

Cal's wedding ring nudged my hip where it lay in my pocket as I climbed the stairs. I pulled open the attic door and waited for Deborah and Gibbes to go first. I hadn't forgotten the first time I'd climbed the stairs with Gibbes while I wore a skirt, and wasn't about to make the same mistake twice.

Deborah paused, looking up the steep, narrow attic steps. "Edith always kept the door locked, so I've never been up here. Not that I would ever go against her wishes, of course. She was a very private woman, and I respected that." A small smile tilted her lips. "Mr. Calhoun never came up here, either, not that she locked the door when he was home. The man couldn't abide a locked door." She rubbed her hands over her arms as if she'd just had a chill. "I always wondered why she didn't use the basement, where the old kitchen and slave quarters were, for her workshop. There was always the potential of flooding, but it would have been a lot cooler." She nodded toward the stairs. "But now I understand why. Her husband was a big man who was fond of his brandy. I don't think he could have managed these steps."

I scratched my head. "I haven't even been to the basement — I've seen the half-moon windows from the outside, but they're covered with dirt and cobwebs. And I know the door's at the end of the back porch — which seems to me an odd place for it."

Gibbes began climbing the steps. "When they added on the new kitchen, they didn't enclose the basement door, although I have no idea why. I don't think anybody's been down there for years. I just remember how dark it was — with old wooden beams on the ceiling, and dirt floors. It would be a nice place to fix up — maybe a rec room for Owen."

"It would be if he were going to be living here. Besides, if it's prone to flooding, maybe I'll just let it stay the way it is. Something less to worry about."

Even to my own ears my protest didn't sound very convincing. I hadn't been in Beaufort very long, but even in such a short space of time I was finding it difficult reconciling the woman who'd sat in Mr. Williams's office crying with the woman who'd willingly gone out in a boat, crossed a large swing bridge in a car, and worn a dress that showed more leg than some bathing suits.

I flipped on the light switch when we reached the top, then adjusted the air conditioner to a lower temperature and a higher fan speed. I still kept it on all day, but had compromised my need for cool air with my New England need to not be a spendthrift by keeping it on the "economy" mode when I wasn't up there. Still, Deborah plucked at her blouse, trying to fan herself, drops of perspiration forming on her upper lip.

"It must have been unbearable for Edith up here during the hotter months. I don't know how she could have stood it."

I looked at Gibbes, knowing we were both thinking about why. What was it about her life that made escaping into a scorching attic to make tableaux of crime scenes seem like a welcome alternative?

Deborah looked up. "It's a sound roof, at least. It would have been a bad thing if it leaked. Imagine the mildew on the cardboard boxes." She spotted the sea-glass table first and walked toward it.

Sticking a hand in one of the baskets of glass, she swirled them around with her fingers like a witch making a potion. "For a long time I thought Edith made her wind chimes to hide what she really did up here — from Calhoun. But she continued to make them even after he died, so I guess she probably had another reason."

She peered out one of the attic windows and smiled. "We've had a few bad storms — like Hugo back in 'eighty-nine. Edith had to pull every one of her wind chimes inside so they wouldn't become projectiles, but she always put them out again. I'm glad to see you're honoring her by keeping them hanging."

I felt Gibbes's gaze on me, but didn't turn around. I didn't have the heart to tell Deborah that the only reason the wind chimes were still there was because I hadn't yet found a ladder tall enough to reach them.

Her gaze scanned the room, finally resting on the makeshift shelves against the far wall. Recognizing what sat on the shelves, she walked directly to the first one and leaned down to see it more closely. It was a 1950s kitchen, not unlike the one downstairs, with a lifelike apple pie sitting on a windowsill, the real glass window cracked half-open. Four bright red apple-shaped place mats sat on the round table, tiny silverware and cups filled with clear cellophane in their correct spots. A braided rug lay in front of the sink, which was half-filled with what looked like soapy water.

The only indication that there was something wrong in this idyllic scene was the back half of a woman, dressed in navy blue pumps, a floral dress, and an apron, protruding from the open stove door.

"Ah, yes," Deborah said. "I remember this one. A case from Greenville, I think. I remember the woman was pregnant." She straightened, a crooked smile on her face. "It wasn't her husband's. But it wasn't he who killed her." Pointing to the open window, she said, "Her lover thought he was being so clever coming in through the kitchen window, carefully removing the apple pie, and then replacing it so it appeared to be a suicide. He strangled her with the ties to her apron before putting it back on her."

Gibbes shoved his hands in his pockets, his eyebrows raised. "But any amateur knows that an autopsy would reveal that she'd died of strangulation and not gas."

"Yes, well, this was in the days before *CSI*, when the average person didn't necessarily know the nuances of murder."

I stepped closer, no longer as afraid of the boxes as I'd been before I knew what they were. Peering inside, I felt like Gulliver in Lilliput, examining a tiny world I was part of but wasn't.

"The knobs on the stove move, and there are replicas of all the food items from the real refrigerator inside the model," Deborah explained. "Edith was very good. I think Frances Glessner Lee would have been very proud to call her a protégée."

"I'm glad she had this for herself. She must have found it very fulfilling personally, especially since . . ." I stopped, unsure where my train of thought was taking me, and unwilling to share it with anybody.

"Especially since what?" Gibbes asked.

I stepped back, pretending to study the shelves. "She seemed to do a lot of sneaking around so that her husband wasn't aware of what she was doing. I find it rather sad that she lived such a solitary life even though she was married and had a child. And two grandsons."

"My grandfather died long before I was born, and my grandmother never talked about him. But I don't think it was a happy marriage," Gibbes said.

I felt him looking at me but couldn't meet his eyes. "Why do you say that?"

"Because there weren't any photographs of him in the house. From the time I was aware of my surroundings, there was nothing of his still here. Which is saying something, because the house had been in his family, not hers. There was no clothing, mementos, baby shoes — nothing." He paused, the air between us waiting. "Not even a wedding ring."

My pocket seemed to burn, and I lifted my skirt away from my skin, feeling blistered.

Deborah's excitement over the rediscovery of the shoe boxes made her oblivious to anything else, and she continued her examination of each one, exclaiming her admiration of every chair that reclined, every appliance that plugged into an outlet, every wind chime that sang.

"I really do hope you'll loan these to the police department, or even the Heritage Society. There is a great deal to be learned here, and that can be done only if they are shared with the public."

"Of course," I said. "I really don't feel as if I have a claim to them, regardless. I'll leave it up to Gibbes."

"I'm sure we can work something out," he said. "Let me think about it and I'll give you a call next week."

"Thank you, Gibbes. I know your grand-mother would be happy to know her work is still being used and appreciated."

Sweat trickled down the side of her face, and dark stains appeared beneath her arms. She began walking toward the steps, having apparently seen all she needed to.

"There's something else I wanted to show you," I said. "I thought about asking you when we visited your office, but I got sidetracked. I'm not even sure this is related to the shoe boxes, but since it was up here in the attic, I'm assuming it is. Maybe you can tell us a little more."

Gibbes retrieved the plane from its place in the corner and set it on the table with the sea glass, just as he'd done before. Deborah began to examine it, noting the oval windows and the people inside, the unfurled steel around the hole on the side of the mottled fuselage that seemed pieced to-gether with thick white papier-mâché and glass. Deborah put her hand to her heart, and I had the fleeting thought that I was glad we were with a doctor.

"Are you all right, Miss Fuller?" Gibbes placed his hand on her arm.

She nodded. "I'm fine. This is just such a . . . surprise. Did Edith make this?"

"We have no idea," I said. "Although we

assume so, because it's up here, and from what we know, nobody else was allowed in the attic."

"Except for Cal."

We both looked at Gibbes, unsure what, if anything, that meant.

He continued. "There's also a bag with the pieced-together wings and about forty or so passengers, some still strapped in their seats, each showing various injuries. Some of them with mud and grass stains on them."

"Do you have any idea what this is?" she asked, her voice distant.

"According to Owen, it's most likely a passenger plane used in the forties and fifties — maybe a DC-six. But that's all."

"That sounds right," she said out loud, although it seemed she was talking to herself. "There was a plane crash here in Beaufort. It was the summer — 1955."

Gibbes nodded slowly. "That's what the man at the antique store said — that the bolt Cal and I found in the marsh could have come from a crash that happened in the fifties. It might be the same one."

"It was horrible." She took off her glasses and rubbed them with a tissue she pulled from her pocket, as if she needed them to see her memories more clearly. "I was a little girl at the time, so I was protected from hearing about most of it, but I did a lot of eavesdropping on my parents and their friends. There were forty-nine souls on board, I believe. All of them perished."

She continued to stare at the fuselage, a distant look in her eyes. "It was low tide, so the pluff mud collected a lot of the wreckage." She swallowed, her hand on her heart. "Our neighbor had a seat with a passenger still strapped inside land in the marsh across the street from his house. The man was dead when they found him, but there were scratch marks in the mud on both sides of the seat, so he must have been alive when he hit the ground. Eight of the victims were never recovered, and two of the bodies went unclaimed and were buried at St. Helena's."

"That's horrible." I stared at the plane model with renewed fascination. "So this must be Edith's attempt to re-create the scene." Looking up at Deborah, I asked, "Did they ever determine the cause?"

She shook her head. "Not that I know of. For a couple of decades they printed anniversary articles in the local paper, but they stopped that in the nineties, I think. Even up until then there were always a lot of theories, but nothing conclusive. The final explanation that the experts seemed to agree with is that something sparked a fire in one of the gas tanks, which exploded just as the plane was flying over Beaufort. It was a hot summer — the hottest summer on record — and they think that might have played a part." She thought for a moment. "I remember one of the newspaper articles mentioning that it was at its cruising altitude of twenty-two thousand feet at the time it exploded, which explains why so little of the wreckage was recovered, and why no definitive cause of the explosion could be determined. So much of the wreckage went into the river and the marshes and was then taken out to sea."

She replaced her glasses on her face. "One of the things that struck me was that it wasn't supposed to fly this far inland, but a little farther east, over the ocean. But there were some sort of military exercises going on offshore, so commercial traffic was rerouted. It added fifteen minutes to the projected flight time, on top of any delays they might have already had. I remembered wondering whether that would have made any difference, if that extra fifteen minutes could have been the trigger or something." She shrugged. "I guess we'll never know."

I had the oddest feeling that I needed to warn these hapless passengers as I looked at them strapped in their seats. Like I could somehow play God and turn the clock backward. But I couldn't, of course. I was like everybody else, forced to watch events unfold beyond our control.

Deborah continued. "One of the last articles about the crash mentioned that flight data recorders weren't required until sometime in the sixties, so it was impossible to determine whether or not the pilots had any warning before the explosion. I've often wondered whether, if this had occurred just a decade later, we would have had enough technology to find out what really happened. It's very difficult not having answers, isn't it?"

I nodded absently as I squinted my eyes, seeing something I'd missed before. "All the seat and row numbers are painted in over the seats. I wonder if the dolls portray real people who were in those assigned seats."

Deborah looked affronted. "If Edith made this, then of course they're accurate. She never overlooked a single detail."

I was barely listening, paying closer attention to the sightless people facing innocently forward. I noticed a woman with a pregnancy bulge under her dress, and a young boy wearing shorts and a jacket and tie sitting next to an older woman with gray curls and a neat hat. I jerked back, an unwilling witness.

Gibbes turned to me with sympathetic eyes. "I'm guessing my grandmother wanted to solve this mystery — that's why the plane was put together in puzzle pieces and why some are still missing. Since she had an 'in' with the police department, she would have had knowledge of each plane part that was recovered and then made a copy of it. The pieces that weren't found, she made of clear plastic."

"Do you know where the plane was flying from or where it was going?" I wasn't sure why it mattered so much to me. Maybe it was human nature to separate the strangers in a tragedy from yourself, to illuminate all that was different between their lives and yours, to convince yourself that such a thing couldn't happen to you.

"It was going to Miami. From New York, I think." Deborah frowned, her glasses dipping low on her nose as she bent closer to examine the jagged pieces on the plane's right side. "This must have been the big secret project she was working on, then. It just doesn't make sense why she wouldn't have shared it with anybody. Her husband died that night; I do remember that — hit a tree with his car. Police think he might have been distracted by the explosion. Anyway, there was really no reason to be so hush-hush about her work, since she didn't have to worry about his disapproval." She tapped her chin, her eyes narrowed as she walked the length of the table to view the plane from as many angles as she could. Looking directly at me, she said, "Knowing Edith, I'd have to say she probably knew something that nobody else did."

The silence in the room grew stifling as the hot air and the quieted voices of the forty-nine lost souls became almost a palpable presence, a growing shadow that threatened to overtake any light in the room. I headed toward the stairs, needing a deep breath of air, and walked down into the foyer and out onto the front porch, Deborah and Gibbes close behind me.

"Are you all right?" Gibbes asked.

I nodded. "I just needed some fresh air."

Deborah smiled. "Thank you for letting me see the attic. I'm sure Gibbes will let you know what our plans are for the nutshell studies. I'd ask for the plane, too, but since there's nothing conclusive drawn from it, I doubt the police department will want it. But maybe the museum will. We'll see."

"May I drive you home, Miss Fuller?"

"No, thank you. And please call me Deborah."

The sides of Gibbes's eyes crinkled when he smiled. "I've known you since I was a baby, and it's a hard habit to break. But I promise to try."

Deborah squinted up at the sky. "It's cooled off some and the exercise will do me good. Thanks again," she said with a wave, then jogged nimbly down the front steps. She walked away with her head down, looking up only to cross the street so she could stroll alongside the water. It was low tide, the sea grass appearing bereft. She paused for a moment and looked up at the attic window, as if expecting to see Edith Heyward in the early evening shadows. Then she continued on her way with her head bent, deep in thought.

"We might be able to find something about the crash on the Internet," Gibbes said.

I started, having almost forgotten he was there. "That's probably a good idea, but we can't do it here. You probably won't be surprised to hear this, but your grandmother wasn't set up for Wi-Fi, or cable, or really anything else that's been invented in the last forty to fifty years. I think there might still be an antenna on the roof, or at least the remains of one. And I have to change my phone plan, because I can't get service inside the house with my current carrier. The e-mails I've managed to send and receive from my smart phone have happened only when I've stood on the garden bench outside — which isn't really practical. I've got people scheduled to be here by the end of the week, but I'm not going to bank on that."

"All right. I'll Google it when I get home tonight and let you know. Assuming you're interested."

I thought of the nameless passengers and how their existence was recorded only in the fading memories of a few people. I'd never had the desire to be famous, but there was a particular tragedy to being forgotten. "Of course I am. Please let me know if you find anything."

Loralee stepped out onto the porch, and in the last rays of sun she appeared pale under her makeup. Or maybe it was just the directness of the sun that bleached out her features and made her eyes a startling blue.

She grinned widely and she was the old Loralee again. "Owen and I are making chocolate sundaes, and we've got two with your names on them."

"No, thank you," I said automatically. "I

need to go through the hutch in the library. There are all sorts of papers and miscellaneous items in there that Gibbes might want."

"Are you sure? I can put it in the freezer just in case you change your mind." Loralee sounded genuinely disappointed.

"I'm sure. I'm not a big ice-cream eater, anyway." I thought my explanation would make things better, but when I saw the look on Gibbes's face, I knew I was wrong.

"All right," she said, still smiling but with a lot less wattage. "I'll tell Owen he can have yours, too. That boy is way too skinny."

"I'd love one," Gibbes said, after giving me a pointed look. "I'll be right there."

Loralee nodded, then went back inside, closing the door. I stared at it, wondering whether it was too late to tell her I'd changed my mind and that I actually liked ice cream, too.

"Why do you do that?" Gibbes's voice lacked any warmth.

"Do what?"

"Push people away. I've known a lot of New Englanders, and while most of them had a definite reserve, they were never like you. Is it something we've said or done? Because I thought that everybody you've come in contact with since you arrived here has treated you with nothing but kindness."

I wanted to shake my head and tell him I couldn't explain, because it was something I'd never been able to say out loud before. *It's because sooner or later everybody leaves you.* I blinked back the sting in my eyes, feeling the power of his words and my involuntary response to them. "I think I've told you before that you know nothing about me, and I don't think that's changed. So don't pretend you do."

"You're right. The only things I know about you are from the stray crumbs you've dropped along the way." He stepped closer. "I also think that you haven't been completely honest with me. I don't believe your story about how you and Cal met. That whole scenario is so . . ." He searched for the word, his hands raking through his hair in frustration. "So *foreign* from the brother I knew that it can't possibly be true."

We faced each other for a long time while he waited for me to respond, but I said nothing. How could I explain something I didn't understand, either? That the man I first met wasn't the man I'd married?

I bit my lip, embarrassed to feel it trembling. "I loved him. I did. And that's all you need to know."

He blew out a long breath, then turned to

go into the house. "I'm going to load up my truck with the boxes in the hall, and then I'm going to have a chocolate sundae. Don't bother to see me out."

I watched him head up the stairs, wondering not for the first time how I'd ever mistaken him for Cal. I closed the door and headed past the stairs and into the study, where the jumbled drawers of the hutch awaited me, my pocket feeling heavy with the weight of Cal's ring. I opened the top drawer and stared into it for a long time, not seeing anything as I willed the tears I'd been holding back since my mother's death to come. But they never did.

CHAPTER 19

Loralee

Loralee awoke with her hand over her mouth, as if even in her dreams she battled the constant nausea and stomach upset that she dealt with during her waking hours. She lay still for a moment, waiting to see if it would subside and trying to remember on which side of the bed she'd placed the garbage can, just in case.

The bedside clock ticked its slow progression through the early morning hours, a sound she was becoming more and more accustomed to as she began to find it difficult to sleep through an entire night. Very carefully she eased her way up the headboard, pausing so she wouldn't jolt anything loose. Once there she paused again, taking stock before slowly leaning over to the bedside table, where she kept a roll of Tums. She chewed slowly, the sound of the crunching tablets loud in her head, then forced herself to swallow.

She'd already started planning for her descent back onto her pillow when she heard Owen's voice. Her mother's instinct pushed aside any lingering stomach upset as she slid from the bed, hitting her toe on the garbage can she'd forgotten was there as she made her way out of her room and into the hallway.

Owen's Darth Vader night-light glowed dimly in the hall, guiding her to his open bedroom door, where she thought she heard very quiet singing. She stopped on the threshold when she realized it was Merritt, and she was sitting on the side of Owen's bed. Loralee propped herself against the door frame, unwilling to interrupt, and listened. And then she almost laughed out loud as she recognized the words from the *Gilligan's Island* theme song.

The song came to an abrupt halt. "I can't remember the next part," Merritt said quietly.

Owen's loud whisper came back with, " 'The weather started getting rough.' "

"Oh, right. Although I think I should stop singing, because I don't want to wake your mother. Unless you need to hear more to make you feel better."

"I'm good," he whispered.

"Good," Merritt said. "Are you ready to tell me why you were crying?"

There was a long pause, and Loralee strained to hear.

"I miss my daddy."

His voice was so full of hurt that Loralee thought she could now explain to people what a broken heart felt like, because hers must truly be splitting in half. She wanted to rush in and go to him, just as much as she knew that Merritt was right where they both needed her to be.

"I miss him, too." Merritt's voice cracked, and it took a moment before she continued. "He was a good daddy. Did he teach you how to swim and how to ride a bike?"

"Uh-huh."

"Me, too. His jokes were pretty lame, though. Did he tell you the one about Ewie Gooey the worm?"

"Lots of times," Owen said. "But I laughed each time so I wouldn't hurt his feelings."

"Yeah. I did, too. I guess that's something else he taught you — to be mindful of others' feelings."

"Did he teach you that, too?"

There was a small pause. "Yes. It's something I'm finding I still need to work on, but I'm trying." She paused, and when she spoke again her voice was thick. "I'm sad that I didn't get to see him before he died — and that was all my fault, not his. But I'm really glad that he had you, and that makes me feel a lot better. I think we can be happy that we both had him in our lives so that he could teach us important things we're always going to need. Maybe we should think of that when we start missing him, so we won't be so sad."

It was quiet for a long moment, and Loralee wondered whether it was time to slip back into her room.

"Merritt?"

"Yes?"

"If everybody was only on the SS *Minnow* for a three-hour tour, how come they all had so much luggage?"

Nobody spoke while Merritt made strangling noises. "That's a very good question. I've always wondered how the Professor could make a working radio out of bamboo but not fix a boat. Boggles the mind, really." Another pause. "You know, *Gilligan's Island* aired way before my time, so I think it's pretty cool that you and I both somehow discovered it and liked it enough to memorize the theme song."

"Yeah, sort of like we were a regular brother and sister, growing up watching the same show but in different houses."

"Something like that." The mattress creaked as Merritt shifted position. "Did I tell you that I used to be afraid of the dark, too?"

"You were?"

"You bet. That's why, when I heard you crying, I thought the night-light bulb had burned out. I remember that happened once when I was a little girl. I was staying with my grandmother and she told me that it was time I got over it. It's not that easy, though, is it?"

Loralee heard the rustle of Owen's head against his pillow as he shook his head.

"So I just slept with a flashlight under my sheets after that, and did so for a very long time."

"Do you still?" Owen asked.

"No. Because somewhere along the way I learned that even the darkest nights are full of light."

"Really?" Owen's voice was slurred with sleepiness.

"Really. Have you ever been outside after dark, when the stars and the moon are out? It's like a filter has slid across the sun. Everything's the same, except all the colors are different. And inside, after you turn off the lights, if you push your fear aside just long enough for your eyes to adjust to the

382

dark, you'll find that you can still see."

"But everything is in different colors," Owen repeated slowly, barely finishing the last word.

Merritt must have recognized it, too, because she stood.

"Merritt?"

"Yes, Owen?"

"You can unplug my Darth Vader night-light if you want."

"All right. But only if you're sure."

"I'm sure."

Merritt stood and leaned down to kiss Owen's forehead. "Good night, Rocky."

"Good night, Mary Ann," he said with a sleepy giggle.

"Why not Ginger? She had better hair."

"Okay. Good night, Ginger."

Loralee smiled to herself at the mention of the hair, thinking that Merritt might not be so hopeless after all, then quietly backed away from the room, pausing at the top of the staircase so she wouldn't be seen.

"Merritt?" Owen's voice slurred again as he called out to his sister.

She paused in the doorway where Loralee had been. "Yes?"

"Or you could leave it on. I'm only ten."

"True. Okay, then, I'll leave it on. Good night," she said again.

There was no response, only the assurance that Owen had worked through his fears with Merritt and had finally found sleep.

Loralee rushed down the stairs as quickly as she could in the dark in her long night-gown, not wanting to be seen by Merritt as they crossed paths to their rooms. She stood in the darkened foyer, opening her eyes wider. What Merritt had said was true — there *was* light. It came from the tall windows where the glow from the street-lights fell inside in ribbons of white. Loralee could see the shapes of the furniture that had become dear and familiar to her already, recognized the wallpaper on the wall trans-ferred from red and cream to shades of gray.

Her fingers itched to write down the words rushing to her head before she forgot them. *Even in the blackest darkness, there is always light shining somewhere.*

A sob rose in her throat, but she held it back. Someone was coming down the stairs, and she didn't want anybody to see her cry-ing. Not because she was embarrassed to cry — a good cry was healthy for everybody. It was just that she didn't think Owen or Merritt was ready to see it.

She tiptoed to the kitchen, grateful for once that she wasn't wearing her heels, then sat down at the table in the dark with her back to the door and began to cry softly into her hands.

The overhead light flickered on and Loralee glanced up in surprise, thinking just for a moment that the ancient wiring had finally gone haywire. Or that the ghosts she suspected lurked in the corners of the old house had decided to show themselves.

Instead she smelled the soft lemon scent of the hand lotion she'd given to Merritt when she'd noticed her cracked cuticles, and quickly rubbed her eyes with the heels of her hands.

"Are you all right?" Merritt asked.

"I'm fine. With all the time spent working in the garden, I think I've become sensitive to something out there. I can barely breathe, and my eyes and skin are so itchy that I couldn't sleep. I hope I didn't wake you."

Merritt moved into the kitchen and took a seat at the table opposite Loralee, giving her a full view of Loralee's face. Merritt quickly hid her surprise as she took in Loralee's puffy eyes and runny nose. "Those are some pretty bad allergies. Maybe you should take something before you head outside again."

Loralee nodded as she reached for a tissue from a box on the table and carefully dabbed at her eyes and blew her nose. "I will, thank you."

Merritt leaned back in her chair. "I suppose that was you I heard in the hallway upstairs while I was talking with Owen."

"Probably. Unless you think it might have been a ghost."

Merritt's face stilled. "There's no such thing." She sounded like a child trying to prove something wrong just by saying it.

"There's so much in this great big universe that we don't understand. But just because we don't understand something doesn't mean it doesn't exist. Kind of like love, don't you think? Many people never really experience it, but they still have faith that it's out there."

Merritt hugged her arms around her middle, something Loralee had seen people do on planes during bad turbulence.

Loralee leaned forward, feeling a bit like Dr. Phil during one of his TV shows. Except he always wore a suit and not a leopard-print peignoir. "You must miss your husband a lot."

The look in Merritt's eyes made Loralee sit back in a hurry. It took her a moment to recognize what she'd seen there. It was *fear.* But fear of what? Acknowledging how much she missed Cal? Or fear that the question would lead to another?

"Why did you say that?"

Loralee shrugged. "I'm usually pretty good at reading people and situations, but I get a lot of mixed signals from you about your husband, and to be honest, I just can't figure it out. Was he a lot like Gibbes?"

"No," Merritt answered without even pausing to think about it. Which meant she'd already been thinking about it a lot. "Except for their eyes and the color of their hair, they are nothing alike."

"I'm taking that as a good thing," Loralee said, bending forward to ease the pain in her abdomen.

"Not that it matters. Cal is gone, and Gibbes isn't a permanent fixture in my life."

Loralee considered her stepdaughter. "You know, if you married Gibbes, you wouldn't have to change the monograms on any of your towels or linens."

Merritt, whose legs had been crossed, jerked up so quickly her knee hit the underside of the table. "What are you talking about? I'm not marrying anybody — especially not Gibbes. I don't ever want to get married again. Marriage . . . it didn't suit me."

"Maybe it's because you just didn't marry the right man. It's pretty rare that a person gets it right on the first try. I was married once, before your daddy."

Merritt rubbed her knee as she looked at Loralee with surprise. "I didn't know that."

"I was still wet behind the ears — barely eighteen. We were married for about five seconds. Mama said I was making a mistake, which of course meant I had to go ahead and do it. And after the divorce I moved back in with Mama and she never once said, 'I told you so.' That's when she said that life is a lot like the interstate, where every exit is an entrance someplace else." Loralee smiled. "And she was right. My divorce made me see that I needed to make some changes, and that's when I decided I wanted to be a flight attendant. And if that hadn't happened, then I never would have met your daddy.

"So, see? Maybe it wasn't that marriage didn't suit you. Maybe you just weren't married to the right person."

"Are you not wearing any makeup?"

Loralee blinked at the abrupt change of subject. Robert had been that way, too — changing the subject when the current one no longer interested him. It must be a New England thing, because Southerners would talk a subject to death until it lay gasping and panting in the dust. And if it were an unpleasant one, they'd just end it with, "Bless your heart."

"No, I'm not — well, except for my tattooed eyebrows and eyeliner. My mama taught me that the first rule to having good skin was to always take your makeup off before you went to bed at night."

Merritt considered her for a moment. "You look pretty without it, you know. Although I think I need to change the bulbs in here — you look a little yellow. Why do you wear it?"

Loralee smiled her flight-attendant smile. "Because I like how it makes me feel — strong, powerful. Confident. It's like a man putting on a suit and tie, I guess, but more fun. You know us Southern girls are born with a makeup brush in one hand and a lipstick in the other."

Despite her best efforts, Merritt laughed, the sound bubbling out of her mouth.

"You should try it sometime," Loralee said.

"I wouldn't even know where to begin. My mother didn't wear makeup either."

Their eyes met in mutual surprise that Merritt's last sentence hadn't come out as an accusation.

Being careful not to push too much, Loralee said, "When you're ready, I'd be happy to give you a starter course." Her gaze dipped down to Merritt's shirt. "What are you wearing?"

Merritt looked down as if she'd forgotten what she'd slipped over her head only a few hours ago. "It's one of Cal's sweatshirts."

"Do you wear it to feel him close to you again?"

Merritt opened her mouth to speak, her lips moving as she thought about her answer.

"If you don't know for sure, then my guess is you wear it because you always have. Does it make you feel good? Or sexy? Or even like a girl?"

Merritt frowned. "It's something to sleep in. I don't need to feel anything but tired when I put it on."

It was Loralee's turn to look surprised. "Do you mean to say that after being married for seven years, it never occurred to you that what you wear to bed should make you feel something?"

Merritt squirmed in her seat. "Cal was away a lot at the firehouse, and it gets pretty cold in Maine. I needed to be warm, and this worked."

"It's not cold here." Loralee looked pointedly at her.

Merritt shrugged. "I don't have anything

else to sleep in — well, except for a football jersey. Besides, I roll the sleeves up so I'm not too warm."

"Well, we can certainly fix that," Loralee said, her mind racing in all sorts of directions, and she was happy to follow it down any one because then she didn't have to think about how bad she felt.

She stood and went to the freezer and yanked it open. Ice coated the surface like the fur on a winter hat. "Make sure your next freezer is self-defrosting. I've already taken an ice pick to this, but it doesn't seem to help."

Reaching in, she pulled out a gallon of ice cream and then retrieved the fudge sauce from the refrigerator. "And you need a microwave." She pulled out a small saucepan from one of the lower cabinets and placed it on top of the stove.

"What are you doing?" Merritt asked.

"I'm making you a chocolate sundae. Isn't that why you came down here?"

Merritt's face was exactly like Owen's when she caught him sneaking cookies from the cookie jar. She turned to tell Robert to look, forgetting once more that her husband wasn't there anymore to share parts of their day, to call attention to the funny things Owen did and said. He was gone, and she'd accepted it and had even learned to live with it. But that didn't mean she'd ever stop looking for him.

Merritt opened her mouth to deny it, but Loralee cut her off with a wave of the ice-cream scoop. "Owen has a sweet tooth the size of Texas, and it had to come from somewhere, because it didn't come from me." She placed three large scoops of ice cream in a bowl. As she poured a good amount of chocolate syrup into the sauce-pan, she said, "I'm a salty kind of person — I love chips and French fries and pretty much anything fried. Robert loved his desserts, that's for sure. He couldn't get enough of my red velvet cake — and Owen, too. I should make one for you. And if half of it is missing when I come down in the morning, I'll know I was right about you."

She adjusted the burner under the pan. "Only one burner works on this stove."

"Loralee?"

"Not that I'm trying to rush you into anything, but a kitchen is the heart of any home. I think once you get the kitchen exactly as you want it, you'll feel more at home here."

"Loralee?" Merritt's voice was insistent enough to make Loralee stop talking and turn to her stepdaughter.

"Yes?"

"Are you sure you're all right? It looks like you're crying."

Loralee touched her face and her fingers came away damp. "It's the allergies," she said, but didn't sound convincing even to her own ears.

"Come sit down, all right? I can make my own sundae."

Too tired to argue, Loralee switched places with Merritt, watching as she turned off the burner and poured the chocolate over the ice cream. "Do we have any candied cherries or caramel pecans?"

Loralee dabbed at her eyes with a tissue. "No, but I'll add them to the grocery list. Maybe some peanut-butter chips, too?"

"Oh, yes," Merritt said as she brought her sundae to the table and placed two spoons between them.

"No, thank you," Loralee said, her stomach already protesting at the sickly sweet smell of it. "And what's a 'pee-can'?"

Merritt paused with a brimming spoonful of ice cream and fudge sauce suspended in front of her mouth. "It's a nut. You know, like in pee-can pie. You're from the South — I'm sure you know what I'm talking about."

"I know what a 'puh-cahn' is. *That's* a nut

393

that you eat. A pee-can is something a soldier takes on maneuvers. If you're going to be living in the South, you need to know the difference."

Merritt smiled as she swallowed her first bite. "Well, no matter what you call them, they taste great with caramel sauce and poured on ice cream."

They sat in a comfortable silence while Merritt ate and Loralee studied her face for future makeup lessons. When Merritt was finished, she washed and dried her bowl and spoon, then put them away before pouring herself a tall glass of water to take upstairs.

"Aren't you coming up?" she asked as she stood by the doorway.

Loralee shook her head. "In a little while. Since your daddy died, I find that I can't sleep through the night anymore. I think I'll watch a little TV for a bit. Hopefully there will be something good on one of the three channels that have any reception."

"Good luck with that." Merritt paused in the doorway, almost swaying with indecision. "Thanks for the sundae."

"You're welcome." She stared into her stepdaughter's blue eyes, and saw her son's. "Thank you for letting Owen and me stay here."

Merritt gave a perfunctory nod. "Good

night, Loralee."

"Good night, Merritt."

She waited until Merritt's slow footsteps reached the top of the stairs, followed by the quiet click of her bedroom door closing. Then Loralee turned off the kitchen light and let herself out into the back garden.

The smell of rain hung heavy in the air, the cloud-covered sky above a moonless and starless dome of black. A storm-born breeze trickled into the garden, the sea-glass wind chimes waltzing in slow circles.

Loralee looked up at the sky, realizing that what Merritt had told Owen wasn't completely true — that sometimes the dark simply absorbed all the light you couldn't see, and you just had to have enough love and faith in your heart to trust that it was there.

She sat on the bench for a long time, her eyes dry as she studied the darkened sky even after the rain began to fall.

Chapter 20

Merritt

I fed the red and white checked material through the sewing machine, the pulsing needle like the mouth of a baby bird. My first two attempts had been disastrous, ending up with knotted thread and clumped fabric. Despite popular opinion, operating a sewing machine wasn't like riding a bicycle. The needle jammed again, pulling on the fabric, my foot lifting from the pedal a fraction of a minute too late to prevent another train wreck.

I knew part of the problem was my lack of concentration. Each inch of fabric, each tiny stitch, every whir of the motor reminded me of my grandmother. Not just of us sewing together, but of the joy we'd felt in creating something. Which brought to mind the letter she'd received, and the handkerchiefs, and how I'd never seen the sewing machine again after that day. I stared down at the knot of fabric bunched beneath the needle, but saw only bright red monograms on a white linen handkerchief.

"What are you making?"

I looked up at Owen and Maris, who'd approached without my being aware, and felt a little offended that they couldn't tell what it was. "A tablecloth."

"Or maybe a drop cloth?" Gibbes moved to stand behind the children, looking over their heads at the red and white disaster.

"Why are you here?" I asked, too annoyed to check my manners.

"It's good to see you, too. I rang the doorbell and Rocky let me in. I just saw my last patient of the day and figured now would be a good time to pick up all the recycling boxes." He indicated the sewing machine. "You need to hold the fabric with a really light touch — don't try to feed it into the needle. Slowly press the pedal to gently pull it forward and you just let the fabric move so it doesn't bunch. Makes it a lot easier."

I remembered my mother and grandmother both telling me the same thing: that I needed to slow down and focus. I sometimes wondered whether they would even recognize me now. Except for the decision to move to Beaufort, my life for the last decade had been a plodding and deliberate existence, every day planned to go unnoticed and unremarked.

Frustrated, I turned off the machine and slid back the chair. "And how would you know so much about sewing?"

Gibbes stepped back as I stood. "Everybody had to take home ec in high school. And shop. So I know how to use a needle and thread as well as a hammer and nail."

"I'm guessing the needle-and-thread thing works out great for you in your chosen profession."

"Yes, ma'am. And I've been told that I'm pretty handy with my tools, too."

Our eyes met as we both realized what he'd actually said.

He laughed, not looking embarrassed at all. "I'm sorry; I didn't mean it that way. Although I refuse to retract my statement."

I put a hand over my mouth, trying to hide my own laugh, and for a brief moment I thought he might actually be *flirting* with me. My laugh died quickly as I remembered that I wasn't the kind of woman men flirted with. At least, not according to Cal.

Flustered, I tried to gather the fabric to tuck it out of the way. I managed to do nothing more than bunch it up so that it would require ironing if and when I ever finished it, but at least I had time to allow my face to return to normal.

"Mrs. Heyward?"

"Yes, Maris?"

"Can you take us to the marina? Rocky says he hasn't been there yet."

"I, um . . . Will we need life jackets?"

"Not unless you're planning on getting on a boat or going swimming," Gibbes said, not exactly hiding his smile. "I think Maris and Owen just wanted to go look at the boats."

I looked at the wide and hopeful eyes of the children, trying desperately to think of an excuse to say no. I wanted to tell them that I'd already paid my dues by riding across the bridge and getting in a boat, but that sounded inadequate even to me. Turning to Owen, I asked, "Is it okay with your mother?"

"She's resting and I didn't want to bother her."

My usual annoyance that I felt when Loralee retreated to her room for a nap was nudged aside by worry. I remembered how tired she'd looked the previous night, and how she'd blamed her insomnia on her stuffy nose and itchy eyes due to allergies. Her explanations made sense, but when I thought of her streaming eyes, I couldn't completely shake off a sliver of doubt.

"Yes, let's let her sleep." I thought desperately for another excuse. "Did you clean up your LEGOs?"

"Sort of," Owen said. "Maris made a castle that looks like a horse stable with, like, one hundred horses that all have names and are owned by a princess. And I made a special cannon that can blow down the doors of the castle but not hurt any of the horses or people. It just blows doors off things."

"So we left them out so we could play with them again later," Maris completed, as if they were already an old married couple.

"There's water at the marina there, right?"

Owen and Maris both tried to hide their giggles behind their hands. "Yes," Owen explained. "The marina is where they keep the boats. In the water."

"I know that," I said. "What I meant is that I can't swim, and I don't think it's a good idea if I'm the only adult with the two of you —"

Gibbes interrupted. "If you wait until I get all those boxes of newspapers loaded into my truck, I'll go with you. I'm an excellent swimmer." He grinned like he knew exactly what I was thinking.

"Yes, yes!" The children hopped up and

down like jumping beans.

I looked at Gibbes, who just shrugged. "Looks like we're going to the marina, then."

We weren't going *in* the water or *on* it — just *near* it. Surely I could do that. "All right. Let me go grab a hat and some sunscreen for me and the children. I'll be right back."

When I reached my room, I caught my reflection in the mirror over the dressing table and for the first time in a while I actually looked at myself long enough to admit that I didn't like what I saw. The ill-fitting blouse and skirt were more than unflattering. They were the kinds of things invisible women wore. I'd worn these clothes and others just like them for years, throwing them on in the morning without thought. Even my own mother, who was as no-frills as mothers got, loved wearing the color blue and the way it made her eyes shine.

I leaned into the mirror, staring harder, remembering a favorite blue blouse I'd worn when I'd first met Cal, and again several times while we'd been dating. And how I didn't remember when I'd stopped wearing it and had moved into the uniform of a woman who didn't want to be noticed.

The flesh rose on the back of my neck as

the air conditioner whirred on, making me shiver as I imagined Cal watching me stare at myself in the mirror. *Never turn your back on a fire.* It was almost as if the words had been whispered in my ear. But instead of Cal's voice, it had been my own.

Quickly I unbuttoned my blouse and slipped out of the skirt, then pulled out the shorts and top I'd borrowed from Loralee that she'd apparently mistakenly returned to my room with my clean and folded laundry. I put them on, my only regret being that I had only my loafers for my feet.

I slathered on sunscreen, then grabbed my hat and the bottle of sunblock before heading downstairs. The recycling boxes had already been taken from the upstairs hallway, and I stopped to pick up a newspaper on the bottom step that must have fallen out.

I placed it on the hall table, planning on giving it to Gibbes, then followed the sound of Owen's voice to the kitchen. Gibbes and the two children sat at the table, the Battleship game box open, and Gibbes was reading the directions.

He stopped reading, then watched as I put sunscreen on Maris's face and arms and then Owen's. "All right," I said. "You guys ready?"

"You guys?" Maris's freckled nose scrunched up.

Gibbes returned the directions to the box and stood. "That's how our neighbors to the north say 'y'all.' Not as easy on the ears, but it gets the job done."

"Really?" I said. "I'll make many concessions to fit in, but I promise you that saying 'y'all' won't be one of them."

Gibbes pretended to look offended. "If I weren't a gentleman, I'd place a wager on that."

"And if I weren't a lady, I'd tell you how little I care about what you think."

"Spoken like a Southern lady already," Gibbes said as he ushered us out of the kitchen. "Before the end of the year you'll probably be claiming that crabbing is a sport and that the season between summer and winter is football."

I almost said that he wouldn't know, since I doubted we'd still be seeing each other by then, but I didn't. Not because I didn't think it was true, but because he was looking at me in a different way than he'd done when we'd first met. Seeing me not as Cal's unlikely wife, but somebody else. Anybody else.

We headed down Bay Street, crossing toward the water at the first light. The blue

403

sky offered no respite from the relentless sun, and I wondered how long it would take me to get used to the heat. The long Maine winters seemed very far away, like a fading dream upon waking. Lying in bed at night, I sometimes imagined the icy taste of snow on my tongue. But then I'd hear the wind chimes and it would be gone, replaced with the tang of salt air.

"Did you know that if humans had the same metabolism as a hummingbird, we'd have to eat a hundred and fifty thousand calories a day?" Owen directed this at nobody in particular, but I thought it was probably meant for Maris.

She wore her blue sparkly sunglasses again, and with her pixie face she looked like an adorable bug when she turned to look at Owen. "We have hummingbird feeders off of our back porch and the little birds swarm all over them. You should come see it."

He looked at me as if Maris had suddenly gone off script.

"Sounds like fun," I interceded.

It was a weekday, so only a few boats were out on the water, the rest docked, bobbing up and down like babies rocked by the waves. I felt none of my fear there, the sun and heat making it easy to forget an icy storm and the freezing water beneath a bridge far away.

It was only when I felt my scar, or saw it when looking in a mirror, or when I found myself missing my mother, that I remembered. But each time the pain lessened, the scar tissue thickening. I'd overheard Loralee telling Owen that every time we remembered something, we weren't remembering the event itself but the last time we'd remembered it. It was our way of creating filters between our past and present, creating what we chose to recall and what we'd rather forget. I hoped she was right. After knowing her for even such a short time, I'd begun to suspect that she was probably right about a lot of things.

It was ebb tide, the pluff mud exposed beyond the small seawall at the side of the marina's parking lot. We walked along the edge, examining the mud and grass for signs of life.

At first glance it seemed still, the grass wilting in the direct onslaught of the sun, the puckered mud thirsting for water. Maris got down on her haunches, her tanned arms around her knees, and the rest of us followed. A flash of movement caught our attention as a tiny crab scrambled sideways from his hiding place by a rock to the thick forest of grass. One of his claws was more than twice the size of the other one, giving him a comic appearance. His lopsided appendages didn't seem to hinder his movement, and he'd disappeared into the marsh within seconds.

"That's a fiddler crab," Maris announced. "Because his big claw makes him look like he's playing a fiddle."

Not to be outdone, Owen said, "Only the male fiddler crabs have the big claw, and if they lose the big one in a fight with another male, the smaller one swells up, and a little one grows where the big one used to be. They wave them around during mating season to attract females to their burrows so they can make baby fiddler crabs. That makes no sense to me, but that's what it says in the science book I found in my room." Owen pushed his glasses up on his nose.

Gibbes nudged me, but I didn't dare look at him, because I was pretty sure I'd laugh hard enough to fall over into the mud. Instead we stayed where we were, looking for signs of life. "It's amazing," I said, watching the tiny crabs scuttle across the mud, their oddly shaped eyes watching us warily.

"What is?" asked Gibbes. "The fact that

female fiddler crabs find oversize claws attractive?"

I pierced him with my "museum curator" look, which I'd once used on busloads of schoolchildren. Looking back at the mud, I said, "No. That something that seems so lifeless is actually teeming with life. If Owen hadn't been telling me all that he's learned about the marsh mud, I would have walked by without really looking."

Gibbes stood, his eyes traveling across the water to the sound. "I didn't figure that out until I got to med school."

"What? That fiddler crabs have odd mating rituals?" I said it before I could think twice.

I was rewarded with a smile that made me look away. "No. That we miss a lot when we're not paying attention. That things aren't always as they appear to be."

I stood to face him, the salt air breathing to life something I hadn't felt in years. Something that felt a lot like courage, but couldn't be. I wasn't brave. Or strong. I just seemed to have a knack for landing on my feet.

"Like what?" I asked, meeting his eyes although I wanted to turn away.

"Gibbes Heyward? Is that you?"

We both turned at the sound of a woman's

voice. A boat filled with people and loud music was approaching the dock closest to the parking lot. The man behind the steering wheel lifted a beer can in our direction as a curvy redhead wearing what could only be described as Daisy Dukes and a bikini top easily hopped out of the boat, landing barefoot on the dock, then jogged her way toward us. I turned to watch the kids, reminding them to stay on the wall and out of the mud, unwilling to be a witness to a wardrobe malfunction that seemed a foregone conclusion.

"It is you," she said, whipping her long hair from her shoulders in case we'd missed a view of her cleavage as she'd run. "You haven't changed a bit, Gibbes." She blinked heavily mascaraed lashes at him. Close up, I could tell that she was much older than I'd originally thought, more likely in her early forties than the twenty-something I'd thought her to be from her clothing. "Don't you remember me?" She smelled like a mixture of cigarettes, coconut oil, and sweat, and I stepped back out of range.

A flash of recognition swept across Gibbes's face, or maybe it was something else. Either way, he definitely knew who she was. "Sandy? Sandy Beach?"

"That's your name for real?" Maris asked,

looking up at the stranger through her sunglasses.

"The one and only!" She threw her arms around Gibbes's neck, pressing her considerable chest against his while his hands did a frantic search to figure out a safe place to land.

Gently he put his hands on her shoulders and pushed her back. "It's been a while."

"It has. I just moved back to South Carolina — been living in Vero Beach the last ten years or so." She waggled her left hand. "Got divorced and decided it was time I come home. Florida was too small a place for me and my ex, if you know what I mean."

I tousled Owen's hair to distract him so he'd close his mouth and stop staring at the woman's tattoo, which looked like a dragon perched on her shoulder, its pointed tail reaching toward her cleavage like a directional arrow.

She looked at me with interest, her gaze dropping to the two children, who were busy staring back like spectators at a zoo. "Is this your wife and kids?"

"No," we both said simultaneously.

"I'm Merritt Heyward, Gibbes's sister-in-law. And this is my half brother, Owen, and his friend Maris."

She smiled at the children, her teeth yellowed with nicotine, before moving her gaze back to me. "Unless there's another brother I don't know about, I'm guessing you're married to Cal?"

As if sensing my unease, Gibbes stepped in. "Cal passed recently, and Merritt has inherited our grandmother's house."

"I'm sorry to hear that." She looked at me again with renewed interest, or what I thought was interest. But there was something else in her eyes that I couldn't identify. She took in my loafers and the modest shorts, lingering briefly on the knit top before settling on my straw hat. "You don't seem his type." Deep creases formed between her brows. "How long were you married?"

I wanted to tell her that it was none of her business. Instead I lifted my chin. "Seven years."

"Seven years?"

I couldn't imagine her sounding more surprised if I'd said we'd had seven children or that I was ninety years old.

She leaned forward, studying me. "You must be a lot stronger than you look, then. I dated him for almost a year and it almost killed me." She stepped back, throwing a glance at Gibbes. "I should have gone for this one instead, but he was just a kid and I didn't want to be one of those women, if you know what I mean." She nodded her head in the direction of the children just in case we weren't sure why she was censoring herself. "Not that it mattered, really. Us girls like the bad boys, don't we?"

"No, not all of us."

She tightened her mouth, accentuating the brackets formed by wrinkles on each side of her face. "Yeah, well, I just figured you did, because you married Cal." She coughed a smoker's cough, taking a moment to catch her breath. "It took everything I had to break up with him — even moved to Florida just to make sure there was enough distance between us. But I figured I was lucky to get away with just a broken heart instead of something else."

It felt like somebody was squeezing me around the middle, stopping my heart and my breath at the same time.

"Sandy? Are you coming? Joe's got a keg at his house — we're moving the party there." The group from the boat was clustered in front of two pickup trucks in the parking lot, carrying coolers and brightly colored beach towels, looking very hot and impatient.

She nodded, then turned back to us.

411

"Gotta go — but it was great running into you, Gibbes. And meeting you," she said to me. Her eyes were a dull green, as if the light had stopped penetrating them years ago.

"You, too," I said, managing a small smile. We watched her walk toward the group, tiptoeing her way across the hot asphalt.

"I wouldn't pay her too much attention," Gibbes said. "There's a reason they used to call her 'Sandy the Public Beach.' " Even though his words had been meant to comfort me, the storm brewing in his eyes matched my own uneasiness.

"Owen, I'm so sorry, but I'm not feeling well — it must be the heat. I need to go back right now. We'll return another time, okay?"

Owen masked his disappointment quickly. "All right. Maybe tomorrow?"

"Maybe." I walked quickly, unaware of the sun beating down on us or the sweat trickling down my face and back. As soon as I got inside the house, I tore off my hat, then stood in the front parlor between the two air-conditioning units, lifting my hair off of my neck, wishing the whir of the appliances could erase the woman's voice from my head. *I was lucky to get away with just a broken heart instead of something else.*

The children rushed in behind me, followed by Gibbes, who shut the door. I kept my eyes closed, hoping they'd keep going.

"Did you save this for me?" Owen said behind me.

Reluctantly I opened my eyes and saw him holding up the newspaper I'd found on the stairs and left on the hall table.

"I think it fell out of the recycling box. Why don't you give it to Dr. Heyward?"

"But it has a picture of that plane on it, and I've been keeping those."

Gibbes took the newspaper and flipped it over to read. After a moment he lifted his eyes to meet mine. "It's about the crash. In 1955." He turned to Owen. "Did you say you have more of these?"

Owen nodded. "Yeah. Mama said it was okay with you if I kept a few because they had stuff about planes."

"Have you read them all yet?"

Owen shook his head. "No, sir."

"Can I borrow them? I promise I'll bring them back to you when I'm done."

"Sure. I'll go get them." He took off up the stairs, his tread light as he crossed the hall upstairs to his bedroom.

"This is odd," Gibbes said.

I turned toward him. "What is?"

"The plane was on its way from LaGuar-

413

dia to Miami when it exploded over Beaufort."

"I know — that's what Deborah told us. Which makes sense, seeing as how, without even looking at a map, I can see that Beaufort would be on its flight path."

He lowered the newspaper, then folded it in half. "But that's not where it originated. It was only on a stopover at LaGuardia, where it was delayed for two hours. It started farther north."

For a moment I imagined I could smell the scent of smoldering fire, of hot ashes falling like rain. *Never let the fire get behind you.* "Where?" I asked.

"Bangor. Bangor, Maine."

I blinked several times, trying to get my thoughts in order, hoping to find something to say about coincidences and the world being a very small place. But my thoughts ran all the way up to the attic room, to the plane model with forty-nine dead passengers and crew representing a plane from my hometown that had crashed in Beaufort, South Carolina. As incongruous as it seemed, I couldn't help but think of Cal's favorite phrase when talking about the causes of various fires. *There's no such thing as accidents.*

I looked up and met Gibbes's eyes, and

knew without a doubt that he'd heard Cal say that, too, and that neither one of us believed in coincidence.

CHAPTER 21

Edith
December 1977

The house carried the scent of pine and cinnamon, owing completely to Cecelia's decorating skills. Garlands artfully wrapped the banister, held in position with oversize red velvet bows, and festooned with pinecones sparkling under a dusting of frosty-white paint.

The enormous Christmas tree in the middle of the foyer reached almost to the ceiling, and C.J. had not been happy about having to cut off part of the trunk so Cecelia could put the gold star at the top. It had been a first Christmas gift from her parents two months after her wedding to C.J., which was most likely the reason for her insistence that it be put on the top of the tree, much as it was the cause for his reluctance.

Deck the halls with boughs of holly . . .

Christmas music sang out from the large stereo console in the parlor as Edith touched one of the beautiful gold and red glass ornaments, the surface reflecting the large colored bulbs that wound through all of the branches — another sore spot for C.J. He would have been happy with a single strand, but had been outvoted by his wife and mother. He'd laughed when Cecelia said that, but there had been a look in his eyes that made Edith worry, an expression that made him appear too much like his father.

Cal began to cry in his room, screaming like he always did when he awakened. Edith paused to see whether Cecilia would go get him. She and C.J. were in their bedroom — the one that had once been Edith's before her son's marriage and his request to have the larger room for himself and his new bride.

Edith had heard arguing behind the closed door a little while before, which was the reason she'd put the Christmas music eight-track on the stereo, hoping to shut out their voices. She'd still been able to hear them, making her wonder whether the old house had absorbed the sound of arguing through generations, playing the same sound track over and over. She still held out hope that Cecelia would be different, that her daughter-in-law would be the one to break the pattern. But since Cal's birth nearly four years earlier, Edith had found herself clinging to that hope as precariously as a sand castle clung to shore.

"Mama!" Cal screamed.

The bedroom door remained shut, so Edith began climbing the steps slowly, hoping her son or daughter-in-law would hear their son before she reached him. It wasn't because she didn't want to be with Cal. She loved her grandson. From the first moment she'd held him and seen his mother's amber-colored eyes, she'd harbored the belief that he was his mother's son. But lately she'd begun to see chinks in her firm beliefs, and the more time she spent with Cal, the more evidence to the contrary she discovered.

She waited outside the little boy's room, listening to the rhythmic thumping against the wall and the squeak of the bedsprings before gently opening the door. He stopped when he spotted her, then sat in the middle of his toddler bed, his eyes puffy from sleep, a plastic yellow and blue shape-sorter ball at the foot of the bed. Several yellow plastic shapes were scattered on the floor, far enough from the bed that they'd most likely been thrown.

He looked at her with disconsolate eyes as she approached and sat on the side of the bed. She ran her hand through his fine, sandy-colored hair, sticky with sleep sweat. He was big for his age, just like C.J. had been, with thick, broad shoulders and heavy legs. C.J. liked to say he was born a USC linebacker, but Edith hadn't had the heart to tell him that a parent's dream for his child rarely came to fruition just from wishing.

She leaned down and kissed his forehead, and he sighed as if giving up his effort to fight whatever battle he seemed to have been waging since birth.

"Did you have a good nap, sweetheart?"

He threw himself down on the bed, kicking the plastic ball hard with his foot. "I don't like that."

Edith retrieved the toy and examined it. It was a baby toy, one that Cal hadn't allowed her to pack away with all of the other infant and toddler toys when they took down the crib and brought in his new big-boy bed. Two incorrect shapes had been forced into the wrong holes and were stuck. She tugged on each one in turn, but neither would budge. She reached for one of the shapes on the floor and lifted it to show Cal. "This is a triangle — see? It's got three sides." She

held up the toy. "Then you find the opening that is also a triangle, and it fits right
in." She gave the shape to the little boy,
careful to make sure that it was correctly
positioned.

"I want it to go there," he said, pointing
to a rectangular opening near the top. "It's
yellow."

She'd already opened her mouth to correct him, then stopped. The top half of the
ball was yellow. And to Cal it made sense
that all the yellow pieces should go through
the yellow holes regardless of whether
they'd fit.

"I see," she said, putting the toy aside.
Since he was an infant, he'd had a clear
view of the world and the way it should
work. If his bottle was too warm or not
warm enough, he wouldn't drink it. If his
shoelaces were uneven, he'd throw a fit until
the shoes were removed and retied. If you
told him you would take him for a walk after
his nap and you forgot, he'd remind you
and make you go even if it was pouring rain
outside.

It worried Edith, and not just because C.J.
had been the same way as a boy, but because
it made the world a difficult place to live in
if your view of it was always black-and-white
— a difficult place for those who believed

that, and for those who had the misfortune to love them.

Edith wanted to think that his strong personality had to do with the fact that he was an only child like his father, and wondered whether having a little brother or sister would help him to see that all things didn't revolve around him, that sometimes your favorite shorts weren't clean yet or your potatoes touched the Brussels sprouts on your plate. Cecelia had tried twice before, miscarrying each time, the last just three weeks earlier. She'd tripped and fallen down the stairs. She'd been far enough along that the doctors had been able to tell that it had been a little girl. Cecelia had taken it well, her eyes dry when they'd brought her home, and she'd immediately gone upstairs and closed the nursery door. It was almost as if, Edith thought, she'd become only a shadow of the bright, pretty girl she'd been when C.J. had first carried her across the threshold.

"I want to play fire truck," Cal said, pointing a chubby finger toward his favorite toy, a large, bright red fire truck with a working siren and a ladder that went up and down.

Edith had mentioned the previous day that she'd play fire truck with him soon, and to him that meant right then. She thought of the Christmas presents she still needed to wrap, and her dress for the party that night, which she still needed to iron. And the seating assignments from the plane, which she'd recently acquired through her friendship with a local newspaper journalist and that offered her so many more opportunities for further study of the crash. But Cal would scream until she'd played with him, so it wasn't as if she really had a choice anyway.

"All right," she said, standing up and lifting him from the bed. She helped him put on the big plastic fire chief helmet, then knelt on the floor next to the truck and waited for Cal to give her orders. He was always the fire chief, and she a firefighter who had to do everything he asked. It was her job to make the Lincoln Log structures that would go up in flames, but it was up to Cal to come up with the reason for the fire. He was very good at placing blame: The candle was left where the dog's tail could knock it over; the man with the cigarette didn't put it out all the way and the garbage caught on fire.

Edith had no idea where his scenarios came from, only that C.J. thought it funny when he read accident reports from the newspaper out loud at the breakfast table, each story concluding with one of them shouting out who was to blame. The only benefit to that, Edith had found, was that Cal had a deep-seated belief that there were no such things as accidents, just people not paying attention.

"Where are your little people?" she asked.

He pointed to a LEGO house they'd made together with enough bedrooms to house the small dolls she'd made for him. He hadn't liked the Fisher Price people because they didn't look real, with no arms, and legs and hair that came off. He liked the dolls Grandma Edith made, because they had painted faces and wore real clothes and had hair that moved. It wasn't that he lacked imagination; it was just the way things *should* be.

"What's burning?" Edith asked.

"A house. Somebody had real candles on the Christmas tree and it got burnt down."

Edith remembered the story from the Sunday paper. A family of six had perished because the mother had wanted to give her own mother a reminder of the Christmases of her childhood.

"All right. Where is everybody when the fire starts?"

He studied the large LEGO house, pointing out all the places the dolls should be.

"Are you going to save everybody?"

He nodded, his face serious. Despite his rather fatalistic outlook toward the cause of the fires he and his imaginary crew fought to extinguish, it was always his goal to save every life. It was the right order of things, the way he saw how to make all the pieces fit together. Edith took a great deal of consolation from this, from his clear knowledge of right and wrong. Surely this meant that despite everything else, he might still find his way in the world.

They played for nearly half an hour — or, rather, Cal played while Edith followed instructions. This was the part of her grandson she enjoyed most, when he was absorbed in his role-playing and he was happy because he could control the miniature world he'd created. His chubby fingers were surprisingly agile at manipulating the small levers on the fire truck and moving the doll-people down the fire ladder. *He'll be fine.* Edith found herself thinking that often, ever since she'd first gone to his crib when he'd been just an infant and found that the reason for his high-pitched crying was that a corner of his blanket had exposed one tiny foot.

"Oops."

Edith paused in her efforts to tie the laces

on the older sister's shoes (Cal had informed her that the sister was going to have a burned leg because she'd stopped to tie her shoes instead of running to safety), and focused on Cal.

Cal held the mother and father dolls in both hands at the top of the staircase. The plastic LEGO flames were still downstairs, where the fire had started in a fireplace that hadn't been properly banked for the night, blocking the front door. Before Edith could ask how they were going to escape, Cal lifted the man's arms and shoved the woman, making her topple down the stairs until she lay facedown on the black and white tiled foyer floor.

"Oops," he said again, but in the deep voice of the father. "It was an accident," he said again, the low rumble of that voice coming from a child sending chills up Edith's spine.

But there are no such things as accidents, she wanted to say. Her thoughts paralyzed her, thoughts that no mother should have about her children. Thoughts that could lead to very dangerous places.

Leaning close to her grandson, she said, "It wasn't really an accident, was it?"

He kept his head down and shook it. "She made the man angry. That's why he pushed her." His voice was small and childlike and choked with tears.

Edith swallowed. "Even when we're angry, we use our words and not our hands, remember?"

Cal nodded slowly. "But sometimes when the man gets mad he forgets to use his words and instead does bad things." He looked up at her and his eyes were bright with tears. "Can you fix her?"

Edith picked up the doll. Even without lifting the nightgown, she could feel the neck lolling loosely in her palm, and one arm was bent in a way it shouldn't have been. "Yes," Edith said, already standing, needing to get out of that room as soon as possible. Wanting to circumvent a tantrum for ending their play session so suddenly, she said, "I'll let you come up to my workroom to watch me work while I fix her." She leaned forward, looking into his eyes. "But it will have to be our secret."

She saw his need for rules and structure battling with his desire to see what went on up in her attic workroom, a place he'd been forbidden since he was old enough to walk.

"Can you do that, Cal? Can you keep a secret?"

"Yes," he said quickly. As if he'd been

asked that before and already knew the answer.

A door slammed in the hallway, and they were both silent as they listened to C.J.'s heavy tread pass their door, then jog down the stairs before crossing the house toward the kitchen. A minute later, C.J.'s car sped out of the garage and down the drive, its tires crunching on the oyster-shell driveway.

Edith slipped the doll into her pocket. "Let's clean up first, all right? And when your mother goes out to the beauty parlor later we'll go upstairs."

He regarded her with a serious face. "Okay."

Edith began making the bed while Cal carefully tucked his dolls back into their beds and parked the truck where it belonged next to the LEGO fire station. They were almost finished when the bedroom door slowly opened and Cecelia stuck her head inside.

"Oh, hello, little man. I thought you were still sleeping."

"Mama!" Cal ran to her with arms outstretched, gripping her tightly around her legs.

Cecelia bent to hug him, their hair blending together. When his father was around, he was much less demonstrative toward his mother, but Edith sensed that their bond went beyond mother and son. Sometimes, it seemed to Edith, it was more about just the two of them in a two-person boat, where they decided how fast and where to go, and there was no room for anybody else. Except when C.J. was around, and his physical similarity to his son seemed to meld them together to form a single person instead of just a team.

"We were playing fire truck," Edith explained, glad the doll was hidden in the pocket of her housedress. She noticed that Cecelia was wearing the emerald green cashmere turtleneck sweater C.J. had given her on her last birthday, but the neck was pulled up as high as it could go instead of being folded over, hiding as much skin as possible.

Cal jumped with his hands held up, wanting his mother to lift him. Cecelia looked too thin and weary and certainly not strong enough to lift her son, but telling her not to would have been fruitless. She bent down and winced only a little as she lifted Cal to her hip.

"Mama, where's your necklace?"

Before Cal was born, C.J. had bought a gold locket for Cecelia and had cut a lock of his own hair to put inside. Only Edith knew that Cecelia had replaced it with a lock of the baby's hair, and she wore it against her heart almost every day.

Before she could protest, Cal was pulling at the neck of her sweater, looking for the chain. Cecelia stopped him, but not before Edith saw the finger-size bruises on the side of her neck, dark spots that looked like insects marching up from her chest.

Edith gasped before she could stop herself, causing both Cecelia and Cal to turn to her. Her daughter-in-law gave a quick shake of her head, and Edith dropped her hand from her own neck and forced a smile.

Reaching for her grandson, she said, "Let's go bake some cookies so when your mama gets back from having her hair done, we can have a nice snack together."

"I've decided to do my hair for the party myself."

Cecelia smiled, and Edith caught the scent of alcohol on her breath, as thin and wispy as smoke from a hidden fire. Of course she couldn't have her hair done. Because then she'd have to remove the sweater.

"Oh, all right. I'll be happy to watch Cal for you." She smiled the same smile others had given her all those years of her own marriage, and she was ashamed. Not because she'd raised a son who was as brutal as his father, but because she had learned nothing and was still as ignorant as those well-meaning people who chose to look past the bruises and see only what they wanted to. To think what they wanted to. To believe they understood and placed blame accordingly.

"Thank you, Edith," Cecelia said as she relinquished her son.

Edith tried to prop the boy on her hip, but he was too big and he slid back to the floor. He looked up at her with his mother's eyes and Edith felt the oddest urge to cry. He didn't break eye contact until she'd given him a little nod, knowing he was waiting for her to acknowledge her promise to take him up to the attic.

Cecelia paused in the doorway, her lips parted slightly, as if the words waited on her tongue. Edith stepped forward, wanting to meet her halfway, to prove that she wasn't the coward she knew herself to be. And suddenly she saw the face of the letter writer, the woman who'd written the word *Beloved* on a folded letter to her husband and tucked it neatly inside his suitcase. The face of the woman Edith had imagined dozens of times, waiting by a telephone for news. Waiting for the sound of her husband's footfall outside the door. And the face Edith saw was Cecelia's.

"Let me help you," Edith said softly, the words floating between them like petals. They could be caught, or allowed to fall to the ground.

Their eyes met, yet to Edith it seemed they were standing very far apart, their lives connected yet separated by an invisible barrier that neither one of them knew how to break through.

Finally Cecelia's lips closed and she swallowed. "I don't need any help. Everything's fine."

Relief and shame flooded Edith, making her want to beg Cecilia to let her help at the same time she wanted to pretend that she hadn't seen the marks on her neck. She felt the absurd need to go talk to the statue of Saint Michael in her garden, to ask him for protection. And forgiveness.

"Grandma, I'm hungry." Cal pulled on her arm, and Edith looked at him gratefully.

"All right, sweetheart. Let's get out of your mother's way so she can get her hair done for the party."

Cecelia ruffled Cal's hair as they walked past her. "I love you, baby," she said.

"I love you, too, Mama," Cal answered automatically as he followed Edith to the hallway and down the stairs and into the

431

kitchen.

Have a holly jolly Christmas . . . The thin strains of music seeped under the kitchen door. Edith's purse sat on the counter, and inside it was a copy of the passenger list she'd finally managed to obtain from the police chief — one more piece to a puzzle that seemed to have an infinite number of pieces. She took some consolation in the fact that she'd already figured out so much about the plane and the crash, much more than the police had. They still thought it had been an accident.

She reached into a drawer and pulled out a cigarette and lighter, taking a drag until she could feel the nicotine replacing her doubts. She hoped she could use the passenger list to determine who the letter writer had been, maybe reach out to her in ways Edith hadn't been able to with her own daughter-in-law. Maybe there was justice in the world, perhaps even a divine reason the suitcase had fallen in her garden.

Edith opened the refrigerator and stared inside. She wondered how Cal's clear vision of justice would interpret her actions, how judges and lawyers would argue against the biblical "eye for an eye" method of righteousness. It was too early to decide, anyway. She knew little more at this point than that the crash hadn't been an accident, and that the anonymous letter writer knew it, too.

Edith took another drag on her cigarette and began pulling out the ingredients to make cookies, seeing the bold black letters on the letter each time she opened the refrigerator door. *Beloved.*

Chapter 22

Loralee

"Remind me again why we're doing this?" Merritt slapped another mosquito on her arm, her face red with heat under the floppy brim of her straw hat. She stood inside the towering arches and columned brick walls of the old Sheldon church ruins, the missing roof and doors making it no less grand than before the fire that had destroyed it.

√ Loralee looked up at the open sky, wondering whether prayers might get to heaven faster without interference from a roof. "It's important that children don't forget everything over the summer that they learned in school the previous year. And field trips like this make history come alive. It's so much more fun and interesting than reading about it in a book."

Merritt slapped at her ankle and glared up at Loralee. "Yes, so much more fun."

Loralee turned away to hide her smile.

She'd doubted Merritt would enjoy today's outing, but she'd been sure she would come once Loralee asked. When they'd managed to coerce Merritt onto the boat ride through the marsh, Loralee had realized that Merritt's usual motivation was not to disappoint anybody. She just wasn't sure whether she'd been that way as a girl, or it was something she'd learned during her marriage.

Owen turned from where he'd been studying the charred bricks on a segment of the wall, his backpack loaded with waxed-paper rolls and gold and silver crayons. "This place is so cool. Is it haunted?"

"There's no such thing," Merritt said quickly.

That was the second time Loralee had heard Merritt say that, making her think about what she was so afraid of. Or maybe Loralee already knew. *It's not only ghosts who haunt us. Our memories follow us through life, surprising us now and again when we are forced to turn around and look behind us.* She'd written that on the back of a drugstore receipt as she'd waited in line at the pharmacy, reminding herself that she still needed to transfer it into her pink journal.

"Yes, there is," Owen said. "Maris says there's an old man at the stables where she rides who rattles the horse harnesses in the middle of the night."

Merritt straightened from scratching at her calves. "Then how does anybody know that if it only happens in the middle of the night? Aren't people usually asleep? Seems to me somebody made up the story to keep burglars away."

Owen considered this. "You might have a point."

Loralee stared at the two of them, wondering whether she was the only one who saw how similar they were in the way they viewed the world. How much like Robert they were.

"There are some really old graves over there," Owen said, tramping across the tall grass and through what might have once been a window. "Can I do a rubbing now?"

"Not yet," said Loralee. "Not until you tell me the significance of this building. Did you read the historical marker near the road?"

Owen and Merritt shook their heads in unison, and if Loralee hadn't been so exasperated, she would have laughed. "The original church was built in 1745, but was burned by the British during the revolution in 1779. It was rebuilt, only to be burned again in 1865."

Merritt stood with her hands on her hips

as she studied the shifting shadows on the old brick walls made by the branches of encroaching oak trees and their sweeping shawls of moss. It seemed to Loralee as if the oaks had grown close to the church over the years to protect it with their long arms, like a mother shielding her child.

"Who burned it in 1865?" Merritt asked.

"The damned Yankees," Loralee said, trying not to grin.

"Really, Loralee?" Despite her trying to look stern, Merritt's lips trembled as they fought a smile. "Not just the Yankees, but 'damned' ones?"

"Daddy said that the only time I was ever to use the word *damned* was in front of the word *Yankees*. But I think he meant the baseball team," Owen pointed out.

Loralee smiled at her son. "Yes, well, and when people talk about General Sherman's march to the sea, they're expected to use it, too. It was his troops who burned the church, although, as you can see, the exterior walls refused to fall." She lifted her face to the sun, feeling its warmth on her bare skin. "I like that, how even a fire couldn't completely destroy this place. I think it's still beautiful. Maybe even more so, because you can see its scars. It tells you the story of where it's been."

Merritt stared at her for a long moment, as if she wanted to say something. Instead she slapped at another mosquito on her leg.

Loralee shook her head. "You were the one who insisted on wearing a skirt instead of the nice pair of jeans I gave you. I'll give you some calamine lotion later, but don't expect any sympathy."

"They were too tight. I couldn't wear those out in public."

"Oh, honey, they fit you real good. You've got such a cute figure, and it's not a sin to show it off. Whoever told you that you look better in the clothes you've got had something wrong in their heads or needed to have their eyes examined. Or maybe both."

She'd said it as a joke, but Merritt's face seemed to close in on itself, like a person pulling the blinds on a window. She turned without a word and headed toward the old cemetery behind the ruins, bending over to examine one of the stones, a stone where Loralee could see that all the words had been washed away by time.

Loralee began walking toward her, wanting to know more, to find out what had happened to the Merritt whom Robert had talked so much about. Loralee was usually a lot more restrained, especially with people like Merritt, who created an imaginary bubble around them at all times, but she didn't have time for gentle persuasion.

She stopped suddenly, a groan making its way halfway up her throat. She pressed down on her abdomen, willing the ache to go away, hoping it was something she'd eaten for breakfast that wasn't agreeing with her. Her hand kneaded the spot as she took deep breaths. Remembering what her mama had told her, she made her mouth smile and waited. *Smiling makes everything seem better, and makes other people think you're up to something.* She wasn't sure that was going in her journal, not completely convinced that the first part was true.

"Mama? Are you okay?"

"Yes, baby. I'm fine. Just a stitch in my side. Let's go find a good stone with lots of words and maybe a picture for you to work on."

With deep breaths, she followed Owen into the cemetery, where old and new stones seemed to be arranged in a haphazard pattern, like a gambler's dice that had been tossed on the sandy soil.

"Why is Merritt staring at that empty stone?" Owen asked quietly.

Loralee bent over, trying to ease the pain, pretending to study the dates on the stone in front of her, much as Merritt was doing.

439

"Because she's working out something in her head. Just because somebody's being quiet doesn't mean they don't have something to say."

"Are you going to write that in your journal?" Owen asked.

Loralee took off his glasses and cleaned them on the edge of her blouse. "Yes, I expect I will."

She placed the glasses back on his nose and watched him dash off toward two large aboveground tombs. One had the roots of a giant oak nudging the base of it, as if in a contest to see which one could claim the ground the longest. Loralee was about to point it out to Owen when she felt a sharp pain, taking her breath away.

"Loralee?"

Merritt's face seemed blurred.

"What's wrong?"

She swallowed the saliva pooling in her mouth. "I might have food poisoning. If I could just sit down . . ." She slid to the ground, leaning against the tombstone of a woman who'd died in 1832.

"Mama? Are there dead people in here?" Owen gently patted the horizontal stone over one of the large tombs.

After a quick glance at Loralee, Merritt answered, "Yes. But if they're really old, I imagine they've all turned to dust by now."

"Can I do the wax rubbing on one of these?"

"Yes. But try to be fast, okay? Your mother isn't feeling well."

Loralee raised her hand in the air. "It's all right, Owen. I'll be fine after I rest a minute. Take your time."

After a worried glance at his mother, Owen pulled out the supplies he needed from his backpack and got started.

Merritt frowned down at her. "Are you sure you'll be fine? You don't look well."

Loralee could feel the sweat beading on her forehead. "If you're going to be a proper Southerner, you've got to work on your conversational skills. I know I probably look like I've been rode hard and put up wet — or worse. You just need to learn how to say, 'Bless your heart,' when you tell somebody they don't look well, or they won't take you seriously."

Merritt blinked at her a couple of times. "You look like you've been dragged for miles through the swamp and hit a few stumps, bless your heart."

Loralee managed a smile. "Not bad."

"Do you need some water? We've got those bottles in the cooler in your car."

Loralee shook her head, then wished she

hadn't. "No. I just need to rest a bit. I wish I hadn't forgotten my purse — I have a delicate stomach, and I always have pills in there for this kind of thing." She paused, catching her breath. "I should be good to go by the time Owen is done." She swallowed, forcing down the nausea. "He takes a little longer than most trying to get his wax crayon over every crevice, like the little perfectionist he is. He gets that from his daddy."

Merritt's face lit up with a smile, a sudden unplanned one that showed a dimple in her left cheek. It was the first time Loralee had seen it, and it made her feel a little better. She pointed at Merritt's face. "Owen has a dimple there, too. The boys in his class used to tease him, so he tries really hard to hide it now, but every once in a while it comes out. I think it's pretty cute."

Merritt nodded, her smile fading. "Something else I guess we got from our dad. Mother used to love it, too. When I was little she would tickle me just so she could see it."

Loralee shifted, pressing the side of her face against the cool stone, grateful for the shade from the gnarled trees above them. She wondered whether the woman buried beneath her thanked the trees on a daily basis for their shelter. Or whether, after death, any of it really mattered at all.

Closing her eyes, she thought of her mother and her long illness. It had always seemed to Loralee that death had come to Desiree in pieces, taking parts of her until there was nothing left but one last breath. She found herself thinking of Desiree more and more lately, especially about how she hadn't been afraid at the end. Loralee knew her mother hadn't had an easy life, but she'd left it with no regrets. She was rich, she said, because she'd loved deeply and knew how to laugh, and that was what life was about. *Everybody dies. But not everybody lives.* Loralee would write that down as soon as she got home. As soon as she was able to sit upright and hold a pen.

"Are you sure you're all right?" Merritt's hand felt cool on her forehead.

Loralee opened her eyes and smiled. "I'll be fine — really." Thinking that talking might distract her from the more and more persistent pangs in her abdomen, she said, "I haven't seen Gibbes in a couple of weeks."

Merritt sat on the ground next to Loralee, avoiding the anthills, taking her time as she brought up her knees before folding her arms neatly around them. She fiddled with the hem of her skirt, looking at it as if seeing it for the first time. The hem had fallen out of it, and Loralee had helped her measure for a new one, subtracting an inch from the length Merritt had given her as she'd marked it with white chalk.

Loralee kept looking at her so Merritt wouldn't think that she'd forgotten she'd asked a question.

"I've been busy with my new job. It's been only a few days a week so far, but I make sure I'm available just in case they call me and need me to come in. I guess Gibbes has been busy, too. And the house has been full of neighbors dropping by to introduce themselves and bringing me casseroles for some reason — we won't need to cook dinner for at least a year, I think — so it's not like we need the company. Besides, now that Gibbes has retrieved all the items from the house that he wants, I don't really expect him to come around anymore."

Loralee sighed, her exasperation almost overriding her pain. "Seriously, Merritt?"

Her chin stiffened just like Owen's did when he was asked to do something he didn't want to do. "I mean, we still have a few of the nutshell studies up in the attic that need to be brought over to the police department, and a couple for the Heritage

Society, but I think Deborah Fuller is taking care of that, so I'm not involved at all."

"Well, I know he's called you a few times, so maybe there's more he needs to talk to you about."

Merritt narrowed her eyes, her sharp dark brows like bird's wings. "How would you know he's called? We don't have a landline."

Loralee closed her eyes and rubbed her abdomen, almost glad for the excuse not to have to meet Merritt's eyes. "You leave your phone all over the place, and when it rings it's just natural that I look at the screen. I was actually going to suggest you get a landline, so you can call your cell phone every time you misplace it. I've never seen a person spend so much time looking for her cell phone."

Merritt didn't say anything for a moment, as if trying to figure out when the conversation had become about her inability to keep track of her phone. "Yes, well, he was looking up that plane crash on the Internet and just wanted to share what he'd learned with me. He left a couple of voice mails that didn't require a call back."

If Loralee had the strength, she would have reached over and smacked Merritt on top of her head to knock some sense into her. "Well, I'd be interested in learning more. Maybe we should have him over for dinner."

"There's really no reason. Everything he found on the Internet and read in Owen's newspapers was pretty much what we already knew from Deborah Fuller. Well, there was one thing he found in one of the newspapers — the debris field was in a twenty-five-mile radius, because the plane was at its cruising altitude when it exploded. That most likely means there was no prior warning to the pilots that something was wrong with the plane. No distress calls from the pilots, either. And, as Deborah pointed out, no cockpit recorders to shed any light on what was going on in the final minutes of the flight. Other than that, we still don't know anything new. It's a closed case."

Loralee thought about the plane model Gibbes had brought down to Owen's bedroom, all of the careful details that must have taken a very long time to get right. "If it were so cut-and-dried, then why did Edith feel the need to make a crime-scene analysis of it?"

Merritt studied her hands, her expression making it clear that she'd thought the exact same thing. "Well, regardless of what she believed, even the police thought it was a closed case. When Gibbes went to talk with the chief about the studies, he asked to see the case file. He flipped through it and said the only thing new in there was the passenger list. And it was definitely marked 'closed.' "

"Edith must have been a very strong woman."

Merritt looked at her. "Why do you say that?"

Loralee shrugged, the movement more painful than it should have been. "Just from what you've told me, it sounds like her husband didn't treat her like she deserved, yet she still managed to have this important part of her life without him. It couldn't have been easy. Mama always said that the easy road is usually the fastest way to hell."

"Was your mother always that judgmental?"

"No. But she was usually right." Loralee smiled but was afraid it might look more like a grimace, so she focused her attention on the gravestone next to her. "Poor Rebecca Saltus," she said out loud. "She was only fifty-one when she died in 1832. That's the only part of her tombstone you can still read."

"That's pretty young," Merritt said softly. She picked at stray strands of grass that had managed to emerge from the ground despite the heavy tree shade. "My mother was only forty-four when she died. I remember at the time thinking that was old, but it's really not, is it?"

"No," Loralee answered. "It's not old at all."

"Mama — I'm done," Owen called from across the cemetery. "Can we go now? It's really hot."

"Thank goodness," Merritt said as she got to her feet, then slapped at another mosquito on her neck. "I think they mislabeled a can of mosquito food as repellent, because they can't seem to stay away from me."

Loralee tried to roll to her knees so she could stand, but the pain was red-hot now, shooting like fireworks up through her chest.

Merritt was on the ground in front of her, her face creased with worry. "Do I need to call an ambulance? You look really sick."

Loralee wanted to say something about how Merritt needed to work on her Southernisms, but the pain seemed to have stolen her voice.

Merritt whipped out her phone, but Loralee managed to put her hand on her wrist to stop her. "No. Please." She took a deep breath. "Just help me up, and don't let Owen see."

Two strong hands gripped her elbows and

gently lifted her up, then continued to hold on as she and Merritt waited for Owen to reach them.

"I did William Bull's grave marker. He must have been an important person, because there was a lot of writing."

"Good job, sweetie." She tried to straighten up all the way, but couldn't. Merritt continued to hold on tightly, even letting Loralee lean into her as they began walking toward the exit. "We'll go to the library tomorrow and look him up and then you can write a report," she managed to say through gritted teeth.

"Oh, boy," Owen said. "Most kids go to summer camp, you know."

"Maybe next year," Loralee said, afraid to make a promise she couldn't keep. "You get to ride shotgun on the way back, okay? I'm going to let Merritt drive us back, and I think I'm just going to nap on the backseat."

Owen was too busy studying his brass rubbing to notice how much she needed Merritt's help to get inside the car, or how the hot leather of the backseat should have burned her if she could only feel it.

Before Merritt closed the door, Loralee touched her arm. "I think you're a lot like Edith."

Merritt gave her a hard look. "Why do you

say that?"

"Because there's a lot of strength and determination in you, too."

"You don't know me."

Loralee wanted to argue with her, to tell her that through Robert she felt as if she'd always known Merritt and the girl she'd been, the daughter she'd been. The survivor she'd been after the accident that had killed her mother. Loralee wasn't sure what had happened in the intervening years — years that she was pretty sure hadn't been good ones — yet Merritt had come out on the other side still kicking.

Instead, she said, "Call Gibbes. Ask him to meet us at the house."

"He's a pediatrician, Loralee." She glanced at the front seat, where Owen was busy studying his wax rubbing. "Why don't we go to the ER instead?"

Loralee shook her head. "No. He'll know what to do."

Merritt looked doubtful, but nodded. She shut the door, then climbed into the driver's seat. "Owen, fasten your seat belt. I can't promise I'm going to follow the posted speed limit." She handed her phone to him. "And please dial Dr. Heyward — he's in the contact directory — and see if he can meet us at the house in about thirty minutes."

He glanced into the backseat with a worried expression. "Are you going to be all right, Mama?"

"Yes, sweetie. My stomach is upset is all. I figure a pediatrician knows all there is to know about tummy troubles."

Satisfied with her explanation, he faced forward again and began scrolling through the contacts on Merritt's phone, apparently a short list, since he found it quickly and hit the call button.

Despite the increasing pain, Loralee managed to smile to herself as she saw Merritt's profile and the determined set of her jaw that reminded her of a bulldog. In a good way.

You are stronger than you think, she thought as she watched her stepdaughter and felt the surge of acceleration as they pulled out of the dirt parking lot and onto the asphalt road. A sharp pain radiated around from her stomach to her back, sucking the air right out of her lungs and making her recall something else her mama had once told her. *What doesn't kill you only makes you stronger.* Loralee closed her eyes and listened to the sound of the tires on the road as they sped back to Beaufort and she prayed for the oblivion of sleep.

CHAPTER 23

Merritt

It was almost dusk by the time we returned to the house on the bluff, and I nearly sighed out loud with relief when I recognized Gibbes's Explorer in the driveway, his tall figure leaning against the side. I pulled in behind him, then stole a glance at the backseat. Loralee was curled on her side in the fetal position, her eyes closed, her hands pressed against her stomach.

Owen's head was pressed against the window, his glasses fallen to the tip of his nose, gentle snores telling me that he was sleeping. After turning off the ignition, I opened the door and bolted from the SUV.

"Thank goodness you're here," I said, happier to see Gibbes than I cared to admit, and not just because I was worried about Loralee. "She's in the backseat and is in a lot of pain. She thinks it's food poisoning."

He was already walking toward the car

453

and had pulled open the back door by the time I reached him.

He leaned in and gently touched her forehead. "Loralee? It's me — Gibbes. We need to get you into the house, all right? I can carry you, but I've got to maneuver you out of the backseat first. Can you help?"

Her hands fluttered like lost butterflies, unable to land, then returned to her abdomen. She lifted her head, the effort too much for her as it quickly fell back onto the upholstery.

Gibbes looked at me. "Has she taken any medication?"

"I don't think so. She forgot her purse here, which she didn't realize until we were almost at the ruins. I know she carries medication in it."

He nodded, then glanced at the still-sleeping Owen. "I need you to run inside and turn on lights so I can see. Find her purse and leave it on the bedside table so I can figure out what types of meds she has in there."

"Do you think any of them will help with food poisoning?"

He sent me a sharp glance. "I won't know until I look. Or maybe something she's been taking is the cause of the pain — I just can't say for sure."

"I hope I did the right thing. I wanted to take her to the emergency room, but she insisted on calling you and coming here instead."

"You did the right thing. If I can't help her, then I'll take her to the ER myself."

He gently slid Loralee out of the backseat, and she began to mewl like a hurt kitten. Unable to stand by and do nothing to help, I headed inside, grabbed her purse from the hall table, then flipped on the outside lights and every single switch I passed as I made my way up to her room. Her bed was neatly made, and I carefully folded back the covers and plumped her pillows. I had just finished when Gibbes entered, carrying Loralee.

He laid her on the bed while I carefully took off her sandals and placed her feet under the covers.

"Does she have a nightgown you can put on her so she'll be more comfortable?"

I thought of the leopard-print peignoir I'd just hidden under one of the pillows and knew that I couldn't do that to either one of them. "No. But I have a bathrobe I can put her in."

It was old, gray, and flannel — three adjectives that I was pretty sure didn't describe anything in Loralee's existing wardrobe, but it zipped all the way up to the neck and wouldn't unnecessarily expose any body parts. I raced to my room to get it, and when I returned, Gibbes turned his back to give me privacy while he went through her purse.

Loralee's eyes were glazed with pain; she seemed barely aware of where she was or what was happening. Her limbs seemed boneless, pliable as I moved them to slip her out of her shirt and jeans. I paused, really seeing her for the first time, noticing how large her joints appeared to be, how caved-in her chest was, her collarbones clearly outlined under yellowish skin. Her abdomen was distended, looking grossly out of proportion to the rest of her.

I zipped up the bathrobe and she immediately turned back on her side, drawing her knees up to her chest. I turned to Gibbes, whose hands were filled with various prescription bottles, while more sat on top of the nightstand, along with a bottle of Tums and one of Benadryl, and a bubble packet of a laxative.

Before I could even form a question, Gibbes said, "Go downstairs and find Owen, and keep him occupied until I figure out what's going on here, all right?"

I nodded, then sped downstairs and out

of the house into the night and found Owen right where we'd left him, in the front seat of the SUV, sound asleep. The yard seemed lit with fireflies, their staccato light show pulsing to music I couldn't hear. I watched Owen sleeping, a soft snore drifting from his slightly opened lips. He looked like a baby, and I felt a soft pang at the thought, realizing that I could have known him as an infant. I slid off his glasses before they fell, then gently shook his shoulder. "Rocky?"

He jerked upright, and I was glad I'd saved his glasses.

"Where's Mama?" he asked.

I cleaned his glasses off on the bottom of my skirt like I'd seen Loralee do, before sliding them back on his nose. "Dr. Heyward is upstairs with your mother, making her feel better." I looked out into the new night, mesmerized by the dance of the fireflies. "I thought we could catch fireflies in the back garden while we wait."

Owen slid from the Navigator and slammed the door shut all in one movement before running toward the house and up the porch steps. "I guess that's a yes," I called out, but he'd already run into the house.

I retrieved the jars I'd found in Edith's closet, the ones Gibbes had said had once

457

belonged to him and Cal, and met Owen on the back porch. The waxing moon was nearly full, eliminating the need to turn on the back lights.

I'd been so busy cleaning out the inside of the house that I hadn't come out to the garden since the first week I'd moved in. Even in the moonlight I could see the transformation Loralee had created. Paths full of bright white stones — stones that I remembered agreeing to and paying for and seeing delivered — led the way through the garden, which no longer seemed full of tall, untamed weeds. Instead it resembled what a garden should be, a place of fragrance and beauty, where delicate flowers could tilt their heads toward the sky in search of light.

A soft blue light settled on the garden, giving the stone bench and the statue of Saint Michael a phosphorescent glow. Even the stone bunny, now sporting a bow tie and vest, seemed more dignified in the moonlight. The fireflies danced and swayed around us, their flashes like tiny beacons punching holes in the night.

Please let her be all right. The silent prayer surprised me. It had been a long time since I'd thought to ask for intervention, and it was the first time I'd admitted to myself that I was worried about Loralee.

"It's not really dark, is it?" Owen whispered.

I shook my head. "Kind of makes the dark much less scary, doesn't it?"

"Uh-huh." He clutched his jar while tilting his head up toward the sky. "Did you know that it takes one hundred thousand years for the light on one end of the Milky Way to make it to the other side?"

"No, I didn't know that," I said quietly, somehow comforted by the thought that light was everywhere, even in the far reaches of the Milky Way, always traveling, always in search of the dark it needed to fill.

"Can we have a contest to see who gets the most fireflies?" Owen asked.

"Sure. Although I will admit to being rusty. I don't think I've done this since I was a little older than you." I'd been with my mother in our front yard. She hadn't had her own jar, preferring to point out the brightest lights for me to pursue. She'd sat under the large maple tree, the one where each year on the first day of school she'd taken my picture as I held my newest backpack and lunchbox. I often wondered whether the tree was still there, or if it was another victim of my father's wish to leave that part of our lives behind us.

"We'll have to have a prize for the winner,

though." Owen pretended to think for a moment. "If I catch the most, I get to have ice cream before I go to bed."

"All right. But what if I win?"

"Then we both get some." He giggled, and I saw the shadow of his dimple in the moonlight, in the same spot as my own.

"Deal," I said, unscrewing the lid of my jar. "Just watch out for that little dip in the ground by the bench. Looks like your mother has been digging a hole."

He turned around to acknowledge the spot before facing me again. I waited for him to take the lid from his jar. "Ready?"

He nodded, positioning himself in a runner's pose, with one leg in front of the other.

"Set." I paused for dramatic effect. "Go!" I shouted. He took off so fast that I was afraid he'd run into something or trip. But he was as sure-footed as a cat, quickly disappearing around the other side of the large oak tree dominating that part of the garden.

"Got one!" he shouted.

Feeling a little silly, I began stalking the garden, waiting for a firefly to alert me to its presence. They were everywhere, busy in their mating ritual of blinking hindquarters. I felt almost guilty interrupting them, but hoped maybe they'd make a romantic connection while held captive in my jar.

"I think I have about a hundred," Owen called out.

I looked down at my own jar, where I had nowhere near that amount. "I think I have about twice that!" I shouted back. I smiled to myself. It was something my father would have done. My mother said he was prone to gross exaggeration, which was probably why she was so exacting in her praise and encouragement. I had sometimes found it deflating as a child, so much different from Loralee's constant building up of Owen's fragile ego.

"I'm not done yet," he called, a definite challenge in his voice.

A hand touched me on the arm, and it seemed as if somebody had suddenly turned off all the light in the garden, and I was alone in the dark with just the feel of hand on my skin. "No!" I shouted, twisting around and raising my arms to protect my face. The jar fell from my hand, hitting the soft dirt by the side of the path with a dull thud.

"Merritt, it's me. It's Gibbes."

I lowered my arms and looked into his familiar face. I was breathing heavily, a thin sheen of perspiration covering my body. I bent down to retrieve my jar, trying to hide my embarrassment.

When I straightened, he hadn't moved. "You need to sit down."

Hesitating only a moment, I allowed him to lead me to the bench, both of us walking around the dip in the ground. I clutched the jar in my lap, wishing I could somehow hide inside.

"How is Loralee?" I asked, steering the conversation to where it needed to be.

There was a short pause before he answered. "She's resting now. She usually takes prescribed pills throughout the day, but today she couldn't, because she forgot her purse. That sort of messed her up, but she should feel much better when she wakes up."

"So it wasn't food poisoning?"

He looked down to where his hands were resting on his thighs. "No. It's not food poisoning."

"Is she going to be all right? I saw her collection of pill bottles. I can't imagine those are all for ulcers."

He continued to stare at his hands. "Although I'm not officially her doctor, I can't discuss her health with you. You'll have to ask her yourself. Just wait until she's feeling a little better, all right?"

"Now you have me worried."

"Loralee is one of the strongest people

I've ever met. She can handle this, and would definitely not want you to be worried on her behalf. She promised she'll be up making breakfast tomorrow morning."

I let out a breath, feeling inordinately relieved that it wasn't as bad as my imagination had led me to believe. "She's awfully thin," I said, remembering what she'd looked like while I'd put the bathrobe on her.

I heard the grin in his voice. "She'll probably take that as a compliment, but, yes, she's definitely too thin. See what you can do to get food in her."

"Well, I know she likes fried foods. Maybe I could learn how to fry chicken."

"That's pretty ambitious, coming from somebody who was raised in Maine. Call Mrs. Williams. She'd be happy to show you how it's done."

I nodded as I desperately sought for something else to say so he wouldn't fill the silence with questions I didn't want to answer. "Who knows?" I said quickly. "Maybe I will be saying 'y'all' before the end of the year. And not thinking it's really so hot when it hits the nineties with ninety percent humidity in the middle of May."

"Do you miss Maine?" His voice was deep but soft and even, perfect, I thought, for a pediatrician. Calming to children yet authoritative to their parents.

"You should ask me that in January. You know what we call our four seasons? Early winter, midwinter, late winter, and next winter."

He chuckled. "I'm guessing it's pretty cold most of the time."

"Yes, but we do have summer. The days are long and filled with warm air that starts to fade after only a few weeks. And it's always chilly in the evenings. Very different from here, but still very beautiful. There's nothing like a blueberry field in winter. The fall turns the plants a bright crimson, almost like blood against the white snow. It seems like another world to me sometimes. Or another life, really."

"Do you think you'll go back?"

I shook my head. "No. I needed to move forward. My father was a pilot and spent his entire life traveling, yet I'd never been outside of Maine. And when I was going through my grandmother's books and found a travel guide to South Carolina, it seemed almost serendipitous when I learned I'd inherited a house here, too. To be honest, I didn't even give that much thought to it — maybe because I thought if I did, I'd change my mind. I just knew it was time to leave, and where I went seemed immaterial."

"Cal was like that, too. He'd never left the state until he left for good. He lived in California for a while, and I heard from him from time to time, how he'd started out being a bar bouncer and then decided to become a fireman. And then I didn't hear from him anymore. I guess at some point he decided to move to Maine, and the rest, as they say, is history."

I felt him watching me, and I turned my head to look at him and saw moonlight reflected in his eyes. "Why are you asking me all these questions?"

"You were my brother's wife, which means you're part of my life now, too, whether you want to be or not. You don't seem very forthcoming with details about yourself, and I got tired of waiting."

I looked away. "There's absolutely nothing to know. Nothing that interesting, anyway."

"I know that you're very brave. I know very few people who would leave everything they've always known, pack up their car, and head to a new town where they know nobody. But I have a suspicion that you have no idea how brave you really are."

"Because I'm not. I just did what I thought I needed to do. Here was this house

I'd never known about, and this place where my husband had been born and raised. The museum where I'd worked was downsizing, and my husband was dead. It's not like I had a lot of options."

"Sure you did. You just picked the hardest one."

"According to Loralee, the easy road is the fastest way to hell."

He smiled, but it seemed he was holding part of it back. "She's a smart woman."

I looked down at the jar in my hands, where the blinking had slowed to a somber pulse, almost as if the fireflies were waiting for some sort of sign. "I've been thinking about that Sandy Beach woman we met the other day. Did Cal really date her?"

"Yeah, unfortunately. That was the type of girl he normally went for."

I felt his eyes on me again, but I couldn't meet them. He didn't need to explain to me what "the type of girl" meant. However she might be described, the most obvious way would be not like me.

"I don't blame you for not believing my story of how Cal and I met. Especially after meeting Sandy. I agree — it doesn't make sense. I'm just left to wonder, Why me?"

"We can't always choose who we love."

A corner of my mouth twisted upward.

"You're starting to sound like Loralee."

"I'll take that as a compliment."

We listened to the sound of Owen running through the garden, shouting out his victory with each captured insect.

Gibbes cleared his throat. "I brought over the folder I've put together about the plane crash. I thought you might be interested."

I remembered my initial excitement at the thought of discovering more about the ill-fated flight. But now I could see no purpose to it. One of the few treasures Cal had brought from his childhood home had been a bolt from the plane. It had once meant something to him, but he was gone now.

I shook my head. "Not really. Not anymore. Now that I know why the plane was up in my attic, I feel there's really nothing else to know. Your grandmother had an affinity for crime investigation, and perhaps believed there was more to the story than what the police came up with, but apparently there wasn't. Case closed."

"I think I have a thousand!" Owen called out.

"I think he's going to win," I said with a smile as I faced Gibbes.

He was looking at me closely, his expression serious, and my smile faded.

"Did Cal ever hit you?"

I remembered once as a child when I'd climbed too high in a tree, despite my grandmother's warnings not to, and couldn't find a way down. Unwilling to have to admit that she was right, I'd decided to shinny down the tree the way I'd seen monkeys do on TV. I'd fallen about ten feet onto my back, miraculously not breaking anything, but knocking the air from my lungs. I felt that way now, gasping for air that seemed too thick to breathe.

"Don't," I finally managed.

"He was my brother, and even though he left here when I was just Owen's age, I remember that he wasn't always a nice guy. He'd lose his temper and become somebody else. He was always sorry later, but that rarely made it better. He had lots of girlfriends like Sandy Beach, girls who were probably used to rough treatment at home and didn't find getting knocked around to be something they didn't think they deserved.

"But you're not like them. I thought maybe he'd changed when he met you. But every time I make an unexpected movement, you jump. And your eyes." He shook his head. "It's like the light goes out in them."

I stood, feeling faint. "I don't feel well.

I'm going inside. Tell Owen to take his shower and I'll have his ice cream ready when he's done."

Gibbes stood, too. "Whatever he did to you, you didn't deserve it. You're a strong, smart, and beautiful woman, Merritt. I don't want to believe that he ever made you feel less than what you are."

"Don't," I said again, stepping away from him. "You don't know me. You don't know what I've done."

Something clanged on the ground, and we looked down and saw the lid of my firefly jar, which in my agitation I must have twisted off. I looked back at the jar in time to see the last firefly lifting into the air, its body glowing brightly, then fading again like a wave good-bye as it disappeared into the branches of the oak tree.

Without a word I turned toward the house and entered the kitchen. I placed the empty jar on the table, accidentally knocking a file folder that had been perched on the edge onto the linoleum floor, a single sheet escaping and coming to rest next to the folder. I bent to retrieve the folder and paper, glancing at the page as I attempted to stick it back inside. I couldn't figure out what I was looking at until I saw the header at the top of the typewritten page.

Northeast Airlines Flight 629, July 25, 1955. List of Passengers.

The purple text was from an old carbon-copy machine, the letters faded to a pale lilac.

I was about to close the folder and return it to the counter when my attention was caught by a single name about halfway down the list: Henry P. Holden, Bangor, Maine.

The fluorescent light above the kitchen sink began to flicker as I stared at the name, the intermittent buzzing matching the tempo of the blood that throbbed in my temples. I closed my eyes for a moment and almost felt Cal's breath on the back of my neck as I recalled his words. *A backdraft is an explosive event caused by a fire, resulting from rapid reintroduction of oxygen to combustion in an oxygen-depleted environment.*

The door opened and Owen ran into the kitchen, followed by Gibbes at a more sedate pace. "I won! I won! I'm going to take the fastest shower *ever* and I'll be down for my ice cream. I'll let you have some, Merritt. And you can have some, too, Dr. Heyward," he added as an afterthought as he raced through the kitchen door and headed toward the stairs.

"What's wrong?" Gibbes asked, shutting

the door behind him.

I held out the paper toward him, my finger pointing to the name.

"Henry P. Holden," he read before lifting his eyes to mine again. "Does that name mean anything to you?"

I nodded. My tongue seemed glued to the roof of my mouth, and it took me two tries to speak. "I'm not sure. I mean, this has to be a coincidence, right?"

"What does?" he asked, his eyes wary.

I swallowed. "Holden was my mother's maiden name. Henry Patrick was her father. Either this is a very strange coincidence, or Henry P. Holden could be my grandfather."

We stood facing each other for a long time without speaking, listening as Owen turned on the shower upstairs, the water pipes creaking and groaning in the walls of the old house, but not loud enough to block out the memory of Cal's words. *There's no such thing as accidents.*

CHAPTER 24

Edith

January 1989

Edith led Gibbes by the hand down the church steps of Saint Helena's and into the ancient churchyard, following his mother's coffin. The old tombstones, some dating back more than two hundred years, leaned together conspiratorially. Gibbes was just two and a half months shy of his sixth birthday but looked like a little man in his black suit and tie, his sandy-colored hair a welcome shot of light against all the black.

C.J. followed behind them, reeking of alcohol either from the previous night or that morning. He'd always managed to stay sober during the week, when he would show up at his law office or court or wherever he needed to be, but on the weekends he was always deep in his cups. But since Cecelia's accident, his weekend binges were ending later and beginning earlier, so that it was hard to determine whether he ever sobered up in between.

Cal was nowhere to be found. He'd been dressed for the funeral earlier at breakfast, looking sullen as he pushed his breakfast around his plate with a fork without apparently lifting any food to his mouth. He'd left the table as soon as his father had come in, and Edith hadn't seen him since.

She'd already told C.J. that she didn't think Gibbes should be at the burial, so she continued to hold his hand and led him out of the cemetery to Church Street, just a short walk from Bay Street and home. She would finish laying out the food in the dining room for the crowd of people expected after the funeral, the family china, crystal, and silver gleaming on the white lace tablecloth, exactly as Cecelia would have liked it.

Gibbes tripped on an uneven part of the sidewalk, and when Edith slowed to help him regain his footing, she saw that his face was streaked with tears. She got down on her haunches and pushed his hair out of his eyes. They were his mother's eyes. Edith had finally gotten her wish: a grandchild who resembled his mother in all ways, including a warm and tender heart. It was up to Edith to make sure it was preserved.

He'd always been a sweet and quiet child,

somehow knowing that his place in the family was as an observer instead of a participant. He watched everything, coming to his own conclusions, and never offered his thoughts unless asked. And Edith was the only one who knew to ask.

"It'll be all right. Maybe not tomorrow or even the next day, but one day it won't hurt so much," she said, wishing she could force sincerity into her words.

"How come they couldn't fix Mama? I want her to come home with me."

She hugged him tightly to her. "The doctors tried, sweetie, but she was too broken." It had been a silly New Year's Eve party, her heel clipping the back of her dress as she descended the stairs on her way out of the house. Edith had been up in the attic, finishing making a wind chime, hearing the arguing through the closed door. She'd wanted to believe it was an accident, wanted to believe that she had not raised a monster.

"I could fix her," Gibbes said with all the sincerity of a five-year-old.

"I wanted to fix her, too," Edith whispered in his ear. "But sometimes people don't know they're broken or that they need fixing."

Gibbes's eyes widened. "I told Cal I could fix her, but he told me to go away."

Edith pulled back. "When did you say that to Cal?"

"After Mama fell and she was sleeping on the floor. Daddy was there, too, and told me to go to my room, so I did. I thought they were going to fix her."

Pinpricks of ice dusted the back of her neck as years of denial and excuses jammed against her conscience. "Maybe when you're older you can become a doctor and fix people. You can do that to honor your mother." She leaned forward and kissed his forehead, then wiped his face with the sleeve of her black coat.

Taking his hand again, she continued to lead him toward the house, pretending that her shivering was due to the winter wind that swept off the river and settled over Beaufort like a cold breath.

She heard a rhythmic pounding as soon as they walked through the driveway gate, following the drive toward the back garden, where Cal stood facing the oak tree. As they watched, he drew back his fist and drove it into the trunk of the tree, making a hollow sound as impotent as his rage. He dropped his fist to his side, and she saw the blood running from his knuckles and staining the oyster shells beneath pink.

"Cal!" Edith called out, realizing it was

too late to shield Gibbes. Dropping the boy's hand, she walked quickly over to Cal and examined his injury. "You probably have a broken finger. Let's get you inside and put some ice on this and get it wrapped."

He didn't move. "I told her to leave. So many times I told her to leave. But she wouldn't. She said she loved him. Can you believe that? She loved him." He turned back to stare at the tree trunk. "It's her own damned fault."

His breath came out in quickly evaporating clouds, carrying his words away.

She grabbed the sleeve of his coat. "Come on, Cal. Let's go inside. . . ."

He yanked his arm away. "Why is there no punishment? You taught me that, Grandma — that every bad deed gets punished. Where's the justice?"

Gibbes had started to cry again, and she moved back to put her arm around his shoulders. She thought of a younger Cal and his fire truck, how punishment had been carefully meted out to those who were careless. But his mother's death had shaken his world order, showing him cracks in the facade of black and white, right and wrong. Edith wasn't sure whether she could glue

476

them back together or if it was fractured forever.

He slid down the trunk of the tree and rested his head in his hands.

Gibbes pulled away from her and approached his brother. "We could go play chess if you want. Or we could go fishing." His voice captured all the hope that an almost-six-year-old could hold that grief was a fleeting thing, an osprey lifting from a tree and flying away.

"Go away," Cal said, and Gibbes's shoulders slumped as he turned to walk back to his grandmother.

Cal looked up, his eyes burning with too many emotions. "I'm sorry."

Edith squeezed Gibbes's shoulders and headed to the front porch. She recognized a familiar figure as they climbed the steps.

"Deborah — it's so good to see you." As predicted, Deborah's mother had lingered for a good ten years before she died, and her daughter had faithfully stayed by her side. It was too late to return to law school, so Deborah remained in Beaufort doing various types of community work and volunteering at the Heritage Society.

"It was a beautiful service. I left early because I thought you might need help before everybody got here."

Edith smiled gratefully. "Thank you, Deborah. I appreciate it."

Deborah leaned down with her hands on her knees in front of Gibbes. "You look very handsome in your suit. Your mother would be very proud of how grown-up you are."

Gibbes regarded the woman with somber eyes, eyes that were the same as his brother's under the same sandy hair. But the resemblance ended there.

"Thank you, ma'am."

Deborah tilted her head to the side, studying the boy. "I've got a little house on Fripp now. Lots of great places for crab pots and net casting and all kinds of fishing and swimming. Problem is, I don't have any little boys to take advantage of all of it. So if you ever need a partner in crime to just hang out on a boat or in the water, just tell your grandmother and I'll come get you."

The first real smile that Edith had seen since his mother's death crossed his face. "Can Cal come, too?"

Deborah didn't hesitate. "Absolutely. I'm a firm believer that there's nothing that a boat and water can't fix, no matter how old you are."

Deborah straightened and faced Edith. "I'm yours — just tell me what you need me to do."

Edith thought for a moment. "I need you to help me hang something." She went inside to the hall table and pulled open the small drawer before taking out a wind chime. Bringing it out on the porch, she held it up so Deborah and Gibbes could see it. "I made this in memory of your mama, Gibbes. So that every time the wind blows, you'll hear her voice."

Turning to Deborah, she said, "Since you're so tall, I thought I'd lift Gibbes up and you can help him hang it on the hook I screwed in yesterday."

"Of course," Deborah said. "Although I think I could use a chair, too." She slid over a small child's chair that Gibbes had long since grown out of but that Cecelia didn't want to part with. Edith had been using it to hold flowerpots.

As Edith handed her the wind chime, it slipped from her grasp and landed on the wood planks of the porch with a clatter. Edith bent to retrieve it, examining each piece of glass.

"Did it get broke?" Gibbes asked, his eyes wide.

Edith shook her head. "No. This glass has been rolled and tumbled about the ocean for years, so it's seasoned and not so breakable. You should remember that — that not all glass is as fragile as it seems."

Edith handed the wind chime to Deborah again, then picked Gibbes up in her arms, wondering how much longer she'd be able to lift him. Deborah guided his fingers as he hung the string around the hook.

"Good job," Edith said. She took a deep breath. "I need you to go upstairs now and change your clothes. Then pull out your overnight bag from under your bed and pack your jammies and some clean underclothes. I'm sending you to the Williamses' for a few days. Maybe longer. Until things settle down here. All right?"

Despite Betsy Williams and Edith's close friendship, their daughters-in-law had not carried on the tradition, even though their sons were around the same age. Gibbes and the two youngest Williams boys were great friends, but Cecelia and Kathy, despite an early friendship, had distanced themselves from each other. Edith guessed the friendship had ended after a combined family trip with the husbands and children, and had always wondered whether Kathy had seen or heard something Cecelia had not wanted her to. Kathy had phoned several times afterward, but Cecelia had never called her back. Kathy had been at the service earlier, and she and Edith had avoided looking at each other, as if guilt and blame had chosen a seat between them.

Gibbes nodded, then headed toward the stairs. She watched him for a moment, wondering how long it would be before he could no longer remember his mother's face or the sound of her voice. The young rebounded from grief more quickly than adults, but that also left them with more time to chastise themselves for forgetting.

She thought of Cal and his bloody knuckles and his cry for justice, and for the first time in a long while she felt her old anger return, along with the sense of purpose that had propelled her into the police department with her first nutshell study.

Turning to Deborah, she said, "I have something I need to see to — would you mind taking the serving dishes from the refrigerator and placing them on the dining room table and then starting the percolator? I'll be right back."

She trudged up the stairs, but instead of turning toward her room, she headed up to the attic. It was chilly in the unheated space, and she was glad she'd left on her coat. She went immediately to the corner where she kept the plane hidden from Cal, who sometimes joined her in the attic to watch her work on the nutshell studies. He enjoyed the attention to detail, and hearing the stories of how the crimes were committed and what mistakes the perpetrators had made that led to their being caught. It appeased his sense of *rightness.*

But she would not let him know about the plane, and what she'd discovered. She had the knowledge to point the finger of blame at the person responsible, but she could not condemn her, could not pass judgment. Because Edith understood her motives, understood that desperation was sometimes all that was left.

Maybe that was why, during the funeral service, she'd kept thinking about the anonymous woman and the suitcase she most likely believed to have been destroyed in the crash along with her letter. How all these years she believed her secret safe. And how Edith wished she'd told Cecelia what she knew, that she wasn't alone. That some women were sometimes pushed to the point of desperate acts if they didn't seek help. Maybe that would have changed things. But hindsight was as useless now as Cal's fists against the stalwart trunk of a tree.

It had been while Edith was thinking about that suitcase that she remembered the missing dopp kit, and that empty space where one might have been. It was the last part of the puzzle she hadn't figured out, the *how*. And suddenly the answer had clarified itself so finely in Edith's mind that she was afraid she might smile in the middle of the service.

She quickly found the bag where she stored the passenger dolls who'd been found outside the fuselage and all of her notes, as well as the passenger list. She placed them on the table next to her sea glass, then lifted her reading glasses to her nose before running her finger down the names. She missed it the first time and so went more slowly the second, her unvarnished nail sliding down the list until it stopped on the name she remembered seeing written in bold, black ink on a luggage tag. *Henry P. Holden.* And then, in very small writing, she wrote down the address she still remembered from memory, and imagined the faceless woman now against the backdrop of a cold Maine winter.

CHAPTER 25

Loralee

Loralee opened her eyes, watching the shadows of the oak leaves shimmy against the wall of her room. The buttery yellow of the sun told her it was later than it probably should be for her to still be in bed, but it seemed her eyelids were the only part of her she could willingly move.

She remembered vague snippets from the night before: of Merritt driving them back to the house and Gibbes being there, handing her medicine and water and talking quietly to her, and then a smaller hand brushing her hair from her forehead. Gibbes knew her secret now, of course. She didn't remember telling him, but he was a doctor and would have figured it out. Loralee knew that with as much certainty as she knew he wouldn't tell Merritt, even if he could. She also knew that he would expect her to do it as soon as possible. Soon. She would tell Merritt soon. She just needed a little more time.

She closed her eyes, assessing how she felt. Her doctor in Georgia had told her to rate her pain level from one to ten, with ten being the worst. Loralee figured the day before had been a six, and that scared her. Because six was almost eight, and eight was the number to dread, the number where Loralee would have to make plans.

Without moving too much, she reached out her hand for her Tums and instead felt a warm hand holding hers and placing the Tums in her palm. She opened her eyes and saw Merritt, in her hideous gray nightshirt, staring down at her.

"Gibbes said you might need this when you woke up."

Loralee nodded gratefully and took two. She studied Merritt as she chewed, trying to pull in her thoughts. "What time is it?"

Merritt looked at the bedside clock. "It's almost eight o'clock."

Loralee blinked. "Why are you still in your . . . um . . ." She waved her hand in front of Merritt.

Her stepdaughter looked down at her chest as if to make sure she knew what Loralee was referring to. "I fell asleep in the armchair in the corner. Owen was worried about you, so I promised I'd sleep in your room to make sure you were all right. I just woke up, too."

Loralee felt her eyes fill, so she turned to the side to put the roll of Tums back on her nightstand. "Thank you. Although I told Gibbes I would be right as rain this morning and making breakfast for everybody. I must have been more tired than I thought."

Merritt sat down on the edge of the bed. "You were very sick. Gibbes told us that you have some stomach problems that you need to take medicine for, and you forgot your medicine when we went to the church ruins. I wish you'd told me — we could have come right back."

Loralee managed to smile. "It was stupid of me, and I'm sorry if I made you worry." Before she could talk herself out of it, she pushed herself up to a sitting position, then waited a moment for her stomach to settle. "It's too late for breakfast, but I can make us up a brunch."

Merritt stood. "Don't be silly. You should stay in bed and let Owen and me bring you something to eat." A half smile crossed her face. "Gibbes and I both think you're too thin and we need to fatten you up. My dad taught me how to make his famous French toast, and I think we have all the ingredients. . . ."

Merritt must have sensed the nausea rising in Loralee's throat, because she stopped.

"Or I can just make you some plain toast. You should have some food in your stomach. And I've heard chicken soup is good for you, too — that it's not just an old wives' tale."

"You know how to make chicken soup?" Loralee asked, her stomach threatening another protest.

"No. But I know we have some cans in the pantry. It just takes a minute to heat up."

"Just toast is fine. But I can go get it. . . ."

She was saved from the effort of standing by Owen bursting into the room, holding up a spiral notebook. "Mama!" he cried, rushing over to the bed and throwing his arms around her. She ached everywhere, it seemed, and her stomach was less than settled, but she wouldn't complain. He smelled of soap and baby shampoo — something he hated but continued to use because that was all she bought, since she loved the smell of it — and his shoulders seemed broader than the last time she'd hugged him. *The greatest moments in life are usually the smallest.* Her mama had told her that once, and in hugging her son, Loralee knew she was right.

Owen pulled back and put the spiral notebook on the bed next to her. "There's my report on William Bull. Merritt told me that if I woke up first, I should work on it. I found a lot of information online, so you don't have to take me to the library."

Loralee hid her smile as she flipped through the pages. "This looks real good, sweetie. I'll grade it later, all right? I'm still a little tired."

Merritt took the notebook and put it on the dresser. "Let's let your mother rest a bit while we go make her some toast. Have you eaten, Rocky? I could probably figure out how to scramble some eggs."

"Dr. Heyward made me pancakes with blueberries. And he let me drink a Coke with it, seeing how it's Saturday."

Loralee wasn't sure whether she was more shocked that a pediatrician would allow a child to drink Coke first thing in the morning or by the fact that Gibbes had come over to make breakfast.

"He made you breakfast?" Merritt asked.

"The refrigerator wasn't running again, and the ice in the freezer was melting down the sides. You left your phone in the kitchen, so I used it to call him," he said, looking at Merritt. "You shouldn't leave it lying around all the time — that's how things get lost. Anyways, Dr. Heyward already took the food out and put it in coolers, but he said the fridge is a dead duck. And then he made me breakfast."

The sound of pans clattering in the sink came from downstairs.

"He's still here?"

Owen shrugged. "Somebody had to clean the dishes."

Merritt looked down at her sweatshirt again, and apparently didn't like what she saw. "I'll be right back."

Just as she reached the door, there was a light tapping on the other side. "Is everybody decent?"

"Hang on a second," Loralee said as she pulled herself out of the bed and made it to her dresser. She grabbed the first tube of lipstick she could find and turned to Merritt. "Hike," she said, tossing it and hoping Merritt knew enough about football to know she was supposed to catch it. And if she didn't, then Loralee made a mental note to give her a crash course. Owen would need his sister to know these things.

Merritt caught it cleanly in her right hand, and then Loralee pantomimed putting it on her lips, just in case she wasn't sure.

What? Merritt mouthed.

She wants you to put it on, Owen mouthed back, imitating his mother.

Merritt rolled her eyes, then yanked off the top and brushed the tube against her upper and lower lips in a straight line instead of following the curve of her mouth.

"Come in," Owen shouted before Loralee had a chance to throw Merritt the tissue box.

"How is everybody this morning?" Gibbes asked as he approached Loralee. She was leaning heavily on the dresser and didn't argue when he led her back to the bed.

"I'm much better, thank you." She slid her legs under the covers, noticing for the first time the bathrobe she was wearing. "Good heavens. I must have really been sick if I let somebody put this on me." She grinned up at Merritt and then stopped when she saw the pink slashes on her lips.

Gibbes pulled the covers up. It was probably too warm in the room for a flannel robe and a blanket, but Loralee was cold all the time now, as if her body lacked the insulation she needed.

Gibbes rubbed his hands together. "I put some pancakes in the oven on warm, in case anybody would like any — and I just put some bread in the toaster, if Owen would like to run down and bring it up on a plate with a glass of water for his mother."

Gibbes smiled at Owen's departing back and then appeared to notice Merritt for the first time. He hesitated only a moment. "Good morning," he said, doing a really good job of not focusing on the lipstick. "Owen tells me you kept an eye on Loralee last night." His gaze fell to the sweatshirt and his expression changed. "You still sleep in Cal's shirt?"

She pressed her lips together. "I need to get changed. Excuse me." She stepped toward the door, but he didn't move out of her way.

"Before you change, I thought I'd ask if you and Owen and maybe Maris wanted to go out on the boat again today. I thought we'd head out to the sandbar, soak up a little sun, maybe even see what we can catch in a net. Loralee should probably rest, and I thought it would be a good way to give her some peace and quiet."

Merritt couldn't quite hide the panic in her voice. "I'll stay with Loralee, just in case she needs something."

"I'll be fine, Merritt. Really. Probably sleeping most of the day so I can regain my strength. Besides, the sandbar is in the middle of the river — not in the ocean. And you'll be with Gibbes and wearing a life jacket."

Owen reappeared in the doorway with a plate of toast and a glass of water and put them down on the nightstand after Gibbes slid the pill bottles out of the way.

Owen must have overheard Gibbes, because he shouted, "I want to go to the sandbar! Maris said it's the coolest place on earth. It's in the middle of the river and you can see all sorts of fish and sometimes shrimp, too."

"Shrimp?" Merritt asked, not as excited at the prospect as Owen seemed to be.

"Yes!" he said. "And dolphins, too. Maris says you can usually see them by the marina, but they're everywhere."

Merritt looked like a little girl, with her smeared lipstick, oversize shirt, and wide eyes. Gibbes must have thought the same thing, because he was trying very hard to hold back a smile.

"I really would like to stay here. If Loralee doesn't need me, then I have to run out to an appliance store and buy a refrigerator — hopefully one that can be delivered tomorrow — and have the old one hauled away."

"I already called Sears and they're open until six," Gibbes said. "I can take you when we get back."

"Yay! I'm going to put my bathing suit on and call Maris," Owen announced as he raced from the room.

"Thank you," Merritt said stiffly. "I appreciate it, but I've already been out on the water once. The creeks and marshes are lovely, and I'm glad I had a chance to see a part of my new home. But I will never like or be comfortable near the water, and I wish you'd just stop trying to force me to do something I don't want to do."

Loralee spotted her pink journal just out of reach on the nightstand. She was filling a page a day now, as if she were in some kind of contest, or maybe a race, but without a marked finish line. At least, that was what she'd thought before, but now she felt like the finish line might be right around the corner. She closed her eyes, committing to memory the words that she wanted to put down on paper. *Forget what hurt you in the past. But never forget what it taught you.*

Very softly, Gibbes asked, "Did Cal know you were afraid of the water?"

Merritt looked like a deer caught in the crosshairs of a hunter's rifle, her feet primed and ready to bolt. The Merritt whom Loralee and Owen had first met when they'd come to Beaufort probably would have. But in the short time they'd known her, Merritt had changed. Maybe it was the South Carolina heat or the scent of the pluff mud that had slowed her gait and widened her smile. It was like a loosening of bones, an opening up of spaces inside of her that weren't empty and dark but instead simply pieces of her heart waiting to be filled. It could be, Loralee thought, this beautiful place of water and bridges and islands that had changed her. Or maybe Merritt was simply responding to being with people who cared about her. It hurt Loralee to think about how long it might have been since Merritt had felt that way.

Merritt didn't drop her gaze, and Loralee wanted to clap. It was a glimmer of the Merritt from the past, the girl Robert had remembered. "Yes. He knew."

Gibbes didn't say anything, his silence meant for her to continue. Loralee could see how he was a good pediatrician, knowing when not saying anything was the best way to listen to children telling him about the bogeymen who lived under their beds.

Merritt continued, her look defiant, as if she expected Gibbes to contradict her. "He even got some kind of warped satisfaction from my fear, like it was a well-deserved punishment for something I wasn't even aware I'd done. He was like that, wasn't he?

Always looking for justification or retribution no matter how convoluted his reasoning."

A muscle ticked in Gibbes's jaw. "Did he ever take you swimming, or try to help you in any way to get over it, or at least manage it?"

Merritt went very still. "Once." She jutted out her chin and looked like she was about to say more, but a shudder ran through her, and for a moment Loralee thought that Merritt might need the garbage can on the side of the bed. Instead she took a deep breath. "It didn't cure me, but it gave him a reason to call me a coward, which I guess I am, since I'm still afraid of the water."

They stared at each other, as if daring the other to break contact, to admit defeat.

"Then why don't you prove him wrong?" Gibbes asked, his words slow and deliberate.

She looked at him as if he'd just suggested she stand on her head and make up a rap song. Her jaw worked as she tried to form the word *no,* but Gibbes was faster.

"Whatever Cal did to try to help you manage your fear, I promise you this will be a lot more fun. And I promise I'll keep you safe."

Loralee nestled back into her pillow, feeling warm and tingly, just like she got when watching her favorite soaps.

Merritt searched the room as if it might offer a reason to say no, but her gaze settled back on Gibbes. She gave a heavy sigh. "As long as we're home in time to go buy a refrigerator."

He smiled, and Loralee hoped that Merritt noticed how knee-weakening it was. "Deal."

Looking as if she were headed for a firing squad, Merritt turned toward the door again, but Loralee stopped her.

"Take that shopping bag from Belk's with you." She pointed to the bulging bag by the door. "I had to return some things I'd bought in Georgia that still had the tags on them, but they were old so I could only exchange them. I don't need anything, so I got some things I thought you might like instead. There's a cute red one-piece bathing suit — in a forties style that I think will look really fine on you."

Loralee was glad she'd waited until all of Merritt's energy for arguing had been used up. Otherwise her stepdaughter probably wouldn't have picked up the bag and exited the room without a word.

She and Gibbes listened as the bag bumped against Merritt's legs as she walked down the hall and closed her door. And then, five seconds later, a loud groan.

"She must have just seen her reflection," Gibbes said with a guilty smile.

Loralee laughed, wondering whether laughter really was the best medicine, because she already felt much better. "Could you please hand me that pink journal and the pen?"

Gibbes did as she asked, and before she could forget, she wrote, *Never give a lady a tube of lipstick without a mirror.*

CHAPTER 26

Merritt

I stared at my reflection in my dressing-table mirror and frowned. The red bathing suit fit perfectly, with its retro-style sweetheart neckline and boy-shorts bottom. Despite how relatively covered up I was, I still felt, well, *sexy.* It was an unfamiliar feeling, like wearing somebody else's broken-in shoes. But I couldn't quite talk myself into taking the suit off and wearing the shorts and T-shirt I'd had on before.

The doorbell rang and I heard Maris's voice. I sighed to myself, realizing that I couldn't back out now. A soft tapping on the door interrupted my thoughts.

"Merritt? It's Loralee — may I come in?"

I opened the door, then stepped back while she gave me the once-over. "You look prettier than a pat of butter melting on a short stack."

"Is that a compliment?" I asked, shutting

the door behind her.

"Oh, yes. And you need to start recognizing them when they come your way so that you say thank-you and don't look so surprised."

She flashed her wide smile, which didn't completely hide the fatigue behind her eyes or the slight yellow tinge of her neck below her foundation line.

Holding up her hands, she said, "Not that you need it, but I bought these, too, since a woman should never go out without accessorizing." A red chiffon scarf, the exact shade as the bathing suit, trailed from one hand and down her arm, a matching red and white striped visor hooked on the index finger of the other.

I looked at them dubiously. "I appreciate it, Loralee, but I think the bathing suit's enough, don't you?"

"Enough what? Enough pretty? Oh, sugar, there's not enough pretty in this world to go around. We have to do what we can."

Not wanting to argue with a sick woman, I stood still in front of the mirror while she wrapped the scarf around my ponytail, tying it in a long, loose bow. "Just like putting the top hat on Fred Astaire." She clasped her hands over her chest. "Red is definitely your color. You look absolutely gorgeous."

"Thank you," I said slowly, still not sure whether I wanted to wear a red scarf in my hair.

Loralee leaned close to me. "See how easy that was?"

"How what was?"

"Accepting a compliment." She smiled again, then turned back to my reflection. "Let me show you how to put on this visor without messing up your hair." Pulling apart the Velcro closure, she adjusted the visor on my head, then refastened it under my ponytail.

"You don't want it to be too high or you look bald, or too low so nobody can see your face. If you had bangs, you'd feather them over the top." Her eyes met mine in the mirror. "Do you want me to cut you some bangs? You'd look real cute, and I've got a way with scissors."

I held up my hand, my head spinning. "Thanks, Loralee, but they're waiting on me downstairs. Maybe later."

"I wish we had time for a pedicure, because I've got the perfect shade for your toes. But I do have a matching red lipstick — I'll even show you how to put it on."

"No," I said a little too quickly, remembering the horror of the earlier lipstick incident. I could still taste the soap I'd used to scrub my mouth to get it all off. "To be honest, I really don't see the point in this if all we're doing is going out on a boat and then sitting on a sandbar."

She gave me a patient smile, the kind I imagined she gave to Owen when he'd said something that was either untrue or beneath his intelligence. "Looking pretty isn't about how people see you. It's about letting people know how you feel about yourself."

I turned to face her. "Did your mother teach you that?"

She shook her head. "Nope. I figured that one out on my own." Putting her hands on my shoulders, she made me face the mirror again. "Do you feel pretty?"

I hesitated for only a brief moment. "Yes. I do."

She grinned her widest grin, then let go of my shoulders. "Great. Then my job here is done. You go on and have fun today. And don't forget your sunscreen."

I slid my shorts over my bathing suit, then picked up the grocery bag, into which I'd thrown a towel and my sunscreen. "Already taken care of."

She frowned at my bag. "We'll have to work on the rest of your accessories. And for heaven's sake, borrow my sandals. Even if they don't fit, they're a good bit easier on the eyes than your loafers with a bathing suit. I left them by the back door."

"All right," I said. I hesitated by the door, feeling a dormant emotion stretch in the place where my heart was. It took a few tries, but I eventually got the right words out. "Thank you. For everything. I know I don't deserve your kindness."

"You're welcome," she said. "Although you're wrong, you know. We all need kindness. Especially those of us who don't think we deserve it."

I remembered how Gibbes had said that he thought Loralee was one of the smartest people he'd ever met, and at that moment I had to agree. Before I could stop myself, I moved forward and hugged her, her bones small and rigid under my fingers. She hugged me back, her hands patting me as if I were a child, as if she understood all the things I wanted to say to her, but hadn't yet found a way to.

I released her and turned away without another word and left the room, hoping I wouldn't trip over my feet because I couldn't see through my watery eyes.

The children's voices floated up to me as I descended the stairs, and then the back door slammed, leaving the house eerily silent. I pushed open the kitchen door, expecting to find the room vacant.

Gibbes was at the counter, the plane's passenger list in front of him. When he looked up, I could see the surprise in his eyes. "Wow."

I almost looked over my shoulder to see whether Loralee had followed me. "Thank you?" I said.

He gave me a slow grin. "That's a start, but next time try it without a question mark on the end."

Ignoring him, I set down my bag and examined the refrigerator, its doors open and the freezer defrosted, the inside dark. My gaze moved to the coolers on the floor holding the iced contents of the refrigerator and freezer. "Do we have an extra one to bring with us?"

"Already packed," he said. "Maris's mother sent one over, along with a watermelon and juice boxes for the kids, as well as a case of mini water bottles. I added some sandwiches and snacks, and when we get to my house, we can fill what's left with beer."

"Beer?"

"You can't go to the sandbar without beer — I don't think that's allowed. I've got some margarita mix, too, if you'd prefer."

"Beer is fine," I said, trying to remember the last time I'd had one, realizing it was probably when Cal and I were dating. I'd found soon after we were married that I needed my senses to be sharp, my reflexes quick.

"Good. And I've got some beach chairs we can bring, too. No room for my volleyball net, but if you want to play, there will be a lot of people looking for teammates."

"What kind of a place is this?" I asked, picturing a large playground in the middle of the river.

"It's about a mile-long strip of sand that's this side of heaven, and a Beaufort tradition. Sundays are usually family day, but since we're going today, just be prepared to see lots of tiny bikinis and muscled torsos."

"I'll try to prepare myself," I said, attempting to smile, but the image of all that water was quietly terrifying me. "Do you go there often?"

"Not so much anymore. After my mother died, Deborah Fuller used to take me out there on the weekends, and Cal would sometimes come, too. But since he was ten years older, he got tired of having me hanging around, so he started going with his friends. I'd come out a lot with the Williamses, too — although usually without Mrs. Williams. I'm guessing she looked forward to having a bit of peace and quiet with three boys at home — and usually four, since I spent more time there than I did here."

A shadow darkened his eyes, and I found myself leaning toward him, wanting to know more. "Was that your choice?"

He shook his head. "Not at first. I thought for a long time that my grandmother didn't want me around and was just trying to get rid of me. It's only recently — since I've been coming back to this house, actually — that I've started thinking about it differently." He drummed his fingers on the counter. "I've been remembering things — little snatches."

Gibbes looked out the window over the sink, where the light wiggled its way through the sea glass and spilled, blue and green, into the kitchen. "I remembered my grandmother making a wind chime to honor my mother, saying I'd hear her voice whenever the wind blew." He continued to look out the window, his thoughts distant. "She told me that people who don't know they're broken can't be fixed. She was talking about my mother, I think."

Facing me again, he said, "There was always so much shouting in this house, so much noise. I think that's why I loved books

505

so much — because it gave me an escape. Cal tried it, too, but he could never block it out. He protected me . . ." He paused, as if the thought had just emerged from years of fog and shadow. "From our father. He wasn't a nice man when he drank."

I shivered, imagining a small Gibbes in that house, surrounded by unhappiness and broken people. And Cal, protecting his little brother.

"The last time my father laid a hand on me was about a month before he died, when Cal hit him back. He never touched me after that. And then things sort of calmed down, and I spent most of my time here, because my grandmother almost seemed to need me. She said I was her last hope, although I can't say I ever knew what she meant by that. Then Cal left so suddenly, and my grandmother just sort of closed up. Wouldn't talk about it. And the letters I received from Cal never mentioned it."

He tilted his head. "When I heard that Cal's wife had inherited the house and planned to move in, I'd hoped you'd be able to fill in the missing pieces. I have to admit that I'm more confused than ever." He studied me closely, waiting for me to speak, as if I could maneuver those sections of the puzzle that evaded placement. But all I had to give him was a shoe box holding a Civil War bullet and a charred bolt from a plane.

"I wish I could help you. I do. But I'm just as confused as you — especially after meeting Sandy Beach. It's like the Cal who lived here with you and dated women like Sandy bore no resemblance to the man who moved to Maine and married me." I swallowed, trying to understand my nervousness. "None of it makes any sense."

"No. It doesn't."

I pointed to the folder. "Did you find anything new?"

He stared at me for a long moment before picking up the passenger list. "No. Still wondering why your grandfather's name is on it, assuming it's actually him. But his being from Bangor makes me think it is." He tapped his finger on the top of the file, thinking. "You said you never knew him, that your grandmother never spoke of him."

I shook my head. "No. I remember Grandparents' Day in kindergarten was when I first realized that people usually had two grandparents. My mother explained that her father had died when she was a baby and she'd never known him."

Gibbes nodded slowly, his gaze focused on the folder. "Deborah probably has access to various archives online — maybe she can find a birth and death certificate for your grandfather — just to confirm it's the same man."

"And if it is?" I asked.

His eyes met mine. "I don't know. A part of me hopes that it's not him."

Because there's no such thing as accidents. The unspoken words floated in the air between us.

The back door burst open and Maris rushed into the kitchen. "Dr. Heyward — Owen needs you. He's hurt himself real bad."

She turned and ran outside, Gibbes and me close behind her. Owen sat on the ground with one leg drawn up, his hands gripping his ankle while he tried very hard not to cry. Gibbes knelt beside him, and I squatted on the other side and put my arm around Owen's shoulders as Gibbes gently probed his ankle. "It's definitely not broken," he said confidently. "It's most likely a mild sprain."

Owen's face fell. "Can we still go to the sandbar?"

Gibbes continued to manipulate the ankle, his fingers carefully pressing on the bones of Owen's foot and shin. "I'm going to ice it and wrap it tightly, but I don't see any reason we can't still go. You'll just have to promise me that you'll keep your weight off of it and, when you get home tonight, you'll elevate it."

"I promise!" Owen said earnestly.

Gibbes stood, then carefully lifted Owen from the ground. I stopped, mesmerized by the scene around me.

I'd been in the garden only at night since Loralee had begun transforming it from a forbidding weed-filled space to what I saw just then. The white stone paths reflected the sun like something from a fairy tale, with bright blooms spilling from low hedges and pots along the curving white trail like spectators at a race.

The stone bunny faced Saint Michael, their expressions giving the improbable impression of their being in deep conversation. I was fairly confident that Loralee had done it on purpose.

But the bench had been moved, the small mound that had tilted the base of both statues transformed into a pile of rocks and dirt beside a shallow dip scooped from the ground — most likely the culprit involved in hurting Owen's leg.

Gibbes followed my gaze as I stared at the indentation in the dirt.

"I'm assuming Loralee did all this?" he asked.

"I had no idea she'd made this so beautiful. I saw the hole last night — it's a lot deeper than I thought."

He nodded, frowning. "Looks like she was trying to level the ground. I'll come back tomorrow and take care of it."

"Look," Maris said, squatting by the hole. "There's something funny in here." She reached in and pulled out what looked like a rectangular piece of disintegrating leather, a small tarnished buckle clinging to it by a single thread.

While Gibbes supported Owen, I reached for the object, the faint odor of soil and rot coming from the ground. Maris placed it in my palm, then wiped her hands on the sides of her shorts.

I brushed away the dirt that clung to it, revealing a small flap that covered a clear piece of plastic. Trace remains of white paper lay trapped behind it, a line of black ink still visible.

"I think it was a luggage tag," I said, turning it over in my hand. "I wonder what it's doing in the garden." My eyes met Gibbes's.

"That's a very good question," he said.

Owen hopped into the kitchen, leaning on the doctor's arm, while Maris raced ahead to open the door and pull out a kitchen chair for Owen to sit on. I stayed in the garden for a moment longer, feeling the weight of the luggage tag in my hand and the decay of years against my skin. I listened as a warm breeze stirred the wind chimes that hung from the back of the house, making them chatter like voices from the past.

CHAPTER 27

Merritt

After all the coolers had been loaded, I stood by the back door of Gibbes's Explorer, waiting for Maris and Owen to get in. I was distracted from my anxiety when I noticed how Owen held the door open for Maris and waited for her to get in before climbing in himself. I was about to ask him why I wasn't getting the same treatment when I looked up to see Gibbes holding open the passenger door.

I realized that without Loralee there, I would be expected to sit in the front seat. I could probably climb into the backseat with the children, and endure their looks as well as any from Gibbes, but I wasn't sure I could live with myself afterward.

"Thank you," I said, putting my beach bag on the floorboard, then allowing him to help me up into the seat. I wanted to tell Gibbes that there was a running board and that I

512

didn't need the help, but I had to admit that knowing he was there was oddly comforting. And a good example to Owen, I thought, feeling fully justified.

As soon as he closed the door, I moved the seat back as far as I could, then secured my seat belt. I briefly wished that I had my life jacket on already, prepared to float in the water if necessary.

After Gibbes began driving, I felt the panic inside me like a moth spreading its wings, filling my throat.

"The seat belt wouldn't fit right if you had your life jacket on, you know. And you'd probably feel a little claustrophobic," Gibbes said.

I stared at him. "How did you know what I was thinking?"

"Your eyes. They give you away. Most children are like that, which is probably why I noticed."

"Are you calling me a child?"

His gaze flickered over me for a brief moment as a smile teased his lips. "Oh, no. Not at all. Just thought you should know that you'd make a horrible poker player. Or police interrogator."

Despite myself, laughter bubbled from my lips, the moth tucking back into its chrysalis. "That's good to know, just in case I ever want to switch careers."

I glanced out the window, surprised to see that we were already almost at the bridge, realizing Gibbes had distracted me on purpose. He looked into the rearview mirror at Owen. "Rocky — tell us some interesting facts that we might not know."

Owen practically bounced up and down in his seat. "Did you know that all clown fish start off as boys and later on in their lives become girls?"

"And seahorse boys have the babies," Maris piped up.

I turned to look in the backseat. "Seriously?"

Two small heads nodded vigorously.

When I turned back around my smile faded. We'd just reached the bridge, the shadows of the side rails flickering as we sped forward. It had come so quickly that I hadn't had time to prepare myself, to begin my breathing exercises.

Gibbes reached over and squeezed my hand before returning his to the steering wheel. "You'd probably rather I use both hands to drive."

I looked down at my lap, where my own hands were pressed tightly together. But I still felt the warmth from his hand, my skin tingling where he'd touched me. I felt better somehow, the crossing made bearable because somebody had thought to hold my hand. The loneliness inside me seemed to shift, allowing in a small shard of light.

Lifting my head, I forced myself to look at the bridge in front of us, at the tall beams and grids of the swing portion, although I couldn't quite muster the courage to look over the side to the water. "You didn't tell me we had to go over the bridge again."

"Well, we have to go to my house to get the boat. It's a long swim otherwise. If you like that kind of thing, there's an annual charity Beaufort River swim each May."

"No," I said quickly. "Although I'd be happy to be a spectator and watch you." The words were said through clenched teeth as we neared the end of the bridge, the talking helping by making me not hold my breath.

"I haven't done the official river swim, but I have done it accidentally."

I looked at the receding bridge in my side-view mirror and felt all of my muscles unclench.

"You did it," Gibbes said softly. "I guess you just proved Cal wrong."

"I didn't say I wasn't afraid anymore. But I did make it across," I said, allowing myself a small smile. Turning to him, I asked,

"How do you accidentally do a river swim?"

Gibbes glanced into the backseat, where Owen and Maris were playing Go Fish with a deck Owen had brought with him.

After raising the volume on the radio, he said, "I was being a stupid teenager. Me and Sy Williams drank a couple of six-packs and thought it would be fun to walk the bridge at night. We were on the pedestrian part, not too high up, and I managed to go over the side."

My heart seemed to flip over and shrink all at the same time. "Was he able to pull you back up?"

"Heck, no. He kept on walking. Didn't even know I wasn't there. He walked home, then got in bed and passed out."

"Your grandmother must have been frantic."

"She didn't know until the nice people in the boat that plucked me out of the water about a mile downriver called her." He rubbed a hand over his face. "I don't tell many people that story, because it's embarrassing to admit that my brush with death was completely due to my own stupidity. But I learned something, too."

I waited for him to speak. Finally I asked, "What?"

"I figure Loralee has probably said this

516

before, but everything must happen for a reason. Maybe being a doctor is part of that. Who knows? Did you ever think that surviving your accident prepared you for something else?"

The panic returned to me, the blinding light that always washed away my sight and replaced it with dark, silent water. "No." I shook my head, trying to erase the image to replace it with the dusty road ahead, the moss weeping from the canopy of oak trees above us. "Please. Don't. I don't talk about it."

"Go Fish!" Owen shouted from the backseat, oblivious to our conversation.

"You didn't drown," Gibbes said carefully.

My hands gripped my bare legs, my nails making crescent moons in the skin. "Because my mother pushed me through the broken window." I dug my nails in harder. "And when I tried to turn back to try to help her, she pushed me away again."

We drove in silence for a while, and I cracked open my window to remind myself that the air outside was warm and dry.

His voice was steady and reassuring, as if he were preparing a patient for a shot. "Until we're parents ourselves, it's hard to understand what a mother will do to protect her child. I see that a lot with my critically ill patients. And I see it in Loralee." He was thoughtful for a moment, weighing his words again. "Be kind to her, Merritt. I think she could use an extra dose of kindness right now."

I turned to him, anger and surprise battling with each other. "I'm more reserved than a lot of people, but I don't mean to be unkind. I don't resent her anymore, if that's what you mean."

He nodded, a muscle in his jaw ticking. "She's a single mother, which is never easy. She appears strong, but I think she could use a little TLC. She's always worrying about others, and I don't think there's anything she wouldn't do for her son if she thought it would be good for him."

I looked down at my folded hands and the crescent marks on my thighs that hadn't yet faded, and listened to the children's loud giggles from the backseat. A reluctant smile tugged at my lips. "Like traveling to another state so Owen and I could finally meet?" I turned my face to the window and took a deep breath of the sticky, heavy air. "That's why I resented her, you know. Because my mother had sacrificed herself to save me, and I did everything I knew to honor her memory."

"And then your father met somebody else,

and you thought he was somehow dishonoring her."

"Yeah, pretty much. He said he'd always love my mother, but that there were so many more years left in his own life and he wanted to live them. It wasn't Loralee — I would have resented anybody my father fell in love with who wasn't my mother. I just couldn't forgive either him or Loralee. It was like I wanted to punish them, to make them suffer as much as I was. Because I'd been there with her, in the water. I was the one who was arguing with her when she lost control of the car."

He didn't say anything, and we listened to the roll of tires on dirt and broken shells, and the sound of children playing a card game. A white egret settled delicately on the side of the road in front of us, its slow, graceful movements seeming to calm the wild beating in my chest. My mother loved birds, had loved to watch them at the feeders we kept around the yard. She would have loved that place, with the exotic flowers and the birds that were eerily prehistoric and tropical at the same time.

I pressed my forehead against the window as we drove slowly by the egret, and it seemed to be watching me with its round yellow eyes, prompting me to continue.

There was something about Gibbes that invited confidences. I'd once believed Cal was like that, too. Maybe that was why I pressed on, wanting Gibbes to hear my story, to offer the absolution I'd never thought I deserved. Or maybe I was still the old Merritt, and was hoping to push him out of my life and get him to leave me in the solitude I'd come to Beaufort to find.

I continued. "I tried to help her, but she was stuck between the steering wheel and the seat. She just . . . pushed me away. She knew I could swim — she'd made me take lessons at an indoor pool when I was a little girl, even though she was afraid of the water herself. So I swam through the broken windshield — that's how I cut my leg — until I reached the surface." I swallowed, tasting the salt air that was so different from home, transporting me away from the cold night and the icy rain so I could remember it almost as if I were watching it happen to someone else. I breathed in deeply, smelling the scent of the marsh mud and sun-heated grass that had once been so foreign to me but had already become so familiar. And I thought of Cal leaving it all behind.

The children were giggling again and I closed my eyes, trying to lose myself in the sound, to escape my thoughts. But the summer air and the gentle presence of the man beside me made the words fall from my mouth anyway. "Cal told me I was a coward for leaving her, just as he'd said I was a coward for being afraid of the water. He said I should have tried anyway."

Gibbes was silent, making me believe that I'd finally succeeded in pushing him away. I tried to console myself, to tell myself that that was what I wanted, but all I could feel was a heavy dread that felt oddly like disappointment.

He didn't look at me when he spoke, and although his words were soft, his hands gripped the steering wheel with whitened knuckles. "Courage isn't about the absence of fear. Courage is doing the one thing you think you cannot do. Swimming away from your mother took more courage than most people have." He stretched his fingers, encouraging the blood to flow through them again. "I think I've told you this before, Merritt: You're a lot braver than you think you are. And you're a survivor. Never forget that."

My spine seemed to soften against the leather seat, the breath I'd held escaping through my opened mouth as if I were expelling demons. It was like being crippled for years and then being told I could run.

"Go fish!" Maris shouted from the back-seat, reminding me of where I was and where we were heading.

Facing him, I asked, "Are you telling me this because I'm about to get in a boat again?" I thought he would smile but was surprised when he didn't.

"In part," he said. "But I imagine there are lots of times in life when you'll need to remember that."

There was something in the way he said it, something in the way he measured his words like doling out cough syrup, that made me believe that he wasn't talking about the boat.

When we reached the house, the children retrieved their bags full of sand toys and towels, and two small beach chairs from Maris's mother, then raced each other to the dock despite Gibbes's reminder to keep Owen's weight off his ankle. Owen responded by hobbling as fast as he could.

I felt lighter somehow, as if something I'd been carrying around for a long time had been jettisoned. I took off Loralee's sandals and allowed myself to feel the soft soil beneath my bare feet, unable to remember the last time I'd been outside without shoes.

I helped Gibbes carry everything to the boat, but allowed him to load it all. I'd put on my life jacket and insisted the children put on theirs, too, but Gibbes waited until he'd gone inside and changed, which made me nervous every time he stepped onto the boat before he did.

He caught me frowning and grinned. "Are you worried that I'll get hurt?"

I frowned back at him. "I'm worried that if you get hurt I'm going to have to drive us back across the bridge."

Gibbes straightened, his eyes serious. "I wouldn't make you do that. Not until you're ready."

Not until you're ready. His words meant that he believed it possible, that I would someday be able to drive across the bridge by myself. Because he thought I was brave.

"When alligator eggs are laid, they're not already boys or girls," Owen announced. "It depends on where the nest is. If it's warm, the eggs become boys, and if it's colder, they're girls."

"Why are you talking about alligators?" I asked, glancing around nervously.

"Because they're all over the place," Maris announced matter-of-factly.

I took a step off the dock and looked at Gibbes, hoping he'd reassure me that they were joking. Instead he said, "They won't bother you if you don't bother them."

"Yeah," I said through gritted teeth. "I think you've mentioned that."

"They're not aggressive like crocodiles," Owen explained. "These are just alligators. I hope we get to see one." He bounced on his toes with excitement, just like our father used to do.

A loud splash caught our attention about thirty feet from the dock, and I reached a hand out toward Owen and Maris, getting ready to pull them away from danger.

"It's a dolphin!" Owen shouted, pointing at where large ripples of water were pulsing toward us, the dock gently bobbing under our feet.

A gray fin appeared above the surface of the water, nearer now and close enough that I could see the sleek texture of the animal's skin, the sun reflecting off the arched back as it dived under the dark water. We watched in silence for a full minute, our patience rewarded as it rose above the water again, its large almond-shaped eyes seeming to be full of human emotions, its long mouth with tiny, sharp teeth curved upward like a smile. It jumped in an arc, showing off its loveliness, then dived beneath the water one last time before disappearing.

"Did you see it, Merritt? Did you see it?" Owen spoke in his church voice, hushed and reverent.

"Yes, I did," I said, my voice almost a whisper. There was something magical and fairy tale–like about that place of black mud and marshes, of insect symphonies and long-legged birds with elegant necks, where dolphins leaped from the water right in front of you. It made me feel as if everything in my life, all the gains and all the losses, had always been leading me there.

Owen continued to stare out at the water, as if by doing so he could make the dolphin reappear. "We used to have a bench swing in our backyard that Mama called her happy place. She says that wherever we live, we should always find a happy place — kind of like 'base' in a game of tag, where you can go and all of your problems and worries can't touch you." He opened his eyes wider, mirroring the ceiling of blue sky that was big enough to fall into. "I think this dock would be mine."

Gibbes placed a hand on his shoulder. "And you're welcome to come here anytime, Rocky." He looked at his watch. "We should get going. I checked the tide schedule to make sure we don't get shortchanged on our time. You can always tell the tourists, because they put in on the side of the sandbar that gets covered up first when the

525

tide comes in, and I want to make sure that we're not right there with them."

Gibbes and Owen helped Maris and me into the boat before settling in themselves. I kept my hands pressed between my knees, trying very hard to keep my mouth closed and not shout in alarm every time Owen or Maris put their hands in the water. I watched the water carefully from under the brim of my visor, keeping an eye out for any alligators that might have the idea of eating children's fingers for breakfast, and felt the soft slap of my silk chiffon scarf against my shoulders as we moved out into the river.

"You okay?" Gibbes shouted over the sound of the motor.

I gave him a thumbs-up, feeling the sun and the spray of water on my skin. I took off the visor and tilted my face, imagining myself rising from the dark depths beneath and guided upward by the light of the sun.

Despite the early hour, the sandbar was crowded as we neared — although not nearly as crowded as it would be in another half hour, Gibbes assured me. It looked like an abstract painting while we were still far away, with splotches of bright nylon colors dotted against the sandy background, and white bouncing shapes tethered closely to the strip of sand, bobbing and dancing to the rhythm of various songs playing at the same time. It should have been garish and loud and overwhelming, but I felt my stomach leap with excitement.

Cal had come there as a boy and a young man growing up. Maybe somehow I'd find in the waves and the sand the boy he'd been, the boy I'd seen glimpses of. The boy I'd loved and the parts of him that had loved me back. If I were to make any sense of my seven-year marriage, I needed to find him.

Because our boat was small, Gibbes was able to maneuver it to the front row of watercraft — including a couple of yachts, a few larger motorboats, and some stump-knockers like ours that looked even older — and dropped anchor in the direction of the incoming tide. He did it with a precision of movement, a sleek show of muscle that made the roof of my mouth like flypaper to my tongue.

He took off his life jacket and tossed it in the boat, then kicked off his topsiders while the children shed their own jackets and shoes. Then Gibbes hopped out of the boat, standing in water that wasn't even up to his knees. He lifted Maris out and then Owen — keeping the wrapped ankle dry was already a lost cause — and watched them until they were completely up on the sand before turning to me. I looked down at the water, wondering how high it would be on my legs.

"Are you going to take off your life jacket?" he asked softly.

I looked at all the people on the sandbar, noticing that not a single one of them wore a jacket. I looked uncertainly at Gibbes.

"I'll hold your hand the whole time and not let go. But I won't carry you."

His words would have provoked anger in me only a few weeks before. But I saw them now not as a challenge, but a direction on a path. A path I'd been wandering ever since the night my mother died.

I quickly undid the buckles of my life jacket, then looked over the edge of the boat. While I was wondering what the most graceful way would be to get into the water, Gibbes placed his hands on either side of my waist and lifted me over. Instead of plopping me in the water as he'd done with Owen and Maris, he held me for a moment, then slowly slid me into the water until my toes touched the soft, wet sand.

"How does it feel?"

His voice was close to my ear, his breath warm on my neck. My tongue was finding it hard to dislodge itself from the roof of my mouth. "Fine," I finally managed, feeling only his hands on my waist and my chest pressed against his.

"Good." He pulled away and took my hand, just as he'd promised, and led me to the sand. When I was safely standing next to Owen and Maris, Gibbes regarded me closely. "If I'm going to unload the boat, you're going to have to let go of my hand."

Embarrassed, I immediately dropped his hand and then organized a relay line to unload the boat as quickly as possible, still feeling the pressure of my hand in his.

We set up our chairs on the creek side of the sandbar so the children could take turns bogging in the mud and then swimming in the river to wash it off. Gibbes had un-wrapped Owen's ankle and laid the bandage out to dry with a promise that it would go back on the second Owen returned to the boat. Although both children were strong swimmers, Gibbes went out with them each time, while I stayed on the sand, watching.

The last time they'd come back from swimming, the children sat in the sand and began making a large castle with a deep moat. Gibbes sat down under the umbrella in the chair next to mine and reached over into a cooler and grabbed a beer, then handed one to me.

"Are you sure you don't want to go swimming? You could hold my hand again." He grinned like he was joking, but I knew he wasn't.

I shook my head. "I waded in the water. I think that's enough for one day."

He took a swig from his can. "You said your mother made you take swimming lessons. You probably still remember how."

I pressed the cold can to my cheek, trying to cool a burning sensation that had nothing to do with the sun. "I know. But knowing how doesn't make me want to dive right in. I just don't like the water."

I felt his gaze on me and turned to meet his eyes. "You said that Cal once tried to help you get through your fear. What did he do?"

Putting the can to my mouth, I drank three gulps, the cold alcohol trickling down my throat and into my bloodstream. I took three more, wanting the alcohol to get to my head quicker so I wouldn't have to remember.

"You don't want to know," I said, my body feeling heavy as I shrank further into my chair.

"I wouldn't ask if I didn't want to know."

With a defiant flick of my wrist, I downed

the rest of the beer, waiting until I could feel the beginning of a buzz as it traveled through my bloodstream and hit my brain.

I squinted my eyes out toward the river, where the bridge connected downtown Beaufort with Lady's Island, and people crossed it by the hundreds every day without even thinking about how high they were, or what would happen if their car slipped off the side.

My tongue felt heavy and slurred my words. "He filled a bathtub full of ice-cold water, and then held my face under until I couldn't hold my breath any longer. And then he let me up just long enough for me to grab a single breath before he did it again."

"Bastard." Gibbes dropped his beer in the sand and leaned forward on his knees. When he looked at me, the sun turned his eyes to gold so that they didn't look like Cal's anymore. "If I had known, I would have stopped him. I would have done something so that he never laid a hand on you." He paused. "Even if it meant killing him with my own bare hands."

"I didn't need you to kill him." I blinked, my eyelids languid in the heat, my brain waves slowed by the alcohol and the rhythm of the waves caused by a passing boat.

"Because I did." The empty beer can slid from my hand and hit his with a tinny clink.

He reached up and cupped my cheek, his thumb rubbing away a tear I hadn't wanted to shed. I'd long ago stopped shedding tears over Cal. But maybe this time I was shedding it for me.

"The night he died, he apologized for hurting me again, and said how he hated himself for not being able to stop. And he told me he loved me."

I dug my feet under the sand, feeling the coolness there, wondering how it would feel to bury my whole body beneath it, how each grain was so small, yet how heavy it would be to be buried alive in it. "I told him that to save us both he should walk into that fire and never come out." I shrugged. "And he did."

He slid his hand behind the base of my skull and brought me toward him, then gently pressed his lips to mine. His face was serious when he pulled back. "I'm sorry," he said. "I'm sorry that you lived through that, and that there was nobody to help you. And I'm sorry that you feel guilt over his death." He sat back, still looking at me. "You are so much stronger and braver than you think you are. I just wish you could see you as I see you."

"Dr. Heyward?" Maris's voice piped up behind him. "Can we stay to watch the sunset? I always do when I'm here with my family."

Gibbes stood. "Not tonight. We have a refrigerator to go buy. But the sandbar isn't going away anytime soon, so we'll come back, okay?"

He took my hand and pulled me up from my chair. "I won't let go, okay? When you're ready to swim, just let me know."

I nodded numbly, then pulled away and began to pack up our things and help Gibbes bring them to the boat.

The sun was still high in the sky as we pulled away, and I watched as the water widened then narrowed into the creeks and marshes of Cal's boyhood, searching for him behind every live oak and cluster of sea oats. I wanted to see him, to remember that boy. And then maybe I could forget the man he'd become.

I turned my face toward the sun again and smiled up at the expanse of sky. *You are so much stronger and braver than you think you are.* I wasn't sure I believed it, but at least I was beginning to feel the world twitching outside my self-made boundaries, burning with possibilities.

CHAPTER 28

Loralee

Loralee gripped the banister tightly, following the sound of the sewing machine in the dining room. It was midafternoon on Sunday, and Owen was back at the sandbar with Maris and her family. The house seemed sad without the noise children usually made, and she was glad for the staccato drill of the sewing machine to fill the silence.

She took two steps, then paused to rest. She'd managed to put on her favorite sundress that fell in an A-line and didn't cinch it in at the waist like she was used to doing. She comforted herself with the knowledge that A-lines never went out of style and were flattering for everybody. She'd already written that in her *Journal of Truths.*

She'd left her high heels in her closet, and wore Merritt's slippers instead. It had taken her a full half hour to convince herself that she couldn't walk in her favorite shoes without losing her balance. She'd been surprised after she'd made the decision how little she cared. It seemed as if her body had already begun shedding its skin, unburdening her of things she wouldn't need.

Loralee paused under the archway that led to the dining room. The walls glowed as light spilled into the room through the freshly cleaned tall windows from where Merritt had taken off the heavy silk draperies and dusty sheer coverings. She'd been removing all the drapes in the house, and had begun rearranging furniture and making lists of things that needed to be done, reminding Loralee of a mother bird preparing its nest.

"What are you making?" she asked as she approached Merritt, her head bent over a long strip of pale blue fabric.

Merritt lifted her foot from the pedal and looked up. "I'm restyling the curtains for the front parlor. This raw silk is old, but still in really good condition, and it's too beautiful to get rid of. I guess the New Englander in me convinced me that I had the skills to redo them."

Loralee leaned over to get a better look. "I kind of liked the heavy *Gone with the Wind* velvet look with the thick fringe, but it's not

535

my house." She smiled at Merritt to show that she was joking — although not entirely.

"I've never seen the movie, but I've heard about it. If you'd like, I could make you a dress with what's left over. Otherwise I'm just going to make some simple long panels with some kind of edging I haven't decided on yet. Although I'm pretty sure it's not going to be fringe. But I'm definitely getting rid of the big balloon swags that were at the top."

"You've never seen *Gone with the Wind*? That's like saying you've never been to a baseball game. Or eaten apple pie."

"I have never seen the movie. Or read the book. And don't look at me like I'm the only one."

"Um-hmm," Loralee said, making it clear that she was sure Merritt was the only person on the planet who'd never seen the best movie ever made. "As soon as you get your new TV and DVD player, I'm going to buy you a DVD so we can watch it together. I'd really hate for you to miss out."

The sound of digging brought Loralee's attention to the window. Gibbes was outside, his shirt discarded on the top of the bench, his drenched undershirt clinging nicely to his chest. He'd paused long enough from his work to lift the bottom edge of his undershirt to wipe his face, allowing her to see an impressive set of abs.

She looked down at her stepdaughter. "That man is *fine*."

Merritt's cheeks were flushed a pretty pink, which meant she'd probably been thinking the same thing. Although it was at least a step in the right direction, Loralee hoped she'd stick around long enough to hear Merritt say it out loud.

"What's he doing?" Loralee asked.

"He's trying to make sure you don't do any heavy lifting outside. We were both rather alarmed that you'd moved the bench by yourself and then tried to level the dirt." She glanced out the window again. "We found a disintegrating luggage tag in the little hole you dug, so Gibbes wanted to see if there was anything else under there before he filled it all in and leveled it."

"He looks thirsty. Maybe you should bring him some sweet tea," Loralee suggested.

"I would if we had any. The refrigerator I wanted is back-ordered, so all we have is the small refrigerator Gibbes is loaning us from his office. I guess I could settle for another model so I'd have something sooner, but the one I selected had every single feature we wanted — including the ice dispenser in the door for Owen — so

I'm willing to wait. Anyway, the one we're using isn't big enough for a pitcher of anything."

Loralee kept her sigh of exasperation to herself. "Then how about a tall glass of tap water?" She looked pointedly at Merritt.

After a quick glance toward the window, Merritt flipped off the sewing machine, then pushed back her chair. "All right. I guess that would be the right thing to do."

Loralee followed Merritt into the kitchen, unable to resist rolling her eyes. She waited while Merritt took a glass from the cabinet, then held it under the cold tap while Loralee admired the cute yellow skirt and pale blue blouse that had been in the Belk bag. Merritt even wore Loralee's sandals since, luckily, Loralee had on the slippers. The old loafers had mysteriously vanished, "accidentally" taken out with the trash.

"I like the outfit you're wearing," Loralee said, leaning heavily on the kitchen table and averting her eyes from the bowl of fruit in the center. Today even the thought of food was making her ill.

Merritt turned around so suddenly she sloshed some of the water from the glass. "Thank you. And thanks for picking it out for me. Although . . ." She paused, chewing on her lower lip.

"Although what?"

"I don't like wearing things that show my scar."

Loralee considered her words for a long moment, realizing how easy it would be to say the wrong thing. "We earn our scars, Merritt, and I think it's only right that we show them off, because it proves where we've been. They're something to be proud of." When Merritt didn't walk away or immediately change the subject, Loralee was encouraged enough to continue. "Besides, you've got a gorgeous pair of legs, and I think it's a downright sin to hide them."

Merritt's lips twitched. "But don't you think the skirt's a little too tight in the bottom, and the top maybe a little snug around my chest?"

Loralee crossed her arms and gave Merritt the look she'd always reserved for those inebriated passengers who wanted to order another drink. "Sugar, your clothes should always be tight enough to show that you're a woman, but loose enough to show that you're a lady." She made a mental note to add that one to her journal. "I'd say you can check both those boxes with that outfit."

Merritt didn't look completely convinced and began plucking and tugging on the fabric of the top and skirt while she headed out the back door, Loralee following close behind.

She watched as Merritt handed the glass to Gibbes, avoiding looking into his eyes, while Gibbes never took his gaze from Merritt's face. There was something different between them today, like electrified air during a summer storm. If it were less humid, Loralee was pretty sure Merritt's hair would be floating around her head like somebody had just rubbed a balloon up and down on it.

Gibbes drank all the water in big, long gulps while both Loralee and Merritt took the opportunity to admire the clinging T-shirt up close.

"Thank you," he said, handing the glass back to Merritt.

Their fingers must have touched, or else Merritt had been bitten by a red ant, because she jerked away, dropping the glass. It hit a pile of dirt and didn't shatter, but Merritt stared at it for a moment as if expecting it to. Then they both bent to pick it up and bumped heads, until finally Loralee stepped forward to get it and end their misery.

"I'm glad you came out," Gibbes said. "I found something inside the hole and I've been trying to dig around it to make the opening wider so I can pull it up."

Merritt stepped closer and looked down. "It looks like the side of a suitcase." She stepped back and this time met Gibbes's eyes.

"Yeah. I thought so, too."

Loralee moved over to the bench and gratefully lowered herself onto it. "Maybe it's from that plane that exploded and rained wreckage all over Beaufort. Maybe it's somehow connected to that plane model Edith made that's up in the attic. They're both so bizarre that they've got to be related. It's like that time Owen's guinea pig disappeared and the neighbor's dog stopped barking at Owen when he rode his bike in the driveway. I knew it had to be because the dog felt guilty about what he'd done to Owen's pet."

Both Merritt and Gibbes looked at her for a moment before Gibbes cleared his throat. "Anyway, it looks like it's leather and has probably been down there for a while. If the whole thing doesn't disintegrate when I pick it up, I'm not sure there will be anything inside that's still recognizable or not covered in mildew."

"Can I help?" Merritt asked.

Gibbes gave her an appraising look that Loralee felt sitting all the way over on the bench. "Sure. Just be careful you don't ruin your outfit. I'd hate not to see it again."

Merritt began tugging on the bottom of the skirt. "You don't think it's too short?"

He grinned. "Trust me, if I thought it was too short, I wouldn't tell you."

Merritt struggled to respond, then just turned her back on Gibbes and marched toward Loralee. Reaching for the glass that Loralee held, she said, "I'm going to go put this in the sink."

Gibbes was still grinning as he watched Merritt walk away.

"Why do you do that?" Loralee asked softly.

Gibbes didn't seem startled by her question. "Because I don't believe anybody has made her feel beautiful or desirable in a very long time."

"Is that the only reason?" she asked, the scent of the moist dirt stinging her nostrils.

The light sparked in his eyes again. "The more I scratch the surface to see what's beneath that crusty exterior, the more I see the person I think she was before she met Cal. And there's a lot there to like."

Loralee beamed. "Y'all had a good time at the sandbar yesterday, I'm guessing."

"We did. Especially the kids. But I learned a lot about Merritt, too."

Loralee sat up straighter, even though it made her stomach hurt. "Like what?"

"Well, she doesn't resent your marrying her father anymore — which I think we both agree is about time. And I learned that my brother wasn't a very nice man."

"I'm sorry," Loralee said. "It's not easy to find out that people aren't who we thought they were, or who we wanted them to be." She shifted on the bench, wondering whether there was a better position that wouldn't hurt so much. "After Mama died, I tracked down my daddy, thinking he must've had a good reason to leave us when I was a baby, and that maybe he'd been trying to find me all those years.

"I found him in a bar in Birmingham, hustling people at the pool table, just living from drink to drink. He spit at me, then told me to go to hell." Loralee pressed her hands against her abdomen, willing the nausea to go away. "That's when I realized that his leaving me and Mama had nothing to do with us at all. He was just born with inner demons that were always stronger than he was. Even my mama's love and a baby daughter weren't enough ammunition to help him fight. I felt better when I left the bar, like I'd just been released from prison, and I finally found my own strength to forgive him."

Gibbes's eyes were full of shadows, like the creek beds at dusk. "You're saying that I should forgive Cal for being a brute and terrorizing his wife?"

"I'm not telling you anything. But it seems to me that you and Merritt have been brought together because of Cal, and maybe in that you can find your own peace."

Merritt came through the back door then, and Loralee was relieved, because she knew that Gibbes's next question would have probably been to ask her whether she'd told Merritt how sick she really was. It was still too early, the cement between the blocks of their new relationship still too wet to withstand any pressure. Her pain level had risen to a seven, but it still wasn't an eight, and to Loralee that meant she still had time.

Gibbes jumped into the shallow hole. "You ready?" he asked Merritt.

"Sure." She knelt in the dirt and put her hands on her thighs. "Ready when you are."

Loralee moved to stand behind Merritt and watched as Gibbes carefully guided the shovel around the suitcase, loosening the dirt to make it easier for him to lift it out. Then, using the shovel like a spatula, he carefully stuck it under one of the shorter ends and gently lifted it. With the shovel handle lying on the ground and the suitcase propped up, Gibbes reached down and grabbed it around the two exposed sides. With an impressive display of biceps, he lifted it to the lip of the hole while Merritt grabbed it and slid it until it was flat against the ground.

"It didn't fall apart, which is a good thing, although it feels pretty soggy." Gibbes stepped out of the hole and brushed his hands together.

The leather of the suitcase might have once been a light brown, but moisture and years of being buried had darkened it to a deep mahogany. There was a large dent in the bottom corner, as if it had fallen from a great height and hit something on its way down. Loralee spotted something beneath a dusting of soil by the handle and brushed the dirt away with her finger. It was a gold-embossed monogram: HPH.

Merritt made a strangled sound in the back of her throat. "Those are my grand-father's initials," she whispered, the words garbled as if spoken through dirt.

Gibbes touched her hand. "We're doing this together, all right?"

Merritt gave him a grateful glance and nodded before the three of them returned their attention to the battered suitcase.

The latch by the monogram was already opened, leaving the two on each side. "If these are too corroded to open, I'll get a saw," Gibbes said as he reached around to the undamaged side. After a brief pause, he twisted the latch. It stuck at first and then, with a grinding pop, stood in the open position.

Merritt held down the unlatched side as Gibbes moved to the other end of the suitcase. The latch on the damaged side was harder, and Gibbes was about to resort to a saw when they heard the pop for the second time.

Merritt moved her hands from the top, letting them hover above the front and side latches like an indecisive bee.

"Ready?" Gibbes asked.

She nodded and together they lifted the lid.

Loralee coughed and held her hand over her face. The smell of rot was strong, reminding her of the cellar of the house she and her mama had lived in during their brief stay in Tuscaloosa. The discarded lives of previous tenants had littered the space that flooded each spring and fall, the forgotten boxes and piles of clothing slowly turning to mush.

When she looked back at the suitcase,

neither Gibbes nor Merritt had made a move to touch anything. A coating of green and black goo covered the top layer of what had once been clothing, a mosslike growth crawling upward across the sides and top like tiny fingers looking for an escape.

"I'll go get the dishwashing gloves," Loralee said as she made an attempt to stand without using any of her abdominal muscles.

Merritt leaped up. "You stay there — I'll go get them." She ran into the kitchen, then returned with the pair of yellow rubber gloves. "I only have one pair, and they're small, so I guess I'm going to have to do the honors."

Gibbes shifted backward to give her more light. "Try to remove the top layer — there might be less damage farther down."

She nodded and, with her lips pressed together, began lifting out limp and soggy button-down shirts, still folded as if waiting to be worn. "My mom used to pack my dad's suitcase this way — with the folded shirts on top and all the small items tucked beneath, so that if it ever opened up he wouldn't be chasing rolled-up socks." She leaned back on her haunches, tilting her head to the side. "But his toiletries kit was always tucked right in the front, so that if he ever needed anything out of it, he could grab it without having to open the suitcase the whole way."

After the ruined garments had been placed on the ground, the rest of the items could be seen better. The undershirts and slacks were still folded, but the creases were crusted with mud and mold, the elastic of the boxer-style underwear bleeding streaks of red and brown.

Gibbes reached inside a pair of black wingtips and pulled out a tie that had been neatly rolled into a ball. The silk was stained with moisture and spots of mildew, but the navy background with light blue diagonal stripes was still visible.

Loralee leaned forward and reached out her hand. "I've seen that tie before."

"It's a pretty common one, I think," Gibbes said. "I probably have one in my closet."

"Yes, it's called the Eton tie, I'm pretty sure," Loralee said, feeling a surge of nausea wash over her that had nothing to do with her being sick. "And I could be wrong, but . . ."

"But what?" Gibbes prompted.

Loralee swallowed. "One of the passengers in the model plane up in the attic is wearing the same tie. He's the one with the dopp kit glued to his lap."

A tic had started in Gibbes's jaw, the sound of the garden's insects somehow quieter, as if somebody had lowered the volume button so the three of them could think. "I'll check that out as soon as we're done here."

Wanting to know where the red staining the underwear was coming from, Loralee moved closer and lifted a corner of the small stack of undershirts, revealing two wilted and yellowed linen handkerchiefs, with a bold red monogram in the corner of each. She pulled them out and turned them over. "Definitely done with a machine."

"What is?" Merritt turned away from her search of the side pockets and stopped suddenly, as if she'd just put a Popsicle in her mouth and was suffering a brain freeze.

"The handkerchiefs," Loralee said, holding one up. "They were done with a machine — that's why all the stitches are so perfect."

"What's wrong, Merritt?" Gibbes asked, noticing that her face no longer seemed to have any blood in it.

Merritt reached over and took one of the handkerchiefs from Loralee and held the monogram close to her face, stretching the fabric taut, staring at it as if she were waiting for it to change.

When she looked up, her eyes were dark.

"I've seen one of these before." She slowly dropped her hands into her lap and turned to Loralee. "I told you about it — when you gave me the sewing machine. I told you how my grandmother and I loved to make things together." She stopped, her chest rising and falling as if her lungs were too busy struggling for air to let her have enough to speak.

Loralee continued for her. "Until that package arrived for your grandmother. There was a letter in it and a handkerchief."

Merritt pushed the handkerchief off her lap as if it were a large insect. "After she read the letter, she stuffed it back in the package, along with the handkerchief, and threw it in the garbage. Then she packed up the sewing machine and put it away. I never saw it again." She slid off the rubber gloves and let them fall to the ground as she stood.

Her hands were shaking as she looked at Gibbes. "How? How is this here?"

He stood and tried to take her hands, but she was too jittery, walking around the suitcase without looking at it. "My guess is that it fell from the plane and my grandmother found it."

Merritt rubbed her hands against the sides of her skirt, trying to erase years of dirt that clung to the suitcase. "That's the only part that makes sense. Then she opened the suitcase before it was buried. That's how she knew about the tie that she put on a passenger in that awful plane model up in the attic. And that's how she knew about the handkerchief. Because she got the address from the luggage tag and then mailed a handkerchief to my grandmother in Maine with a note — a note that said something that made my grandmother crawl into herself and stay there for the rest of her life."

Merritt clutched her head with both hands, as if she were afraid it might explode if she didn't hold it together. "How is this possible? That my grandfather's suitcase — assuming it's the same Henry P. Holden — is buried in the backyard of the house where my husband grew up one thousand miles away from where I met him? There's a connection here that I'm not sure I want to know. This suitcase was buried, hidden because somebody never wanted it to be found." She shook her head, as if it were a snow globe with all the words and thoughts swirling around in random patterns.

"We can figure this out together," Gibbes said, but Merritt backed up toward the rear porch, out of his reach.

"I need to be alone right now. I need to figure things out on my own." She ran up the steps and through the kitchen door, letting it bang shut behind her.

Gibbes stared at the closed door before shifting his gaze to Loralee. "What just happened here?"

Loralee struggled to keep standing, leaning heavily on the back of the bench. "She's not used to sharing her emotions, and when they all demand to come out at once it's confusing. Just give her some time to sort things out, and to realize that she's not alone."

"Let me help you upstairs, Loralee; you look exhausted."

She wasn't going to argue with him. "Thank you," she said, her eyes resting on the open suitcase, remembering something she wanted to put in her journal. *Secrets, like chickens, always come home to roost.*

She took a step toward Gibbes and her knees went wobbly as a pain she'd not yet experienced seemed to split her in two, the insides of her eyelids illuminated with white-hot heat.

She was aware of Gibbes's arms around her, gently lowering her to the bench, and then heard his soothing voice. "I'm calling an ambulance."

Loralee shook her head, trying to find the strength to push at his chest. "No — Merritt can't know. . . ."

But Merritt was already running back down the steps toward her, Loralee's name on her lips, as her eyes flew back in her head and another pain slashed through her. Her last remembered vision before the pain consumed her was that of a worried Gibbes and Merritt staring down at her as a plane flew overhead in the blue sky behind them, long white streaks trailing behind it.

Chapter 29

Merritt

Fires in buildings are dark, not bright. The black smoke quickly blocks any light from the flames themselves, and a person trapped in a burning building may become disoriented because he or she cannot actually see to evacuate.

I opened my eyes in the visitors' lounge at Beaufort Memorial, gasping not from thick, dark smoke but from imagining my lungs filling with icy water too black to allow any light from above. I stood and began pacing around the perimeter of the room, Loralee's sandals gently tapping the flecked white linoleum. I almost laughed as I realized my thoughts had moved to the waiting room decor, another sign that Loralee's presence in my life had affected me in more ways than one.

Stopping, I looked down at my feet in her sandals, almost expecting to see her pretty toes and the dark pink polish she wore on her toenails. My bare nails seemed so inadequate, so . . . hopeless. A middle-aged woman, the only other occupant of the waiting room, snored softly as her knitting slowly slid from her ample lap into a blue and green puddle like a dying sweater.

Gibbes had been called to the pediatrics floor soon after we'd arrived at the hospital. He'd wanted to stay but I'd told him to go. I wanted to be alone. I wasn't sure why, except that since I was a little girl, being alone had always been my defense mechanism. My father had once called me an opossum, hiding from the world. It had been years before I understood the rest of what he'd meant: how closing my eyes didn't mean the world couldn't see me. That it still revolved despite my best intentions. But understanding and accepting were two different things.

Gibbes had driven us behind the ambulance, the car heavy with silence fueled by guilt. *He'd known.* Before the ambulance came, Gibbes had sent me upstairs to get one of Loralee's medicine bottles — a bottle half-full of five-milligram tablets of morphine. *Morphine.* Half an hour before, I had thought Loralee simply had a delicate stomach.

Maybe, deep down, I'd known she was much sicker than she'd let on. The evidence had been right in front of me for weeks. But I was so good at hiding from any truth I couldn't face that I'd gone along with her charade, ignoring all the obvious signs so we could both pretend that everything was all right.

I had asked Gibbes a dozen questions, each one answered with the same pat response: *She's very sick. She needs you to be strong right now.* In the part of my brain that could still reason, I knew Gibbes couldn't have shared her condition with me, couldn't tell me what I needed to be strong *for.* But his words were like heavy storm clouds on the horizon, promising a rain for which I was not prepared.

Loralee was the only one who could have told me, but I couldn't be angry with her. Because every time I thought about how sick she must be, I thought about Owen and that everything she'd done was for him. And I remembered how much I'd wanted her to go away when she first appeared on my doorstep. I wished she were with me right then to tell me something insightful that her mama used to say about regrets and looking backward. But all I could hear were the snoring of the woman in the waiting room lounge chair and the distant sound of a man's voice on the PA system reminding me where I was.

"Mrs. Heyward?"

I looked up to where a petite black woman in khaki pants and a bright pink and yellow floral shirt stood on the threshold, a clipboard in her hands and a photo ID around her neck.

"Yes, I'm Merritt Heyward."

Her tight smile was more efficient than warm, but I imagined working in a hospital had taught her how to do that. "I'm Carmen Tanner, with social services. The nurses here have made Mrs. Connors comfortable and she's ready to see you. I just have a few questions for you first. Why don't we sit down?"

I sat in the nearest seat and Ms. Tanner sat next to me. "You're Mrs. Connors's next of kin?"

I looked at her, startled, ready to tell her my rote response that I had no relatives. "She's my stepmother — my father is deceased. She has a son." I paused. "He's only ten."

She nodded. "You're his legal guardian?"

"No. I mean, I don't know. He's my half brother."

She jotted something down on the clipboard. "Mrs. Connors has given me permission to discuss her care with you."

"Oh. Sure. Of course." I was too embarrassed to tell her that all I knew for sure was that an oncologist had been called in to see Loralee and that she'd been taking a five-milligram morphine pill every four hours that had been prescribed to her before she'd even left Georgia. Before she'd shown up on my doorstep.

The social worker continued. "I'm recommending hospice care for Mrs. Connors. Before you leave today, I'll have a folder of information for you to go through with the patient so you can make the best decision. . . ."

"Hospice? But that's for . . ." I couldn't force myself to say the words.

"End-stage care," she finished for me. "To help manage the pain."

I stared at her dumbly, waiting for my brain to process her words. "Wait," I said, holding up my hand, as if it were big enough and strong enough to stop the oncoming clouds. "All I know is that she has cancer. I don't even know what kind."

"She has stage-four ovarian cancer. Unfortunately it has spread to other organs." Ms. Tanner's eyes were kind, but couldn't hide the fact that she'd seen this before, had said these words before. I wanted Loralee to have been the first, the only one. As if her being singular would bring her to the attention of those who could save her.

"But why hospice? What about chemo and radiation and all those other things they do for cancer?" My calm, no-nonsense New England demeanor had packed its bags and left me with only images of ancient oak trees that wore their grief in the gnarled bend of their limbs.

She must have sensed my rising hysteria, and placed a hand on mine. "Mrs. Heyward, I'm sorry. This is a very aggressive cancer. Unfortunately Mrs. Connors discovered it only after it had spread." Ms. Tanner flipped up a page on her clipboard. "She pursued other treatment options in Georgia, but she and her doctors agreed that although she might prolong her life slightly, it wouldn't increase her quality of life. I believe that protecting her son from an extended illness was a strong motivator for her." She paused a moment, waiting for the wave of grief to pass through me, to carry with it the sediment of guilt and remorse before settling in the pit of my stomach. Her voice was gentle when she continued. "Once the cancer has spread, there is nothing that can be done except to make the patient comfortable."

I bit my lip hard, trying to keep it from trembling. "How long does she have?"

Her expression was sympathetic. "You'll need to speak with Dr. Ward, but I will say that once a patient reaches end-stage, it won't be long. Maybe a month, maybe a little longer."

I jumped up, unable to sit one second longer. "May I see her now?"

"Of course. She's in a private room, and there's a lounge chair in there that can be converted to a bed if you'd like to stay the night."

"Thank you, but I should be with her son. Somebody needs to tell him, and he shouldn't be alone."

She regarded me with kind eyes, as if she knew long before I did whom that somebody needed to be. "I'll have the information for you at the nurses' station when you leave, along with my card and cell number. Call me if you have any questions — any questions at all. You'll need to let me know what you and Mrs. Connors decide concerning her care."

"Thank you," I said, then followed her from the room and down the brightly lit corridor of patients' rooms, passing a janitor wearing headphones mindlessly polishing the linoleum floors, the sound oddly ordinary. I had the strongest compulsion to whip the headphones from his ears and shout at him to pay attention, to stop taking for granted even the most mundane tasks.

Carmen Tanner pushed open a door and stepped back, allowing me to enter. She put a gentle hand on my arm, then left the room, closing the door behind her.

I noticed very little about the room except for the single bed with a person lying on it, an IV drip in the back of her hand. I almost didn't recognize Loralee. She seemed to have shrunk, her life diminished under the fluorescent lighting. I wanted to throw open the window, allow in the sunshine and fresh air, to immerse her in a garden of pretty and fragrant flowers where fireflies danced at night. Her breath came in little gasps, as if her lungs were filling with fluid, and I wondered why I hadn't noticed it before.

Her hands rested on top of the bedclothes, her wrists and elbows looking swollen compared to the size of her arms. Her skin was yellow against the bright white of the pillow, her blond hair flat and dull. I wanted to deny that this person in the bed was Loralee, but then her head turned and she smiled that big, beautiful smile that I had once hated.

"Thanks for coming. Is Owen all right?"

"He's with Maris. Her mother, Tracy, said he can stay as long as we need him to. I told him that I would bring him to see you as soon as I could." I looked up at the white ceiling, willing my eyes not to betray me with tears. I was an expert at hiding my tears. Seven years of being married to Cal had been a good teacher.

"Thank you," she said.

I had to take a few deep breaths before I could look at her. "You're pretty damned good at hiding things. Even in plain sight."

Her smile faltered. "I guess my secret's out. I'm so sorry, Merritt."

I sat down in a chair and pulled it up by the side of the bed. "Don't you apologize to me or I'll feel even worse." I placed my purse on my lap, ready to go as soon as somebody let us know this was a huge mistake, and we could go home. "I'm thinking you're not really broke, and you just used that as an excuse to move in with me." I almost laughed. "Why didn't you just tell me? In the beginning, when you first came here. I wouldn't have turned you away."

"I know that, Merritt. But I couldn't. You would have taken us in because it was what you thought should be done. Or what you thought your father would have wanted. But

I wanted you to do it because you believed in your heart that you *could.*"

"Could do what?" I asked, too distraught to be embarrassed about the sob in my throat. "Watch you die?" I hadn't meant to use that word, but it propelled itself from me like a dart seeking its target.

She smiled softly. "So that you could help Owen through this. Take care of him after I'm gone. Be a mother to him."

I shot up from my chair, my purse falling with a thud to the floor. "I'm not a mother. Mothers make the right decisions; they know what's best for their children. They're strong." I stared at her, the next words unspoken but understood. *Like my mother. Like you.*

Her eyes sparkled, as if all the light that had seeped from her body had settled there. "You're strong at the broken places."

I looked at her, surprised she knew Hemingway. Then again, there was very little about Loralee Purvis Connors that didn't surprise me. I returned to my seat, somehow depleted. "You're wrong. I don't have a clue how to be strong." I paused, trying to control my breathing and to find the right words. "But I can promise you that I will take care of Owen the best way I know how. I don't want you to worry for one second about that."

She opened her hand on the mattress, and I put my own hand into hers, her fingers sending me a feeble squeeze. "Thank you." She closed her eyes and I waited for her to fall asleep, but after a moment she began speaking. "You are capable of so much love, and you are worthy of it, too. I think I know who is responsible for making you forget that, and I'd like to open up a can of whoop-ass on him."

A laugh that sounded like something between a bark and a sob escaped from my mouth. "Please don't make me laugh. Not now. Not . . . here."

A smile teased her lips. "My mama used to always say that laughter is the best medicine. I'd like to add chocolate to that, though. Not that I think I could stomach any right now."

"How can you joke at a time like this?"

"Because I'm not sad about dying. I've had the most wonderful life. You know how some people come back from a vacation and they're sad because it's over? I just smile because it happened."

"Did Hemingway say that, too?"

She shook her head. "Dr. Seuss, I think. You need to brush up on your Dr. Seuss. Owen will grill you on it."

This time I didn't even try to hide my sob. "I don't know what to do."

"I don't know much about this dying thing, either, but I've learned that if you just keep moving forward, even if you're stumbling or being dragged, you'll eventually get to the other side."

I squeezed her hand and watched as her eyelids fluttered shut. "You can do this," she whispered.

"I'm not that strong," I argued. "Broken places or not. But I will do my best for Owen." After a moment, I added, "For both of you."

Loralee had already fallen asleep, and my words slid unheard to the linoleum floor, then rolled into the empty corners of the room.

I stopped walking, struggling for breath, and quickly searched my brain for an innocuous fire fact. *Smoking is the primary cause of death by fire in the U.S. The second-most-common cause of fire deaths is heating equipment.*

I sucked in a deep gulp of air saturated with the scent of the marsh. I looked around and realized I'd somehow managed to walk from the marina down to Waterfront Park. I'd been dropped off at the house to pick up my car before getting Owen, but had been stopped on the porch by the sound of the wind chimes. I remembered the first time Loralee had seen them and had called them mermaid's tears. I ran back down the steps and just started walking. I was surprised that I'd walked this far by myself so near the water, surprised that I found comfort in the sound and smell of it.

I remembered sitting at the kitchen table while Loralee worked with Owen on his math, and her telling him that our bodies were made of more than fifty percent water. Maybe that was what brought us back to the water, even if it was the one thing we feared the most. Or maybe it was the simple fact that we'd floated for nine months before birth that made us seek that memory of water and the one time in our lives when we were truly content.

I looked down at my hands, where I expected to find my purse and instead found only crumpled brochures and information sheets about hospice care and ovarian cancer that had been given to me by the social worker.

A motorboat skipped across the water, a man at the wheel and a woman with a long, flowing yellow scarf shooting out behind her. I wanted to shout at them, to make them stop. I wanted everything to stop. Loralee was dying, yet the world insisted on turning.

I stumbled away from the water toward a large grassy spot in front of an open-air stage. A band was setting up, and there were about ten people milling about, running cords and moving equipment, each with his or her own job. They had an air of competence about them, the confidence of knowing what had to be done, and I felt an odd envy as I watched them.

In other spots near the stage, food vendors were setting up for a busy night. The Water Festival was in full swing, but it seemed like a world removed.

I sat down on one of the long rows of cement steps that led down to the grassy area and stared up at the blue sky, wondering why there weren't any clouds.

"Merritt?"

I shielded my eyes with my hand as I looked up at Gibbes.

"What are you doing here?" I asked ungraciously. I wanted to be alone, to lick my wounds in private. To pretend that if I hid long enough the world would stop and I could get off.

He sat down next to me without waiting for an invitation. "Deborah Fuller called me from her car and mentioned she'd seen you walking down Bay Street toward the marina. I left my car at your house and followed the boardwalk until I ran into you. You wouldn't answer your phone."

"Sorry you went to all that trouble. I'm not good company right now."

I studied the stage again, seeing it transformed bit by bit, like watching a flower bloom. I felt Gibbes looking at me but didn't turn my head.

"How'd you get home?"

"I hitched a ride with a nurse who lives on Charles Street. I didn't want to wait for you. Like I said, I'm not good company right now."

I wanted him to leave, wanted him to understand that every time I looked at him I saw my own failure to recognize someone's needs besides my own, my inability to hold on to anything precious in my life, to admit that everything Cal had ever said about me was true.

Unable to take a hint, Gibbes stayed where he was, his elbows on his knees as he watched the stage setup. "Do you dance?"

I whirled to face him. "What? No. I don't dance."

"They're having a bunch of bands coming to play beach music during the festival, and everybody will be here to shag."

"Excuse me?"

He sat up, bracing his arms on his hands. "Shagging as in the South Carolina state dance, not the *Austin Powers* shagging."

I stood. "Loralee is dying. I really can't think of anything besides that right now — especially not dancing."

He stood, too. "I know. That's why I mentioned it. Before I left the hospital I went to see Loralee. She told me that you want her to come home with you, where she can be near Owen. Even with the hospice nurses, it will be hard on you. She asked me to take you out. To take your mind off of things."

If anything, that made me feel worse. "She's a saint, isn't she? Even while she's dying, she's worried about other people."

"True. But you're the one who's bringing her into your home."

"Like I could leave her to die alone? Surrounded by strangers?" I shook my head. "Not even a consideration."

He was looking at me steadily. "You don't have to do this by yourself, you know. I'm here — call me anytime. Even if it's just to shout at me because you need someone to shout at."

I shook my head. "I'll be fine." Looking at

my watch, I said, "I've got to pick up Owen and figure out what I'm going to say to him. I just have no idea what that's going to be." I began walking back the way I'd come, along the walkway that bordered the river, which no longer seemed so threatening in comparison to the other monsters out there.

His long strides caught up to me just as his cell phone rang. He answered it and spoke briefly before hanging up. He was silent for a moment, and I felt his brooding presence beside me.

"What?" I asked.

"Deborah found out something, but I told her it could wait."

I stopped, breathing heavily as I realized I'd been practically running, feeling nearly sick to my stomach from the heat and the worry. The grief. "Is it something that might distract me from thinking about Loralee? Because maybe I need to hear it right now, if only so I don't stand here in the middle of the walkway and throw up."

Gibbes briefly looked behind me toward the water before turning back to me. "She found your grandfather's death certificate. Cause of death was listed as a plane crash, July twenty-fifth, 1955." He paused. "His was one of the two unclaimed bodies."

"Unclaimed? But he was married. Why

wouldn't my grandmother claim his body?"

"That's a very good question. And he's buried in Saint Helena's churchyard."

"Here," I whispered.

"Yes."

I stared at Gibbes without really seeing him, thinking about the South Carolina AAA book I'd found in my grandmother's things after she'd died, and the way Cal had spotted me on the street and followed me to the museum to meet me. How whenever he looked at me it seemed he was expecting to see somebody else.

"Are you all right? Do you need to sit down?" Gibbes asked.

"Please, I need to be alone."

I turned around, then quickly walked away from him, not slowing down or stopping until I'd reached the front porch, oblivious to the sweat mixing with the tears running down my face. The wind chimes swayed and sang, their marred and stained surfaces, earned from tumbling about the ocean's waves for years, strangely beautiful. They reminded me of something Loralee had said about our scars, and how we should be proud of them because they showed where we'd been.

Reaching up, I touched the bottom stone on one of the chimes, wrapping my fingers around it, feeling how hard and ungiving it was against my skin. *You're strong at the broken places.* I let go of the stone and walked up the steps and sat in one of the rockers. Pulling out my phone, I dialed Maris's mother to let her know I was coming to get Owen. After I hung up, I listened to the wind chimes while I tried to figure out how to tell a ten-year-old boy that his mother was dying.

CHAPTER 30

Loralee

Loralee lay back against the pillows propped up on the headboard of the antique bed. She still felt bloated and nauseated, but the pain had lessened so that she felt well enough to smile at the hospice nurse as she took her vitals and checked her medications. Her doses of pain meds had been significantly increased — way past time, according to Dr. Ward — but not to the point where she couldn't think or talk or still be a part of life. She intended to do all three until her very last breath.

Owen said that he wouldn't have known any different except that she spent a lot of time in bed. He spent most of his waking hours watching her with his father's blue eyes, as if by being vigilant he might be able to prevent whatever came next.

She thought that way of thinking most likely came from his father's side, seeing as how Merritt had been behaving the same way ever since Loralee had come back from the hospital, hovering like a fly over fried chicken at a Sunday picnic. Even now, she sat in the chair in the corner of Loralee's room as if she didn't trust the nurse to know her job.

But Loralee wasn't going to find fault with Merritt, because she'd been the one who'd had to tell Owen how sick his mama really was. Loralee was grateful, because her little boy had been prepared and strong when Merritt had brought him to the hospital to see her, and that had given her heart comfort, had told her — as if she hadn't already known it — that Merritt would make a terrific mama for Owen. It was at that moment that she'd allowed herself to not give up exactly, but to stop fighting so much. She wanted to leave this world the way she'd come into it — not in a Walmart parking lot, of course, but without a lot of fuss. Her own mama had been a good example of dying with grace. They'd been watching their favorite soap on TV, and when Loralee had returned from the kitchen with a glass of sweet tea, it had looked like her mother was sleeping. But she wasn't. Loralee had seen enough of death to know when only the shell of a person was left behind. Sort of like a lightbulb that had just been switched off but was still hot to the touch.

"You've got a good bedside manner," Loralee said to the nurse. "And such a beautiful voice. I like listening to you hum my favorite hymns while you work."

The nurse took off her glasses and let them dangle from a long strand of colorful beads over her ample bosom. "Thank you. I do think it's my calling, but it's patients like you who really make it worthwhile. I must say, though, that I've never had such an accepting patient."

The nurse, whose name was Lutie Stelle, and who Loralee had already discovered was recently divorced with two small children, and who lived with her mother, was about Loralee's age, short and plump with warm brown eyes.

"Maybe because I'm not afraid of dying."

"Loralee," Merritt said with reproach as she stood and walked to the bed.

Loralee turned to the nurse. "My stepdaughter doesn't like me saying that word, but I'm all right with it. We're all dying. Some of us are just lucky enough to know when."

The nurse considered her for a long moment. "You've got a strong faith. I also think you are wise beyond your years. I hope you've figured out a way to share all your thoughts with your son."

"Don't worry about that." Loralee patted the pink *Journal of Truths* that was never out of reach those days, and which had only a few empty pages left. She'd already written in it that morning as she'd watched Merritt sleeping in the chair she rarely seemed to leave. *You will never be truly happy if you keep holding on to the things that make you sad.* And then she'd added, *Hemorrhoid cream is the best cure for enlarged pores on the face and nose.* Because beauty advice was always practical. Yes, the journal was intended mostly for Owen, to teach him things she wouldn't have time to. But it wouldn't hurt for him to know about beauty and fashion, too. The future women in his life would appreciate it.

Gibbes had come to visit Loralee every day since she'd come home, but Merritt always made sure not to be around. It seemed to Loralee that all the good things she'd seen happening between Merritt and Gibbes had been erased the day they'd rushed Loralee to the hospital. Merritt refused to talk about it, but Loralee could almost believe that Merritt was punishing herself for feeling happy, that she felt guilty for moving on with her life. As if she were personally responsible for her husband's death and Loralee's cancer. Or for the hurricanes and earthquakes that rocked the Earth on a regular basis.

The nurse packed up her things, said her good-byes, then left, seeing herself to the door, leaving Merritt and Loralee staring at each other.

Merritt gave her a tight smile. "Owen's with Maris and her family today. They took a trip out to Hunting Island so Owen could climb the lighthouse. I gave him my iPhone to take pictures to show you." She paused. "He didn't want to go at first, but I told him it was okay, that . . ."

She stopped, her face horrified at the words she was about to say.

"That I wasn't going to die today?" Loralee gave her a warm smile. "I'm glad he went. He needs to have as normal a life as possible. I'm glad he has a friend, and I think Maris and her family will be a good comfort for him."

Merritt's lower lip trembled as her face compressed in an effort to keep her emotions under control. There was so much of Maine still in the girl.

"You are going to give yourself a heart attack if you don't let yourself cry, Merritt. And then where will we be? Beaufort Memorial won't know what to think if we both end up there again with you the patient this time."

An unplanned laugh escaped from Merritt's mouth. "Let me refill your water pitcher."

"Actually," Loralee said, taking a moment to gauge how she felt, "I'd like to go downstairs and sit on the front porch while I still can. It's not so hot today, and there's a nice breeze. I know that because the wind chime Owen had Gibbes hang outside my window is chattering like two old ladies at a church social."

Loralee carefully sat up and slid her legs over the side, practically falling off the bed in her rush to put on her slippers — the ones that technically belonged to Merritt — before Merritt could not only get to them first, but slip them on Loralee's feet.

"Do you need a sweater?"

Loralee looked at her stepdaughter, trying hard to have gracious thoughts, knowing Merritt's concern came from the right place. "If I find that I need it outside in ninety-degree weather, I'll be sure to let you know. What I do need is some lipstick."

"I'm sorry. . . ."

"It's all right, Merritt. We're all learning right now."

At least she'd convinced Merritt that she didn't need to wear her stepdaughter's hideous robe and instead was in a comfortable pair of yoga pants and a cute royal blue T-shirt. Merritt grabbed a lipstick from the dresser and handed it to Loralee. "How about this?" she asked, holding up Loralee's favorite shade, Hello Dolly.

"You're a quick study."

Merritt pulled off the cap and rolled the lipstick up — too high, but she was trying — then handed it to Loralee, who put it on without a mirror because she'd done it so often she could probably do it in her sleep.

Handing the lipstick back to Merritt, Loralee stood and put her hand on the corner of the dresser to steady herself, feeling slightly dizzy. "You can give me your arm. I think it's the bird food that I've been eating, and the meds have made me a little weak. I'll even let you help me down the steps."

Out on the porch, Merritt settled her in a rocking chair and stood watching her for a moment, as if to see whether Loralee remembered how to rock. "Maybe you shouldn't have quit your job," Loralee suggested.

"It was only part-time, and it wasn't really what I wanted to do anyway. This way I can be with you all day."

"What about that job Deborah Fuller told you about?"

"The acquisitions manager at the art gallery? That's not official yet — probably not until after the first of the year. It's not a guarantee, but Deborah said she'd put in a good word for me." With her gaze focused on the river, she said, "Although I don't want to go to work full-time at first."

Loralee knew she was thinking about Owen, and how hard it would be for him without his mother. She wanted to reach over and pat Merritt's hand, but held back. Merritt liked to pretend that she was a lot harder and pricklier than she really was, and for the time being Loralee would go along with it.

"If you're up to coming downstairs again later, we can see the Water Festival's opening-day fireworks tonight. Gibbes said they're really spectacular."

She wasn't sure whether she could find the strength, but she nodded anyway, determined to be there. Gibbes would carry her if she asked. "Owen loves fireworks. I swear that's the only reason we took him to Disney World — because he'd heard those were the best in the world and he wanted to see for himself."

A large delivery truck slowed as it approached the front of the house, then carefully pulled into the driveway. Merritt stood, and it appeared for a moment that she might start clapping. "It's my new refrigerator. Finally! I've run out of room to store all those casseroles people keep bringing over."

She walked down the steps to greet the driver and his passenger, her face as animated as most women's would be at a shoe sale. Loralee sat back in her chair and watched as the men loaded up the refrigerator on a dolly and wheeled it toward the house before hauling it carefully up the front steps and into the kitchen.

It was the first time she'd been completely alone since her trip to the hospital, and while the men and Merritt were busy unloading the new refrigerator and packing up the old one, Loralee kicked off her slippers and pressed her bare feet onto the floorboards of the porch. It had been too long since she'd gone barefoot. Back in Gulf Shores she'd mostly run around barefoot, not because she didn't have shoes, but just because it felt so good.

She remembered nighttime games of Kick the Can and Monkey in the Middle, the hot nights and sticky mornings just happy memories now. She wanted to make sure

that Owen knew how to play those childhood games and could teach them to the
new friends he would make there. Loralee
would have to tell Merritt the rules, since
she was running out of space in her journal,
but, knowing Merritt, she'd take notes.

She breathed deeply, smelling the wet air
that was a part of any coastal town just as
much as the sand and water were, and she
was reminded again of her girlhood. She
stopped rocking, and after deciding that she
felt strong enough to stand and walk, she
moved slowly down the steps, holding on
tightly to the railing, and into the front yard
until she was beneath the ancient oak tree.
Bracing one hand on the solid trunk, she
tilted her head to see the silver-white leaf
bottoms that always seemed to be winking
when the wind blew. The tree had probably
been there long before any of those houses,
and maybe even before the river had decided
to burrow into that corner of the world. And
it would definitely still be there long after
Loralee had passed from this earth. It was
comforting, somehow, the permanence of it
that was so much like the love between a
mother and child.

The cool grass in the shade of the tree felt
good on her bare feet, so good that it didn't
bother her that passersby in cars thought

she must be crazy, hanging out like that in front of the big house, wearing nothing but a T-shirt and yoga pants, her hair dull and lifeless but still long. She didn't consider herself a vain person, but her hair had always been her crowning glory, and she was bound and determined that she would meet her Maker with long hair.

She really wanted to cross the street to the marsh, to put her feet in the water one last time. Except she knew she'd already used up any extra reserves of strength and would most likely collapse in the middle of the road, giving Merritt a heart attack wondering where she was.

I'm ready. The thought was so loud in her head that she imagined for a moment she'd spoken. Since Robert's death and her diagnosis, she'd had onc singular goal, one singular prayer. She'd even sworn that it would be her last and only prayer, asking that she could hold it together until she'd put Owen in a place where he would be loved and happy and well cared for. She'd taken a huge risk coming there, her only hope being that the little girl in the pictures and stories Robert kept close to his heart still existed in the broken woman she'd met on the porch of that house.

"I'm ready," she said softly to the tree and

the air and to the place prayers went. She quickly said one more prayer, which technically didn't break any promises, because it was for somebody else, then pushed off the tree and waited for a moment until she felt steady enough to walk back to the porch.

She'd barely made it to her chair when the men reappeared with the old refrigerator strapped to the dolly, Merritt following closely behind and muttering something about her wood floors. Loralee tried to catch her breath, to fill her lungs with air so she could ask one of those men to carry her back up the stairs.

The round-edged refrigerator looked even more antique in the bright light of day, much as she imagined the old countertops and cabinets looked against the brand-new stainless-steel model now in the kitchen.

One of the men tilted the dolly back as far as it could go, preparing to lower it onto the first step.

"Wait — stop a minute."

The men looked annoyed, but Merritt ignored them and bent to get a better view beneath the refrigerator. Screwing up her face, she stuck her hand into what looked like fifty years of dust and cooking grease that had managed to congeal beneath the appliance, trapping something on the bottom, and peeled off what appeared to be a folded piece of paper, yellowed and brittle with age. Strings and clumps of dust fell from the paper as Merritt shook it, then sneezed.

The men continued on their way back to the truck, but Merritt didn't raise her head.

Worried by her silence, Loralee wheezed, "Whatever that is, I'm thinking it's been stuck under the refrigerator for a long time."

Merritt looked at her with the eyes of a child who'd just realized she was lost in an unfamiliar place. "There's only one word written on the front. 'Beloved.' " Her hands shook, rattling the page. "I think I recognize the handwriting."

The rear gate slid down and clanged shut, and then the beeping sounds of the truck reversing came from the driveway, but neither one of them looked over.

Merritt collapsed into the rocking chair beside Loralee's, then carefully unfolded the letter and began to read.

July 25, 1955

My darling Henry,
You will never see this letter; yet I feel compelled to write it. It is my farewell letter to you, the last words I will ever

address to you whether or not you see them. Today our mutual misery will be over for eternity. Or at least until we meet again in the next life, wherever that will be. I will admit that I haven't planned much further than today.

I love you, Henry. I have since the first moment I saw you. But, you see, I hate you almost as much as I love you. And I know you must feel the same way, because when I count the bones you have broken of mine, like a lover counts petals from a flower with, "He loves me; He loves me not," I always come up with a different answer.

I cannot live with you any more than I can imagine living without you. But we have a daughter now, and it is her protection that has charted my course. I could not bear to see you lay a hand on her, and know that I was responsible for not protecting her.

My handwriting is shaky, but still legible. As you know, it's not because of nerves — I'm quite calm now that I know that I'm going through with this. It's because two of my fingers are numb because of nerve damage received when you slammed my hand in the car door because I didn't exit the car fast enough for you. That was the proverbial last straw as I envisioned the tiny hand of our daughter suffering a similar fate.

It was an easy thing, especially for a bright girl who always did well in science, to make a bomb and set an alarm that would detonate after your arrival in Miami, after it is securely stowed in your trunk and you are driving away to your next adventure with your latest lover. It was an easy thing to pack it with your toothpaste and shaving cream, then place it in your suitcase, tucked in among your neatly ironed and folded clothes. Just as easy as it will be to latch your suitcase after I've placed this letter inside and hand it to you, then watch you stow it in the car trunk. It will be easy up until the moment I watch you drive away from me for the last time.

You are my beloved, and always will be. Forgive me.

J

Loralee stared at Merritt, wondering whether she'd ever seen skin so pale, so bloodless. "You know who wrote that?"

Slowly, Merritt nodded. "Yes," she said, carefully folding the letter like the edges were giving her splinters. "My grand-mother."

Chapter 31

Edith
October 1993

Edith finished the tiny stitches on the Eton tie, knotting it off by hand. It was perfect, the dimensions proportional to the real height of Henry P. Holden. She'd been to his interment, and that of that poor woman from Pittsburgh. Or was it Poughkeepsie? It had been nearly forty years, and some of the details were getting foggy. Both unclaimed victims had been buried at the same time in separate graves, at the charity of the parishioners of Saint Helena's.

The names had been printed in the newspaper, and when she'd seen Henry's name, recognized it from the luggage tag, she knew she had to go. She'd almost called the funeral home to suggest bringing a fresh suit of clothes, but then realized that she couldn't. Not ever. But she'd remembered to ask the undertaker how tall he'd been, so that when she made his doll replica, it would be exact. That was how she knew how long the tie needed to be and where it would fall when she'd placed Henry in his seat on the plane.

But the funeral for the man she'd never met but knew so much about had been years before — before C.J. had grown up to be just like his father. Before Cal was born and then Gibbes. Before Cecelia had died. This last was what had convinced Edith that she couldn't be a passive bystander anymore, quietly working in her attic to solve a crime from bits and pieces of discovered wreckage. Her silence since the crash and the discovery of the suitcase and the letter had been just that — passive. But Cecelia's death had pushed Edith to reach out to Henry's widow — the faceless woman whose first name began with the letter J. Not to condemn her. Never that. Edith knew too well what J. Holden had been through. Knew how each beating had diminished her, had warped her thinking to the extent that she could place a bomb on a plane and not expect anything to go wrong. Could not anticipate anybody else getting hurt. Nobody except somebody who'd lived that life, who'd felt her own psyche lessened, would know that.

No, Edith had reached out to Mrs. Holden to let her know that she was not alone. That she — and Cecelia — and doubtless countless others formed an odd sisterhood. One where the members survived in secret and sometimes even enacted a revenge that was as stealthy as the violent acts they'd been forced to endure.

Edith slid open the makeshift drawer she'd created beneath the sea-glass table for odds and ends. Among the rubber bands, buttons, paper clips, and glue, she kept one large envelope identical to the one she'd already sent to Henry Holden's widow.

Every once in a while, Edith toyed with sending her another letter. Maybe she hadn't received the first one, the one with the handkerchief Edith had taken from the suitcase and the note from Edith explaining that she knew how the plane crashed. How the killing of innocent people had been an accident but the death of Henry P. Holden was not. That the secret would forever be safe with her.

Using her thumb and forefinger, Edith picked up the small dopp kit she'd painstakingly made, with tiny replicas of combs and razors and little soaps made from slivers she'd taken from C.J.'s bar of soap he'd left by the sink. With a tiny dab of model airplane bonding glue, she stuck the dopp kit in Henry Holden's lap.

Over the years, while working on her plane model, putting each piece together as it was discovered buried in the marsh or in a farmer's field, that one niggling fact wouldn't leave her alone. Henry Holden's suitcase hadn't contained a dopp kit, although there'd been an indentation among the tightly packed items just big enough for one to fit. It wasn't until Edith had read a newspaper report about the plane's two-hour delay at LaGuardia that it had begun to make sense to her.

Technically, the dopp kit shouldn't be on Henry's lap. But she was vain — vain about her attention to details and the small objects she'd made for the kit. As long as she knew that it was wrong, that the actual dopp kit had been obliterated, vaporized in the first second of the blast by the bomb neatly tucked inside of it. Luckily for Edith, it hadn't been in the suitcase, where it was supposed to have been. If it had, she never would have found the suitcase in her garden. Instead, Henry Holden had retrieved the dopp kit after his dutiful wife had dropped him off at the airport and presumably given him a chaste parting kiss. He had retrieved it because he was going to Miami and was

— possibly? probably? — going to see somebody where a closer shave might have been required. Something he could take care of once they were in the air, in the tiny onboard bathroom. So he'd taken it out before checking his suitcase to be loaded beneath the plane.

The dopp kit, so carefully packed by his loving wife, just like the rest of his things, had stayed in the overhead space, ticking away, while Henry and the other forty-eight passengers and crew on board waited at La Guardia before finally taking off again two hours past the time they were supposed to.

Edith often found herself during the day timing how long exactly two hours seemed to be. She'd make a note of the hour, and then get busy with a task, looking up periodically to see how long it was. She supposed that sitting in a plane during the boring hours in flight must have seemed interminable to Henry and his fellow passengers. But she found herself often wondering whether, had they known that those two hours would be some of their last minutes, the time would have passed by so much more quickly.

Two hours. It haunted her. And oftentimes she wondered whether those two hours haunted Mrs. Holden, too. Wondered when she'd realized her horrible mistake, her flaw in reasoning that had killed so many innocent people. The simple fact remained that if the plane had not been delayed, they would have reached Miami on time. And Henry would have been driving away from the airport — alone? — with his suitcase and dopp kit in the trunk of the rental car at the time the bomb was supposed to detonate. Or perhaps he would have opened the dopp kit midflight and discovered the little extra item his loving wife had packed there. Yes, it haunted Edith. Almost as much as she imagined it haunting Mrs. Holden.

The mistake in judgment was the only justification that Edith had as to why she hadn't told the police when she'd finally figured everything out. The death of all those passengers had been an accident. The death of Henry P. Holden had not been; albeit, in her opinion, it had been justified. Cecelia's death had simply firmed her conviction.

"Edith!" Cal shouted from somewhere in the house, followed by a loud slamming of a door that Edith felt all the way up in the attic. He'd started calling her by her first name shortly after his father's death, when he'd assumed the role of man of the house. She didn't like it, but didn't make the mistake of letting him know.

Edith turned off the lights in the attic and hurried down the steps to the upper level. Ten-year-old Gibbes stood in the hallway holding his book bag, still wearing his school uniform, having just returned home, his eyes wide.

"Edith!" Cal shouted again, something dangerous in his voice. He'd been working in the garden, digging holes for her new rosebushes. It was his day off from the firehouse, and he'd wanted to do physical labor to work on his muscles. She'd planned on hiring somebody, but the roses were already there, waiting inside burlap bundles to be planted.

"I'll be right there," she called, then froze as she listened to his heavy steps in the hallway below, and the sound of something solid being dragged against wood floors. *Dear God, no.* He wasn't supposed to be digging near the bench. But maybe he'd decided that that was where the roses should be, despite what she'd told him. *No, no, no.* Panicking, she turned to Gibbes. "I need you to go to your room and shut the door and lock it. Don't come out until I tell you to. Do you understand?"

Gibbes nodded and ran toward his room, but turned back. "What if you need me?"

"Don't come out." She kissed his forehead, then headed down the stairs, pausing only a moment until she heard the lock turn in Gibbes's door.

She thought she could smell the moist earth and the acrid odor of rot before she reached the bottom of the stairs, then nearly gagged on the stench and her own fear when she saw Cal in the foyer holding the suitcase, a trail of dirt leading from the kitchen.

When he saw her, he slid the suitcase toward her, the metal hinges scraping the wood floor. "This is from that plane, isn't it?"

His voice was low, and to an innocent bystander it wouldn't have been threatening. But it made Edith's skin feel as if ants had dug a hole and begun to march beneath it.

There was no point in lying. Edith had found that agreeing with Cal regardless of whether he was right or wrong was the best way to go. "Yes. It fell in my garden the night the plane exploded."

"Then why is it *here*? Why didn't you give it to the *police*?" He had a way of emphasizing his words to make sure you understood that you had done something wrong and he was about to call you on it. And that he

596

expected retribution for your wrongdoing.

For all the years she'd carried her secret, she'd never once imagined she'd be having that conversation. After she had mailed the handkerchief and letter, she'd kept nothing of the suitcase's contents, nothing to give her away. It wasn't that she'd forgotten about it; it was more like knowing that the family silver was in the dining room breakfront without actually looking at it.

She cleared her throat, trying to figure what half-truths she could tell him. Because his sense of justice and rightness, of punishment and retribution, were still tangled up in his childhood belief that everything was black-and-white, good or evil, right or wrong. There were no shades of the truth. Unless she could somehow manage to make him believe that justice had actually prevailed. She looked down at where the suitcase lay on the ground, smelling the tart scent of fresh soil, and saw the name tag. Her eyes met Cal's and she knew he'd seen it, too. Had probably already memorized the name and address just as she had. She still knew it. Could recite it without having to think very hard.

Keeping her voice calm, she said, "I didn't think his widow wanted the police to have it."

He reached down and gripped the name tag, then wrenched it loose with a single hard tug. He looked at her with an expression that was half triumph, half sneer. "Is she the one? The one who put the bomb on the plane?"

She felt like she'd been punched in the stomach. But she had experience with that and was able to stop herself from reeling, keeping her eyes on his. "Yes," she said calmly. "How did you know?"

He took a step toward her and she dropped her eyes, but didn't move back. "I know what you've been doing up in the attic, Edith. I saw the mangled bodies and the blown-apart plane, even though you tried to hide it from me. I even made my own LEGO airplane so I could pretend I was working alongside you, helping to solve the mystery. And I saw the shoe-box model you made of a woman in her kitchen making a bomb with sticks of dynamite and an alarm clock. You destroyed it, didn't you? Right after Mama died you destroyed it. It's just taken me this long to figure out why." He thrust his finger at her, jabbing her in the chest. "I assumed you'd demolished all the evidence so nothing could ever be proved. But I was wrong." His face was half jeer, half incredulous disappointment.

Edith kept her voice calm. "The damage had been done. People died, but it was an accident, Cal. You do know that, don't you? She didn't mean to blow up the plane — that wasn't meant to happen. She was sick in her head. You don't understand what happens to a woman's mind — a woman who's been beaten and belittled for so long that she can't think straight anymore. She can only think in the present, and not anticipate things going wrong — just the single focus of ending her torment. And all those people who died — there was no way to bring them back. I wanted that poor woman to find some peace, although I don't know whether she ever could."

Edith knew before he spoke that her words would not sway him.

"No matter what you say, or what trials you think you've been through in your life and at the hands of my grandfather, nothing, *nothing* justifies you being an accessory to murder. Yes, that's what you are. A *murderer.* You knew the plane's explosion wasn't an accident, and you found out who had caused it. But you kept it to *yourself.*"

She broke her own rule and raised her voice. "Because I felt a kinship toward her. She left a letter in the suitcase. He hurt her, Cal. Like your grandfather hurt me. Like your father hurt your mother. Except she had the courage to make it stop."

Without warning, he reached up and slapped her hard on the face, knocking her down. "You don't even know her first name," he spat.

She looked up at him and wiped the blood from her cut lip. "I didn't need to. Because I could have filled in the blank with half a dozen names. Like Cecelia."

Cal took a step toward her, and she closed her eyes so she wouldn't see the next blow, but refused to shrink back.

"Grandma?"

Gibbes's voice came from the top of the stairs.

"Don't come down here, Gibbes. Not if you know what's good for you," Cal called out.

Edith opened her eyes. "Go back to your room, sweetie," she managed, tasting blood in her mouth. "I'm all right."

Cal looked down at her, his eyes softening as if seeing her for the first time and wondering why she was on the ground and bleeding from her lip. He knelt beside her and tucked her hair behind her ears, then pressed his forehead against hers. She realized that he was crying, his tears warm and sticky on her face.

"I'm sorry," he whispered. "I'm so, so sorry." He pressed his forehead against hers even harder, as if he could melt inside her and disappear.

She reached up and placed a hand on his cheek. "I know, sweetheart. I know."

"I can't . . . I can't let this go. You know that, right?"

"Please don't, Cal. Let it be. I have carried this knowledge on my shoulders for all these years. Let it die with me. No good can come of it."

He took her head in both his hands, and she felt the power in them and the gentleness, too. He'd always been that way, ever since he was a little boy playing fire and deciding that everybody would live, and that the perpetrator was caught and blame and justice correctly attributed. It was a fatal flaw in his character, the thing that would one day destroy him.

He pulled away and stood. "I have to leave. I can't stay here anymore, knowing what I know. Knowing what you've done. I don't know where I'm going, or what I'll do, but I can't stay here."

Edith scrambled to her hands and knees, pulling herself up using the hall table, her limbs heavy and sore. "Please stay. We can work through this. Do some kind of penance together — community service, maybe. Something good."

"You know I couldn't live like that — knowing that somebody got away with killing forty-nine people and that my own grandmother has known all these years. Somebody has to pay."

"You will, Cal. In the end, you will. You don't know when to stop."

He turned away from her and headed toward the stairs.

"Where will you go? Will you try to find her?"

He stopped without turning around. "I don't know. I just can't stay here with you. I don't know what could happen the next time I lose my temper."

"You need help, Cal."

His shoulders sagged. "I know. Or maybe just leaving this place will be all the help I need."

She didn't call him back, knowing she could never change his mind. As soon as she heard his door shut, she picked up the suitcase and the torn tag and hid them behind the parlor sofa to rebury later, to make sure they would never be found. As she walked from the room she stopped suddenly, almost running into Gibbes.

"You're bleeding," he said, touching her chin.

"I know. I bumped into something. How clumsy of me."

He looked at her with his mother's eyes, and it was as if Cecelia were looking at Edith with understanding and compassion, and for the first time Edith felt as if her silence had at least given her a moment of triumph, a small restitution paid for Cecelia's sake. She simply didn't know whether it had all been worth it.

Gibbes put his arms around her waist, then patted her back as if he were the adult. "It'll be all right, Grandma. That's what you told me when Mama died, remember? It'll be all right. Maybe not tomorrow or even the next day, but one day it won't hurt so much."

They listened as drawers were opened and slammed shut upstairs in Cal's room, and then heard the sound of a suitcase sliding out from under his bed. Edith took Gibbes's hand, then knelt in front of him. Her heart ached as she brushed her fingers against his soft cheek, and he looked at her with his mother's eyes. She had failed to save Cecelia, had failed to raise good men. Gibbes was her only hope, her last chance. "I'm going to take you to the Williamses'.

Go on upstairs and pack your overnight bag with a couple of changes of clothes. If you need more, I'll bring them."

"Why are you sending me away? Did I do something bad?"

She shook her head, then kissed his forehead. "No, sweetheart. You're the only one who hasn't." She touched his face, wishing she were strong enough to start over, to do a better job with Gibbes. But she was tainted with too many ghosts, haunted by the daughter-in-law she couldn't save and the faceless passengers on the doomed plane. She'd thought she could justify what had happened, telling herself it was an accident, that being physically and mentally abused by someone you loved did awful things to the way you saw the world. But it didn't matter anymore what she thought; Cal had discovered her secret and would enact his own twisted sense of justice, and she was helpless to stop him.

She looked into Gibbes's golden brown eyes and saw Cecelia. "I want you to be happy, and I know you can't find that here, or with me. At least not right now. Promise me that you'll be happy, that you'll see the good in people, and seek forgiveness first. Can you promise me that?"

He nodded solemnly as his arms slid from

around her before he turned and headed slowly up the stairs. He stopped and faced her again. "Can I come back here? Is this still my home?"

"Yes. Always. But right now the Williamses can give you the family and guidance you need and that I have failed to provide. I hope you will understand it one day. That you will forgive me for all my failures."

He studied her for a long time before continuing his ascent as Edith stood at the bottom of the steps, listening to the sounds of her two grandsons packing their belongings along with the final pieces of her heart. She'd thought of the useless energies of her life, all wasted, all misunderstood. She would be alone until she died. It was all she had left to do. It would take years, she supposed. Wasn't it true that only the good died young? It would be a fitting punishment for a woman who'd only ever wanted justice for the silent victims of crimes people never spoke about, and those who were only whispered about in confidence.

She stepped out onto the porch and took a deep breath of the fall air that already carried a hint of cooler temperatures. The afternoon lay still in the curve of the river where her beautiful house perched on the bluff, the low tide exposing stagnant pluff mud and listless grass. She felt like that now, sensed her own outgoing tide with each breath.

The wind chimes hung limply, hollow shells of the tumultuous journey that had brought them to her. She willed them to move, to let her know that all of her efforts hadn't been in vain, but they remained motionless, mocking her.

She turned her back on the river and headed into the house, but paused on the threshold as she felt the stirrings of a breeze at her back, imagined the gentle swaying of the wind chimes behind her. She closed the door without turning around, listening for the faint sound of the glass stones as they whispered together a soft good-bye.

CHAPTER 32

Merritt

I set down the suitcase on the dirt floor in the corner of the basement beneath the house, then placed the plane model and the bag of dolls and debris next to it. Last, I placed the letter on top of the suitcase, balancing it so that it didn't rest flat as a reminder that I wasn't finished with this — with the suitcase, the letter, the victims of the plane crash. With the memory of my grandmother. *My grandmother.* The woman who'd placed a bomb in her husband's suitcase, expecting it to explode when he was safely in Miami, and had inadvertently killed forty-eight other people.

It was a horrible tragedy — no, an unspeakable and horrendous tragedy, albeit one that was more than fifty years old, the memory of those lost mostly faded by now, the survivors of their loved ones older now, or dead. Dealing with it would have to wait a little longer, because right now a ten-year-old boy was about to lose his mother, and I had to somehow find the resources I didn't believe I had to be strong enough for both of them. I ignored the inner voice that continued to prick my conscience that said there were other, darker reasons for my reticence, an old, familiar voice telling me that I was a coward.

I climbed the steps to Loralee's room, picking up a shopping bag in my room on the way. I paused on the threshold, listening to her labored breathing, her body emaciated except for the rounded dome of her belly. In the weeks since she'd been in hospice care, I'd seen Loralee gracefully surrendering her life bit by bit. She'd shrunk so much that I doubted she weighed much more than Owen. She'd sent me to Victoria's Secret to get pretty nightgowns in the smallest sizes, but even those seemed to dwarf her.

The cancer had spread to her liver, which was what had caused her skin to yellow, and had continued its insidious and invasive spread to other organs. She didn't get out of bed anymore, even to make her two laps around her room to "keep her girlish figure."

Her bed was littered with Owen's LEGOs and the Harry Potter book he was reading out loud to his mother. He didn't like being away from her, and it would be only after Loralee told him to go to Maris's or head to the store with me that he'd reluctantly leave her side. Several times I'd found him sleeping on the floor in the hallway outside her door, bathed in the light from the Darth Vader night-light, keeping the encroaching darkness away.

Gibbes came by almost every day if his work schedule allowed, usually bringing her flowers, and stayed for a bit to talk with her and to Owen. I always found an excuse to be in some other part of the house, because every time I saw him I thought of the letter. And how the truth kept nudging me, wanting me to face things I wasn't ready for. I hadn't shared the letter with him, not yet. I simply didn't have the courage to watch him put the pieces together, and to confront the aftermath.

The television was on low, showing one of Loralee's favorite soaps — one in which even I could now name the characters and who was sleeping with whom. I watched it for a few minutes, then walked over to turn it off.

"Just turn down the volume, please," she said.

"Sorry — I thought you were sleeping."

"I was mostly thinking."

I sat down on the side of her bed. "What about?"

"About what I want to be buried in." She paused to catch her breath. It was difficult for her to talk, and she paused often between sentences and sometimes words. "I've got a really pretty pink suit with a bow at the collar; I'll show you which one. And I want my hair down and curled the way I like to wear it — nice and big. Will you take care of that for me? I want Owen to remember his mama looking her best."

"Loralee," I began, feeling the ever-present sob in the back of my throat.

"And I want you to wear red. Go buy yourself a new dress, and every time you wear it, I want you to remember me and how fabulous we both looked at my funeral."

A half sob, half laugh erupted from my mouth. "All right. What about Owen?"

A soft smile fell on her lips. "He'll probably pick his little-man suit with the striped tie, but if he doesn't that's all right. Let him wear what he wants to. Maybe he'll rebel and wear tennis shoes or something. There's nothing wrong with that. A show of independence now and again is a good thing."

Her breath rattled as she tried to suck in air.

"Got it," I said, wishing I had my own journal to write down all of Loralee's child-rearing tips and general wisdom. I had a strong feeling I would need it.

"Where'd you put the suitcase?"

"In the basement. For now. Along with the rest of it."

She didn't say anything, but I knew she wanted to. Since we'd read the letter, she hadn't said one word about it, and it must have taken all of her strength to keep it inside. I stood and began tidying the items on her dresser, waiting.

Pushing herself up against the pillows behind her, she said, "Lying in bed all day gives a person lots of time to think, and I do believe I have finally figured out something important."

"And?" I braced myself.

It took a moment until she was ready to speak again. "As you know, my mama taught me a lot. But lying here watching so much television, I've finally figured out that everything I've ever needed to know in life I learned from my mama and my soaps."

"Really?" I said, turning around to lean against the dresser.

She nodded, her nostrils flaring as she

struggled to breathe. "I'm watching these people and it's basically the same thing over and over — people never learning from their mistakes so that they make the same ones again and again." She paused. "And then there's people who make mistakes, acknowledge them, and then keep picking at that mistake like it's an old scab, so that it never goes away and they can't go forward. And then there's those who stick their heads in the sand, pretending that everything is fine and that nobody can see them there with their heads stuck right there in plain view, and believing that they already know what people think and therefore there's no point in laying their cards out on the table for discussion."

She sounded like she'd just run a mile. I poured a fresh glass of water from the pitcher on her nightstand and helped her drink before I began my rebuttal. "If that last part is about me not telling Gibbes about the letter, I told you — that's temporary. I'd rather just focus on you and Owen right now. I will eventually show him the letter and everything else, and give the suitcase to the police."

I wanted to tell her that I was still wondering at the truth — the truth that involved the path that had brought Cal and me together, that had started long before we were born, the threads already woven together and knotted in places. At some point I would have to attempt to unravel them, to pick apart the knots and confront my seven-year marriage to a man who'd married me only because he'd been looking for somebody else. But I couldn't lie to her, even with a grain of truth. She deserved my honesty, so I kept silent.

She looked at me with tired eyes, but eyes that still had so much light in them. "I get it — you want to cross the creek one stone at a time. But you don't have to cross the creek alone, you know." She smiled the smile that was part joy, part friendship, but wholly honest. "I'm running out of time here, and I just can't wait until you're ready to ask for my opinion, so I'm going to give it to you whether you want it or not."

I opened my mouth to protest, but she actually shushed me as if I were an errant child.

It took nearly a minute for her to gather strength, but not nearly long enough for me to prepare myself.

"I know you don't like saying his name, so I will. Cal found out that his grandmother knew who and what had really brought down that plane, and that's why he left —

either because he couldn't stand living with his grandmother anymore, or because he was looking for some warped kind of justice. He found you instead, and you feel like a dummy because you married him, having no idea what his story was — believing you were on an even playing field because you both came from pasts you didn't want to talk about."

She'd paused often during her speech but took a long rest now, breathing deeply, her chest rising and falling, but the look in her eye told me I shouldn't interrupt.

She continued. "Knowing you, you feel responsible for your grandmother's actions, and maybe even just a tiny bit feel like Cal's taking his anger out on you was justified in some crazy way. It is well documented that women in abusive situations adopt a warped way of thinking just so they can manage their lives. Like telling a person so many times that they can fly that one day they believe it and jump out a window.

"But Cal loved you, Merritt. Even you admit that. Why else would he have married you? When he discovered that your grandmother was dead, he could have let it be. Maybe he thought that you could redeem each other — and maybe for a bit, you did. But he was sick, honey, and I don't think anybody could have changed him. He knew it, too. He walked into that burning building on his own two legs, of his own free will. Don't you be hanging that around your neck, either, because that's just wrong. We make our own choices, and he made his. And now it's your turn. Show Gibbes the letter and take it from there. You are not the guilty party here, and I promise you that Gibbes won't think less of you or want to punish you." She took another deep, rattling breath. "You've been dealt a tough deck of cards, that's for sure, but it's time to pull up your big-girl panties and move on. Like my mama used to say, you can't move forward if you always have one foot on the brake." She closed her eyes, as if all her energy had been completely emptied.

My whole body shook with anger. "You have no right," I began, then faltered, because I didn't know what else to say. She had every right, simply because there was nobody else.

"Good, I've made you mad. But you've got to get louder than that so I'll pay attention. Go ahead and yell and scream at me and tell me I'm wrong." She paused, wheezing in and out as she struggled for a deep breath. "A good hissy fit every once in a while is good for you. And if you want to cry your heart out about all the injustices in the world, then do that, too, but come over here first so that I can put my arm around you and pat your shoulder while you cry. Crying alone is never recommended."

I began to sputter, hot, angry tears I didn't know how to shed somehow finding their way down my face.

She held up her finger, her voice now considerably weaker and making me feel even worse. "And the last thing I'm going to say on this subject — unless you actually ask for my opinion on it — is that you should give Gibbes a break. Not only is he not too hard on the eyes, but he's smart, and funny, and kind — not to mention great with Owen. If you would just stop putting up walls where they don't belong, and wondering whether he sees you the way you think Cal used to see you, I think you two would make a nice couple. And for heaven's sake, show some leg once in a while, and use a bit of mascara and lipstick. You have no idea how pretty it will make you feel."

I stood there, crying harder than I ever remembered crying, feeling like the little girl I'd once been whose mother had made her swim away. *You are so much stronger and braver than you think you are. I just wish you could see you as I see you.* I still had doubts that Gibbes was right, but maybe it was time I stopped fighting the words I didn't want to hear. Maybe Loralee was right, too, that I'd had one foot on the brake for far too long.

She patted the bed next to her and I curled up at her side, being careful not to jolt her, and let her stroke my shoulder while I cried and hiccuped until I couldn't. We lay there for a long time in silence, the irony of the situation suddenly hitting me and making me laugh.

"What's so funny?" she asked, a smile in her voice.

"That I just let a dying woman comfort me. As Owen would say . . . awkward."

She laughed gently, and I tilted my head to look at her, amazed that I no longer saw her as my enemy, as the woman who'd stolen my father from me, but as a friend. The kind of friend who let me cry on her shoulder despite her own pain.

"Is that what you meant by 'opening up a can of whoop-ass' on somebody?" I asked.

"Pretty much. Except I went easy on you, seeing as how you're family."

"Bless my heart," I said.

Her shoulder shook beneath my head. "You're learning, darlin'. You're learning." She looked at the bag I'd dragged up on the bed with me. "What's that?"

"I brought you a surprise."

She smiled again, and I saw how the wattage hadn't dimmed. I hoped Owen saw this, noticed how strong his mother was, how she counted every blessing even when the basket of blessings was almost empty. That was something she'd said to me when I asked her why she kept smiling, and then she'd written it in her pink journal.

I sat up and upended the bag and watched as the DVD set of *Gone with the Wind* spilled out onto the bedclothes. "I'm tired of being the only person in the world who's never seen it. Since we finally have a DVD player and it's conveniently located in your room, I thought now would be a good time."

"It's always a good time to watch *Gone with the Wind,* and I happen to have time right now."

I took off the wrapping and removed the first disk before placing it in the player. I returned to the bed and plumped up Loralee's pillows before fluffing the extra ones and placing them against the headboard next to hers. "You ready?" I asked, holding up the remote control.

"Not yet. We definitely need a box of Kleenex in the bed between us. I've never gotten through this movie without using at least half a box."

I slid off the bed and retrieved a box from her dresser. "These are for you, then. I never cry at movies. Ever. Besides, I don't think I have any tears left."

"Uh-huh," she said primly as she leaned back against her pillows.

I pushed "play," then pressed the "next chapter" button to get through the opening credits.

Loralee put her hand on my arm. "What are you doing? The music score is the wings of the movie — it's part of the experience."

I looked at her dubiously. "All right, if you say so." I lay back next to Loralee and we listened to the opening strains of the theme song as she pressed a tissue into my hand.

Four hours — plus five potty breaks, two food and water breaks, and two phone calls — later, Loralee was sound asleep and I was staring at my lapful of used tissues. My phone pinged and I saw it was a text from Gibbes saying he was at the front door and could he let himself in. I responded yes and waited for him to find me in Loralee's room.

I hit "pause" on the remote and looked up to see him standing in the doorway. He held a paper bag with liberal dark spots of grease on the bottom that smelled like heaven. I was glad Loralee wasn't awake to comment on how my nose and eyes were red and that I probably should have at least brushed my hair or put on lipstick.

"I didn't want to wake her, which is why I didn't ring the doorbell." He glanced from me to Loralee, then back again. "Have y'all been wrestling?"

I snorted through my nose, too exhausted to care what I might look or sound like. "*Gone with the Wind.* I just got to the part where Melanie dies. Please tell me it gets happier at the end."

"You've never seen *Gone with the Wind* or read the book?"

"I know. I'm an anomaly. That's why I was watching it."

He took the remote from my hand and turned it off. "Let's just say the ending is inconclusive." He held up the bag. "I brought something to eat."

I looked over at Loralee, who still appeared to be sleeping. In a loud whisper, I said, "It smells fried. I don't think she's . . ."

"Not for her — for you. I know you've been taking care of Owen as well as making Loralee's meals and getting her to eat as much as she can, but I'm thinking you probably haven't been paying much attention to your own needs."

I felt my spine stiffen, but Loralee's words about putting up walls came back to me, and I settled against the pillow. "I am pretty hungry. I usually eat with Owen, but he's at Maris's tonight. I did have some popcorn while we watched the movie." I jutted my chin at the bag. "What's in there?"

"A shrimp burger and hush puppies from the Shrimp Shack over on Saint Helena. Best food you ever put in your mouth. The shrimp is fried before it's put in the burger, so you might overdose on grease, but you're with a doctor, so it's all right."

"Good to know," I whispered back, picking up all of the used tissues before carefully sliding off the bed. "Let's go to the kitchen and grab some plates." I glanced over at the clock. "She won't need more meds for another hour."

I made to move past him, but he didn't budge. "Have you been avoiding me?"

I looked anywhere but his eyes. "I've been busy."

"I know. I see this a lot with caretakers, how they make themselves sick because they're too busy taking care of other people. You need to take time for yourself."

"There's really nothing else I want to be doing." I met his eyes for a moment, and then glanced away, not yet ready to take Loralee's advice. I wasn't sure I ever would be.

"Another band is coming next weekend to Waterfront Park, and they're expecting shag dancers from all over the state. It should be fun."

"I told you — I don't dance."

"Great. Because I'm a great teacher."

"I don't —"

"She'd love to," Loralee interrupted.

"You're supposed to be asleep," I said before facing Gibbes again. "I really can't. I think I was born with two left feet. Besides, I don't have anything to wear."

Loralee grinned widely. "I think we were just saying how much you needed a red dress. Problem solved. And I get to do your hair and makeup."

Knowing how much the thought probably excited her, I didn't argue. Instead I picked up the remote and handed it to her. "I'm going downstairs to eat an early dinner, but I'll be back as soon as I'm done. You can finish watching the movie if you like. I was at the part where Melanie dies."

"Did you cry?" she asked.

"Like a baby."

She opened her hand and I squeezed it.

"And you feel better, don't you? Having a cry is good for you."

I looked at her closely, seeing how translucent her skin had become, how sharply her cheekbones jutted from her face. "Are you feeling all right?"

"Just a little uncomfortable. We can ask the nurse tomorrow about upping some of my doses. But I'll be fine for tonight. You two go on and have your dinner."

I started to move back, but she held on to my hand, bringing my head closer to her. "You are strong enough. And he's not Cal," she whispered.

Impulsively, I leaned down and kissed her cheek. "Thank you," I said. "For everything."

She winked at me, then mimicked putting lipstick on her lips with her finger, and I rolled my eyes before turning away and snatching up her tube of lipstick on the dresser before leaving the room.

"Don't forget to use a mirror," she called back, her voice weak but still audible.

I felt my face heat while Gibbes struggled to hide his laugh with a cough as we headed down the stairs.

Chapter 33

Merritt

I sat at Loralee's dressing table, staring in the mirror at a prettier version of myself than I was used to seeing. Loralee sat on the bed behind me, propped up to get a good view of my face's reflection. She told me that I needed to learn how to do it myself, but we both knew she was too weak to hold her arms up for long enough to curl my hair or flick a mascara wand through my eyelashes.

"Is the light on the curling iron green yet?" she asked. Her voice was reed thin, but still held the unmistakable twang of Alabama behind each syllable.

"Which one's the curling iron?"

She at least had the energy to roll her eyes. "It's the one with the round barrel. The flat one is the straightener."

"I could just wear my hair in a ponytail and not worry about either one," I suggested, already exhausted from the makeup lesson. Who knew that making one's face look natural took so much effort?

"There are no shortcuts to anyplace worth going."

I turned to look at her. "Is that in your little book?"

"Not yet. But I don't think I have the strength to write in it."

"Would you like me to do the honors?"

She nodded, and I stood to retrieve the pink journal and the pen that she always kept nearby. I opened it, surprised to find that all the pages were filled with her elegant handwriting. I flipped to the back and read her last entry. *Try to remember that the best days of your life are still ahead of you.* I blinked back the sting in my eyes and held the pen poised over the page. "You've only got half a page until the book is filled. I'll have to go find you another one — although I don't know how easy it will be to find another pink journal."

She didn't say anything, and I didn't look up as I wrote, my handwriting looking large and childlike next to hers. *There are no shortcuts to anyplace worth going.* "There," I said, closing the book and sticking the pen in the last page. "I think there's room for one more."

"Thanks," she said. "I'll start thinking of a good one. An appropriate one for the end of the book."

"Of volume one, anyway. I have a feeling you've got a few more journals in you."

"That's for sure," she said, her breath rattling. "Can I ask a favor?"

"Of course. Anything."

"After I die, can you make sure that Owen gets my journal? That's why I've been doing it, so that he'll sort of still have me even after I'm gone. I want you to read it, too."

"Sure," I said, working hard to keep my voice steady, and even managed a smile. I turned back to the mirror. "Are we done here?"

"Almost. Just pick up the curling iron — don't touch the metal part or it will hurt like the dickens, and I speak from experience — and twist it into those front sections of your hair like I showed you." Her breath came in gasps, her chest rising and falling. It was difficult to listen, but I also knew that Loralee's favorite thing to do was talk, and I wasn't about to tell her that she couldn't.

I did as she told me, although with questionable results, and returned the curling iron to the dresser before unplugging it and the straightener. I made a move to stand, but she called me back. "Don't forget the hair spray — in this humidity you have to spray it to death or you will look like a drowned rat in less than thirty minutes. Don't be all delicate on me now; hit that pump and just keep going."

There was a fog of hair spray around my head by the time I was done. I quickly fanned at it to make it dissipate before it reached her. "What is that — shellac?"

"Just about. You can only get that brand at beauty-supply stores — and I think a few of the contents are probably forbidden in some countries, but it gets the job done."

I glanced sideways at her to see whether she was joking, but before I could ask, the doorbell rang. "That's probably the nurse. She said she could stay until we get back — which won't be late — so you won't be alone. And the movie Owen is seeing with Maris and her dad is over at nine, and he should be home shortly after that." I slid her cell phone closer. "But you can still call me at any time, all right?"

The doorbell rang again and I went to answer it, finding Lutie Stelle at the door, and Gibbes walking up behind her.

"Well," Nurse Stelle said as she stepped inside. "You look pretty as a picture. Let me see that dress."

I gave a little twirl, just enough so the full skirt swished about my knees. It was deep red, my "signature color," as Loralee called it, having an almost Jackie O. look to it, with a portrait collar and a tightly fitted bodice. I'd gone shopping by myself, but had taken more selfies in one day than I had in my whole life and sent them to Loralee until she and Owen selected what they both considered the perfect dress. I couldn't imagine wearing it to a funeral, and refused to think beyond getting through the coming night.

Gibbes closed the door behind them and gave a low whistle. "It's not going to matter if you can't dance. You can just stand still in that dress."

Remembering what Loralee had taught me, I bit back any arguments and just said a simple, "Thank you." I noticed the bouquet of flowers in his hands. "I'm assuming those are for Loralee? Come on up — I think there's room in the vase from the flowers you brought last time."

We all headed upstairs, where Loralee greeted us with one of her big smiles. I noticed she'd put on some of the lipstick I'd left on her nightstand.

Gibbes kissed her cheek as I arranged the flowers in the vase and moved them to the dresser so they'd be closer. Nurse Stelle settled herself in the chair by the bed and began checking the clipboard and re-arranging the medicine bottles.

"Don't you worry about us," she said. "We'll hold down the fort until you get back — and no need to rush. Loralee and I always have a good time, don't we?"

"Just don't have too wild a party," I said, leaning in to kiss Loralee's cheek. "I don't want Owen coming home early and being scandalized."

"We'll try not to," she said, looking up at me with bright eyes. "Good-bye, Merritt."

It wasn't until we were outside again that I wondered at her choice of words, but I didn't dwell on it. If there was anything Lo-ralee had taught me, it was not to dwell on things. In the week since we'd had our "come-to-Jesus meeting," as she called it, I still hadn't found a way to tell Gibbes what I knew, or prepare myself for the conse-quences. I knew she was probably hoping it would happen that night, but when his hand touched the small of my back as we headed down the porch steps, and I smelled the clean, fresh scent of his shampoo, I knew I couldn't. If that was to be the only night we'd have, then I didn't want to ruin it with confessions and recriminations. Or memories of a husband who'd never let me wear red.

"Would you like to walk?" he asked. "We could drive, but it might be hard to find parking."

I pointed my toe, showing off my new red ballerina flats with the tiny bows on the top. "These are perfect for walking, and it's a gorgeous evening, so I say we walk. And maybe, if you're lucky, I'll trip and hurt my foot so that I won't be able to dance."

He threw back his head and laughed, then tucked my hand into the crook of his arm. "You probably aren't aware that it's illegal to live in South Carolina and not know the state dance."

"I think you've mentioned that. Although they might need to change the law after tonight."

As we approached the marina, Gibbes stopped. "Are you okay to walk along the river, or would you prefer we stick to Bay Street?"

I stared down at my shoes for a moment, thinking. "I'll be okay to walk by the water. I just have to think about Loralee and I realize my fears are pretty pathetic in comparison."

I put my hand on his arm and we resumed walking past the marina to the waterfront, both of us lost in our own thoughts. It had been a warm day, but not too hot, and a cool breeze now blew off the water as the sun began to paint the clouds with streaks of red and orange. The distant sound of live music came from the park, and my heart sighed. It was almost as if for a long while all the things that made my heart beat had been silenced by the things in my life I couldn't control. But as my skirt swished against my legs, and I felt the salt-tinged air on my face and the solidness of Gibbes's arm beneath my hand, I allowed myself to loosen up and to believe — even just for one evening — that both feet were off the brake.

"Have you been over to Saint Helena's churchyard to find your grandfather's grave yet?"

His question startled me. "No. I'm not . . . I mean, maybe eventually. I'm just focused on other things now, taking it one day at a time. I plan to give the suitcase to the police, but not yet. I need a little more time to think things through." I stopped walking, making him stop, too. I looked up into his eyes, still hoping I could find answers that were more palatable than the ones I already had. "Do you remember anything about the day Cal left? Anything he or your grand-

631

mother said to you?"

He looked away for a moment, the sun shining in his eyes. "I remember mostly how I felt — lonely. And unwanted." The light made his eyes almost translucent, and I imagined I saw clouds moving behind them. "But like I said before, being in the house so much lately has helped me remember other things, too."

"Like what?" I asked, trying to hold my breath, trying to see Edith not as an accessory to a crime, but as an abused woman who'd sought love and restitution in a world she didn't fully understand.

"My grandmother told me to be happy." He rubbed his hands over his face. "But it's what Cal told me that I've been thinking about lately. 'Never let the fire get behind you,' he said. I haven't thought about that for a long time, and I guess I'm still trying to figure out what he meant."

I remembered what he'd told me as we stood outside the Heritage Society. "And you said Cal called Edith a murderer."

He nodded slowly. "Yeah. I can't figure that one out, either."

Tell him now. It wasn't Loralee's voice in my head this time, but my own. I didn't want to be like Edith, dwelling in the past and living in exile in the old house on the bluff, with only my guilt and secrets to keep me company. And I had Owen to think of, the brother I'd happily pretended didn't exist for ten years but who'd now become so precious to me. *You can't move forward with one foot always on the brake.*

I tilted my head back, his name on my lips. "Gibbes . . ." I began.

I hesitated, my old fear of stepping past my boundaries, of swimming away from the safe place, paralyzing me, making me think of Cal and the coward he believed me to be.

But then Gibbes kissed me, his lips soft and warm against mine, and I stopped thinking about Cal, and my fears, and everything else except the feel of Gibbes's hands gently cupping my head as if I were a rare and precious treasure.

He lifted his face away from mine.

"Why did you do that?" I asked, breathless.

He didn't remove his hands. "Because you're a beautiful woman and it's a warm summer night, and you're wearing that dress. And because I've been wanting to do that for a very long time, and I think I might just do it again."

And he did, but this time I put my arms around his neck and let him draw me closer, kissing him back. I felt wanted and desirable and even pretty. I imagined curling up with Loralee later and telling her thank you. Mostly, though, I felt the long-dormant stirrings of desire, and want, and gratitude to this man who'd never demanded more from me than I was ready to give.

"Get a room," somebody from a crowd of teenagers called out as they passed us.

We broke apart and I was sure my face matched the color of my dress.

"You ready to cut some rug?" Gibbes asked, reaching out his hand.

"Excuse me?"

"Dance. Are you ready to dance?"

"Only if you're ready for a good laugh," I said, putting my hand in his.

"I'm always ready for that," he said, leading me down the boardwalk and the grassy area to where bodies were already moving in tandem and the music seemed to dance across the water like a skipping stone, rocking the anchored boats with its rhythm.

I found that I recognized a lot of the music as old standards like "Double Shot (Of My Baby's Love)," "Too Late to Turn Back Now," and "Band of Gold." Maybe it was my ability to sing along with the lyrics and anticipate the beat that saved not only my pride but also Gibbes's feet. I made sure we stayed in a back corner, far away from the very experienced dancers — whom I'd have been content to just sit and watch all night — as I counted out loud to the eight-beat count, "One-and-two, three-and-four, five-six," always reminding myself that each beat meant a different foot.

His left hand held my right, giving me a firm, guiding pressure to remind me when to turn and when to avoid an oncoming pair of dancers.

"Remember — your weight should be toward the balls of your feet, and you're supposed to pretend that your shoes are magnets and the dance floor is made of metal, so that you just sort of shuffle through the steps." Gibbes smiled as I ran into him again before stepping back with my left foot.

I allowed myself to laugh and to make mistakes, becoming bolder as Gibbes laughed along with me, gently leading me instead of criticizing me. A thought occurred to me, and I stopped moving, causing Gibbes to pull me toward him and off the dance floor so we wouldn't get trampled by the other dancers.

"Are you all right?" he asked, concern in his voice. "Can I get you something to drink? Or eat?"

"No, thanks. I'm just hot. Can we go sit on one of those benches on the boardwalk?"

I took out a tissue from my small evening purse — the purse borrowed from Loralee and the wad of tissues suggested by her — and handed one to Gibbes, then took one for myself. It was full dark now, the lights from the boats on the water twinkling like fireflies.

I tilted my head back and pressed the tissue against my face and neck, finally understanding why Loralee insisted on waterproof makeup in the summertime. "I just realized something — something about your grandmother. She made a lot of mistakes, but she did right by you. Maybe she's the reason you're a good pediatrician, and the kind of person who accepts — although grudgingly — his brother's widow even when he thinks he probably shouldn't." I shrugged. "It's something to think about, anyway."

"Maybe," he said, seeming to weigh the word and what it might mean slowly in his head. "What's making you so philosophical tonight?"

I leaned back on the bench and noticed the nearly full moon, pregnant with possibilities and the power to conduct the music of the tides. I kept my gaze focused on the moon, at the way it sheltered us all from the dark like a mother's hand, and let it bathe me in its blue glow. "You. And Loralee. This place, too."

I imagined for a moment Edith at her attic window, looking out at the same moon, attempting to protect a woman she'd never met, and setting off a chain of events she could never have foreseen. And I thought of my own grandmother, lost and alone, making the only choice she believed she had to protect her daughter — *my mother* — and inadvertently damaging so many lives. There were no heroes in their story, but neither were there any villains. And nobody had learned anything. *Yes,* I thought. That was the sticking point. I couldn't nudge myself past it with the belief that it had all been so pointless. Both Edith and my grandmother were gone. What good could come from resurrecting their ghosts?

"Do you really believe that everything happens for a reason?" I asked.

"Yes," he said. "But I also believe in free will. That our lives are what we make them."

Our eyes met, the glow of the moon filling the space between us, and all doubt left me. He leaned forward for another kiss, and my phone rang. I jerked back, quickly scrambling to retrieve it from my bag, knowing it could only be Owen or Loralee.

I looked down at the unknown number, identifying only the Beaufort area code. When I answered, I recognized Nurse Stelle's voice immediately, and suddenly it seemed as if the moon had fallen from the sky.

I didn't remember how we got back to the house, only that we must have run the whole way without stopping. I didn't even recall digging out my key or putting it in the lock or running up the stairs. My whole memory of that awful night was just of Loralee's peaceful expression, the hint of one of her glorious smiles still lingering around her mouth.

She looked as if she were still sleeping, and I half expected her to tell me to turn on the television or put on some lipstick. The pretty pink-and-lace nightgown I'd bought for her at Victoria's Secret lay loose around her neck, making her look like a little girl wearing her mother's clothes. I felt Gibbes behind me, his hands strong on my shoulders.

The nurse stood and I saw she'd been crying. She'd known Loralee for only a short while, but I suppose Loralee had that effect on most people. She wasn't somebody one easily forgot. "I already called her doctor, and the coroner is on his way."

I nodded, not sure I could trust my voice.

She cleared her throat. "I see this a lot, when a patient knows it's time but they don't want to upset their loved ones. They wait until everybody's where they want them to be." She sniffed and brought a tissue to the corners of her eyes. "I hope it brings you some comfort to know that she didn't die alone. It was so sudden, like . . . like she knew. She reached for my hand and I held it the whole time, and then she smiled at me, closed her eyes, and went to sleep. It was so peaceful and quick, I didn't have time to call you. But I think she wanted it that way."

I walked toward the bed with the absurd notion that if I spoke Loralee's name, she'd open her eyes. I leaned over her to brush her hair off her face, and one of my tears fell toward the bed, landing with an odd splat.

Looking down, I saw her pink journal cradled against her side, the pen lying next to it as if she'd just finished writing. Carefully I picked up the journal and opened it to the last page. There, right beneath the one I'd written just a few hours before, in a very shaky and light hand, was Loralee's final piece of wisdom. *Life doesn't get easier.*

We just get stronger.

"Oh, Loralee," I whispered. How was I going to get through the rest of my life without her? Without her wisdom and advice? And how could I be the mother she wanted me to be for her son?

"Owen," I said. "I've got to go get Owen. I need to be the one to tell him."

"Let me come with you," Gibbes said. "You shouldn't be driving."

Any courage or knowledge I believed I'd somehow attained fled, leaving behind the old Merritt who would always be afraid of the dark. "Yes. Thank you." My mind raced, trying to make lists and find order to distract me from the growing numbness. "I'll call Maris's dad, tell him that we'll pick Owen up at the theater and that we're on our way. He needs to say good-bye."

I turned to the nurse, not sure what to say, and she took the journal from my hands. "I'll stay with her until you get back. You'll need to tell the coroner which funeral home."

I nodded numbly, my grief like a fist that had grabbed hold of my lungs, strangling the breath from me.

Gibbes and I said our final good-byes to Loralee and then we left the house. As I stood outside I looked up at the moon again and saw heavy clouds drifting across its face, hiding the light and casting the dark night all around us.

Chapter 34

Merritt

Thunder rolled across the sky as my cell phone rang and I let it go to voice mail. It was Gibbes again, and although I'd seen him at the funeral and several times since when he came to check on Owen and me, we hadn't really talked. Maybe it was the New Englander in me, but I didn't want to talk — to anybody. Judging by the number of people who'd stopped by with casseroles and Jell-O molds, the Southern way to grieve was through food and talking. If it weren't for Owen, I would have simply sat in the silence and listened to the echo of the doorbell.

I glanced down at my cards and then at Owen across from me at the kitchen table. "Go fish," I said.

He just looked at his cards as if he didn't understand what I was saying and then back up at me. "Is it okay if we quit? I don't feel like playing."

"Okay, Rocky. That's fine." I began gathering up the cards.

"And I don't want to be Rocky anymore. I decided I like Owen better."

I smiled. "Good choice. I like it better, too." I finished stacking the cards, then slid them back in their box. "Would you like to watch a movie? We could call Maris and see if she wants to come over later and have pizza and popcorn and watch with us."

He shook his head. "No, not tonight. I just . . ." He looked at the new refrigerator, as if hoping it could finish his sentence.

I took his hand, wishing that Loralee were there to tell me the right words to say that could make it better for him. But all I had was me. "Owen, it will get better — I promise. One day you will wake up and that weight on your chest won't be as bad, and you'll be able to breathe in a little more air than you could the day before. And then you'll know that it's getting better."

He rested his chin on the table. "You promise?"

I nodded. "I promise."

"I miss her." Tears welled in his eyes and I quickly blinked back my own. One of us had to at least pretend to be strong.

"Oh, sweetheart, I miss her, too." I wished

again that she were there to offer some helpful piece of insight or her mama's wisdom that would make sense out of her not being there.

"Can we go visit her? There're some pretty flowers she planted in the garden, and I want to bring them to her."

I sat back in my chair, relieved to have some plan of action. "Absolutely. We can go whenever you want — but let's wait until the storm blows over, all right?"

He nodded. We hadn't been back to the cemetery since the funeral, where I'd worn the red dress, and Owen his little-man suit, and Loralee had looked beautiful in her pink suit and with her hair teased and sprayed big around her head just like she wanted. Gibbes had laughed when I'd explained why, and somehow the sound didn't seem out of place at Loralee's funeral.

My phone dinged, letting me know Gibbes had left another voice mail. My thumb hesitated a moment before I dropped my hand back to the table. "You can ride your new bike, too, when you visit the cemetery. I'll have to come, but I can just hover in the background and you can pretend you don't know me."

I was rewarded with a small smile. Gibbes had brought over the blue bicycle a couple of days after the funeral. It had been his when he was Owen's age, and it was just sitting in his garage. He'd fixed it up, oiled the chain, and pronounced it good as new when he'd delivered it to Owen. And because I was taking my new role as guardian very seriously, I'd gone to Walmart and bought my own bike — in yellow — and helmets for both of us.

Slowly he slid his chair back from the table. "I think I'll just go up to my room and play with my LEGOs for a little while."

"All right. Just let me know if you need anything or if you get hungry."

He nodded, then slowly walked out of the kitchen, his sock-covered feet quiet on the wood floors.

I stood in the kitchen for a long time, wondering what I should do, then headed up the stairs to pull all the paperwork Loralee had left, including guardianship of Owen and handwritten notes about what sort of education she envisioned for him, as well as the funds and accounts that were already set aside for that purpose.

I paused at the top of the steps, then detoured toward Loralee's room. The nurse had stripped the bed and remade it with a quilt she'd found in the closet. But the rest of the room appeared as if Loralee had never left, with her clothes hanging in the closet, the scent of her perfume still lingering in the air, her makeup and hairbrushes resting on the dresser.

One day I'd have to pack up her clothes and shoes and personal effects and decide what to save for Owen, and what to part with. But I couldn't do that yet. It would almost seem like watching her die twice. I stood in the doorway, unwilling to go in, unwilling to admit that it was empty. My gaze fell on the bedside table, which was cleared of all pill bottles and rolls of antacid tablets. All it contained now was a small pink clock, a vase of wilted flowers, and Loralee's pink journal. I'd somehow managed to forget about it, or to push it so far from my brain that I'd pretended to forget about it. The journal belonged to Owen, but Loralee had wanted me to read it, too.

I took a step forward to get it, but stopped. Reading her words, hearing her voice, would probably be more than I could take. I headed back toward my room, leaving the journal where it was. It would be there when we were ready for it.

I sat on top of my bed with Loralee's papers as well as my notebook of ideas — something Loralee had suggested and labeled for me — and tried to think of practical things, like schools for Owen as well as plumbing and appliances and heating and air systems. And refinishing basements. I'd decided to turn the basement into a rec room for Owen and his friends, a fun boy retreat with a place for gaming (Gibbes's idea) as well as a Ping-Pong table and something called Foosball (again, Gibbes's idea; he apparently got all his ideas from his college fraternity days).

But I was too easily distracted by thoughts, the same ones that had kept me up most nights since Loralee's death. They were a mixture of grief, and uncertainty about my ability to be a good enough mother to Owen, and my indecision as to what to do about the suitcase and the letter in the basement.

I yawned, realizing I was too tired to make any decisions about anything in my current state. I wasn't usually a nap taker, but I figured it might be my only option, since I wasn't able to keep my eyes open.

The thunder had been replaced by the steady beat of rain against the roof, as good as any lullaby. I picked up my phone to set an alarm for thirty minutes — assuming I could sleep that long — and saw the voice-mail sign on the screen. I touched the button, then listened to Gibbes's message.

"Hey, it's me again." Pause. "If you want me to get lost, just tell me. But I'd really like to talk. I miss her, too, and maybe if we . . . I don't know." Another pause. "Anyway, I wanted to let you know that I'm going on a fishing trip with some friends of mine, and the cabin we usually stay in is pretty much off the grid, with no cell service. There's a gas station about three miles away, though, where I can get a few bars. So if you need me, call and leave a message and I promise I'll check in a couple of times a day. Tell Rocky I said hi."

I listened to the message three times just to hear his voice, then hit the "end" button. I'd call him back later, if only to tell him that Rocky was back to being Owen. I dropped my phone on the bed beside me and lay back on my pillow, the sound of the rain the last thing I remembered hearing before I dropped off to sleep.

I woke up to evening sunlight from the window blasting me in the face just as a heavy roll of thunder shuddered around the house. I sat up, blinking my eyes and belatedly realizing that I'd neglected to set my alarm. Lightning pulsed outside, followed by another blast of thunder a few seconds later, the sun dimming only slightly. *The devil's beating his wife,* I thought, hearing Loralee's voice.

I searched for my phone, vaguely remembering dropping it on my bed before I'd passed out, finally finding it tucked under one of my legs. I was in the middle of a stretch when I looked at my screen and saw that it was after six o'clock, the realization dawning on me that I'd been asleep for almost five hours.

I leaped from the bed, then headed toward Owen's bedroom, calling his name, wondering whether he was hungry and feeling bad, and if he hadn't wanted to awaken me to let me know. Yes, he could probably make his own peanut butter and jelly sandwich, but he wasn't supposed to. That's what I was there for.

"Owen?" His door was cracked open, so I knocked and waited for a response. "Owen?" I tried again after a moment, pushing open the door slowly. His room looked like it belonged to a military cadet, with bedclothes tucked in at neat angles, all of his LEGOs in color-coded bins against the walls, his latest projects displayed on the bookshelf along with Cal's.

"Owen?" I called again, louder this time, checking in his closet and under the bed just in case.

I ran down the stairs, calling his name, pausing only long enough to hear him reply. But I heard only silence. I looked into all the downstairs rooms before heading toward the kitchen and then into the garden, where all the blooms and leaves bowed their heads from the weight of the raindrops, seeming to me as if they were in mourning, too.

"Owen?" I called, hearing my own rising sense of panic.

I moved quickly through the house again, calling his name, then out the front door and to the side of the house. "Owen — please! Answer me!" I used the gate to cut through the garden, moving rapidly toward the basement door, feeling the emptiness of the room before I'd hit the last step. The suitcase and plane model seemed to mock me, using Cal's voice: *Coward.* I backed up, then quickly retraced my steps.

I ran upstairs, checking in the attic and the bathroom this time, calling Owen's name again and again. I felt the rising panic begin to bubble over into my reasoning, and I found myself questioning Loralee's decision not to get Owen a phone yet because he was only ten.

I was about to run downstairs again when I backtracked to Loralee's room. I hadn't checked in there, knowing Owen's reluctance to enter it was as strong as my own. I stood on the threshold. "Owen? Are you in here?"

I waited, hearing the sound of the rain against the window and the soft ticking of the pink alarm clock by the side of the bed. I was about to turn away when I noticed that the journal was missing. I entered the room and got down on my hands and knees to look behind the nightstand and under the bed and came up empty.

Where could he have gone? Wherever Owen was, I had to assume the journal was with him. In desperation I called Maris's mother, although in my heart I knew she would never have brought Owen to her house without speaking with me first. The whole family had come to Loralee's funeral, and I knew their offer to call them for anything had been sincere.

Tracy hadn't seen or heard from Owen, and neither had Maris, but she promised to let me know if they did, and asked me to let her know if I needed her to go out and start driving around looking for him.

I thanked her, not ready for my thoughts to go in that direction yet, not wanting to think of a lost Owen wandering the streets of Beaufort in the rain, his mother's journal tucked against his chest. I started to call

Gibbes, but stopped, remembering that he wasn't available, and suddenly felt completely helpless and alone.

I closed my eyes. *Think.* The cemetery. I'd check the cemetery first, and if I didn't find him there, I was calling the police. He wasn't a runaway. He wasn't a troubled child. He was simply . . . gone.

I grabbed my purse and headed toward the detached garage with the sagging roof. It was big enough for my car and our new bikes, keeping them out of the heat of the sun and the elements. I slid into the driver's side, my gaze scanning the walls of the garage, which were mostly coated with layers of cobwebs, except where Gibbes had cleared them off to make room for the two bikes and two hooks for our helmets. I stopped. Owen's helmet and bike were gone. He was somewhere on his bike, in the rain.

Terrified now, I backed out of the garage and sped over gravel to the street and headed toward Saint Helena's churchyard. I was looking for his bike now, which might make him easier to spot, and found myself saying prayers I hadn't said since I was a little girl.

The sun was on its final descent, and although the rain had stopped, heavy clouds hung dark and threatening as I parked my car along the street outside the church and raced in through the gates. Raindrops clung to the junipers, sycamores, and sculpted myrtle branches that hovered over the graves, a storm-scented wind shaking them loose until they fell like tears onto the stones and sodden earth.

The last rays of sun escaped through the winding paths between graves as I found my way to the mound of dirt marking the interment site. It was still covered with wreaths and bouquets, the ground raw and fragrant like the suitcase had been when Gibbes had pulled it from the hole.

No bike, no tracks, no sign whatsoever that Owen had been there. The full panic that I'd managed to hold at bay so far threatened to engulf me, to take me back to the helpless woman I'd been while married to Cal.

Think. Think. Loralee would have known what to do. *But Loralee isn't here.* I stumbled blindly out of the cemetery, watching as dark clouds obliterated what was left of the sunset and everything turned to gray.

I made it back behind the steering wheel before the sky opened up and rain pelted down, thudding against the metal roof and windshield. My hands were shaking as I picked up the phone and hit "redial" to call Gibbes's number. It wasn't until his voice mail picked up and I heard his voice that I remembered he wasn't there. That he was "off the grid" and would be checking in only a couple of times a day.

I threw my phone onto the passenger seat, then pressed my forehead against the steering wheel hard enough that it hurt. *Think. Think.* Lightning flashed, illuminating the world for a brief second, the limbs of the oak trees lining the road stark against the angry sky.

I thought of Owen, out in the storm by himself somewhere. Missing his mother. Maybe wondering where I was and why I wasn't coming to get him.

"Owen!" I yelled inside my car as the sky went black again. And that was when I knew where he was. I saw him so clearly, standing on the dock watching the dolphin sluice through the water, feeling the ripples beneath my feet. And I heard Owen's voice. *We should always find a happy place — kind of like "base" in a game of tag, where you can go and all of your problems and worries can't touch you.*

I immediately turned the car around and headed toward Bay Street. I'd been to Gibbes's house only twice, but each time

I'd spent so much time studying the road that I was sure I could find it again. It was only a few turns, and then a long dirt drive to his house. *And a bridge.* My foot nearly slipped from the accelerator, but I moved it back again, gently pressing on it as I neared the bridge, which was lit up clearly against the night sky.

What if it's open to let boats go through and I have to stop in the middle? I pushed the thought away, telling myself I'd think about it later, feeling a little like Scarlett O'Hara.

I thought of calling Gibbes again, and then as quickly as I dismissed that idea, I thought of Deborah. Deborah would come immediately; I knew that. But Owen was my brother, and he needed me *now.*

I flicked on my signal to turn right onto the bridge, hesitating long enough that the person behind me felt compelled to tap his horn. Slowly I moved forward onto the foot of the bridge, my hands gripping the wheel so tightly that I could barely feel them. My body shook while bile rose in the back of my throat. *Breathe. Breathe. Breathe.*

The rain had abated slightly, but the wipers continued at high speed, my hand refusing to let go of the steering wheel long enough to change the setting. *Thump, thump, thump.* I hated the sound, hated the way it reminded me of the sound a car made as it slid against the side of a bridge, the sound it made right before the car plunged over the side into icy cold water.

Breathe. Breathe. I was almost at the midpoint of the bridge, and it was closed, so I didn't have to stop. Because if I had to, I wasn't sure whether I could go forward again. There was a lot of traffic on the bridge, moving slowly, but as I approached the second half I wanted to get off *now*. *Move,* I said in my head to the white SUV in front of me. "Move," I said out loud, my voice trembling, my forehead drenched in sweat.

You are so much stronger and braver than you think you are. The sob broke from my throat unexpectedly, my tears hot and sudden on my skin. "Move," I whispered to the car in front, my foot slipping from the accelerator again and then punching on the brake. The vehicle behind me honked and I wanted to stop then. To park my car and get out and run back the way I'd come.

You are strong at the broken places. I blinked quickly, clearing my vision, and remembered Loralee saying that to me, remembered how I'd wanted to argue with her. "Move," I said again to the back of the SUV, but with less conviction this time, my wipers beating back and forth, back and forth. *Courage is doing the one thing you think you cannot do.* The words came to me in a rush, not as if they'd been spoken, but almost as if they'd taken up residence somewhere in my brain.

My breathing slowed, my hands loosening on the steering wheel. I neared the end of the bridge, aware of the lights along either side of me but still not daring to look away from the road directly in front. The traffic surged forward and I went with it, following the cars until we'd left the bridge and were back on solid ground again.

Blood pounded in my ears, and I thought for a moment that I should pull over to catch my breath, to make sure I wasn't going to do what Loralee had feared and give myself a heart attack. If the muscles in my face hadn't been so frozen, I probably would have smiled at hearing myself say those words in my head with a soft Alabama accent. But I couldn't stop. Owen was out there in the dark night, alone and maybe lost, and I was going to find him.

The rain had lessened to a light drizzle, and I finally pried my fingers from the steering wheel and switched the wipers to intermittent. On the back roads of Lady's Island the dark wedged itself between the trees like a fist, obliterating all light and making it difficult to navigate by landmarks. I flipped on my high beams, allowing my headlights to illuminate a wider path. I tried not to dwell on the occasional pair of yellow eyes in the underbrush by the side of the road as I looked not only for landmarks, but for a blue bike and a red helmet and a little boy who was too far from home. My only hope was that Owen had managed to make it to Gibbes's house before nightfall, and that he'd thought to find shelter on the porch.

I came up to a road on my right, recognizing a seventies-style ranch house with brightly colored Christmas lights hanging from the sagging front porch. I turned, knowing I was headed in the right direction. I pushed the accelerator down, unaware of my speed, just needing to get where I was going. The long drive at the front of Gibbes's property loomed ahead, and I pulled in at the metal mailbox I remembered, the relief spreading through my joints and expanding my lungs.

Dirt, gravel, and mud flew from the back tires as I tore down the road, afraid to slow down just in case my car got mired in the muck. A single porch light glowed in the distance and I began to get worried all over again. *What if he isn't here?*

I skidded to a stop in the drive and threw the car in park. Leaving the keys in the ignition and the headlights bright, I ran from the car to the front porch. "Owen? Owen — it's me, Merritt. Are you here?"

But the porch was empty, the rocking chairs still. *Not here. The dock.* I jumped off the porch, feeling my shoes squish in the mud, then ran toward the dock. "Owen? Owen? Are you here?"

"Merritt?"

Did I imagine that? I stumbled over something, nearly tripping in the mud, but managed to catch myself. It was Owen's bike. "Owen?"

"I'm over here. On the dock."

I turned toward the dock to where the whole creek was illuminated by the soft glow of Beaufort's lights reflecting off low clouds. I saw Owen then, at least the outline of him, wearing the yellow rain slicker his mother had bought for him, the same one that he'd told me in confidence nobody — especially no boys — wore past second grade.

"Owen!" I cried, running down the dock, then catching him in my arms as he grabbed mine and squeezing him as tightly as I could until I heard him struggling for breath. I pulled away from him, but neither one of us wanted to let go. "Are you all right? Are you hurt?" I went from being relieved to angry to worried, then back again, unable to settle on a single emotion.

"I'm fine," he said, his voice choked with tears. "I just . . ."

"You needed to touch base. I get it; I do. But I was so scared. . . ." I crushed him against me again, unable to finish my sentence, afraid the fear would return. I knelt in front of him. "Don't you ever leave without telling me where you're going; do you understand? Never. I was so worried."

"I'm sorry, Merritt," he said, wiping his sleeve across his nose. "I didn't want to wake you up, and I thought Dr. Heyward would be here and he could call you. When I got here it wasn't dark yet, but then it was and I was too afraid to go to the porch because I couldn't see anything. I was just feeling so sad. . . ."

I brushed his soaking hair off his forehead. "I know. Me, too. But we've got to look out for each other. It's you and me, right? Like Thing One and Thing Two?" I'd been studying up on Dr. Seuss, and hoped I'd made the right reference.

"Yeah," he said, and I felt him smile.

"Promise me you'll never do that again."

"I promise."

Something dropped from his jacket onto the dock and I leaned forward to pick it up. It was a book wrapped inside a plastic bag. "Your mother's journal."

He nodded. "I started to read it, but it began to rain and I didn't want it to get wet. It made me feel better, though. Like she was sitting right here, talking to me."

I reached up and straightened his glasses. "She'll always be a part of you, you know. And I know I'll never replace her, but I promise to do the best I can."

"I know." He tugged on my arm, turning around to face the water, and it wasn't so frightening anymore. *Courage is doing the one thing you think you cannot do.* "You were right about something," he said.

"About what?" I stood, but held his hand, afraid to let go.

He pointed across the water toward Beaufort, and the glowing lights that softened the darkness on the dock where we stood. "About how it's never really dark. How there's always light somewhere if you look hard enough."

I started to cry again, from relief, and grief, and all the things I had learned in one stormy night. I hugged him to me, still not believing that I'd found him. "I love you, Owen."

"I love you, too, Merritt," he said, his voice muffled against my shoulder, but I didn't let go, knowing that in a few years he probably wouldn't let me hug him anymore — at least not in public.

Something dropped onto the dock, and when I stepped forward to retrieve it, my toe kicked whatever it was and then we heard the unmistakable sound of something hitting water.

"Was that the journal?" I asked in panic, then realized I still held it.

"No. Just my glasses."

I looked at him, hoping my parenting skills wouldn't be judged by my actions of a single day. "Great. Do you have an extra pair?"

"No. I had one, but I lost them."

Keeping my arm around his shoulders, I led him off the dock to my car. "I guess we'll go see about a new pair of glasses first thing tomorrow."

"Or I could get contacts," he said, looking up at me hopefully.

"We'll see," I said, sounding so much like my own mother that I almost laughed.

"Merritt?"

"Um?"

"I think we're going to be okay."

"I think so, too." I kissed the top of his head and opened his car door. "Your bike won't fit in my car — I'll ask Dr. Heyward to bring it back."

He nodded, then tilted his head toward the clearing sky, spotting a single star. "Did you know that when you look at stars you're looking back in time? That's because the light from the star takes millions of years to reach the Earth, so you're really seeing how it looked millions of years ago."

"Smart kid," I said, rustling his hair.

He grinned at me, and it was his mother's smile. Owen slid into the car and I closed the door, looking up just as he had. Loralee had shown us both the importance of looking up, of seeing the beauty and the good in unexpected places. And in ourselves.

The rain had finally stopped, the clouds shifting positions in the sky, making room for more stars that managed to push through the darkness and illuminate the places we were once afraid to see.

CHAPTER 35

Merritt

October 2014

I stood on Gibbes's back porch under the newly hung wind chime that Owen and I had made, staring out over the marsh. I wore only Gibbes's shirt — having not quite adopted Loralee's belief in wearing an elegant negligee to bed — but I did feel incredibly sexy in it. The heat from the coffee mug I held warmed my hands against the early predawn chill as I took a sip, watching as morning rose over Beaufort.

Dawn wasn't a bright, sudden event there, but more like a slow exhalation. It was comforting and familiar, the soft gold light now a part of me. It had become home, the gray Maine mornings of my childhood a fading memory. I took a deep breath and let them go, finally setting free the girl who'd once emerged from an icy river and never stopped blaming herself.

The door behind me opened and I smiled. Owen was camping with Maris's family for the weekend, returning in time for the fundraiser, leaving Gibbes and me alone. His warm hands rested on either side of my waist as he pressed his bare chest against me and his lips brushed the back of my neck.

"Aren't you cold?" I asked.

"Not anymore." He kissed me again, and I felt his laugh rumbling against my skin.

He rested his head against mine and we waited in silence for the final breath of dark to give way to the light. Autumn in the Lowcountry settled softly on the marsh, painting it with strokes of ochre and yellow from the wind-tossed seeds of the cordgrass. Birdsongs changed as new visitors from up North searched for winter homes, and others sought shelter farther south. The wooden tombstones of upended oyster boats in summer had disappeared and were plying the creeks and estuaries, looking for beds to crack.

It seemed as if I'd always lived there, that the short summers and russet autumns of Maine were from another life. In many ways, I thought, they had been. I was confident now in the boat, and had navigated it by myself enough times to not be afraid anymore. I'd seen one alligator and countless dolphins on my journeys, and had learned the landmarks to find my way back. Loralee would probably have had something to say about that, something about the heart bearing a compass that always pointed toward home. I'd have to remember to write that in my own journal, the one I'd started after the night I'd crossed the bridge. I watched as the horizon trembled with new light, and imagined I was on the boat again, trees parting and the river bending into the liquid mystery of the marsh, its secrets submerged and exposed with the patterns of the moon.

"Did you sleep?" he asked.

I shook my head. "Too nervous. What if nobody comes?"

"Of course they will — I've never met anybody who could turn down an invite to a Lowcountry oyster roast. Besides, the Cecelia Gibbes Heyward Women's Shelter is a good cause. And you're a local celebrity. How could they stay away? Don't forget, too — Deborah Fuller knows everybody in town and will make sure they're here and bringing donation checks."

I closed my eyes and leaned back, his arms firm around me, and knew he wouldn't let me go. It had taken reading Loralee's journal for me to find the courage to show Gibbes the letter, to admit to him the kind of woman I'd once been, the kind of person who'd allowed herself to fall in love with a lie. *Life doesn't get easier. We just get stronger.* Loralee was right. I was stronger. I'd crossed more than just a physical bridge that night in the storm. She'd been right about so many things. I only wished I'd realized it earlier.

Gibbes had gone with me to the police station with the suitcase, the plane model, and the letter. And never once had he regarded me with Cal's eyes, making me wonder how I'd ever thought he would. He'd been the one who'd figured out that Cal had wandered California for more than ten years before he went to Maine. An entire decade during which he'd fought his demons, tried to forget his need for retribution. But in the end he'd lost the battle, and had come to find justice and found me instead. I had been an easy substitute target for the rage he felt toward my grandmother and an unpunished crime. A rage that had been twisted and complicated by the unexpected love we'd found together. I held Gibbes closer to me. Edith had sent him away to save him, to make sure he had a happy life. In that one respect, she'd done the right thing.

I tilted my head, breathing in the scent of him. "Thanks for letting me use your house for the roast. I just had no idea how long it would take to paint the outside and inside of a house." I thought about my newly painted porch overlooking the bluff, each wind chime rehung as soon as the paint had dried according to Owen's numbering system, which he'd devised so nothing was hung in the wrong spot. Fall flowers shot up from the pots and planters that lined the refurbished brick steps and illuminated the front door with bright splashes of color. Remembering Loralee's love of gardening, I thought it was a little bit like looking at her smile every time I approached the house.

Gibbes nuzzled his morning stubble against my temple. "I promised Owen that I would never sell this house, because of the dock. And you've made all those nice curtains and slipcovers and pillows — although why so many pillows have to go on a bed, I have no idea. They just get knocked to the floor." I felt him smile. "So I guess we're stuck with two houses."

"What are you saying, Dr. Heyward?"

"Well, Loralee did say that if you married me you wouldn't have to change the monogram on any of your linens."

I turned around to face him. "Funny, she said the same thing to me." I tilted my head. "Was that a proposal?"

"Not yet. I need to get Owen's permission first."

I kissed him gently on the lips. "Good. That will give me time to think about my answer." I placed my head against his heart, the strong beat thrumming against my ear, and thought again of paths and compasses. About how our paths had crossed long before we were born, our stories as tangled and meandering as the waterways that had brought us both back to the starting point. *Everything happens for a reason.* I smiled, thinking of Loralee.

"I'm proud of you, Merritt. I know none of this has been easy for you." I felt his kiss on the top of my head.

The story of the crash of Flight 629 and my grandmother's role in it had made the local news, which had brought it to the attention of a national magazine. I had expected recrimination about what my grandmother and Edith had done, but there hadn't been any. There was nobody to prosecute, no more bodies to bury. At least there were no more questions for those still living, no more wondering. In the deepest parts of the night when I lay awake, I found solace in that.

The story had somehow propelled me into an unwanted spotlight as a sort of spokesperson about abusive relationships. I was uncomfortable there, knowing I hadn't found the courage at the time to walk away from my own personal hell. I'd be more comfortable in my role of sewing instructor at the shelter as soon as the funds were made available. Until then I shared our stories — Edith's, my grandmother's, mine — to let others know they weren't alone. That there was help. That they all possessed within themselves the courage to do the one thing they thought that they could not.

"Thank you for being there for me. I couldn't do any of this alone."

"You could," he said softly. "But I'm glad I'm here."

I looked up at the wind chime and watched the glass twist and twirl, thinking about Edith, Cecelia, and my grandmother. I studied the mottled surfaces of the sea glass, seeing not dull glass but weary travelers who had learned to absorb the light and reflect it outward.

It is in darkness that we find the light. I itched to write the words in my journal, to fill the pages with everything I'd learned, how we are all tumbled about by the waves of life, earning scars that show where we've been. And we learn. With each scar we learn. With etched faces we turn toward the light, unbending and unbreakable, strong at the broken places.

Gibbes kissed me, his lips hard and searching, and when I opened my eyes I saw only Gibbes, his brother's ghost now laid to rest. I had found Cal after all, in the waterways of his boyhood, and it was here that I'd finally learned to let him go.

ABOUT THE AUTHOR

Karen White has written eighteen previous novels, including four in the Tradd Street mystery series, set in Charleston, South Carolina. Her previous novel, *A Long Time Gone*, was published in June 2014 and debuted at number 24 on the *New York Times* bestseller list. She lives near Atlanta, Georgia, with her husband, two children, and a spoiled Havanese named Quincy.